P9-DGN-219

ALSO BY SHERWOOD SMITH:

INDA
THE FOX
KING'S SHIELD
TREASON'S SHORE

and coming soon:
BANNER OF THE DAMNED

SHERWOOD SMITH

Coronets and STEEL

DAW BOOKS, INC.

DONALD A. WOLLHEIM, FOUNDER

375 Hudson Street, New York, NY 10014

ELIZABETH R. WOLLHEIM

SHEILA E. GILBERT

PUBLISHERS

http://www.dawbooks.com

Jacket art by Matt Stawicki.

Book designed by Elizabeth Glover.

DAW Books Collector's No. 1521.

DAW Books Inc. is distributed by Penguin Group (USA).

First Hardcover Printing, September 2010
1 2 3 4 5 6 7 8 9 10

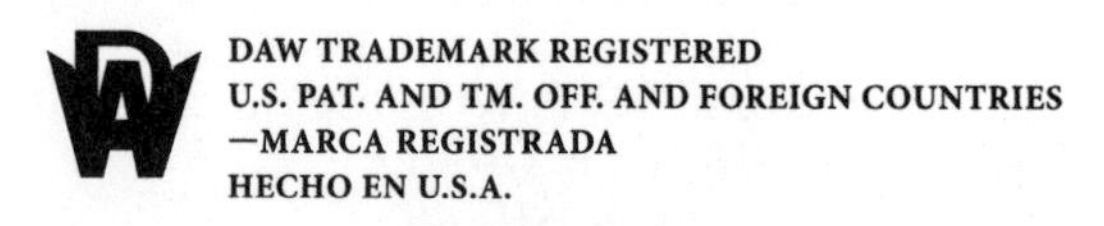

PRINTED IN THE U.S.A.

With a tip of the hat to Anthony Hope.

ACKNOWLEDGMENTS

My grateful thanks to various beta readers—especially Kathleen Dalton-Woodbury, Hallie O'Donovan, Marjorie Ferguson, Jodi Meadows, Tamara Meatzie, Beth Bernobich, and Rachel Manija Brown.

ONE

TOO MUCH IMAGINATION was tantamount to lying, that's what my grandmother taught me. So when I first got that sense that someone was following me, of course I ignored it. It was only my imagination. Who'd waste time following me?

Here's what happened.

My first day in Vienna, Austria, I made an appointment with a genealogical research company in a fine old building in the heart of the city.

"*Guten Morgen, Fräulein Murray . . .*" the genealogist greeted me in German.

I replied in my university-trained German—clear and formal— "I am trying to track down my grandparents' families. The name is Atelier. My mother was only two when she and my grandmother left Paris, but she thinks she might have been born here in Austria."

The woman picked up the first item in my meager evidence, which was a photocopy of a grubby, much-folded form typed on a manual typewriter that had had a fading ribbon. It listed my grandmother as Aurelia Atelier, age twenty-two, and my mother as Marie Atelier, age two, citizens of France—these forms were all many refugees had as ID. The next item was a photocopy of a portrait of my grandfather, a handsome blond man with a crooked, rakish smile. The woman looked from that to me and back again, her brows lifting.

She was too professional to make personal remarks, but I already knew how much I resembled him: tall, slim build, pale hair, honey-brown eyes, crooked jaw with a single dimple in one cheek when I smiled. In the photo, my grandfather was wearing an old-fashioned military uniform with the brass buttons, the high collar, the epaulettes and gold braid all tailored like a second skin.

She laid that aside and glanced at the last bit of evidence: two opera tickets for the Staatsoper in Vienna, date 1939.

When the genealogist looked up again, pencil poised, she switched smoothly to French. "What is your grandfather's given name?"

"Daniel. We don't know anything about his family, or where he was born." It was a relief to use French, the language I'd grown up speaking with my grandmother. "The only thing my mother knows about my grandfather is that he flew a bomber against Russia at the end of World War II."

"This is not a German uniform," she said. "It is not even Austrian from the period before Germany annexed it. I would say this design predates the First World War."

I leaned forward, my forearms pressing against the tension in my middle. "There is no record of him in the French army . . ." I paused, remembering a conversation with my mother from three months ago. We were sitting in the hospital waiting room, talking about Gran—and about how little we knew of her life. *The only thing she ever told me about my father was his name, and that he flew against the Soviets at the end of World War II. I asked if he was a Nazi, and she got mad. "Not all German soldiers were Nazis." She was seriously bent out of shape, and wouldn't say any more. Ever.*

That was more than I'd gotten out of Gran. She never talked about her past.

I looked up at the woman. "It's possible he was a conscript in the Ostlegionen. You know, the foreign-born soldiers sent by the Germans to stop the Russian advance."

"We can research that." The woman touched the photocopied ID paper with her pencil tip. "You mentioned Paris. Did you consult a genealogist or archive there?"

"Yes." My throat had gone dry. "I spent three weeks there. I found a million Ateliers, but none of them ours, and no French forces flew against Russia at the end of the war, at least that I could discover. Which is why I'm here."

As she told me what she could do and what the initial cost would be, I fought back the urge to tell her to hurry, that I couldn't afford to stay. I didn't want to sound like an obnoxious *me first* American and I suspected she wouldn't care that my grandmother hadn't spoken in four months.

What, a sensible person would ask, had that to do with genealogy research?

She photocopied the photocopies and wrote down everything I gave her. I plunked down an initial payment, thanked her, and left. I held in the impulse to urge her to hurry. Everyone wants their business to come first; it's human nature.

So I thanked her and left.

As I walked out into the clear sunshine, I tried to shake loose of all that tension. I'd taken steps. I'd put a pro on the case. Surely they knew where to go and what to look for.

I looked around at the pale stone and warm brick-accented buildings with their grand rows of tall windows and Palladian carvings. Not far away, a spire rose above the rooftops. Was that the famous St. Stephen's Cathedral?

I hadn't done any sightseeing yet, so why not walk back to my pensione? I'd pass by the oldest and grandest monuments in the city, and I needed to sort through that oppressive fog of emotion.

The problem was that I couldn't explain the sense of urgency that drove me, even to myself. It had begun that day four months ago when my grandmother lay restlessly in her bed, a hectic flush in her thin cheeks, her eyes glittering with fever as she gripped my hand with fingers still strong after decades of piano playing.

Retourne au pays, Aurelia Kim! Tu dois aller voir si ils sont en sécurité . . . Je dois savoir s'ils sont en sécurité, parce que . . . on ne peut pas se soulager la blessure . . . Ta mère—

"—your mother is too gentle," she'd whispered. "I cannot send her to heal the breach."

What breach? With her family? His family? Surely not with my grandfather, as she'd kept that silver-framed picture of him by her bedside as long as I could remember.

"Yes, the picture was there when I was a little kid," Mom had said during another conversation, as we waited in another specialist's office, hoping to find out why Gran had recovered from the fever just to sit there in her chair, staring out the east window.

Mom cocked her head, her short frizz of blond hair the same shade as my long mane. "She wouldn't talk about our life before we got to California. When I was little we read together. When I started school we talked about that. My schoolwork, my friends. Music, when we went to the Music Center—when we could afford the tickets. And later, we talked about all the recipes I was learning in the pastry school, before I hooked up with your dad."

Gran and I had been close, as she'd been my primary caregiver while my parents worked. I was named for her. When the weeks turned into a month, then two, then three, and the doctors did their medicalese versions of throwing up their hands, I made the decision to find her family myself.

My parents agreed, Mom because she was preoccupied with worry about Gran. She didn't do worry well, and she was desperate for something that would work. Dad agreed because he was Mr. Mellow, and if I felt I had to do it, that was good enough for him.

Even if we had to go into hock to manage it.

So here I was in Europe, and with nothing. *Nothing.* To show for it.

I walked faster along the grand boulevards of Vienna, though I knew I couldn't outpace my sense of failure.

And that's when I met my first ghost.

TWO

I SET OUT without a goal, taking any turn that looked interesting. The buildings along the broad streets got bigger and finer, the aqua baroque domes and elaborate statuary giving way to a square that I recognized from pictures: I'd found my way to the Michaelerplatz and the grand arched entrance to the Hofburg, the imperial palace of the Hapsburg emperors.

The gold and white entrance extended in a wide curve, flanked by mighty-thewed mythological statues. What did it feel like to live in such a place? For the first time in weeks the driving sense of urgency eased up a little.

I paused, wondering if I should hunt up a tour or cruise the place myself when a waft of chilly air startled me; the sun was so warm. A young woman more or less my age walked through the huge arched entry, twirling a silken parasol over a roguish flat hat of the 1760s that crowned a high white-powdered wig of elaborate curls. Instead of a walking dress she wore a square necked sacque, the rich satin skirt divided in front and gracefully looped back over a brocade underskirt.

She looked like a swan among the bobbing gray pigeons and busy brown wrens of people in modern clothes. It surprised me that no one paid her the least heed—but maybe Austrians were used to reenactment dress, or they were more sophisticated than LA students like me.

As she passed, she cast a laughing glance at me, her eyes crescents of merriment, her cheeks dimpled on either side of a secretive smile, as if she knew a good joke—or was playing one—then the parasol hid her face as she tripped away, her skirts swaying.

She had to be going somewhere interesting. I decided to follow her.

The young lady minced along in her high-heeled shoes with diamond buckles. While I followed about fifty paces behind, I considered talking to her. If I saw her interact with anyone else, I'd know it was all right to talk to her; she might be like those Disney characters who walk around the park but they don't speak, so as not to ruin the atmosphere.

She stepped daintily across the Michaelerplatz at a drifting pace. I stopped once or twice to twirl around on my toes in an effort to take in the sheer enormity of the Hofburg, to banish the Disneyland feel and see the place as the private home of power it once was. Though I knew from years of reading history that power does not automatically bestow happiness, and royalty was not exempt from personal tragedy, the romantic sweep of royal palaces is inescapable. At least to someone like me who loves the stylish and romantic face of history.

I was thinking over dramatic events that had happened in this very space when I discovered that the palace buildings were behind me. People streamed in all directions. When the crowd thinned, I found we'd reached a station for the red and white streetcars called "Bim." This was the Schwedenplatz. A string of fast-moving people left the tram, dividing me from my quarry.

Gone! So much for Supersleuth Murray.

On the other hand, I was right before the underground station that listed Schönbrunn Palace along its route. Of course that woman would be going there. Schönbrunn had been the Versailles for the imperial family for two hundred years. There had to be either a reenactment or a movie being shot there.

The ride to Schönbrunn Palace did not take long—but this is where I first got that twitch between my shoulder blades, as if I was being watched. Or maybe even followed.

Too much imagination was tantamount to lying, that's what my grandmother had taught me. So after a couple of glances at other riders, when no one met my eyes or looked like a creepy stalker, I tried to shake the feeling. It had to be my imagination—imaginary payback for my having followed that reenactment actor.

Schönbrunn was smaller and brighter than Versailles. I paid for the German tour, figuring the swift speech of the guide would be good practice. As I walked from room to room and viewed the furniture the inhabitants had used, and the things they had touched, and the windows they had looked out of, I gained an odd, swift sense of substance or essence, not quite immanence. It was the visceral conviction that if I walked through the right door, or closed my eyes and breathed in the faint, complicated scents, I'd find myself in the same place but in a different time, and there would be the young Prince Joseph, or the restless, brooding Prince Rudolf. Or Napoleon, or Maria Theresia. Or the beautiful and unhappy Empress Sisi.

When the tour ended, and I hadn't found sign of a reenactment or a setup for a Hollywood-style shoot, I followed the crowd back down the marble stairs. Maybe something was going on in the gardens? Not long after the shadows of the geometrically tended maze closed around me I got that shoulder-crawling sense again, as if I were being watched from the many sun-glittering windows in the warm golden walls of the palace.

No one in sight. Of course not! It was my imagination—spoiling my enjoyment. I got up, hoping to leave my overactive imaginings behind, and walked farther on, but the feeling stuck as close as my shadow as I neared the fountains.

I sat down with my back to a wall and satisfied myself with a thorough scan. Nothing to see besides tourists, none of whom were the least bit interested in an American student in old jeans, a cotton blouse, and sandals, her blond hair swept up in a practical knot.

A second scan away from the palace, and there was the actor again. She strolled on the Gloriette monument, her parasol twirling in the golden rays of the sinking sun, the heavy satin of her sky blue gown gleaming.

The slanting afternoon sunlight limned the trees of the park with golden green light, casting the palace into shadow when I reached the Gloriette. I climbed up the stairs onto the roof of the belvedere, which is a triumphal arch with colonnaded wings at either end, topped with military trophies. Built on a hill at the other end of the palace's extensive garden, it affords a view of the palace and the gardens. I wandered to the rail, trying to imagine its famed inhabitants standing there with the pride of ownership.

When hunger reminded me of the long trip back to my pensione, I turned away from the balustrade I'd been leaning against.

A short, dapper older man stepped toward me. I gained a hazy impression of a broad build, a short gray goatee, and a Tyrolean blue–collared gray suit before he smiled and addressed me in a vaguely Slavic-sounding language.

Whether on purpose or inadvertently, his angle of approach had cut me off from the rest of the roof.

He stretched a hand toward my arm as he spoke. I jerked away and snapped in English, "Get lost, creep!"

The man started back as if I'd slapped him, his face creasing in dismay.

What's up with that? I'd been propositioned a couple times in Paris, but that had been at night, when I was alone. I stalked away, furious at being hassled during broad daylight—and at a *monument.*

My mood stayed grumpy until I got back inside the city and sat down to dinner at a small corner gasthaus. The *Kurier,* Vienna's newspaper, had been left at the table. I picked it up while waiting for my food and discovered that the London Ballet was coming to the Opera House.

I'd had to give up dance when Gran's situation worsened, as we couldn't afford for me to study two sports, and anyway I had to take my share of helping to nurse Gran when Mom was at work and Dad handled the household errands. A ballet . . . totally frivolous, when I had to make every euro stretch, but . . .

The cloud of urgency, disappointment—failure—closed in until I compromised with myself. If I skipped a couple of meals, that would even things out.

When I got back to my pensione and asked where I should go to purchase a ticket, the manager offered to arrange it for me. "Get me the best seat you can," I said.

If you're splurging recklessly, at least do it right.

THREE

THE NEXT DAY I took the Bim to the Staatsarchive to see how much detective work I could accomplish on my own.

Zip. But I'd tried, so I left feeling virtuous, returned to my pensione to drop off my folder of evidence so I wouldn't have to lug it around, and set out on foot to do some more sightseeing.

Within three blocks of leaving the pensione, I once again got that sense that I was being watched.

Glad of those strenuous years of ballet and fencing, I went into power walk mode, dodging around slower pedestrians like somebody on inline skates. Good workout, I decided after a few blocks, though not as good as a fencing match.

Then I remembered the date, and my mood soured even more.

Today was the championship tournament. The senior fencing team at UCLA would be there—everyone except me. Our coach had been disappointed when I'd announced that I wasn't going, that I was leaving for Europe the day classes ended.

My teammates had been surprised—some dismayed—but hardest to take was how my oldest friend, Lisa Castillo, had looked away, her expression closed. She didn't actually say "Whatever," but I'd felt it.

I tried to explain, but how do you explain to someone who's always regarded you as a bit flaky—incapable of practical goals—a sense of urgency that you cannot even define to yourself?

To Lisa I was flaking out yet again and letting the team down. It had continued to bother me while I tramped fruitlessly through every Paris archive I could find. When I got on the train to Vienna, I started a letter to her and another teammate to explain, but I ended up at the train window, watching the Bavarian countryside roll by with its occasional glimpses of tiny ancient villages gleaming creamy gold against their emerald setting; Austria seemed another world and time away from the eternal sun of Los Angeles and Lisa's goal-oriented energy.

Modern practicality and old-world romance, that summed up Lisa and me. Living on the same block, Lisa and I had played together as kids. We'd shared rides through middle and high school when we both started fencing; she loved the sport for its precision, and I loved it because I could pretend I was Douglas Fairbanks Jr. She liked Tom Stoppard and the Coen brothers, while I'd rather rewatch Colin Firth's *Pride and Prejudice* or Ronald Colman's *Prisoner of Zenda.*

She had planned out a life in investment stockbroking when she was twelve, to break the family blue-collar cycle; I'd bounced majors from French to German to linguistics to comparative literature, and I'd been about to change it back to German so I could research the origins of the fairy tales Gran had told me when I was small. None of those majors was ever going to boost my family out of our falling-apart little house in Santa Monica.

The last thing Lisa said to me was, *"Kim, I seriously hope you get whatever it is you're looking for. But dude, you're never going to find Mr. Darcy."*

I walked even faster, until the hairpins holding up my bun began pricking my scalp at every step, and my hair threatened to come loose and fall down my back.

Then I slowed. Why was I running, anyway? I walked into the nearest coffeehouse, ordered a delicious cold-coffee-and-cream *Einspänner* and sat with my back to a wall, glaring at anyone who came within ten feet of me.

When I left, the feeling was gone.

There was no news from the genealogists the next day, or the one after that.

I'd nearly reached the end of my resources: if the genealogists found anything, they were going to have to mail it.

At least I had the ballet to look forward to. But . . . what to wear? The afternoon of the ballet, I searched through my suitcase as if something appropriate had sneaked in when I wasn't looking. Nope. Just my familiar LA jeans and tees, chosen for ease and comfort, but totally wrong for the Vienna State Opera House. I sat down on the bed and examined my meager stash of cash. If I stretched my once-a-day meal plan to an entire week, I could buy something nice to wear.

Walking up the narrow old streets to Mariahilferstrasse, I got that feeling again! This time it was sharp, like a cold finger poking my neck.

I plunged through the door of the nearest dress shop, throwing a fast glance over my shoulder as I ran. Was that the guy with the beard again, vanishing into a hat store across the street?

Totally weirded out, I decided to buy something in that shop, if the prices weren't astronomical, and then go straight back to my pensione until it was time for the ballet.

The store had that distinctive aroma: part new carpet, part good fabric, and part zillion-dollar perfume that suggested *expensive.* And there I was in old jeans and a faded cotton top. Bracing myself for the inevitable rude treatment from salespeople who work in snobbish places, I assumed an air of confidence and waltzed in.

Sure enough, a conspicuously affronted expression settled over the features of the woman who minced with measured pace toward me, but then her eyes widened and the downturned red mouth stretched outward into a dignified but definite smile of welcome.

I said politely, in my most formal German, "I need something for the ballet tonight. Thanks."

She nodded, almost a bow, and in fifteen minutes I had exactly what I wanted: a lightweight, simple but well cut jersey dress in a cedarwood brown that matched my eyes. It was flattering, and—I reflected happily—it would roll up into a small sausage in my suitcase. Meanwhile the manager waited on me herself, to my amazement, with a manner of distant deference. Once (when I was in the dressing room and was pulling fabric over my head, so sound was muffled) I thought she addressed me by a different name, but then I wondered if she might be talking to someone else. At any rate I didn't respond, and she didn't repeat it.

When I was ready to go she murmured something about an account in so discreet a voice I couldn't hear her, but stopped when she saw the euros I held out. She stared as if she'd never seen money before, then took the proffered bills.

Back at the pensione, I got ready, wearing my hair up in a chignon instead of the usual practical knot, and put on my heeled sandals instead of my sturdy walking sandals.

I arrived at the Opera House to find that the pensione had kept their promise, bagging me a first-rate seat midway along the lowest balcony with an unimpeded view of the stage.

I sank back in my plush seat and surveyed the ornate glory of the Opera House. Observing the muted colors and fine jewels of the gathering patrons, I let my imagination relax, and it promptly superimposed a vivid image: Edwardian gowns and slick-haired men with monocles and faultless tuxes or splendid military uniforms, the air heavy with the scents of musk and ambergris and heavy florals and beeswax candles. They exchange nods and fan flirts with other titled patrons, and after watching the curtain roll up, anticipate a cozy à deux supper afterward in a nearby palace. Or, if one were more daring, a *very* cozy à deux supper in a quiet and lamplit cafe . . .

I landed back in the present when an elderly couple arrived in my row. We exchanged polite nods over the unoccupied seat next to me and I turned to the stage, relieved that that the single empty seat would guarantee my isolation.

The lights dipped and I settled back contentedly—and a shadow moved on the edge of my vision.

I glanced up as a man dropped into the seat next to mine. Ordinarily I would have glanced away again, but two things caught my attention. One, the way he took his seat. He didn't plump down like a shuffling student collapses, he did it with an air of grace and proprietary negligence. Rather as if he owned the seat. Or the Opera.

The second thing was his expression. He was looking directly at me. I met grayish blue eyes narrowed in humor and . . . irony? The shadows in the corners of his mouth, the slight lift to his chin signaled *gotcha.*

I was instantly on guard. His expression altered to a reflective surprise that was almost as immediately veiled.

Uh-oh. My glance had turned into a stare. *Thought he recognized me,* I decided, turning my attention firmly to the stage.

The lights dimmed, and King Kong could have been sitting next to me for all the awareness I gave to anything but the ballet. I was caught up in the powerful enchantment generated by music and movement merged. Having studied dance since I was five, I was unable to watch passively; my soul went down to flit among the *jetés tours* and *grandes,* leaving my body to tense unconsciously until my toes were bunched in my sandals and my hands twitched in my lap.

When the lights came up for the intermission I relaxed back in my seat, drawing a deep breath.

Then a light baritone voice at my side asked—in French, the familiar *tu*—what I thought of the ballet.

I gave my grandmother's French shrug, said something noncommittal, and he went on to ask if I would like to join him in a drink.

The definite tone of familiarity was not intimate or insulting. It was more like recognition, which was too unsettling for me to feel anything but wary, and so I refused, again politely. But firmly.

The exchange was brief, but I managed a fast check-out. He had a quantity of beautifully barbered collar-length thick dark hair, fine-stranded and glossy, a square face with classically refined bones, and he wore an expensive-looking dark suit. He'd turned slightly in his seat; a well-shaped hand lay negligently on the balcony. On that hand I saw a big, square-cut sapphire, glittering with the unmistakable bling of the Real McCoy. I perceived irregularities in the face of the stone—the carvings of an honest-to-historical-romance signet ring. The ring, his posture, even the marks of tiredness under his eyes and smudging his aristocratic cheekbones (The Smudge, I decided, of Dissipation) . . . he would have been perfect in Pelham black and ruffles.

I cut my gaze away, but not before the thought hit me: *Mr. Darcy.*

"You're laughing," he said in French. "What is it, my invitation or my accent?"

His tone was only mock-insulted; a smile curved his lips, but his brows lifted slightly in question. Again, I got that sense that something was going on, and I had no clue.

"Neither," I said. "But you can speak English if you want." His French was good, but his diction was more English than French.

Sure enough, he went on in English that sounded like he'd been educated at Oxford or Cambridge as he made a comment about the performance, to which I readily replied. I was tempted by my surroundings (which I felt required some dash) to fake a British accent for the fun of it. But my courage failed me and I replied in my bland Los Angeles accent, until the lights dipped and I turned my attention back to the stage.

Nothing marred my enjoyment of the rest of the performance.

When it had ended, I clapped until my hands smarted as the principal dancers took bow after bow.

When I stood up, I discovered that Mr. Darcy was gone.

FOUR

HIS IMAGE LINGERED. So, as I walked back to my pensione, the air soft and the lights twinkling in the trees, I let my imagination spin out a story that had to be more interesting than his real life as a lawyer or software salesman or insurance guy. I dressed him in Corinthian garb and imagined him gambling all night at White's with Lord Alvanley and Charles James Fox, then, having either won or lost fifty thousand pounds—his reaction would be the same for both—he would get up from his table with that same cool air, and in the dim light of dawn embark on a curricle race up the Great North Road. Or a duel at dawn in the Place des Vosges in Paris.

Next morning, the first thing I saw in the bleak light was my wallet. My flat wallet. I would never regret the ballet, or the dress (so I told myself) but I could only stay through one more night if I wanted to get to Scotland and tour Clan Murray's old hangout.

It was with a sense of defeat that I shoved my wallet into my jeans pocket and set out for one last sightseeing walk, stopping first to buy a few postcards. I wouldn't waste the money at an Internet café to tell Mom and Dad that I'd failed as Lord Peter Wimsey.

I found a bench along the flower garden outside the fairy-tale Gothic-spired city hall to write my cards. I still hadn't finished those letters in my suitcase. The nice thing about postcards is, they're shorter.

To Lisa and Kara, I wrote, *Hope you kicked ass at the tournament. My quest so far is kicking my ass.* On Lisa's I added, *So I went to the ballet as consolation. And guess who I saw? Mr. Darcy. Too bad my name is not Elizabeth!* The last card was to Mom and Dad. *No luck so far, but this time I put a bloodhound on the trail right away. Another day of sightseeing, and if there's no news, then I'm off to England, then Scotland.*

At least Blair Castle—which my dad had told me was the ancient home of the Murrays—surely hasn't up and vanished, I thought in disgust as I wandered across the Ring, which had once marked Vienna's medieval city wall.

I found myself on the elegant Kärtnerstrasse and reflected on how baroque it was that the most exclusive street in Vienna—the Rodeo Drive of Austria—was named Graben, or "graves." When I reached the ancient New Market area, lined with grand stone buildings, many with carved corbels and statuary, I was distracted by the distant rise and fall of men's voices singing.

The prospect of hearing Gregorian chant in an ancient stone cathedral drew me like a magnet. I found a mailbox and deposited the postcards still clutched in my fingers, then discovered I had reached the unobtrusive entrance to the Kaisergruft, the Hapsburg emperors' crypts below the austere Kapuzinerkirche. Time to pay the Hapsburgs my respects, having admired their city.

As I entered the royal crypt I left summer—time—behind. The air was cool, the light soft and gray. I thought I caught a whiff of incense as I slowly stepped in; the chanting had vanished, but this crypt was below the church proper.

I was not alone. As often happens overseas, the other tourists were Americans, their LA voices out of place in this ancient stone vault.

A family stood around as the father read to them from a guidebook. *Crack, snap!* That was a teenage daughter, bored eyes and tight clothes, cracking gum at her dad with intent. Two younger kids fidgeted and whispered behind a mother who hushed them crossly; the father's voice droned on, mispronouncing all the ancient names.

"Yeah, they're *all* corpses!" The boy poked his sister in triumph. "Wonder if any of 'em are in glass, like that gross church where Richard the Lionheart was locked up."

The girl gave a small shriek. The parents hushed them as the older girl drawled with detached teen enjoyment, "Oh Gooooo-oood, Joshua, that's grooo-ooss." *God* and *gross* were full-on two-note words.

As they shuffled by it felt like the timeless atmosphere closed in behind them, as the present swallowed them up.

Then I stepped through an arch into the baroque splendor of Maria Theresia's tomb. The silence here was resonant, or maybe it was the still air that only changes incrementally over the years. The giddiness sparkled at the edges of my vision as my gaze ranged over the tomb the empress shared with her husband, their carved semblances sitting atop the enormous sarcophagus, turned toward one another in eternal gaze as an angel watched over them; thrill zapped along my nerves. I stood a few steps from someone I admired—but 250 years created an impassable gulf.

Yet when I blinked there was her stout figure, impressive in swaths of baroque dress, as she gazed on the unfinished, ornate casket, as she gave a short nod, then indicated the wall nearby, which had been hollowed out.

No. There she *wasn't.*

I remembered my fourth grade field trip to the San Juan Capistrano Mission. The bus got lost on the windy street leaving, and we ended up overlooking the beach not far away. Excited to show off my knowledge, I pointed to the girl my own age in Acjachemen dress looking out over the sea, a row of kiicha huts overshadowed by elderberry trees lining a stream that tumbled down the rocks.

The kids didn't pay any attention, but the teacher said in that voice you learned early meant they didn't believe you, "*Very vivid imagination you have there, Kim! You may write a story about her for your trip report, if you like.*"

And when I got home and told the family, Gran asked, "*Did anyone else see the little girl?*"

"*No.*"

"*Then she was not there. Aurelia Kim, if you make up little stories, people will not believe you when you do tell the truth.*"

Wasn't that right around the time she stopped telling me those fairy tales about Fyadar and Xanpia—

A noise, the scrape of feet, the murmur of voices broke into the memory. I leaned against a stone, the giddiness sharpening briefly to dizziness, then it was gone. The hollowed wall beyond the empress' gigantic sarcophagus was actually a narrow niche containing a plain coffin.

Adjacent to the royal pair lay another plain coffin, remarkable only in its total lack of ornamentation. To my surprise it did not belong to Maria Theresia's governess Gräfin Karoline Fuchs-Mollard, who I knew was the only nonroyal person buried in that crypt. It held another emperor—Maria Theresia's heir, Joseph II.

I stared at the plain casket surmounted only by a simple cross. Here lay the remains of a life of intense bitterness. He was an absolute monarch, brilliant and filled with enlightenment zeal, married to his beloved at a young age, yet he lost everything that mattered most. He wanted his epitaph to read "Here lies Joseph II, who failed in every undertaking." At least he was spared the horrible death of his sister, Maria Antonia, renamed Marie Antoinette when she crossed the French border as a young teen.

The sound of the American dad's voice reading out loud snapped me out of reverie. I approached the narrow niche that I had thought a much larger space. Here I discovered the governess' quietly elegant coffin with a heartfelt inscription by Maria Theresia. How powerful the empress was to have overborne tradition in order to include this woman among royalty. And how odd, my imagining a room beyond this narrow niche—

"Awww, Dad, that's gro-oss. Let's *gooo*-oooh." The kid's whine echoed. The teenager's opinion was rendered with an expert triple-snap of gum. But he said coaxingly, "C'mon, kids, only a couple more. This is history! Pay attention and you'll get an A next year for sure!"

I moved on, thinking about the trappings of empire weighting what was unmistakably human flesh. Was the most powerful of all the Hapsburg emperors, Charles V, interred here, or had Philip II buried him in the Escorial in Spain? The other tourists had moved in the opposite direction.

Silence settled over the dim, austere alcoves as I continued my search, a silence which gently extinguished the sense of immediacy. Even my breathing was muted.

Then the leisurely ring of hard heels worked slowly into my awareness. I whirled—and stared into the shadowed eyes of my seatmate at the ballet the night before. He was tall.

"Contemplating memento mori?" he asked with a slight smile, *contemplating* in French.

He's not surprised to see me.

This awareness startled me so much that I said randomly, continuing my previous train of thought: "As it happens, I'm beginning to wonder what Ariosto was trying to do for Charles V and his empire in *Orlando Furioso.* Chivalry as it should have been?"

His brows lifted slightly and he gave a soft laugh. "And never was. Every time Orlando turned around, there was another monster. Or an evil knight."

I did the Mick Jagger point-and-shoot toward Maria Theresia's magnificent sarcophagus, a gesture I'd learned from my old hippie dad. "So Ariosto, and Spenser, too, weren't dolorously mourning the great days of parfait knights and quests?"

The guy gave me the strangest look—like I'd sprouted a banana out of my forefinger, or had begun chanting in Martian.

Stung, I said, "The conflict. Tension. Between the ideal of the mystical union of religious and temporal power—unity of empire—and real politics of those days."

"You mean Spenser and Ireland?"

"Bigger than that. Or smaller. Ideal versus reality. Code versus behavior. Underneath all the cross-dressing fun and the glorious fights . . . well, I wonder if people always look backward rather than ahead when they sense their world splintering—"

In the dimness of the alcove, his expression was difficult to define. Oops! In my enthusiasm I had switched to English, the language in which I'd debated these subjects at UCLA. I felt like a pompous twit, yapping at a perfect stranger. "Sorry. Didn't mean to bore," I said stiffly.

His lips parted. Before he could speak the teenage girl's voice echoed slightly from around the corner, "Wow, Dad! She was only seventeen, and he shot her? How sick is *that?*"

Mr. Darcy and I rounded the corner to the alcove where Franz Joseph and his family were interred. There stood the teenage girl, grinning at Mr. Darcy. She snapped gum at him in exactly the same manner her great-great-great grandmother might once have snapped her fan, and walked slowly away, the thong strap above her lowrider tight jeans seesawing up and down with every roll of her skinny hips.

"Hell," he said softly, his eyes narrowed in sudden humor as he turned away. "What was that?"

"Just follow the smacking gum, Humbert, and you'll find out."

He gave a soundless laugh, then sent me another glance of surprise that swiftly turned speculative. "So you've read Nabokov." It wasn't quite a question.

In the background the father's voice droned unheeding as he read a flaccid account of the unhappy Mayerling story. As if in epitaph, the little brother chortled in a loud voice, "The bones come out on Halloween! *King* bones!"

"Moooom!" the little girl wailed.

"Quiet, kids," the mother hissed. "Listen to Dad! This is real history!"

"I'd rather watch TV," the boy muttered.

"Yes, I've read Nabokov. I've even read Patrick Dennis." I was about to add *thanks to my dad,* but when I saw a searching gaze instead of the expected smile, my laugh did a belly flop.

The tightness about his mouth changed to mild enquiry. "Shall we have a coffee?"

The timeless mood had splintered, landing me squarely back among my fellow humans—including one I couldn't make sense of. Coffee—public place. I took in that handsome face, and thought, *Oh, what the hell. Maybe he'll turn out to be boring.*

So I said, "Okay."

FIVE

OUTSIDE WAS BRIGHT light and color, a brisk breeze, noise, movement. Mr. Darcy walked beside me in silence. I sent a couple of fast checkouts his way, trying not to be obvious about it. He was wearing a tailored jacket over an expensive white shirt worn open at the neck, gray slacks, good leather loafers.

I let him lead, as he knew the territory. And then the question came. He didn't ask for my name, which one might expect. Instead he asked a different personal question, in German—familiar mode—"Do you make that pilgrimage often?"

The *du* pronouns, I had learned since my arrival here, were used more widely among strangers, young people anyway, than we'd been taught in school. But his tone was familiar as well as the verb form, as if we'd known each other for years.

I shot a look at him. In the full light of day those marks in his face that I had fancifully attributed to dissipation the night before now seemed more like ordinary human exhaustion.

"To the Kaisergruft?" On his nod of assent I went on, "That was my first visit." Bothered by that *"often,"* and by his unexplained switch to German, I threw back what I sensed was a challenge by asking in my elementary-school Russian, "Do you go there often?"

I would have liked to have said *Do you make that pilgrimage often?* but I didn't remember the word for "pilgrimage."

Damned if he didn't answer, and in such good Russian I almost couldn't follow him because of the speed of the words. "Looks like every tourist in Vienna had the same idea," he said, pointing to the expensive Graben cafe he'd chosen. It was packed.

He switched back to English. "Unless you've a favorite place, I'll show you another crypt, shall I?"

We turned toward St. Stephen's Cathedral, then merged into the stream of late afternoon Kärtnerstrasse traffic.

"You're leaving Vienna soon?"

"Yep."

"Where're you staying?"

"A pensione. Where are you leading me?"

"The Zwölfapostelkeller. It's nearly old enough to have claimed their patronage."

"Dude! Sounds awesome," I said with enthusiasm; I had not been to any of the famed weinkellers. Sightseeing I enjoy on my own. Drinking alone I do not.

On the other side of the cathedral we twisted and turned, finally ending up in a narrow street, Sonnenfelsgasse. *Keller* means basement: down we went, three stories worth. Over an ancient brick archway was set a stone carving dated 1561. A heady combination of odors embraced us: wine, bread, people. Revelers made congenial noise in the wooden booths.

As we entered the ancient stone-ceilinged vault of the Brunnenkeller, lined with booths down both sides, my guide signaled a waiter who was bustling by. I didn't hear the order because a burst of laughter from a neighboring booth drowned the voices. Six or seven older men with rosily flushed faces squeezed jovially round a table meant for four.

Mr. Darcy touched my elbow. "This way."

This way . . . *who?* Something about his not asking my name irked me. Like he already knew, or assumed he knew. I decided to see how long before he asked, and I wouldn't help by asking his. It wasn't like I had anything else to do—and he sure was fun to look at.

We found an empty booth and slid onto the hard, high-backed benches. The table appeared to be a couple hundred years old; as I breathed in the complexities of the air that giddy sensation came back, bringing brief, vivid images: young people in Empire-style clothes, heads bent in earnest conversation, fingering the unchanged rough stone wall, and wondering what Napoleon would do next; youths in German versions of Cavalier coats and long tangled hair speculating what it would be like to be ruled by a woman emperor; and most brief, young fellows in ruffs worrying about what that madman Luther was doing up in the north, nailing his 95 Theses to the castle church door in Wittenberg.

I blinked and the images vanished.

I ran a thumbnail absently along old grooves in the top of the table as the waiter appeared and set down a liter of white wine with two heavy, wide-based glasses. "White wine?"

Mr. Darcy paid, then poured out the wine with a practiced gesture. "Kremser," he said in that tone of *you know that as well as I do.* "From the Kremser district."

"I've never tried it," I returned promptly, resisting the temptation to ask if I had to give a secret password before learning his name.

He lifted his wineglass with an ironic air. "Prosit."

I tried to come up with a suitable reply—and laughed. "Skumps!"

I sipped. Usually I don't like white wine, but this was light and smooth.

"Skumps?"

"What, you don't recognize it? The toast of kings."

I was rewarded with an enigmatic smile and a short question in a Slavic-sounding language that sounded familiar. But you hear a lot of languages around a university.

I shrugged, then sipped again. And because I couldn't figure the why of his language quiz, I did what I usually do: turned the situation into a game, and gave him the resounding alliterative verse describing Grendel's death.

"*Beowulf.*" He lounged back on his bench. Then smiled, his blue gaze watchful. "Where the hell did you pick that up?"

"Where else? At school."

"Which would be?"

"UCLA."

He reached for the liter and poured out more wine for us both. "Tell me about UCLA."

I described the history and linguistics departments, moving with wine-loosened enthusiasm to some of the pet eccentrics on the faculty and among the grad students there and in other departments. His gaze was steady on my face as he listened. He said nothing until I finally ran out of gas and snatched up my wineglass to wet my dry mouth.

"You say you learned your French there?"

"Nope. That I got at home." And because it felt awkward to be chatting about school and home without the usual niceties of manners, I dropped the game and gave him a Subtle Hint. "My name's Kim, by the way. Kim Murray."

"Kim," he repeated in an odd, ironic voice.

"Something wrong with it?" I sounded more belligerent than I felt. *Whoa, better slow down on the wine.*

"Nothing at all."

"Do I have to pass a test before you tell me yours?"

"Alec. I apologize, I thought I had." The irony was back, distinctly.

"I'm betting you were an Oxbridge student, and before that, you went to one of those ancient schools that the British call public but are actually private. Not to mention mega-posh. Am I right? Was it Eton?"

"Downside." He lifted a shoulder, his tone that ironic one again—like I already knew that, and who did I think I was fooling?

So I said chirpily, "I've never met anyone who went to one of those. Tell me! Was it really a seething den of slashy passions, like in Alec Waugh's novel, or was it sadistic like C. S. Lewis' school, or . . ." I waved a hand. "Was it all jolly games fun and tuck-shop treats and rags, like Chalet School and Billy Bunter?"

He sat back, gaze distant; his cell phone vibrated insistently. Then he blinked, his attention back on me. "A combination of all things is probably somewhere near the truth. I expect you get what you're looking for. Could be said for any school."

"And you?" I asked, steepling my fingers.

"What I got from them is an excellent education. What I looked for . . . was growing up and getting on with my life."

My ear caught among the pure upper-class British words a subtle twist, distinctly non-English. Russian?

I snickered. "Are you a Russian spy?"

His brows twitched upward, then he smiled. "No. Are you?"

The wine-fueled laughter was hard to stop—not that I tried hard. "No way." I smacked my chest with a thump. "Solid American citizen, that's me! You've an accent," I added. "The way you said 'education.' The linguistics profs train students to listen for those clues, you see," I repeated the word *education* but my wine-loosened tongue couldn't reproduce either the British or the other accent.

His gaze was steady under an ironic brow lift. "Like they trained you to speak French?"

This time I didn't use Dad's point-and-shoot, but my grandmother's airy, elegant gesture. "I told you, I learned my French at home. In fact, I scraped up my tuition money this year by student-teaching *je suis, tu es, il, elle est.*"

"Do all Americans speak French at home?"

"No," I said softly as I remembered my grandmother smiling proudly at me. "Grandmère's English is okay but she never spoke it with me. She used to say, *'Though times have changed and changed again since I was small, I don't believe you will ever be sorry to speak French like a Parisian lady. This is the only gift I can give to you, Aurelia Kim—'* "

He set his wineglass down with a precise movement, and despite the roar of noise in the background I heard the ring of glass on the hardwood, which broke my reverie.

I sighed. "I never got what she meant by that. She was always doing things for me."

Alec's gaze was steady, reflecting the glitter of the atmospheric candles set in sconces. His expression was assessing in a way that I found odd.

"Sorry. I'm babbling," I said. "But I usually don't drink during the day. Hey," I made a discovery. "We killed that whole liter! And," I added, "I need to make a restroom run."

"I can show you where it is."

"You're on."

We wound our way back through the increasing crowds of patrons and up two flights of stone steps.

When I came out Alec was there, lounging against the wall, cell phone in hand. When I stepped near he snapped the cell shut and straightened. I bit my lips and said, "I could've found my way back. Actually we were done, weren't we? I know I'd best not drink anymore, so I think I'll shove along. Well, it's been—"

"How about a last toast. I ordered a half-liter, and I'd better pay for it, at least."

I peered up into those enigmatic light blue eyes, looking for the warning smirk or leer that would herald the usual come-on.

Nothing. No expression at all.

"Oh, may's well. One more. *Only* one." I shrugged recklessly. "And then I'm outta here."

"Thank you." He gestured politely for me to go before him.

Presently we were at the booth again, and there was a half-liter, with fresh glasses. "Catch the waiter's eye?" Alec murmured as we slid in.

Obligingly I leaned out, watching a trifle blearily as the waiter appeared and served the loud gentlemen. Finally I succeeded in catching the waiter's attention, and sat back in triumph as Alec placed a full glass before me. Alec paid, then raised his glass in a silent salute.

I said, "To Vienna!"

"Vienna," he repeated. He reached across the table and touched his glass against mine, then with a quick movement he drank his wine off.

I started to follow suit (with a suitable flourish) but stopped halfway. I'd drunk too much already, and besides, this wine was different, subtly bitter. I put my glass down and tried unsuccessfully to suppress a shudder. "Okay, I'm done," I said. "Whew, that stuff is too dry for me."

"I apologize for the taste."

"No problemo! Not your fault. Probably a newer bottle than the last." I smiled, but the room had turned stuffy and warm. I drew in a slow breath. "Well, Mr. Da—" (cough) "—um, Alec. It's been nice."

If he noticed the slip, he gave no sign. "I'll walk out with you. No wish to stay and drink alone."

"Okay." I laughed inanely as I slid out from my bench.

Once again I was giddy, as if I had grown to a height of seven or eight feet. Light gleamed brightly off people's faces, glasses, watches, clothes, and the shadows behind them grayed and blurred, overlaying the guests here with more fanciful images of people in historical costume, as if my imagination was channeling the past.

I didn't think I was *that* drunk, I thought blurrily.

A strange sense of distance—a recklessness—swept through me and I threw my head back to look up at Alec's face. He was right behind me. I stumbled, and his hand moved swiftly to my arm to help me restore my balance.

"Thanks. Ech. I feel strange. But it was fun," I rambled on. "I must say," I added, my tongue ranging as freely as my thoughts, "if this was a pickup—and I'm so glad it's not—it was the weirdest I ever had."

"Did you want to be picked up?" he returned, smiling. "Watch that step," he added under his breath.

"No. Yes. No. Don't want complications," I mumbled, staring up the stairway I'd come down a few minutes before without any problems. It seemed to stretch up for miles. "Oxygen, that's what I need. No air in here." I tried a dramatic turn, and stumbled. "Came along cuz . . . you seemed like Mr. Darcy. Not Mr. Darcy." In case he misconstrued, I added, "Byronic villain."

This caught him by surprise, and he laughed. It was a quick, genuine laugh, unlike the guarded countenance he'd shown me during our conversation. His smile was singularly attractive.

"Um," I said appreciatively.

"Last flight." He steered me with care.

By the time we reached the top, he was half holding me up. "Wha's hap-pening?" I croaked, my lips feeling icy-cold and stiff.

"Door's here," Alec said kindly.

Sweet, cool air washed across my face as he guided me outside.

I sucked it in gratefully—and my knees buckled. At once two

strong arms picked me up; my head rolled to the side, my perspective whirled.

From the increasingly confusing shadows emerged a green car with unfamiliar smooth lines. Alec stepped toward it. He opened the back door and smiled at me.

"Huh?"

"Let's go home, Aurelia," he replied gently, as the shadows merged and my eyelids drifted down.

SIX

PRISONER OF ZENDA.

If you're thinking my experiences so far match that hapless scion of the Elphbergs and Rassendylls—well, just wait.

I woke up groggily and slowly, to find myself stretched out on a narrow bed with another bunk a couple of feet above me. A steady rhythm penetrated into my aching brain . . . *lank-lank, thunk-thunk . . . lank-lank, thunk-thunk* . . . as my bed quivered—

A train? I was on a train?

I've been roofied.

Adrenalin burned from my aching brain to my feet. I threw off the light blanket covering me and sat up. My head throbbed as a sharp odor of stale wine drifted up from my clothes.

I was still wearing my clothes, right down to my sandals.

Okay, good news? I hadn't been molested.

Bad news? *I was on a train in the middle of nowhere.*

I took in the tidy, impersonal compartment of a wagon-lit, trying to comprehend that I was awake. And here.

Next to the bed someone had thoughtfully put a couple of bottles of Evian. I grabbed one and barely had the strength to twist off the top.

I chugged the water and sat back, breathing gently, as the residual pain gradually began to diminish. After I finished the water I felt well enough to look around. I sustained another nasty shock when I spotted my suitcase lying on the suitcase rack.

Memories surfaced murkily: laughing uncontrollably in the pensione lobby; being unable to stand on my own and thinking it terribly hilarious; the blaring voice echoing through the loudspeaker at the train station as I tried to walk across the wide, glaringly lit main hall with—

I winced and shook my head despite the headache. My hairclip was loose, yanking on my scalp. I removed the clip and my hair rolled down and hit the bunk behind me with a soft *plop.* Massaging my scalp slowly, I thought back. I remembered stumbling and laughing, my arm up around a male shoulder as a strong hand gripped my waist . . . my own flat but enthusiastic soprano joining a pleasing light baritone in singing old Beatles tunes.

Why?

I glared at my suitcase. I never told Alec where I was staying, yet the green car had driven straight to my pensione, with me giggling drunkenly in the back of it. Rubbing my eyes, I tried to remember what the voices around me had said, and I remembered nothing. Nothing but those Beatles songs . . . and the vaguest, most ephemeral memory of a voice floating somewhere nearby as at last I stretched out and shut my eyes, "Sleep well, Aurelia. We'll talk tomorrow."

Right, I thought, planting my feet on the floor. *Like hell we will.*

Ignoring the throbbing in my head, I pulled the suitcase onto the bed and unzipped it. There were my clothes, pretty much as I had left them. But my passport, my plane ticket for the return home, even the letters to Lisa and my folks that I'd begun on the train between Paris and Vienna, all were gone from the side pocket where I had kept them. I slapped my jeans pocket—my wallet was missing as well.

I yanked the zipper shut, jammed my hair clip back over my coiled braid to anchor it, and stalked to the compartment door.

I reached toward the handle to slam it open, then froze. Wait a minute. Whatever's going on, no one knows I'm awake yet. This might be an advantage.

There was a small window beyond my shoulder, with the shade modestly pulled down. I put my eye up to the crack between the shade and the window and peered out.

In one direction I saw an empty train passageway with windows looking out onto swiftly passing hilly scenery. Not so in the other direction. Leaning against the window staring out was the gray-bearded man in the Tyrolean suit whom I had seen at least once in Vienna after our encounter on the Glorietta at Schönbrunn.

A kidnapping, I thought. No, an honest-to-Regency-romance *abduction*. But why me? I was neither rich nor important.

One thing was for sure, I wasn't going to hang around long enough to find out why.

Surely someone nosed in to check on me from time to time. They would in a mystery! I retreated to the bed and stretched out under the blanket again while I tried to plan my next step.

What do I know? An English (?) guy who calls himself Alec, possibly teamed up with a short man who wears a Tyrolean suit, abducted me, and stuck me on a train—?

Anything else: zip.

Not much to go on.

The *lank-lank, thunk-thunk* was gradually slowing. Not a minute later my door clicked and slid slowly open. My heart started thumping but I kept my breathing even and my eyes shut. Five or ten seconds that seemed like half an hour passed and then the door quietly slid shut again. *Click.*

I sprang up. Grabbed my suitcase. This was an old train car, with windows that opened. I forced my shaking fingers to ease the window down.

A quick glance over my shoulder showed the curtain trembling in the new current of air that rushed into the compartment. I stuck my head out again, the air buffeting my face. If I was going to jump, I had to do it before they pulled into whatever station was coming up.

I leaned farther. Hilly pastureland and no people or houses in sight.

The train is slowing. Has to be now.

I levered my suitcase out, swung it, and dropped it as gently as I could, shoved a leg out, the other, then—carefully—my head, clinging to the upper part of the window with my fingers.

Count to three. Hold my breath, tighten my guts. I braced my feet against the side of the train, and—*one, two, three!*—jumped.

And hit with a thud that knocked my breath out. I tumbled like a rag doll, terrifyingly aware of the roaring clash of train wheels nearby. When I stopped rolling I lay gasping, grateful to be alive, until the last few cars passed. Then raised my head. My vision swam as the train thundered on down the track. No alarms sounded; no sudden braking sent up sparks.

I wavered to my feet. One shoulder throbbed like a buffalo had stomped it, and a stone or something had gouged my rump during my roll down the embankment. I was amazed that I'd made it.

I began a lead-footed lope back along the tracks to find my suitcase. It seemed a mile away, though it was probably only five hundred yards, if that, and it was surprisingly intact, aside from one of the wheels being bent.

As I straightened up I caught sight of a patient group of cattle on a hillock on the other side of the tracks. The creatures stood motionless, watching me. When you only see cows on TV, you don't notice that they are *large.* Cow attacks are not a big part of TV action sequences, but I was too shaky to take any chances. Doing a one-eighty, I struck out in the opposite direction. The cockeyed suitcase wheels promptly tried to roll in different directions, so I picked the thing up by its handle.

I was in a river valley of some kind. Squinting upward, I spotted the sun glaring through a whitish haze low over the horizon.

Morning. East, that way. Wait. What if it's sunset? I could have slept through an entire day without knowing it.

But there was a look of morning to the dew glistening on the weeds and grasses around me, and to the butterflies and bees moving about their day's business.

The agenda: one, finding some sort of civilization and getting the authorities to put me in touch with a U.S. Embassy; two, getting something to eat.

Seemed easy enough.

Then the grind of an engine and the crunch of gravel startled me. A vehicle! Should I—no, wait. I'd been kidnapped. It seemed unlikely that the Evil Alec and his bearded minion could be pursuing me—but then I would've thought it unlikely to go out for a drink and wake up on a train to God knows where.

I scrambled off the road and flung myself and my suitcase behind a shrub. Half a minute later an ancient, spectacularly rusted and decrepit pickup truck rattled by, with fifteen or twenty chattering guys squeezed bouncing and jouncing onto the back. It disappeared down the road, kicking up gravel and dust and spewing out enough diesel exhaust for five buses.

I coughed, waving at the blue cloud, my empty stomach lurching in protest. Those guys were probably workers on their way to the daily job—expected if it was morning. But I'd woken up on a train, when I should be buying my ticket to London.

"That does it. Never so much as mention Ariosto in public again," I announced to the air. Somehow talking out loud to myself was comforting.

A town lay on the other side of the river valley—I made out a church spire and the golden-walled buildings so common in this region—but (being a Los Angeles native) I was certain I'd find what I wanted long before I had to walk that far.

I picked up my case and started hiking through the adjacent field so I wouldn't have to worry about the road.

When I first left for Europe, I'd been proud of my careful packing. Thus far, my suitcase had been easy to roll from station to hotel, hotel to station.

As I trudged across the rough field, the suitcase's weight seemed to increase by increments of ten pounds. Shifting it from hand to hand, I passed vista after vista of pretty scenery—rocks, fields, short tree-shaded cliffs, small flocks of sheep—and no houses or people.

The sun shone squarely on top of my head when I stumbled over a rock and sprawled heavily in the tall grass.

I groaned, rolling over and shading my eyes against the noon sun. Could have been an LA sky: bright blue except for blotchy clouds moving in grand unison—

Patchy clouds. At home, those usually preceded rain.

"Oh, great." I added some speculation about the genealogy and probable postmortem fates of blue-eyed Alec and his Tyrolean friend.

That felt good, but didn't do squat for fixing my situation. So I sat up. My head thrummed sharply, no longer from drugs and wine but from thirst and hunger. I scratched irritably at my legs and picked the worst of the stickers from the hems of my jeans. Then I got to my feet again, wincing as I tried to swallow. My tongue felt like a gym sock that had successfully evaded the laundry for the entire championship season.

I need water. And soon.

Where?

A line of trees grew along the edge of the hill below me. Hadn't I read in some book about finding streams near trees?

I opened my hands. On each palm a double line of new and angry blisters stung painfully. My suitcase felt like someone had inserted a dozen anvils into it.

The air was too warm and humid for me to take the clothes out and carry them, or wear them, so the last alternative was to hide the suitcase and come back for it. The sun was directly overhead so I was unsure of my direction, but to my right I noticed a cliff with an odd granite pattern topped by two distinctive scrub pines.

I fixed the landmark in my mind, pushed my suitcase under a bush with yellow flowers, oriented myself in relation to that cliff, and started off downslope at a much faster pace.

The trees grew alongside a stream trickling over mossy rocks. Stumbling toward it, I thought *typhoid, dysentery,* and my lips stayed resolutely closed as I dropped to my knees, put my hands down in the cold rush, and splashed my hot face, thinking with intense regret of that second Evian bottle left on the shelf back in the train compartment.

Two small birds chattered shrilly in protest, shot out of a low shrub, and zipped into the sky.

My gaze dropped back to the water longingly, my modern hygienic worries wavering until I noticed things floating along the top of the water. Nothing overtly nasty. Grass, leaves, pieces of bark, bits of sheep wool. With my luck, those sheep I'd seen back upstream used this water for a bathtub and a toilet as well as a drinking fountain. Ew.

Pick a direction, I thought, as my skull pounded rhythmically. Any direction. All roads lead to hell.

On the other side of the stream stretched a wide field, a circle of low farm buildings in the center. The fields surrounding the buildings had been plowed under and neat rows of crops grew. My giddiness grew, light shimmering over the bobbing backs of workers in the field.

They could have been medieval, or workers from the Thirty Years' War, ears wary for the distant thunder of armies riding heedless across their fields. No matter whose side they were on, armies were always bad news for the farmers as well as their livestock and crops.

As I neared, the light coruscated like heat waves. Was that a tractor? No, a hay stack.

My isolation broke when the workers straightened up to stare. The men wore homemade work clothes; the women long, dull-colored dresses, their hair hidden under kerchiefs. I felt as if I'd fallen into a time machine and back a century.

I licked my dry lips before attempting a polite smile. A couple of younger men nudged each other and exchanged comments in a guttural tongue, then grinned at me. Two of the women, one young and one old, stared back at me, radiating stony disapproval.

I consciously straightened my backbone as I met the eyes of the oldest woman. Overhead, a flock of large brown birds squawked by. The woman's brown, creased face did not change. I pointed to my mouth and croaked, "Water? Wasser? Eau?"

She flicked her eyes to the younger woman; as if they communicated by telepathy, the younger one nodded shortly to me and beckoned for me to follow.

"Do you speak German?" I asked in that tongue as we started across the fields.

Her tightly compressed lips didn't move as she gave her head a shake. She seemed to be about my age. Her hair was bound under a kerchief, and she wore an old, coarse apron over her dark blouse and skirt. A crucifix lay on her breast, swinging with her long strides.

She did not look at me until we neared the low, ramshackle buildings. We walked into an unfenced barnyard, and there was a pump with its own roof.

On a shelf above the water pump sat a wooden bucket with a ladle in it. She lifted the bucket down. It was filled with water. She dipped the ladle and held it out to me.

It was warm and tasted slightly flat, with a seasoning of wood. I sucked it up greedily. When I handed the ladle back her face had changed, and she said something in a language I did not know. When I shrugged, she dipped the ladle and helped herself to a slug.

"Thanks," I said, and repeated it in German.

"You are real," she said in a Germanic-sounding dialect. But as she said it, a shaft of sun lanced down, and for an eye blink I could see right through her.

Thoroughly unsettled, I started on my way again; her footsteps faded as she strode back toward the fields.

Another hour or two along, the countryside began to roughen. Steeper inclines and larger rocks slowed me down, but there were more trees to shadow me intermittently from the white glare of the midday sun.

After toiling with increasing labor and decreasing speed, when I finally blundered onto a road, I stayed on it. The sky was hidden by clouds. I had long since lost sight of my suitcase-cliff, but I did try to memorize all the subsequent twists and turns of the road. I was too tired to care about cars, and I had had it with foraging through fields.

The road wound upward at an ever steeper incline until it narrowed as it entered a village perched on the side of a forested slope. Scenic as all get-out, but my feet were not appreciating the wild, Brontëian heights. The buildings were old, low, made of stone, with small windows and thick walls covered with a plaster painted that golden color so common in the south. They had to be centuries old—most were crumbling and mossy. The single street was cobbled only from about five hundred yards before the village started until the same distance past the last house.

The white glare had diminished somewhat, but the humidity remained. I squinted against the headache that blurred my vision. No signs evident, either on the street or on the houses. No people, either. My ankles, still sore from the impact of jumping off the train, jarred with every uneven step on those cobblestones. But I scarcely noticed. I was too creeped out by the sensation of being watched from behind those dark, blank windows.

In the last, low, old building, a swarm of flies circled lazily in an open door. I took a few steps toward it. Nothing was visible from outside. The thick air smelled of unrefrigerated meat. From within came sounds—the scratch of a wooden chair on a flagstone floor, the clank of something metallic being set on wood.

Someone was in there, looking out at me. And not in welcome, or wouldn't they call something to me? Instinctive fear—a woman alone, no ID, no help in sight—prompted me to back away and continue on. Two more small houses, a sharp right turn—and I was out of the village. I paused for a fast scan: no street lights or electrical wires.

All right. Maybe I'd be better off finding a place that had upgraded their communications tech to at least the level of 1900.

I trekked about a mile along the road, which had narrowed to a single lane. A steep, tree-shadowed cliff rose sharply to my left, an equally sharp hillside slanted below toward an unseen stream tumbling away. Gradually I became aware of the rustle of leaves rising above the hissing roar of the unseen stream below. The high tree branches overhead tossed in a rising wind that I did not feel around me. The branches cast no shadow, and in the distance thunder muttered, dying away to a low rumble.

A bluish flicker gave me a nanosecond of warning before the skies opened on my head with a world-shaking thunderclap. I made an abrupt about-face and started marching back, opening my mouth to get at least some good out of the drenching downpour.

Maybe I was better off risking the village. Except . . . how far would I get with no money? Sorely regretting the magic talisman of cash, I won't go so far as to say I felt naked, but you get the idea.

Well, I was rounding the sharp corner on the outskirts of the village when the raindrops ahead lit up in sparkling beams about four feet from the ground: car lights.

My discomforts had driven The Enemy out of my mind for the greater part of the day, and even now I couldn't believe they would try to chase after me, much less be able to find me. Last night seemed a totally separate nightmare from this. Nevertheless I sprang between the last pair of cottages, pressing close to the wall as I sidled along its rough contour (I can still feel that crumbling plaster under my palms) until I reached the front corner. I peered around as the car stopped outside the butcher shop.

The driver flung open the door, got out, slammed the door shut, and strode around the front of the car toward the building. As he passed briefly in front of the car lights his profile was illuminated.

It was Alec.

He looked even more tired, and decidedly more disheveled, than he had the night before.

I gloated—*Ha! Ha!*—and then oops! I was standing next to a sheer wall, as exposed as a bug on glass. I scuttled to the back of the cottage and stood at the edge of a vegetable garden, peering back. Presently came the *thunk!* of a car door shutting. The engine roared to life, then the accelerating car shot down the lane, sending mud flying in all directions. Good riddance.

So now what?

Not onward, obviously. Or back. When he got far enough to realize even a marathon runner could not have covered that distance, what choice but to retrace?

I ran down the road until I was out of sight of the village. Then, facing the slope below, I drew in a long breath. "Here goes nothing."

And I was so right.

Slipping and oozing down a mud-running mountainside is nothing I would have enjoyed even if I hadn't been tired, hungry, lost, scared and semidrowned in a full-on thunderstorm. I bumped and slipped and rolled and fell, then climaxed my trip with an ignominious splat as one foot plunged into a hole (filled with slimy mud) and stuck. I fell face-down in the mud, my ankle wrenching excruciatingly.

For a long moment I lay there in the mud, cursing with Catullan fluency.

Good as it felt, it got me nowhere. So I sat up and faced into the rain, which at least washed some of the mud off my face, though my eyes stung and my teeth gritted from the load I'd already taken aboard. Then I checked my ankle. My years in dance had taught me a bit about leg and foot injuries. A light sprain was my guess. Not enough to be serious—as long as I kept from walking on it.

"Right," I said to the thunder. "What now?"

I was sitting there, massaging my foot and debating what bright idea to try next, when twin glares emerged from the darkness below and to my left. A square, black car loomed out of the dark gray rain and crawled along slowly. From one of its windows a powerful beam flashed up and down along the slope I was on.

There was no way they weren't going to find me.

Wincing against the headache, I forced myself to my feet. To hell with fate, destiny—or inevitability. The Murrays may go down in defeat, but they go down fighting, my father once said, and so I began inching my way back up the cliffside, as the sweep of the flashlight moved closer and closer and then lit up the area around my silhouette on the muddy incline.

The light passed on—and then jerked agitatedly back as the car slammed to a stop. I peeked over my shoulder.

Two car doors flew open, and two tall male figures leaped out, one burly and one slim.

I meant to hustle up the hillside, but another hidden pothole caused my throbbing ankle to twist. The wrench knocked me to my knees.

The two men reached me.

Alec said something in that Slavic-sounding language as two different hands gripped my arms and helped me to my feet. I jerked my arms violently free, shouting, "Don't touch me!"

—and fell back with a *splorch* into the mud.

The big guy backed off and trained his flashlight on me. Alec reached into the light and pulled me to my feet again. I stiffened, ready to claw and bite—and he waited. Offering no violence. I knew I couldn't win any fight here, in fact a try would probably do more damage to me than to them. All right. So I'd bide my time.

Alec must have felt my decision through his grip on my arm, for he shifted his hand to under my elbow. Support.

The car was preferable to a muddy hillside in the middle of nowhere in pouring rain. I sighed, and cooperated as he started slowly downhill. "Ow. Ow. Ow," I groaned under my breath.

Now that "what comes next?" had thus summarily been taken out of my hands, my temper kindled again, and at every painful, squishing step burned brighter.

"Come along," Alec said grimly when at last we reached the car, and he thrust me into the front seat. The bulky man snapped off the flashlight and got in beside me without once looking at me. Alec slid in behind the wheel on the other side and slammed the running engine into gear with a blow of his palm that told me a lot about the state of his own temper. The car boosted forward with a roar that pressed us all back into our seats.

SEVEN

SO THERE I WAS. *Me.* Aurelia Kim Murray, law-abiding citizen of Los Angeles, California, squashed between two strange men in an unfamiliar car in the middle of God knows where in a deluge, and soaked and mud-smeared from braid to sandals.

And I hadn't done anything to deserve it.

I kept my eyes focused front and center. The road was scarcely discernable beyond a windshield under full blast as if sprayed by a fire hose. As the silence grew protracted I said through chattering teeth, "There anything to eat in this hearse?"

"No," Alec replied.

I'd said it to be goading; if he had offered me anything I would have turned it down with comprehensive disdain. I knew it was stupid to want to pick a fight. I should be afraid, but I wasn't—yet!—my Murray temper was up, and if I didn't do something to discharge the righteous anger simmering in me I would explode.

The car screeched around a narrow turn. I glanced at Alec's hands, which were steady on the wheel. He knew what he was doing, all right, so I said snidely, "You'd better slow down if you don't want to burn tracks from here to Texas."

"Would you prefer to ride in the boot, Aurelia?" he responded pleasantly.

"Why not? It would be a lovely finish to a swell day," I snarled back, and was pleased that despite my clacking teeth my voice sounded corrosive enough to blister cement. "And the company much preferable."

He kept driving.

A sign flashed by, Slavic names spelled in Roman letters, and numerals representing kilometers. Names all unfamiliar, distances meaningless.

We sailed on for a time in the increasing downpour. Occasional lightning spilled across the windshield in splashes of brilliant liquid light; the thunder drowned the grinding car engine.

We were in a taxi. There in front of my knees was the meter, dark and silent. They had commandeered a square black Mercedes taxi of the type so common all over Germany and Austria.

A surreptitious glance to the right: the big man glaring through the windshield, his heavy jowls looking like they had been carved from weathered granite. Rain gleamed on his short salt-and-pepper hair, and his huge hands gripped his knees. He might have been about seventy, even older, judging from the deep furrows in his face, but he looked twice as tough as most Marines half his age. On my left, Alec's profile was equally stony; there was an implacable look to the cut of his mouth, his jawline. Even the fine strands of damp black hair drifting down across his forehead added to the general ambience of anger.

They're mad? I fumed silently. *They're* mad?

The burly guy addressed Alec in that language I'd heard twice, once the night before and once at Schönbrunn. Alec replied in it, slowed the car, and without warning whipped us into a tight U-turn that pressed us all to one side. He drove on a way and then turned sharply onto a half-hidden access road, flinging us in the other direction.

Water dribbled coldly down my scalp into the neck of my sodden blouse, making me shiver. "Ugh," I snarled.

The car rolled onto a wider paved road. The speed picked up. Alec said, in English, "Tell me, Aurelia, was that your own idiotic idea or did your damned brother put you up to it?"

"Brother?" I sat bolt upright. "That explains it. You're as crazy as a bag of alligators!"

There was silence for the remainder of the trip.

My eyes stung increasingly as the muddy water in my hair drained down into my face. So I was pleased to see how the wet from my clothing spread outward to dampen my companions' portions of the car seat, and I hoped I smelled like a swamp.

The muted lights of a city loomed up, scarce white and yellow arcs that looked alien and uninviting, unlike multicolored neon America. Another road sign flashed by, but the window directly in front of me was steamy enough to haze the words. The storm slowly broke up, the rain and thunder intermittent, as daylight began to fade.

My eyes stung so sharply I had to shut them. I pulled my foot up onto the seat and began massaging my ankle.

The two men held a short exchange in that language (was that a Latinate word for night?), and a few seconds later Alec slowed the car and parked it. I kept my eyes shut until the car was stopped; my temper had cooled enough to leave a numbing, aching exhaustion, but when I opened my eyes to see sunset colors purpling a now benign sky, I let out a slow breath of relief. The vanished sun eased the sensation that I was trapped in a time warp, and that this day would never end.

Okay, time to shake the goon squad. First a quick scan. We were in a crowded parking lot beside a huge, cream-colored Gasthaus with a bright flowering hedge bordering it. Beyond was a paved street, and on the other side newer buildings sat in a civilized cluster.

Alec shut off the engine and got out. He held out his hand to help me out. Naturally I scooted the other way, as the big man was already out and heading for the trunk. I forgot about my ankle and nearly took a header when it promptly gave out.

So much for making a dash. I caught myself on the open door and when Alec came round and silently held out an arm I snapped, "In about two seconds I'm going to yell and scream."

"This is an inn. A public one," he said with strained sounding patience. "The idea is to hold a consultation in comfort before we progress any further."

Comfort. "All right. Consultation I'll go for," I snapped, still hanging on the car door. "In comfort. I'll wait here while you set it up," I said in an unsubtle attempt to test the boundaries of the apparent truce as I propped my throbbing foot in the doorframe of the car.

Alec's answering smile was ironic, but he only lifted his head and said something to the other man somewhere behind me before walking off to the inn's entrance. I leaned my forearms on the top of the car door and put my chin on my folded fingers as I breathed deeply of the heavy, wet-grass-smelling air. The trees and plants around the perimeter of the building and parking lot were pleasingly green and newly washed.

The car shifted as the trunk clunked down. The burly man hove into view, muscling two handsome suitcases and a matching overnight case tucked under a massive arm. He trod on around the side of the building without a glance in my direction.

Aware of my total lack of kick-butt chick ingenuity, I did not even check to see what Mr. Big was up to. My foot hurt so much I wouldn't be able to outrun a one-legged rooster. *Talk? All right. I can't run, but I can talk. And he won't like what he's going to hear.*

So I bolstered my courage with this stirring resolution; secretly, I was heartened to see that my first (and, I hoped, last) taste of Durance Vile was to take place here and not in some sinister old castle with five centuries of mildew and no plumbing.

The Gasthaus appeared to be clean and prosperous. Two of the three floors sported rows of bright-flowered window boxes.

Comfort . . .

And then I remembered my suitcase, lying in the middle of some soggy field. "Crap, crap, crap," I moaned.

Right on cue Alec reappeared. His brows quirked at my exclamation, but all he said was, "I've engaged three rooms. This place is said to have fairly decent food. There is only one bath in the second story, which is where the rooms are, but," he smiled, "you shall have it first."

I let go of the car door, stepped away and slammed it shut with a thrust of my hip. As Alec extended a hand I shrugged away. "No, I'll walk, I'll walk."

He fell in step beside me as I limped painfully across the parking lot, around the corner of the building, and past a row of windows, each framing patrons seated at tables. I made the mistake of glancing inside. Sure enough, every single person at every single table seemed to have nothing to do but get an eyeful of my mud-crusted form.

I sneaked a glance at Alec's sharply averted face. From the set of his shoulders, the muscle in his jaw, I could tell he was trying his best not to laugh. Argh.

Inside we were greeted with a heavenly aroma of fresh bread, braised onions, and beef stew. We crossed an old-fashioned, painfully clean lobby, off of which was the dining room full of hungry travelers ranging from yammering toddlers to stolid oldsters.

Alec said, "Stairs this way."

"Wonderful." I eyed the pretty folk-pattern tiled steps as if they were a pit of snakes. There was a good sturdy rail, at least, so my progress up the steps was no harder than it had been from car to front door.

On the first landing I paused to rest as three people came down from above and passed me by, then I made a depressing discovery: true to the European way of counting, the second floor was, in fact, the third floor—at the top of a narrow double flight of stairs.

Alec must have been watching; he waited politely for the people to pass him, then without any warning picked me up.

I squawked, "Hey! Put me down."

"What's the matter? No one's around to see."

"It's gotta be against the Villain's Code," I retorted.

This time he did laugh.

As soon as we reached the top Alec set me down and walked on toward an open door, leaving me to limp in his wake.

The third floor was an attic suite. Under a sharply slanting roof there were four rooms, a WC, and a bathroom, all opening off a small square landing. Apparently Alec had taken them all over. One of the rooms was in the process of being set up as a sitting room; I reached the open door to see a stout woman in a shiny black widow's dress and kerchief directing the movement of tables and armchairs by two sweating young men.

She broke off when she saw me and gave a shriek. Backing toward her chairs as though to protect them with her life, she burst into rapid-fire Slovene.

Alec soothed her protests in stilted but adequate Slovene by promising that the "young woman" would not touch her beautiful furniture until she had bathed.

"That's cool," I said, "but I lost my suitcase. After this hypothetical bath what do I wear, a toga made out of Madam's curtains? Or is a bath towel acceptable outerwear here?"

Alec said, "Kilber will have put one of my valises in the bath for you by this time. Go along. Please make use of whatever of my gear you wish. We'll be served dinner up here," he added.

"I'd rather know what's going on right now," I replied, but without my earlier heat. Only the most incompetent villain would stage scenes of Unmentionable Mayhem in such a setting. And as I'd rather be clean, dry, and warm before tackling any "consultations," I limped into the bathroom and locked the door.

Then slid under the doorknob the single chair with the Vuitton case and folded fabric placed on its seat.

The bathroom was a narrow room next door to the WC, with plain plaster walls and a sink below a small mirror, lit by a lone bulb hanging from the high ceiling.

The tub was a monster on feet, nearly the size of a Jacuzzi—without the jets and other goodies. I turned the century-old knobs so the water splashed in at its mightiest trickle, but at least it ran hot enough to steam gently and invitingly.

As the water dribbled in I turned my attention to the stuff The Enemy had made available for my use. Since I had no clothes or supplies my scornfully high-handed repudiation of Alec's offerings would have to wait for another opportunity.

Two thick, neatly folded towels sat on top of an also neatly folded dressing gown of a soft, extremely expensive combed cotton. I shook it out and held it up, hoping there would be a barbaric dragon embroidered on the back, or at least some vulgarly ostentatious intertwined initials over the breast pocket, but it was unrelieved deep midnight blue. In the case were soap and shampoo, pricey French brands, and a comb and a silver-backed brush—the frame probably a hundred years old, judging from the etched patterns, the bristles new and natural.

The water was deep enough to climb into, so I peeled off the clammy, gritty clothes, unpinned my hair, and lowered myself into the water. Oh, that felt good! I lay there, soaking long enough to feel my aches and bruises ease. Even my ankle and shoulder felt considerably better by the time I reached for the soap and shampoo and began to degrime myself.

Rinsing thigh-length hair in a bathtub with water pressure a step up from a drip required patience. Then it was time to turn my attention to my clothes. My underthings and top were easy to wash out, but the jeans presented a challenge. Not sure if I should use soap lather or shampoo I finally used both. Big mistake. Ever tried to wring jeans out by hand? Especially with blistered palms? Finally I gave up, hoping they'd dry by morning.

I used a towel to wrap my hair into a turban, straightened up the bathroom, and put on the dressing gown. It was roomy; I wrapped the sash firmly around my waist, rolled the sleeves back to my wrists, slipped the comb into one of the huge pockets and my hairclip into the other pocket, then hobbled out.

Madam and her minions were gone. The door to the parlor was open. Alec sat with a teacup in one hand and a newspaper in the other. He, too, wore last night's clothes.

"Which is my room?" I asked truculently, to cover my embarrassment.

"There." A nod behind him.

I opened the door to a small, charming bedroom with a high four-poster single bed, a table and chair, and a wardrobe in the corner. The door latched on the inside. I draped my wet clothes over the chair and table and the bedposts, then limped back into the makeshift sitting room and sank into a large upholstered armchair next to the table.

Despite the situation, a sense of well-being suffused me when I discovered a fresh pot of tea waiting.

Alec excused himself, and for a long time I sat back in the deep, comfortable chair with my fingers wrapped around the warm teacup, staring at the window across the room and ignoring the growling of my stomach.

When I finally raised the cup, my lip against the rim, I thought, what if there's something in it?

Down crashed the cup, and my mood.

That was when Alec reentered the room, damp clean hair swept back from his brow, the rest of him elegant in a pair of charcoal slacks and a white dress shirt.

His eyes were marked with tiredness, his gaze light and cool and alert as he addressed me in that pleasant, curiously familiar tone. "I ordered dinner to be brought up at eight because I thought you'd be a lot longer in the bath than you were. But then, without your usual battery of cosmetics I suppose there isn't much to do beyond the basics, is there?" He dropped tiredly into the other chair.

"My usual battery of cosmetics?" I repeated. "I've never worn makeup, except for dance recitals. You keep *doing* that. I would like to know who the hell you think I am."

"And I would like to know if it's money, fear, or perversity that inspired you to run this game on us. Or is your brother behind it, as I've suspected all along?"

"First tell me who my brother is supposed to be, and I'll tell you if I've ever met him," I retorted. "Seems to me you're the one running games, all this yap about brothers and makeup. Take the clue bus, Gus! I. Am. Kim. Murray."

"Aurelia—" he began.

"All right, *Aurelia* Kim Murray. How did you know that, anyway? I never use it."

His face tightened, even more skeptical. "You're enjoying this charade, damn you; do you know what it's done to my father, to your parents?"

"*My parents,*" I stated, revving up for battle, "are happily at *home,* waiting for my latest postcard to hear about my *wonderful* trip to Europe, *and they will be furious* when they hear what happened to me, and by the way, what did you put in the tea? Is this supposed to be round two?"

A ridge of color touched his refined cheekbones, but he pressed his lips tight, as if holding in his own nuclear-powered comeback.

I went on with exaggerated patience, "I'm beginning to think it's a waste of time, and what I should contact is not an embassy but the guys with the straitjackets. Look. For the millionth time I am Kim Murray, born and bred in Santa Monica, California—"

"Yes, so it states in that fascinating pile of fiction I found in your valise. What I want to know is where you managed to obtain such a realistic passp—"

"You *did* thieve my stuff! You thieved it, and you *nosed through it!*"

His mouth twisted. "And most interesting I found it."

"You rat bastard!" I exploded out of my chair, fist aimed straight for that scornful face.

He flung up a hand and caught my wrist.

For those two glorious seconds I'd forgotten my hurt ankle, until it promptly collapsed under me. But for Alec holding my arm I would have fallen into his lap. His grip kept me upright but the jolt caused the towel turban rocking unsteadily on my head to tumble off, and my hair rolled down over my shoulders and across his chair.

The effect on Alec was so odd my rage shifted into overwhelming confusion. I stared down at his face, which had changed from sardonic disbelief to astonishment and then blankness. Devoid of any expression whatever.

So there we were for a long moment, me leaning on the chair, him sitting in it, my wet hair draped in limp wet waves over us both as his eyes traveled slowly up the hair to my face, and then to the clean pink part on my scalp.

He released my wrist, pinched his fingers to his brow, and rubbed his eyes slowly. His expression was the remote one I'd first seen at the ballet.

And when he spoke, the scorn and disbelief were utterly gone.

"What was your mother's maiden name?" he asked.

EIGHT

"ATELIER," I SAID NUMBLY.

He watched in silence as I sank back into my chair, pulled the comb out of the dressing gown pocket, and began to comb out the tangles. His eyes followed the movement of my hand with the comb, his expression still blank. Finally he said, "Where was she born, and when?"

"During the war. We're pretty sure in Paris, but it might have been Vienna. That's one of the things I was there to find out."

"Your maternal grandparents' names?"

"Aurelia and Daniel Atelier. Are you going to tell me why you ask?"

"Yes," he said, his gaze flicking from my face to my hand to my face again. "Go on, please."

"There isn't much more." I shrugged. "Mom thinks she has an early memory of a flat in Paris that had a lot of flowers, though she's not certain. Her first real memory is aboard the ship coming over to the States, probably when Gran was widowed. All she knows about my grandfather is that he was sent to fight against the Russians."

"Does your mother remember him?" he asked quietly.

I frowned in concentration. "Maybe. She doesn't know if it was real or a memory she made up from looking at his picture, which always sat on Gran's bedside table. Said he was tall. Thin. Laughed a lot. Smelled like tobacco, which would be a real memory, wouldn't it? Gran never smoked."

I hesitated, sure I was being boring, but Alec listened intently. So

I went on. "I have a copy of the picture in my suitcase . . . which is out in a field somewhere, argh, argh, argh. Anyway, she also has a picture of my mother when she was a toddler, but I didn't bring a copy of that, as I didn't think it would lead anywhere. Mom's wearing this amazing antique-looking baby dress, all lace and pearls, that I guess had been Gran's. Mom thinks they sold the dress during the war." I shrugged, but he was listening closely.

"Your grandmother and mother came across to the States when?"

"In forty-five, right after the war ended."

"Were they alone? How did your grandmother survive once they arrived?"

"They were alone, and Gran first was a governess, teaching French and deportment and the like to some rich girl. When that family came to Los Angeles, she quit and taught piano for years and years."

Alec let out a low whistle, his eyes narrowed. "Easier to believe—no." He shook his head, rubbed his eyes again. He muttered something short and pungent in that Slavic language I'd heard a few times, then his hand dropped. "I haven't slept in four days. I can't think."

He gave me that real smile again, but this time between it and any sense of aesthetic appreciation lay the matter of a superlatively rotten twenty-four hours. "I knew that powder was a stupid idea, but I didn't know how stupid until this morning. This afternoon. Now." His hand passed over his face, fingers briefly pressing his eyelids. "I beg your pardon. For everything, beginning with that damned dosed wine."

I stared stonily back at him. "Not that it makes it okay, because it doesn't, but you had a reason?"

He leaned his head back against his chair and said, "Aurelia von Mecklundburg is probably capable of imitating an American accent, and she could have bought a forged passport, the California clothes, and all the rest, but the one thing she could not have done is grow her hair a meter and a half in less than six months."

"Aurelia von Mecklundburg?" I repeated, totally confused.

He nodded, his blue gaze appraising. "You are her size, and shape, you have the same complexion, and you've got the same eyes the color of honey. You've even got the same single dimple in your left cheek when you laugh and the same mole on the nape of your neck. You could be her twin. You could be her!" And, as I stared in disbelief, he went on with some of the old irony, "I wondered what had inspired her to whack three years off her age in the passport, yet dress like—well, like a student from California. But Aurelia—or Ruli, as she likes to be called now. Still trying to get used to it. She's what the French call BCBG."

Bon chic bon genre—not merely the height of fashion, but always perfectly put together. I nodded, for neither observation would fit me. "Well, I must confess my style in haute couture could best be summed up by 'LA laid-back.'" I laughed. "Meanwhile, is craziness contagious?"

"So you've never heard of Aurelia von Mecklundburg?"

"Never."

"Armandros Danilov von Mecklundburg?"

"Nope."

"Marius Ysvorod?"

A shake of my head. "Wow, when they were first graders, did it take half a week to write their names?"

"How about—" His tone softened, more tentative. "—Maria Karoline Sofia Aurelia Dsaret?"

"Nada. Except the name Aurelia, of course. Must be a more widely used name than I'd thought."

"Particularly in Dobrenica. Heard of it?"

I rubbed my forehead, trying to call up an image of the age-battered European map tacked to the wall above my desk. "I think, um, ah I might have heard of it. Only there was something funny about it, but I don't remember what. It would be one of those little Eastern European burgs swallowed up by the Germans during the war, and the Soviets after, right? Somewhere in the Carpathians?"

"Somewhere in the Carpathians," he repeated, smiling.

Then I remembered the train, and I said slowly, "You weren't taking me there, were you?" And at his nod, the comb dropped out of my numb fingers. "What?" I moaned. "Nothing makes any sense at all."

He glanced down at his watch. It was a thin, discreet type that cost a year of my parents' salaries. "We've a few minutes till eight. Why don't you drink your tea. I could use some myself."

He leaned down, poured a cup of the now lukewarm tea, and drank it straight down.

I picked up my own cup and gratefully sipped.

He put the cup down and said, "I'll give you the rest of it over dinner. No interruptions. Right now I'd better see to some things." He held up his cell and left.

I reached for the tea, then heard clatters and thuds lumbering up the steep stairway. Madam and her helpers toiled in, bearing heavy trays of food. They set places for two; Alec reappeared as they finished. No sign of Mr. Big.

Alec sat down, politely said, "Bon appétit," and I devoted myself, with the dedication inspired by nearly twenty-four hours of enforced abstinence, to a splendid dinner. Slovene-style veal stew with corn dumplings, sharply spiced, and savory chicken *Djuvec, Sarma* in cabbage leaves . . . My mouth waters today when I think about how good that meal was.

The atmosphere had altered from anger to truce. For a while neither of us spoke, except about easy things—the food, the rain. At last I sat back, toying with the last few bites of the layered apple *gibanic*. He was already finished.

One of Madam's waiters brought fresh coffee, steaming tea, and a small golden bottle of cognac. He set these down on the low table, carted away the dishes, then he left.

Alec passed me a cup of tea then poured himself some coffee and laced it liberally with the cognac.

I settled back, curling up my feet, and cradled my cup in my hands. "Well, that was a great meal," I said. "But. I'm not ready to be grateful. Good as it was I'd rather not have to whet my appetite with a hundred-mile hike."

"A hundred-mile hike," he repeated. "I thought it was typically perverse of you—being, as I thought, Aurelia—to have learned courage at this late date. Imagine poor Emilio's shock on entering that train compartment with a peace offering of tea to find you gone and the window open—"

"Hah!" I gloated. "So what is this Aurelia von Whatever's terrible crime?"

"She disappeared without word or trace about a month ago. A couple of months before she and I were to be married."

"Married? You?" I snorted, almost slopping my tea, and as he signified assent I could not resist adding, "Well of course she'd take off! Who wouldn't?"

Humor creased the corners of his eyes. My cracks had no power to provoke, now that I wasn't his Aurelia.

I sighed. "So the next question is, why are you chasing after somebody who has obviously changed her mind?"

"Because it's not so obvious."

"What? If your courting manners are much like what I saw today . . ."

He made a quick, impatient gesture. "You do not understand the situation. She may not have changed her mind. I think it's been changed for her. If it has been changed. When we spoke in March she was willing enough to get on with it—" He set his coffee down, got up, and moved to the window. He glanced over his shoulder and added, "—though no more enthusiastic than I was." He flashed that sudden smile again. "The motivation for this event, I feel constrained to add, is mostly political."

"Political?" I squawked. "Politics? Political marriages these days? That's stupid."

"But politics are always stupid," he retorted promptly.

"He shoots, he scores!" I gave him a double-finger point-and-shoot. "Okay. So we know I'm not involved in whatever mess you've got going. I guess you could say it's none of my business. But I'm curious, and—" I patted his dressing gown significantly "—not going anywhere, and since you're the reason why I'm not going anywhere, I think you owe me an explanation."

"I do owe you an explanation," he agreed, as outside rain began tapping gently at the window again, and far away lightning flickered. "You said you know little about Dobrenica."

"An isolated country like the Falklands and Granada and Kuwait that you never hear about until the superpowers steamroller them in their own pursuits, except this one doesn't always show up on old maps. I've always assumed that that was because of the way kingdoms swapped borders and allegiances back in the bad old empire days."

"Yes," he said—somewhat ambiguously.

At the time, I didn't notice, but plowed right on, eager to show off my two cents' worth of knowledge. "Apparently they speak a weird combination of ancient Latin and Slavic that drives the purists nuts when they try to isolate origins. The USSR controlled it, right?"

"Yes. Until relatively recently, too. To sketch in the background, Russia is the ancient enemy, persistent enough through medieval times that Dobrenica became part of the Hapsburg Empire somewhere in the fifteenth century. For one reason or another—" He hesitated, then went on. "The empire's control was nominal. As a kingdom protected by the Hapsburgs we existed in relative peace until the empire and its world crumbled after World War One. There succeeded a number of desperate years—"

"Like the rest of Europe."

"Yes. Germany overran Dobrenica early in the war. The Dobreni conducted a constant losing guerrilla war, using long outdated weapons. And at the end of the war Stalin rolled over us from the east." He lifted a shoulder in a slight shrug, but anger tightened his lips. "Those leaders who could left the country to make plans for regaining independence. We were prevented from gaining freedom as much by internal conflict as by being overrun by the Soviets."

"But now you're free, right?"

"Yes. Mostly. There are some dodgy treaties, but leave that aside. To Aurelia. Two families have been traditionally involved in Dobrenica's affairs—"

"You mean, like, ruling families?"

"Yes. There are five 'ruling' families, with numerous cadet branches, but since the treaty with the Hapsburgs two families, the Dsarets and the Ysvorods, have been predominant—with the von Mecklundburgs their equal in ambition and influence. The former two traditionally passed the crown back and forth until the early twentieth century when the Dsarets ruled."

"So Aurelia is a—a lost princess?" I had to laugh at the unlikelihood of such a thing existing in a world dominated by fast food and reality TV.

"No. But she is descended from an important ducal family, which is why the marriage was proposed. An attempt to unify the two families. And factions."

"Wait a minute. What's your last name?"

"Ysvorod."

"So the title went from the Dsarets, to—your father?"

"Yes. That is, he was never formally crowned, but he didn't lay down the title. Since the war and occupation he's been king-in-exile."

"So." I tried not to laugh. "That makes you a crown prince?"

He smiled as he leaned on the back of his chair, the signet ring glinting cool blue. "Is that so astonishing? Or did you expect golden spikes to protrude from my skull like antlers?"

"You have to admit crown princes are a dying breed," I said. "Particularly in the States."

"Oh?" he replied. "I thought that's where a lot of them ended up after the revolutions at home."

"Only if they didn't keep the royal treasury. I think the rich ones all go to Paris. Or buy islands. So you and Aurelia are the high-born scions of two venerable houses. But how's the Romeo and Juliet stuff relate to politics? I mean, does it matter to anyone outside your social circle which heir marries which heir?"

He gave me his ironic smile. "Step down for a moment from the democratic high ground and consider the nature of power and of the reasons why men follow other men, even to their deaths—"

"Or women. Okay, go on. Though, as far as ruling families are concerned I feel like thrusting a caveat in here, from your own Lord Acton. Uh, yours as in where you were raised, not born—"

"Superficially correct but fundamentally unsound," he said. "Even with the oft-forgotten modifier *tends to.* Power is not the equivalent of corruption. You can find enough examples of rulers who had unlimited power and who ruled with a steady hand. Charles the Fifth comes to mind. The type of man, ah, person, if you will—"

"I will."

He flicked his fingers up in the fencer's hit. "And you are right, even if the roads to power used to be different for women than for men. Anyway, the type of person who usually seeks power is corrupt from the start, or at least carries the seeds of corruption among his motivations, if not in stated intentions."

"We definitely see that at home," I said. "No royal families, but there sure are powerful ones. Go on."

"I am not arguing that birth selects for the best rulers. I don't believe there is any foolproof system. Human nature is too wild a variable."

"With you so far. So . . . back to your princess."

"We are in many respects back in the nineteenth century in Dobrenica. Earlier, even. For good and not so good reasons. The people still have faith in their rulers and the rulers are still trained for their positions from birth. This being the case, the leading families serve more strongly than ever as the symbols of freedom, of independence. I will not go into the background alliances and personalities, but suffice it to say the marriage would be the equivalent of a truce between two factions, a badly needed truce. We were splintered during and after the Second World War by more than Hitler and the Russians."

"Tell me, where does Aurelia's so-called rotten brother fit in?"

"I didn't say he's rotten, but he represents his family's views . . . to a degree."

"By which you mean he's against this 'truce'?" I made air quotes. "And against you?"

"Yes, to both."

"So he's corrupt, and you're not?"

His brows went up slightly. "What is it you have in mind?"

"I'm thinking," I stated, "of drinking a last glass of wine and waking up on a train."

NINE

"QUITE RIGHT." Alec returned to his seat. "I apologize again. It was inexcusable." He reached for the coffeepot, his brow tense, then he said, "Shall I replace the generalities with specifics?"

"I'm here."

"In March Aurelia agreed to the marriage, which was to take place on a national holiday, September second. She left in spring to visit Paris to buy new clothes."

He paused again, obviously considering his words.

"A month ago I got a frantic phone call from her mother. They were to meet on the Côte d'Azur for their customary holiday together. No show, no word. Messages flew all over the map. Since her brother Tony was apparently somewhere in the Baltic, or the Mediterranean, or the south of France, her mother begged me to find her, and I had to drop everything and go search. Aurelia has always been predictable. Never vanished like this. I got people to search all her family connections, from Greece to Paris."

I leaned forward. Weird as it sounded, his story was at least beginning to come together.

"From Aurelia to you. Few days ago while I was in Florence I got a call from Emilio to say he found you in Vienna. Standing in Schwedenplatz, waiting for a streetcar, and you walked right past him as if you didn't know him. He followed you around while I extricated myself without causing alarm. The planes were down because of weather so rather than wait, Kilber and I drove like hell for Vienna. Meanwhile you were behaving in a manner that seemed peculiar in the extreme."

"Peculiar," I exclaimed. "Yeah, right."

Alec smiled. "She would never walk nor visit tourist sites. Nor would she ever take the underground. When she shops or calls on people she hires a car or takes a taxi. You went out to Schönbrunn. He followed with great care, then picked a moment without witnesses, on top of the Glorietta monument, to approach you."

"And I thought he was trying to proposition me."

"So I gather," Alec said, smiling. "Poor straitlaced Emilio! That pretty much left him gobsmacked. He followed you back, even more cautious than before, to discover that you were staying under a false name at a cheap pensione rather than the family flat. The only thing you did that restored his faith in his sanity was to go shopping at one of Aurelia's and Aunt Sisi's favorite stores on Mariahilferstrasse—"

"*The account.*" I snapped my fingers. "I wondered if I'd heard wrong. And I only picked that place because I saw him! No, wait. Was that after?" I remembered that weird poke in the neck, but I wasn't about to talk about that. "Never mind. Sorry. Go on."

"He asked the clerk what you bought and was told you'd paid cash for a frock in order to attend the ballet. The ballet? Aurelia never attends the ballet, unless it's a gala. We could not figure it out. I asked Emilio to find out if tickets were sold through your pensione. Yes. One. So I told him to get a ticket for the next seat so that one of us could meet you there. Talk to you."

"Huh."

"I arrived in Vienna after driving through without stopping. Emilio begged me to be the one to meet you, so I stopped long enough to change for the ballet, expecting—anything but to be treated as if I were a total stranger. I began to think I'd gone mad. Not possible we found the wrong person. You look the same, you speak French with that same perfect Parisian accent she's gone on about all these years. Not the idiomatic French of people our age, but the posh accent of a generation ago, the accent my aunt thinks proper for someone in our position."

Gran's accent, I thought.

"I'm thinking, perhaps you're carrying on like this because someone is watching. Maybe I've interrupted some expected meeting. This is precisely Tony's type of game, so when you refused to go to the bar with me, I took off to wait for a better time, out of the public eye."

He set the coffee cup down.

"Kilber watched the pensione all night while I dealt with a lot of phone calls—meanwhile you didn't go anywhere else, or meet anyone. Your window finally went dark. The only thing left was to try to contact you again. While I was on the phone all morning, Emilio followed you and hovered while you scribbled postcards. But our cloak-and-dagger efforts stop short of tampering with the mailboxes. Then—to the Royal Crypt? Once again we were expecting a rendezvous. We watched. No one except tourists went in. Kilber mentioned carrying sleeping pills. They used the ground pills in wine during the Soviet days when things got desperate. Said if you're in trouble you can't get out of, it's one way to get you out with a minimum of fuss. He backed me up, watching for—anything—as I tried once more to contact you."

He smiled at the ceiling. "More of the false identity, and you said 'dude.' I don't think Aurelia has ever heard it, in her circles."

"Well, my Gran doesn't like slang and worked hard to educate me out of it. But it slips out."

"Then there was your verbal fencing—Ariosto—Nabokov. I feel like I'm in a Jean Genet play. I suggest the Zwölfapostelkeller. I don't know what to expect, but you come along easy enough, as if this is a casual tourist encounter—but you hint that you are leaving Vienna soon. Kilber follows, waits outside, after mentioning his potion again. I waver. Was your hint about leaving the city soon a slip or a warning?"

"Whoa."

"When you said your name was *Aurelia* I thought, it has to be a warning of some kind, and I've got to get you out of there. This decision is based on the logic of twenty-four hours' lack of sleep on top of drinking half a liter of wine. And so, while you are in the ladies', I go outside to Kilber, get his powder, order the half-liter of wine, drop the powder in a glass."

I grinned. "Would've served you right if someone had grabbed the glass."

"That occurred to me as I waited for you to come out. Nothing funny about it at the time. There was also the prospect of getting you out with the least amount of attention. Then, when we had managed that, and had fetched your things from the pensione, there was the fun of getting you across the train station."

I laughed. "And then I disappeared."

His own laughter showed in the narrowing of his eyes. "At the same time you were scrambling out the window of that compartment, I was drinking my sixth cup of wretched coffee while trying to work up the nerve to face Aurelia's quite justifiable ire before I tried to find out the reason for the masquerade. When I sent Emilio in with a peace offering of tea, he found an empty compartment and an open window. So began the chase around the countryside in search of you. And when we did catch up, you still persisted in the masquerade." He spread his hands. "I thought you were doing it to piss me off. So there you have my story."

"And now you have to do it all over again."

He glanced up with mild inquiry.

I gave him the hairy eyeball. "You do intend to give me back my stuff, my papers and money, that is, as my clothes can't be helped? So I can enjoy what remains of my trip?"

"I was going to offer to drive you out tomorrow—seeing as it's raining right now, and you must know that you are perfectly safe—to try to find your bag. If you remember where it is."

"Of course I remember where it is. That is, from the village with the stinky meat I do, anyway."

"St—oh. Yes. I think I know which you mean, the last one we were through before finding you. Strange dialect out there, they said something about you walking through trailing ghosts. I have no idea what that particular idiom means, but the point is, they were terrified of you. Anyway if we don't find it I'll replace your things before you do go your way." He rubbed his fingers across his eyes and stood up in a leisurely movement. "What a long, hellish day!"

"Another question."

"Yes?"

"Why did you want to know my mother's last name?"

He picked up the coffee cup and balanced it in his hand, a curious gesture. He did not want to answer my question. "Can it wait until morning?" he asked finally. "We both need sleep."

"Yeah." I sighed, tiredness overwhelming me in waves. As he said, we weren't going anywhere.

"Good night." He flicked up a careless hand and turned to the door.

"Good night."

He went out. I eased to my feet, turned out the remaining lamp, and began limping slowly to the bedroom allotted to me.

My feet creaked on old, much-scrubbed floors as I felt about for the lamp; yellow light flared as the other bedroom door opened. Alec stood in the doorway, his shoulders leaning against the frame. "A moment," he said.

I stiffened and folded my arms squarely across my front. The yellow light from his room shone in a golden haze through some of his fine dark hair, but the rest of him was in silhouette.

"I won't be able to sleep unless I also apologize for having riffled through your personal effects."

I reached back to switch on my lamp. Dim yellow light slanted out softly across his face, but it didn't reach his eyes. I propped my bad foot against the door behind me as I said, "Oh, it's okay. Not like anything there was *personal* personal. If it had been, maybe you would have figured things out sooner." Or maybe not. There seemed to be crucial bits missing from his story. But it was too late to ask. "So . . . Well, let's forget it."

"Thank you."

"Okay," I said awkwardly, embarrassed. And because I was embarrassed, I had to get back to humor. "My turn."

He'd straightened up, his hand on the door, but leaned again. "Question?" his voice was light, his expression hidden.

"You said 'my people.' Does that mean you have minions?"

His head tipped back against the door and he laughed. It was a quick laugh, hardly audible, but genuine, his voice warm.

"You'd better ask them," he said with a casual wave.

"I have too strong a sense of self-preservation to ask that Kilber if he's a minion."

Alec's humor faded. "Ah, Kilber. If you were to ask if he was my father's minion, he'd agree with pride. As for the rest, despite the evidence that I regret more every time I think about it, let's say we're not completely stuck in the past. Good night."

I fluttered my fingers and shut my door. And locked it.

TEN

ON A CLEAR, pleasant morning I woke, swung my feet out of the bed, and experimentally set the bad one down. Swollen and ached like it had been kicked by a buffalo.

I hopped across the room to my clothes. In Southern California they would have been completely dry by midnight. My undies were damp and limp, but bearable. I picked up my jeans. Wet. Cold. Even in the uncertain light from the high north-facing window the seams were gray with—and slick and slimy from—unrinsed soap. The top was almost as bad. Ew.

After pulling Alec's dressing robe back on, I yanked my door open and hobbled to the bathroom—where I found a brand-new toothbrush and some unopened toothpaste labeled with Slovenic lettering.

When I reached the makeshift sitting room I found Alec drinking coffee and reading a newspaper.

He stood up courteously. "Good morning. Sleep well?"

"Yes," I grumped as I hunted fruitlessly for the comb I'd dropped the night before. "Despite my foot. And blistered palms. And I can hardly wait to slog all over Eastern Europe searching for my no doubt wet and mildewy suitcase while wearing cold, wet, slimy, gritty jeans." I finally spotted the comb, lying neatly on a side table next to a tray of fresh tea things.

"Sit down. Drink your tea. Breakfast will be along shortly. As for clothes, you can have some of my own. I can't vouch for their fit, but they are clean. Put the others out and Kilber will take them to a laundry for you."

Which is what happened, and with an orderly, matter-of-fact haste. Whether or not these toffs are trained to smoothly manage all the ridiculous logistical flaps in getting rid of one day and beginning another while on the road, I don't know. Maybe it's nothing more high-bred than the possession of cash. But an awesome breakfast appeared and then its remains disappeared, then that silent, burly Kilber drove off in the battered borrowed taxi with an armload of miscellaneous stuff (including my wet jeans and top), and finally Alec and I descended through the inn to the parking lot to find a beautiful light green Daimler waiting for us. Probably (I bet myself) with a full tank of gas.

Alec's subdued brown slacks were too long, and the white shirt volumes too large—which was a fashion statement some places in LA. My biggest problem was trying to fit my sandal on without hurting my ankle.

"Shall we find a doctor?" Alec asked, watching me wince and hiss.

I shrugged. "What would they say? Wrap it and stay off it? I already know that. I've done this before. It'll be okay in a day or two, as long as I don't try any more marathons. There." I'd adjusted the buckles, and I set my foot down. Then I rolled up the dragging cuffs of his elegantly tailored slacks.

The result looked terrible, but when I straightened up and eyed him he said merely, "Ready?"

"Lead on!"

As we climbed into the Daimler I said, "Nice ride. I'm surprised you wanted to mess around with trains."

"It was much easier, under the circumstances."

Much easier to cross the border with a sleeping woman in a train cabin attended by a bearded minion standing helpfully outside with passport and ticket, as opposed to a groggy prisoner in a car who might make a fuss.

"Ri-i-i-ght," I drawled.

He flashed that quick grin. "I apologize. Again."

"Okay, okay. I'll stop harping on it, since you did explain, and you're about to make up for it."

He started the engine, which hummed with the unmistakable expensive-car lack of grinding noise. "Where to?"

"I think I can manage from that last village."

"Then that's where we'll start." He pulled away from the inn, driving with the skill but not the speed of yesterday. I relaxed into the contoured seat and watched the pleasantly rolling hills move smoothly by.

The sky was partly clear, but the streaky gray clouds that drifted westward promised another front on the way. The air was balmy and a trifle humid. Inside the car the air-conditioning made it cool and pleasant.

The silence was so curious, almost timeless, yet with a sense of promise. No, of proximity.

Alec's profile was somber and his gaze seemed far more distant than the road. Driving on automatic pilot.

I discovered my hand gripping my other arm. I forced my hands to relax in my lap. Safe topic? "Um. About the pensione. Did you grab my stuff and skip out, or did you pay my tab?"

"We settled up, of course." He seemed amused. "I thought I had convinced you I'm not part of an international gang of desperate criminals. You can go back there with impunity."

"Good to know at least that Interpol is not out hunting my blood. I wish I wish I'd known, because I would have gone to a ballet every night."

He laughed.

And his temper remained even and pleasant throughout the next three totally useless hours. I had been certain I knew where to go but once we started out from that village, each turn, each cliff was familiar—until I got close. Then it turned frustratingly unrecognizable.

Several times I tried exploring anyway, each time hobbling out of the car only to stare around helplessly. The worst moment was when I was so certain I recognized the curve of hills above that farm where I'd gotten the drink of water. There *was* a farm, but the only buildings in view was a cluster of plain houses built sometime in the early twentieth century, and a tractor growling away in the distance.

After the fifth dead end he said, "On the other side of the railroad tracks there's a Gasthaus that's supposed to have great food."

I sighed. "Haven't you got better things to do? You've got to find your Aurelia."

"I'm waiting for a call." He touched the pocket where he kept his cell phone—one of the super expensive ones with satellite everything, I'd noticed. "Which isn't likely to come in before afternoon. Until then the least I can do is place myself and my car at your disposal. We might begin to replace your belongings."

"That's all right. With my own cash back, I'm ahead since you paid off the pensione. All I need is another pair of jeans and a couple of T-shirts since my trip is almost over. But before I depart," I said, "you did promise to tell me why my grandmother's married name was so important. What the connection is between my name, her name, and your Aurelia?"

"When we stop. Will that do?"

"I can wait that long." I sat back, and tried to breathe out the annoyance of my still-missing suitcase.

I turned my attention to the gentle hills, so green compared to the parched desert landscape beyond LA's endless urban sprawl. I enjoyed the expensive car that he guided so smoothly. He was a good driver, something my father had taught me to be. But driving at home was fraught with tension, what with 24/7 traffic and with the constant fear that my elderly VW would break down on the freeway. You have to have been negotiating LA traffic in a junkmobile older than you are to fully appreciate spectacular scenery in a ride like Mr. I'm-a-Crown-Prince's.

I watched his hands on the wheel as he steered us with hardly a check through a knot of erratically driven dilapidated vehicles that seemed to want to play me-first through an intersection of three roads.

Hands. He had beautiful hands, I thought, studying the shape of his long fingers so casually resting on the wheel, the latent strength there, enhanced by the unconscious grace of his movements.

I shifted my gaze to the window. Didn't it figure! Now that he'd removed himself from the Villains' List, my radar was on full force, its object a guy so different from my world we may as well have been from different planets.

And in a couple hours I'll never see him again.

It was right about then that his own radar must have sent him some signal because he said, "Problem?"

"Oh no," I said airily as my thoughts flailed wildly for a suitable subject. "So tell me about the king biz. How do you train a king anyway? It's not like there's a king school tucked up somewhere—or was all that stuff you told me in the Weinkeller a lot of gas?"

He smiled. "No, it was all true. I did grow up in England, which is where my family escaped when the Soviets took over. Though many of us went back to Dobrenica during the long vacations, slipping over the border. My father considered that part of my education." He glanced aside, then said, "As for the other, I think I can safely sum it up as mostly committees and compromise."

"What? No 'off with your head'? What good is being a king if you can't order everyone around?"

"You can. But every order—every action—has consequences. Unlimited power only belongs to dictators these days. Still there's enough left that one had better know what one is doing."

I found it difficult to wrap my head around the existence of kings in the blandness of modern times. "Hey, that sounds like all work and no fun."

He gestured, the light catching on his signet ring, which glimmered with intense, cobalt blue light. "You know about vocation and avocation, right?"

Memory: my wild-haired father sitting in the kitchen, when I was about ten, the Beatles playing in the background, Dad waving a clock tool as he talked. "My Dad said once that if you couldn't have the job you loved, then you got one that supported whatever it was you loved."

"Your father does what he loves?"

"Well, since he lost his job when his newspaper went chapter eleven, he repairs rare old clocks. But his avocation is the Roman Empire. The entire garage is filled with his replicas, right down to the last detail. Battles, buildings, you name it, he's got it. When it comes to Xenophon, Thucydides, Horace, and the Plinys, he can quote you chapter and verse. My mother does cake decorating—and sometimes works for caterers who do fancy Hollywood parties, to pick up the slack. What about your mother? You haven't mentioned her. How does she figure in?"

"She's dead," he said. "Died when I was small. A yachting accident."

"How horrible! I'm sorry I brought it up."

"It's all right. It was one of those political marriages you were deploring. She was many years younger than he was. Once she met her part of the bargain—produced me—she handed me off and pretty much went her own way. I don't remember her at all."

"Was she also from Dobrenica?"

"Yes. Here it is," he said, turning the car up a steep, narrow track that led to a beautiful half-timbered inn perched high on a hill. "How about a beer?"

"Cool."

A wide terrace with the ubiquitous *Cinzano*-umbrella shaded tables fronted the inn. We threaded our way to one side of the terrace, which afforded a breathtaking view of an old town built on the banks of a meandering river, the mellow gold of the walls sun-warmed. Beyond, green hills jutted up in picture-postcard perfection; in the hazy distance the silhouette of a ruined castle crested the top of a hill higher than the others, looking in the heavy gray mist like a mirage from the fourteenth century.

Two large brown birds screeched overhead, flapping energetically. Alec leaned back in his seat, his blue gaze contemplating the line of distant hills until a waiter appeared and set down two heavy frost-sided and foam-crowned beer mugs.

Alec picked one up and lifted his glass in salute. I remembered another toast in a weinkeller. "Skumps!" And after a long and delicious swallow, "When I said that, did you think I was dropping hints about kings?"

His eyelids lifted humorously, which made his eyes gleam blue in the bright sunlight. "At that point I was half-inclined to strangle you."

"I did it because you did this." I mimicked his gesture with the wineglass. "With such an air. 'Skumps!' was how the two kings toasted one another in Disney's *Sleeping Beauty.* My favorite film when I was in the second grade." And, after another tasty cold sip, "It's amazing how good the beer here is." I set the mug down.

"May I ask a personal question?"

I was surprised, then wary, then came the tide of heat. "Sure. But I reserve the right not to answer."

"Fair enough. Why do you wear your hair that long? Is it a . . . a family characteristic?"

"No. Yes. Kind of. Mom I guess had long hair when she was young, but she chopped it off when I was born. Dad's is still long. Gran's is also long, as long as mine, though it's gone silver. I used to love watching her brush it out, and, oh, I don't know."

I didn't want to admit that Gran used to call mine princess hair. It sounded so twee, if you didn't know Gran, and you hadn't heard the way she said it, which to my childish ears sounded . . . sad.

"I thought it was romantic, and it's easier to deal with in my sports, because you pin it up. Short hair gets in your face and sticks to your neck. My dad says that life is too short for petty conformity like haircuts. But when I got bubblegum in mine when I was five, and had to have it cut off, Gran was so upset I got upset, and he cut his in sympathy. Neither of us have cut it since. Okay, that was boring. Sorry."

Alec's expression was that odd, slightly puzzled intent look I'd first seen at in the Kaisergruft. Then his face smoothed into politeness.

I said, "She—Ruli, your Aurelia—has short hair, I remember. Well, shorter than mine, so we're not alike in that."

He hesitated, and again I got that feeling that he was sorting words before he said, "Her mother was quite angry when she cut hers."

"She's three years older than I am and still lets her mom tell her how to do her hair? Never mind, people's family dynamics always seem weird to outsiders. Hey. You said you'd tell me about how she connects to the Ateliers."

The polite blandness faded, leaving that expression of slightly guarded, slightly watchful, always polite distance. The sense of ease between us had vanished. I could not define how. But I could feel it.

"I asked you," he said, "if you'd heard of Aurelia Dsaret."

"And I said no."

"Let me tell you a story, and you tell me if you see any connection. It begins in Dobrenica. Between the wars. With the birth of two daughters to the queen. Aurelia and Elisabeth Dsaret were identical twins, that being common every couple of generations in the Dsaret family. Also common were their names, as family continuity is traditional. They were nicknamed Lily and Rose."

"Okay, Aurelia is Lily, and Elisabeth is Rose. Got it."

"The eldest by some minutes was Lily, so she was designated heir to the throne. Whether she was constantly reminded of her exalted future responsibilities or simply because she was naturally sober in character, she grew up grave and quiet and studious. Her sister Rose was the opposite: mercurial, with a taste for jokes and play and pretty gowns and the like. When they reached their midteens, Rose especially attracted a crowd of well-born young fellows. Ah, I should mention that Lily had been accustomed since childhood to the idea of her eventual marriage to Milo Ysvorod."

"Milo? Ysvorod—isn't that your last name?"

"Yes. Milo is my father."

"Oh!" I digested this first sign that a story about people in a remote place and time related to anyone here and now. "But, didn't you give me another name last night?" I frowned, trying to recall.

"Marius Alexander Ysvorod of Domitrian. Domitrian is the title, when the family isn't on the throne. It's my name as well. He was called Milo by family and friends."

"Got it. Okay, she was expected to marry your father. How did she feel about that? Did anyone ever ask?"

"They'd been friends from childhood. They were all teens when World War Two began. Despite the increasingly dire reports elsewhere in Europe, the princesses were introduced to court at the age of sixteen, as usual. Every night was filled with dancing, music, parties. Word got out that court functions were fun. That drew the attention of Count Armandros Danilov von Mecklundburg, who was heir to his much older brother Karl-Johann, the Duke of Riev Dhiavilyi. Think of them as Armandros and Johann."

"Okay, got it."

He went on, not looking at me but at the ancient, winding streets of the town below. "Armandros had been racketing around Europe, wherever sport was fast, expensive, and dangerous. He also had a reputation—" He stopped, looking at his empty mug. He'd downed that entire beer.

"As what? A con man? A jerk? What?"

"He was what my father called 'a bit of a lad.' His own family branded him a hellion, irresistible when he wanted to charm. Followed by tales of numerous exploits ranging from the adventurous to the scandalous—including, apparently, two duels by the time he was eighteen. He had a temper, and courage to match. Anyway, he came on strong with the princesses. When the king's disapproval of his activities in general and this in particular reached him, he responded by making it a point of honor to court them. In this he had the enthusiastic cooperation of the princesses. And he was skillful enough that—" He broke off to signal for more beer.

I picked up my own mug, watching him over the rim. His profile was elegant, inscrutable; he sat so still the glinting reflection in his signet was a steady blue gleam. The humidity intensified, underscoring a subtle sense of expectancy; he'd fallen into a brief reverie. I didn't know if he was listening to some voice of the past, or choosing his words, but when he lifted his gaze, I flicked mine past him at that ruin. Not a ruin. In the slanting rays of the sun it shimmered oddly, its crenellations even between towers—

I blinked hard. When I looked again, it was a ruin.

"What is it?" Alec leaned forward, all his attention on me.

I was afraid he'd think I'd gotten squiffy on two sips of beer. "Looking at the, um, ruin." I forced my attention back to the Wicked Armandros. Picturing a tall, sinister but handsome guy, maybe with one of those pencil mustaches and a monocle, I said, "I think I know what comes next: the good girl Lily fell for bad boy Armandros. Am I right?"

"You are."

"And so—?" I prompted as the waiter set another mug down and Alec handed him some money.

"And so—" He turned his head as someone behind us let out a lungful of smoke, which hung for a time in the motionless air. "—her father felt it necessary to remind her of her duty. The union between Lily and Milo was increasingly important . . . for various reasons. The most obvious being the troubles elsewhere in Europe."

He stared down at that second mug of beer while I thought to myself, if he drinks that I'm either taking his keys away or walking back.

His fingers ran up and down the frosty side in an absent movement as he said, "They were supposed to marry when she turned eighteen—he was a year older—but there was talk of moving the wedding up."

"Because nobody wants to put on a big royal wedding in the middle of a war. I get it."

He paused, looking away, then back. "Right." He went on quickly, "Young as he was, Milo had proved to be capable and strong, so the king, whose health was failing, gave him increasing responsibility in the government. Lily as well, but when she wasn't busy she spent more time with Armandros, whose reputation was as dismaying as were the ambitions of his powerful family."

He turned the beer mug around and around, his body tense, sparking my awareness of how his arms shaped the shirt. You'd think the king biz wouldn't lend itself to much beside royal decrees and throne warming, but it was clear that Alec was in shape.

His glance flicked my way and I turned to gaze at the ruin, half-obscured in fog. Or was that a tower?

"Is there something interesting up there?"

"No ruins in LA. Real estate costs too much." My face burned; maybe he thought I was bored. How to tell him I wasn't without sounding like a dweeb? "Go on, please. Armandros was hitting on Lily, and she was into him."

"The king sent court home for Easter Week, and the royal family withdrew to their retreat." He shifted in his chair, his profile toward me as he studied the ruin, wreathed in drifting vapors. "Easter morning, Lily rode in the royal carriage next to Milo for the procession to the cathedral in Riev. Bowing and smiling. Those who had watched anxiously relaxed. But not long after, Lily laid down her titles and went into exile, all in the space of a day."

"Exile?"

"Rose told her friends that her sister tried to break her betrothal, but the king forbade it. You can imagine the scandal. Lily said that honor left her no recourse: she had made a vow to Armandros, and she respected Milo too much to marry him when she had given her hand and heart to another."

"That sounds so . . ." *So teenage?* Everyone laughs at teenage emo-drama, but this one sounded too real, too heartbreaking for jokes. ". . . so desperate," I finished. "Back to the Evil Count. He was after a title, right?" The combination of strong beer, the soft garden-scented air, and my awareness of the man sitting an arm's length away made the moment hyper-real. "So this connects to my grandmother how?"

"Princess Lily—no longer princess, as she had renounced her title—left the country."

I felt the impact of his gaze as a tingle through my nerves. "I know a bit about old-fashioned families and how they operated," I said. "She was driven out by scandal, and he stayed behind to marry the other princess, right?"

"You're partly right," he said, looking away again, this time at a hawk riding high on the slow, warm air currents. "Lily moved in secret to Vienna, right before the Germans took over Austria."

"Vienna. Whoa," I said, the tingle changing to one of those chills of apprehension that get you along the backs of your arms and your neck.

When I shifted my gaze to the ruin, there was the tower again.

I turned in my seat so I couldn't see it.

"Vienna," he repeated, again with the hesitation, almost reluctance. "For a time," he said slowly as he tracked the drifting hawk. "The war halted communication from the homeland. She fled to Paris."

My guts tightened, and I rubbed my hands together, trying to shed tension. "To Paris?"

"Yes. With a daughter. Who was called Marie, in the French manner."

Golden fire tipped the edges of the hawk's wings as it rode the high currents. The bird's head flicked back and forth, back and forth, scanning the ground for prey. The chill had frozen me.

"Right before the war ended, the house she'd lived in was found gutted by flames from a nearby bombing, and Lily and the child had disappeared without a trace. It was impossible to ascertain whether or not they had been inside the house when the bombing and fire had occurred."

Numbly I said, "So that Princess Lily was my grandmother, is that what you're saying but not saying?"

"It's possible." He pushed away the beer. "Did she ever mention anything at all about any of this? Speak German, even?"

"Never. I never heard one word of German from her." I shook my head firmly. "Even when I was studying it and practicing it. All she said about Europe was how beautiful Paris had been in the spring, and how much good French was an asset to a young lady. But Gran had saved a single Viennese memento: a pair of concert tickets."

"Which is what brought you to Vienna?" His voice was sympathetic.

"Yes. Well, that and a vague memory my mother had, of a . . . conversation about Vienna, Germany, the east. More like an argument, not that she understood any of it. Anyway, when I had zero luck in Paris, off I went to Vienna to put a genealogist on the trail. Well." I took another deep breath. If I decided to believe that his princess was Gran, how to tell Mom? Call? E-mail? Wait until I got home and tell her face-to-face? I said, "She must have adopted France as her new country when she married Grandfather Atelier. That is, *if* Gran is your missing princess. It would explain my resemblance to your Aurelia, who I'm going to think of as Ruli, so my brain doesn't explode. Who is she, Rose's granddaughter?"

"Yes."

"So she has good French. Too. Taught by somebody of Gran's generation, am I right? So our accents and vocabulary are pretty much the same?"

"Yes."

"Well! You'll certainly have a great story to tell her when you do catch up with her. Funny, how genes will do that. I wonder if her mother looks at all like mine, and for that matter, what all the various fathers and grandfathers have in common."

"Would you like something more to drink?" he asked.

"Not beer. Despite my performance the other day, I don't drink much and rarely during the day."

He indicated his untouched beer. "I think I'd better switch to coffee as well. Shall we order lunch?"

"Now that you mention it . . ."

The humid air was motionless, heavy. We ate the savory Slovenian food and talked easily on a range of subjects, discovering odd things we had in common (a fondness for early Beatles' music—his favorite tutor had played it all the time, like my Dad had when I was a kid); a partiality for Victor Hugo and Alexandre Dumas, whose works we'd both devoured as teens, and how much funnier Dumas was read in French; oh, I don't remember what all, because I was mostly trying to impress the sound of his voice on my memory.

Behind him, the fog slowly whorled around the ruin, but that did not explain why I saw the outline of a castle, and then a ruin. So I turned my chair so that my back was to it.

When I straightened up, I found him regarding me in silent question. I blurted, "Have you ever done any fencing?"

His expression blanked. "A little. You mentioned sport. You took up fencing?"

Guys with blades—paging Dr. Freud! "A lot. With the trophies to show for it." I threw in my trophies to get away from any possible imputations of Freudian symbolism, but now I sounded like a blowhard. So I blathered on, "I wanted to be Geena Davis in *Cutthroat Island* when I was a kid." He gave me the expected laugh, then I changed the subject. "Do you like swashbuckler movies?"

We went from movies to music, and the awkward moment passed.

Meanwhile the fog had retreated, replaced by a menacing army of thunderheads stealth-marching overhead. When the sky was covered, they loosed their arsenal in a spectacular bombardment of lightning, thunder, and hail.

The waiters hastily closed up the terrace against the rising wind. We climbed back into the green Daimler and, shutting the noise of the storm out, began the return drive.

Daimler. Why did he have to drive such a cool car? Why couldn't he dress in plaid pants held up with a cowboy belt and wear his hair in an honest-to-eighties mullet?

We were silent as he maneuvered through the few cars and hurrying pedestrians on the narrow, rain-streaming streets. After he turned onto the smooth and uncrowded main road I watched the *swish-swish* of the wipers in their hypnotic sweep as I struggled not to stare at his hands.

Geez, why wasn't he shorter than Napoleon, round as a beachball, balding, a cheery avuncular guy? Except a short, beachball-shaped, balding, cheerfully avuncular guy in a mullet and cowboy belt who spoke with that *voice*—warm melted chocolate when he was smiling, the whisper of silver when his mood had shifted beyond that invisible wall of good manners, hiding whatever he was feeling, the smooth edge of steel when he was angry—would be exactly as compelling.

Lightning-bright rain scattered across the windshield in diamonds; the thunder was merely a distant muffled rumble in this car. Tension seemed to ride between us, slow lightning on the sensory plane, as I tried not to remember his laugh from the night before, slightly husky, sparking gold with delight—I'd heard many guys laugh, but not once had anyone with a single sound managed to whack me behind the knees.

I thumped my arms across my chest and dug my nails into my palms.

Concentrate, Murray! Okay. So I had trouble believing Gran had been, like, a *princess,* for heaven's sake. But when on impulse I half turned, meaning to ease the atmosphere with a joke about California and kings, my gaze zipped straight to the tight grip of Alec's hands on the wheel, and then to the tightness of his shoulders.

Then the problem wasn't me, surging with enough pheromones to fuel an entire high school cheerleading squad. Something was wrong, I sensed it, but didn't even know how to ask. Or if I had a right to ask.

And so I shut my eyes and forced myself to think through what I'd been told so I could repeat it coherently to my mother. But what might be her questions? Would I be able to get Alec's e-mail address, or was this the last I'd see of him, and this connection with Gran's past, tenuous as it seemed, would vanish like it had never happened?

My trip was to find missing family, and here was the possibility Gran had had a twin, leading to a real family somewhere in this part of the world. There could be nothing wrong with family questions. Right?

I said, "Back to the Wicked Count. You did say he married Rose, so your Aurelia, Ruli, is their granddaughter."

"Yes."

"I'm glad—if Lily was Gran—she got over him, and found Grandfather Atelier."

Sw*ish-swish.* Lightning flickered. Thunder rumbled.

I said, "I know Gran loved him a lot. That picture I mentioned. I wish more than ever my copy wasn't lost, so I could show you. Anyway, she's kept it on her bedside table all these years, and she used to smile at it, both Mom and I grew up seeing that. But anyway, the sinister duke, or count, or whatever he was, I'm glad he was forgotten."

Lightning again. The rain was so heavy it was nearly impossible to see beyond it, though the airtight car kept most of the noise out. I felt a curious sensation, as if the car was a ship and we were shooting through water (or maybe through space) with no land or civilization within light-years. Alec's silence as he drove magnified the quietness of our little space in the eye of the storm.

I'd run out of words, my mind running a private YouTube of dancing princesses, evil counts, duels, desperate cross-country races against the backdrop of war. But this wasn't movie clips, it was real—it had happened—and my quiet, piano-playing grandmother had been at the center of wrenching changes as a desperate, loving sixteen-year-old girl.

Alec spoke. "I don't know if this is a bad idea or a good one. But I wonder if you'd consider a plan I've in mind."

"A plan?" I repeated, thinking of Gran, mustachioed dukes, and Paris.

"Yes." He glanced quickly at me, his face impossible to read. "It would require a week or so of your time, but I'd pay for it."

"A week—where?"

"A couple of days in Zagreb. A beautiful city. Maybe a day or two in Split, then to Dubrovnik, known for its ancient fortress and polished marble streets. Ruli likes the night life. From there you could go on to Greece, or Italy."

"What? Wait!" It was then that I thought of Rudolph Rassendyll, and shook free of the shroud of emotions, of questions I could not ask. Shades of *Prisoner of Zenda!* I said recklessly, "You want me to impersonate your Aurelia? How cool is that?"

"Yes," he replied in a neutral voice. "What could be cooler?"

ELEVEN

MY RECKLESS MOOD lasted about ten seconds. After all, I was no Rupert of Hentzau.

So who was?

My mind bloomed with questions. I reached for the most immediate one. "At least it's not a coronation. Maybe I should be asking why you can't let Aur—er, Ruli go her own way, treaty or no treaty."

"It's not so simple," he said, scanning the road.

"You keep saying that. The way I see it, she apparently doesn't want to marry you, so you let her go. I'll bet there are plenty of other titled ladies who'd be happy to take her place, if you have to have titles."

"First I find her," he said. "Then she tells me what she wants to do—ah," he exclaimed with satisfaction. "There it is."

"What? We're not going back to the inn?"

"No, I thought we'd take a short detour. Take in the view of Verezc from the Cheneska ruin."

"The ruin?" I tried to hide my complete lack of enthusiasm. That place gave me the creeps, though maybe it was only fog and tiredness making me see things. "In a thunderstorm?"

"It should lift any time. Look. Behind us there's blue sky." He glanced at me in mild question. "You have an objection to the ruin?"

I was not about to say I'd been weirded out by fog tricking my eyes. "No, I'm fine with it."

He drove smoothly and without apparent effort up a narrow road of hairpin turns; I wondered if narrow roads and hairpin turns were as normal in Dobrenica as traffic is in LA. The storm pounded us in unabated strength, occasional blasts of wind rocking the car and splashing torrents of rain over the windows. As he drove he gave me a short history of the ruined castle. I only half-listened; I wanted to get back to his switcheroo idea. But he avoided discussing it, and I began to wonder as the green car at last nosed smoothly into a wide, clear space ringed by a low stone wall, if it had been a kingly joke.

Or maybe he remembered the story of *The Prisoner of Zenda* and realized his part would have to be one of the villains. Ha ha.

Alec drove up to the wall. ". . . and so it was abandoned as an outpost in 1848 and left to stand. The family could not afford to rebuild it and live in it. The succeeding governments have claimed it since."

"Interesting." I peered into the purple gray rain-shrouded hilltop parking lot. "And affords an awesome view of twenty-five feet."

"Look over here."

He pointed southward, through his side window. Sure enough, the long, pale gray mass retreated, leaving patches of sky of that peculiar light aquamarine color I've always thought of as swimming-pool sky. Appropriate enough, considering I've only seen it before or after thunderstorms. To the north the slate- and green-tinged clouds roiled toward the horizon.

All right. I was here. Let there be mysterious walls and towers if it dared.

I opened the car door and was met by a rush of heavy, wet grass–scented air. The last splatting drops of rain stung my face and hands, tickled my scalp. Then a fresh, pure breeze seemed to end the rain, like a magic hand waving benignly. The clouds broke up and straight ahead a rainbow arched ethereally bright and clear across the valley. To my left shafts of golden sunlight touched the mossy, gray crumbling walls of the castle, stippling the contours with warm color. I stooped and rubbed my fingers over the solid wet stone.

"Reality check?"

"Not many castles in LA."

"Dobrenica is even more beautiful after a summer storm."

"Does Cooks book bus-tours there?"

He smiled.

Light shafts widened and blended into general brightness as the sky cleared. I sighed finally and said, "An impersonation sounds swashbuckling as all get-out, at least in stories. What would be the purpose in reality?"

"To sting her into reappearing on her own, if she's hiding from her mother, or even from the idea of marriage. Far more likely her brother's mixed up in this somehow, though he says he talks to her as little as possible and never asks where she's traveling. Except when he wants to avoid being in the same city. If you were to show up and be seen by people who know both brother and sister, we might be able to call his bluff."

"The brother again."

"The brother again," he agreed. "Do you want to walk around the ruin?" He held out his arm.

"Better not." I lifted my foot to the low parapet and pulled up the trouser cuff. "I thought so—it's swelling up again. I shouldn't have been so bullheaded about hiking around looking for that stupid suitcase. Anyway, it's pretty enough right here." I turned around and sat down on the damp stone. "Though," I gloated up at him, "you will have to dry clean these pants."

"A small price to pay to give you pleasure," he returned promptly, with a bow and a suave hand gesture.

I snorted. "So what exactly would I be doing?"

"You'd be enjoying the sights, the casinos and clubs, and you'd be spending money on clothes."

"What would this brother have to say to me should we meet?"

"There will be no meeting," he replied. "Tony seems to be incommunicado. His family says he's yachting in the North Sea, except one of their townhouse staff told Emilio that he's on a wine tour in France. He's notorious for losing cell phones, so he could be anywhere, even holed up in his castle. But he's not here."

"He has a castle?"

"Nearly a thousand years old."

"Is it sinister?" I asked hopefully.

He laughed. "It's quite large. And it does sit on a peak called Devil's Mountain. Anyway, by the time he would hear about your appearance—as Ruli—you will have embarked—as yourself—safely on your trip. I'll send you back to your starting point, I hardly need to add—by plane, or a cruise to Greece and up to Italy, where you can catch a train to Vienna, or wherever you choose. If Tony does turn up in the vicinity, I'll send you immediately on your way."

"The rest of her family? Any close friends?"

"They will be dealt with individually. You won't meet them."

"So it's not only the brother you want to fool?"

"Tony and his people, yes."

"Minions again!" I couldn't help laughing, and he smiled, but it was a quick, preoccupied smile.

"We'll be on watch. You won't have to speak to them, should we see any. And once you're gone, since they don't know of your existence, they can't come after you."

"I'm not scared," I scoffed. "I'm trying to figure if this disguise, which does sound fun, would be doing my namesake—who may be a distant cousin of mine—any good."

He stood a few feet away, staring over the valley.

When he didn't speak, I added, "I also don't care to figure as an ignorant pawn in a political skirmish, especially if I'm not to hear the other side."

He turned that reflective gaze on me as he asked mildly, "Then why are you considering my plan?"

It was my turn to look away. I gazed out over the valley, rubbing absently at my aching ankle. "You're not going to tell me all the nasty political ramifications, are you?"

"Do you want to hear the nasty political ramifications?"

I hesitated. *This stuff is real to him. His country and its problems are real to him.* I said, "Look, I want to be reassured, if possible, that nothing I do is going to jeopardize Aurelia, er, Ruli. Much easier to think of her as Ruli, otherwise this is way too weird."

"Meaning I would be willing to jeopardize her?" he asked, brows lifted. Then he smiled, a quick, rueful smile. "I beg your pardon. I know you mean well, and I honor your scruples. But rather than talk up my high principles, let me remind you that she has been missing for some time. From before we ever saw you. Or we never would've seen you in the first place. If they do have her, I hope to force them to let her go."

I nodded. "Good enough. When do we start?"

"As soon as we get you some gear." He tossed his keys lightly on his palm. "Shall we return to the inn?"

As we sat down at a small table in the Gasthaus dining room, Alec told me that we'd leave for Zagreb in the morning.

Those two men I thought of as Graybeard and Mr. Big had made appearances throughout the day, but they did not join us.

"Those two men of your father's," I said.

"They've worked for the family for many years. Kilber was with my father during the war."

"Yes, that's what I wanted to ask. They must have been super young. Like teenagers. And it was Kilber who slipped you the roofie-juice the other day?"

"I must say, he rather surprised me," Alec admitted, and he blushed, which made me feel slightly less annoyed about the incident. I was beginning to believe that he didn't go around drugging people. I'd been the unlucky first.

For *him.*

"In the war years they all started young. He told me that that sort of trick was a leftover habit from years of dodging Russians."

My resentment had shifted to Alec's henchman. "Somehow, with that face, it doesn't surprise me."

"Kilber only speaks a few words of English, or he'd join us, and Emilio departed on an errand earlier this afternoon. I suspect you'll like Lavzhenko Emilio. He too is a Wodehouse fan, but he prefers the Mulliner stories to Bertie and Jeeves."

"And I suppose that Kilber character reads E. F. Benson while disposing of bodies—drugged or otherwise? What is that, his last name or first? The 'kil' part seems most apt."

"His first name is Klaus, but at home professionals go by last names. First names are only used by family. Kilber saved my father's life several times during the early Russian years, and he does not like the idea of killing people. Which is why he would use that sleeping pill ruse to knock 'em out."

Wartime. A totally different paradigm. "All right. Got it. One of the good guys, in spite of his pills."

A smiling waiter delivered plates of spiced Serbo-Croatian food, and for a time I was too busy to talk. But I did think.

When the coffee was served I said, "You know, I can't help wondering about Ruli . . ." Then I stopped in case he was worried about eavesdroppers. I cast a look about me. We were alone except for an elderly couple giving their food their undivided attention.

Alec sat back inquiringly, the sapphire on his ring glinting cool blue.

"I was wondering how much I truly look like her, or if you don't know her."

"Both," he replied. "Physically you're much alike. In personality, you're not at all alike. Yet, if I'd known her as well as I thought I did, I should've suspected the truth long before I was forcibly convinced."

"Did she grow up in England, too?"

"Only through childhood. In her early teens she was shifted to boarding school in Switzerland, then in Paris, where she spent all her holidays with her mother. When she finished school, they spent their time traveling around Europe to visit friends and relations. Winters in the south, the rest of the year between Vienna, Paris, Berlin, and London. Occasionally even back home. Though I understand she'd begun a nightlife on her own a year or two back. That's when she decided we were to call her Ruli, as Aurelia was hopelessly old-fashioned."

"And I take it she teased you because your French is school trained?"

"She was annoying about it for four or five years when we were all in our teens. Then her attitude changed. Tony told me that someone had taken her aside, pointed out that a true sophisticate wouldn't mention the accent but let it, ah, speak for itself. He took revenge by loudly complimenting her in public on how good her accent was."

"So you spent time with her family?"

"The holidays when I was not with my father, until I was about eighteen. Not long after that my aunt moved to the Paris flat on a more or less permanent basis."

"So you haven't seen Ruli much in recent years?"

"Not much," he agreed. "Don't worry. Always have a cigarette in your hand. Look bored, never smile outright. As I said before, no one would ever imagine that a double exists. They'll supply all the belief necessary. You have the force of recent memory to convince you of that, right?"

I choked on my coffee. "What a story to tell at home! How's her German and her Slavic languages?"

"No Slavic languages. Her German is school trained—much like yours."

"How does German fit into your background, anyway?"

"German was the language of government, and French the language of diplomacy, until the Second World War. Leftovers from the Hapsburg era. The Dobreni have caught up with nineteenth-century nationalism enough to want to be governed in their own tongue, but all our parents thought it necessary for us to learn German as well as French."

"I don't know any Dobreni."

"Anyone who would want to speak Dobreni to you is going to be intercepted by one of us. Shouldn't be a problem."

"And what about her short hair? I won't cut mine."

"If you put it up the way you did for the ballet in Vienna, it'll be fine. She still wore her hair up for formal occasions, which is why I was fooled."

"But we won't be doing anything formal, will we?"

"No. Remember, no one will be looking for anything strange. It will seem a new whim."

When we went upstairs a surprise was waiting for me: not only were my jeans freshly laundered, but a pair of expensive new suitcases (empty) plus a makeup case (not empty) and an overnight bag waited in my room. Lying next to them was a department store bag containing a pretty cotton nightgown and a matching robe of soft rose. In the makeup case I found a load of goodies: toothbrush, soaps and shampoo, hairpins of every imaginable kind, and a handsome cedar-backed brush and comb, plus a formidable battery of hairspray and cosmetics.

Alec leaned in my open doorway, grinning. "How's Emilio's taste?" he asked.

"Well, fine, I guess! Except . . . ." I brandished a bottle of crimson nail polish in one hand and hair spray in the other. "My look is pretty much beach casual, so I've never been into any of this stuff."

"But Ruli is."

I snapped my fingers. "Of course! So this is my disguise kit."

"D'you like the frock?"

"Where?" I turned to the wooden wardrobe in the corner, opened it. There hung a dress, a belted cotton print in shades of blue. "Oh, that's pretty."

"He said the dress store owner picked that out when he described your coloring and approximate size. You can shop wearing it. My aunt never permitted Ruli to wear jeans, though she might now. But we'll stick with what I remember. Be on the safe side."

"Gee, this is fun," I enthused.

He smiled. "I'll tell Emilio you're pleased."

"So that was Emilio's mysterious errand?"

"One of 'em. Emilio's married, with a daughter and daughter-in-law. I thought he'd make sensible choices."

"Well, give him my thanks," I ended a trifle awkwardly.

Alec gave me that airy salute. "Good night."

"Okey-dokey." I shut the door. "Good night."

TWELVE

THE NEXT MORNING, bright and early, we were off. Emilio carried down my new badges of respectability and I wore my new dress, and unfortunately my ruined sandals. My ankle was less swollen, and I kept my pace sedate.

Alec was behind me on the stairs. He said, after a few seconds, "You never mentioned any duels with desperados—other than myself—the other day."

"What?" I stopped, surprised to hear the guardedness back in his voice. "Desperados?"

"On your hike." He brushed his fingers over my shoulder. His touch was fleeting and impersonal, but it sent sparkle-fire down my nerves.

"Oh," I said as offhandedly as possible. "That mighty bruise. I forgot. Looks awful, huh? Maybe I'd best get some blouses with sleeves."

"How did that happen?"

"When I jumped out of the train. Got another biggie, too, on my butt." I laughed; he smiled, but his brows contracted in quick concern.

The big Daimler smoothly ate up the miles under Alec's hands, and the time passed agreeably; the three of us talked about favorite books, movies, local history, and the like.

Alec was right about Emilio. I apologized to him for my rudeness on the Glorietta monument at Schönbrunn, he apologized in turn for disturbing me, and after that we got along fine. He never called me by anything except Mam'zelle; he seemed earnest, and a trifle shy, and it was impossible for me keep seeing as a sinister and evil villain a guy in his seventies whose face lit with joy when he talked about Gilbert and Sullivan operettas.

Zagreb was old and modern in a fascinating jumble. As soon as we got to the city center Alec turned over the car to Emilio and he took a taxi to some unnamed destination while Emilio and I embarked on a massive shopping campaign, all paid for by Emilio from a fat wallet. Shoes imported from Italy—clothes from all over Europe—it was a shopaholic's heaven . . . but cool as the idea was to be spending someone else's money, it felt weird picking out clothes according to a stranger's taste. A stranger who looked like me.

That second night I rolled my papers and cash in my jeans and LA top and tucked those into a corner of one of the suitcases. That small roll was my reality check.

We all met back at a grand hotel called the Regent Esplanade, the name of which reminded me ridiculously of San Fernando Valley shopping malls. The resemblance stopped at the name, of course. This place was solid with early-twentieth-century charm, the colors variations on warm gold, with high ceilings, arches, elegant chandeliers, the works. I practiced my Aurelia act, steadied by the knowledge that she'd only stayed there once or twice; her infrequent visits to Zagreb were to see some second or third cousins.

Alec said nothing until we were alone at dinner (Emilio having thanked me for a pleasant afternoon and disappeared, destination unspecified), then he gave me some mild coaching.

At the end of dinner he said we would begin the charade the next day, and he excused himself politely—after requesting me to confine myself to my room. I was prepared for that. On my shopping foray I had found a bookstore with a small section containing French novels. So I'd made a few random selections.

After we parted I sat in the expensive room, propped my foot on a hassock, and opened the first of my books. It was late when I became aware of my tired eyes and stiff neck. I stood up and stretched. My foot hurt much less than it had.

Someone tapped briefly at my door.

Surprised, I called in French, "Who's there?"

"Alec."

I opened the door. He made no movement to come in. "I saw your light on and stopped to ask how your evening was, if there is anything you need?"

"I've got a question for you." His brows lifted interrogatively and I went on, "If Princess Lily was the heir, and she gave it up, why didn't her sister take over the throne, and her descendents after her?"

He said, still standing in the hallway, "Princess Rose's daughter was disinherited right after she was born. Shortly after that the king abdicated and turned the throne over to my father."

"Ah, I see! So that's why you and Brother Tony are at odds! He wants his mother's rights, huh? Why not give 'em back?" As soon as it was out Alec's expression shifted to that ice-smooth facade and I knew my flippant surmise was a mistake. Worsened by the late hour.

Alec said lightly, "The proverbial American knack for solving everyone's problems after thirty seconds' perusal. Tell me, does the solution come with foreign aid?"

I slammed the door in his face.

No, I don't want to hear your nasty political ramifications, I'd said to him. I knew I'd set myself up for that zinger—but that didn't make it any easier to take.

After a restless night I marched down to breakfast the next morning, ready to apologize—or take the next train out, depending on his attitude.

I found Alec sitting at a table in the dining room. When he saw me he laid down his newspaper and stood up.

"I'm sorry, I didn't mean to be a jerk—" I began at the moment he said, "I beg your pardon for my rudeness."

We eyed one other—the tension was gone.

With one of those sudden, rare, real smiles, he opened his hand toward a chair in invitation. "May I pour you some tea?"

No hint of *droit de seigneur*.

I sat down. As we got our tea and coffee, he said, "Shall we discuss today's agenda? Emilio and the car are at your disposal. He says there are a number of streets whose shops you haven't seen yet."

"O-kay," I said slowly.

"Daunting prospect?" He seemed on the verge of a laugh.

"We-ell," I drew out the word. "I like pretty new things as much as anyone. But most of this stuff is so . . . so high end. And it costs a fortune. What will we do with it when the switch is over? I can't see myself in a two hundred dollar blouse grading student papers, or grubbing under the hood of my junkmobile wearing shoes that cost half a grand."

He laughed. "Night and day . . . night and day."

"I guess I'd feel better if you donate them to some good cause," I finished awkwardly.

"We'll do whatever you want."

I felt uneasy again, that sense of proximity, and yet there was the possibility of trespass. *I am not Ruli, I only look and sound and dress like her.* "What's on the menu? Anything besides scrambled eggs and calves' brains?"

After breakfast, I found Emilio waiting for me in the lobby. He was dressed in a quiet brown suit, his expression earnest as he stood up at my approach. "Good morning, Mam'zelle," he said with a funny nod like a short bow.

Alec had obviously talked to him about the shopping, for Emilio offered me a drive through the countryside instead, which I accepted with relief. The weather was balmy as we drove along narrow country lanes, some juddering the car with ancient cobblestones laid down before tires were ever invented, others hastily covered with tarmac to ease the movement of some army crossing from here to there, and patched afterward. We passed picturesque old villages apparently little changed in three or four hundred years, and two ancient, crumbling churches that were at least a thousand years old. Probably older.

We stopped at one of these. Inside, kerchiefed and black-dressed widows knelt and prayed, as their foremothers had done for a thousand years. The rough, aged artwork in these churches showed the influence of Eastern Orthodoxy as well as Roman Catholicism. The sense of mystery, of the numinous, made my tourist-gawking seem inappropriate. Perhaps it was the otherwhere-absorbed motionlessness of the figures at the wooden rails, partly perhaps the utter silence in which my scraping steps and rustling clothes sounded preternaturally loud . . . or maybe it was Emilio's unthinking crossing of himself as he entered and bowed his head reverently.

When I walked out the sunlight coruscated in a familiar way, making me giddy, as if a slight quake rolled the ground, and I stopped short, staring at a dust-covered box coach, all black. Even the horses were black, and the liveried servants at their heads wore black armbands.

The sunlight flared with glaring coronas around Edwardian-era silhouettes that walked slowly toward me. Another blink and they vanished, leaving me staring at the dusty road, grass on one side, an ancient churchyard on the other, while my head reverberated like a sonic boom.

"Mam'zelle? Are you ill?" Emilio's voice broke the grip of excitement—fear—sorrow, yanking me from the aftermath of Sarajevo in June of 1914, and thrusting me back in the now.

I hadn't had that giddiness since I'd sat with Alec looking up at the castle ruins. I'd ascribed it to exhaustion plus beer, worsened by the residue of Kilber's sleeping pill.

This weird sense of stumbling briefly in and out of time was nonsense, of course. "Fanciful." More serious was the concern in Emilio's kindly face. In my experience, people who express real concern worry more if you say, *Oh it's nothing.* If you don't want to cause them to worry at it further, then you have to give them a plausible reason.

"I stumbled. And, well, the truth is, I happen to have an overactive imagination. What are we seeing next?"

Emilio accepted this clumsy answer and drove me to an open air market, where we cruised the dealers offering spectacularly complex and colorful Persian rugs. He knew a lot about textile art.

In midafternoon as a drizzling rain seeped over the landscape we found an old, jumbled used bookstore. I prowled among the dusty stacks and shelves in the dimly lit airless cubbyholes. Wishing I had the cash to buy bags of books, I picked up a pair of slim volumes of Russian and Serbo-Croatian poetry, and then I made my big discovery: a small, green-bound German-Dobreni dictionary. It was almost a century old, printed (as it stated in red and black *fraktur*, complete with crest) in 1890 by order of Alexander IV, King of Dobrenica. Would he be my something-great-grandfather? I wondered, feeling strange.

I didn't tell Emilio. I wanted to study it in private, maybe even figure out a sentence or two to surprise him with—if we were around one another that long. But mainly I intended to take it back to LA and give it to my mother when I told her Alec's strange story.

When we got back to the hotel I curled up with the dictionary. Alec knocked on my door at about six and asked if I'd like to go down to dinner with him. He looked tired as he asked politely if I'd had a nice day, etc. etc. and I responded with equally ironclad politeness.

Before we entered the dining room, we stepped out onto a terrace, where crowds of smokers talked, laughed, and drank. In the reflected light from the enormous bank of windows, he pulled from his jacket a slim, richly gleaming gold case with two diamonds glittering in light scrollwork along the edges, and with a wry quirk to his brows, handed it to me.

"What's this? Oh!" I flicked it open and saw two rows of aromatic white cylinders lying inside. "I forgot. She smokes."

"You know how to handle a cigarette?"

"I've seen enough old Joan Crawford movies that I think I can manage to fake it with the proper old world air."

His eyes smiled as he handed me a solid gold lighter. The metal was warm from being in his pocket. I maneuvered it awkwardly in my hand as I said, "This I'd better practice with. I never could figure them out."

His smile deepened to a grin. "No need. Her mother trained Ruli to never light her own cigarettes if there is a man present. It's a proprietary act, don't you see? She produces a lighter only as a hint to a slow escort. Flash it around. Ruli used to play with hers, I think as a way to break her childhood habit of chewing her nails."

"Okay," I said, feeling silly as I pulled a cigarette from the pretty case. "Try lighting it."

I put the cigarette in my lips and leaned forward. His hand moved toward my face with the lighter, up sprang a flame which came closer—closer—my eyes crossed trying to stay focused on it, and belatedly I remembered to puff. Rather than draw the smoke into my lungs, I held my breath for a second or two, then blew it out slowly. It burned the inside of my mouth, hot and acrid.

"Good job. But—" He was on the verge of laughter. "—you needn't watch. I won't burn your nose, or miss the cigarette." Then he added in mild enquiry, "What are you doing?"

I had put out the cigarette and was in the midst of laying it back in the case.

"Saving it for later," I answered, surprised my intentions were not clear. "I don't need Ruli props right now, and I'm sure not going to finish it. Yeccch, my mouth tastes like the bottom of a birdcage."

"Ruli would never reuse them." He shook his head and stretched out his fingers to twitch the cigarette from mine.

The touch of his fingers on mine gave me a small inward shock. I slapped the case shut and made a business of slipping it into the handbag until I recovered. Then I grinned. "You'd best keep an eye on me in case I leave it somewhere behind. Remember, I'm not in the habit of lugging smoking kafuffle around."

"Kafuffle," he repeated, smiling as he flicked the cigarette into an ashtray.

"Dad's word," I said. "Gran hated—hates—cussing. My dad picks up words that get around vulgarity, like fewmets and minions. He was a newspaper minion before he got laid off."

"Kafuffle," he repeated under his breath and chuckled as we went inside to dine.

After dinner we took a taxi to stone-facaded nightclub. Outside the doors Alec shot me an inquisitive look. "Ready?"

"Lead on." I followed him in.

Noise and smoke blasted at us. The place was nearly as dark as the cloud-smothered sky overhead, and super crowded. Loud music thumped inside my chest, played through mega-amps by a combo on a small stage. The small dance floor was crammed with people. In the hazy darkness they seemed to be struggling at Sisyphean labors. We threaded our way through, and somehow Alec found a table. Drinks appeared. Alec sat back to watch the band as I self-consciously pulled out a cigarette. He took the lighter and lit it with smooth expertise. The flame brightened his face briefly, and he gave me a salute, a private gesture between the two of us. Then the lighter snapped the flame out and Alec sat back.

Talk was impossible. I watched the band, and Alec watched the people. I was too nervous to risk meeting any eyes, so I tried puffing the cigarette, but my breath was so nasty I waved it around instead. At one point his chin came up and he lifted his drink in salute to someone behind me. I resisted the impulse to turn my head, but I thought, *They're here already!* Then I remembered that Ruli, if not Alec, had distant relatives in this city.

With his other hand he touched my arm and, my heart banging counterpoint to the band, I nodded over my shoulder in the general direction he'd sent his salute. It was impossible to identify one among the mass of light-limned silhouettes, though it did appear the crowd was flowing around a thickset man who stood against a far wall. The owner? He was swiftly hidden from view by approaching dancers, and I straightened around again.

Another drink, another cigarette, which burned down nicely all by itself, more noise—then Alec touched my arm again. I understood from the jerk of his head that we were free.

Outside I gulped in pure, cool, sweet air. "Made it out alive!"

He laughed. "Not accustomed to the club scene, I take it. What do you do for fun in Santa Monica?"

"I curl up with hot cocoa and Jennifer Crusie. Jane Austen on a big night. Why are you laughing?"

"I'm not, I'm not," he assured me, but the smile lines around his eyes betrayed him.

There was no malice in his amusement, so I said, "My friends and I tend to sit around talking, or we go to small theater plays. When we have the cash and no school deadlines. Who was that guy?"

"Brother of a second cousin, one of her new flirts."

"All right, we flushed one vulture. Now what?"

He beckoned to a prowling taxi. "I don't know if he knows what's going on, but I expect he's either going to call someone, or call on us, or both. But we won't be here. First thing in the morning we leave Zagreb."

And we did. Again it was Emilio, Alec, and me in the Daimler. We drove straight to the coast, to a fantastically beautiful hotel in Opatija on the Kvarner Bay, near Rijeka. I was amazed that a Communist country had once allowed such flagrant pandering to bourgeois luxury, for the place boasted of its establishment 150 years ago. Alec told me that the Dalmatian coast had been an aristo playground long before Soviet-style Communism stomped down its heavy boot; wealthy people had been going there to recuperate from their excesses for over a century.

"Ruli's well known here," he said as he stopped the engine. "Her favorite retreat from . . . family surfeit, let's say. Got her firmly in mind?"

"Curtain up!" I waved my manicured, scarlet nails, then reached for the car door.

He flicked up a warning hand. "Wait! Remember, she's the daughter of a duchess. Duchesses do not open their own car doors." So I sat there feeling like a fake while he walked around and opened the door for me.

I had pictured myself waltzing into the hotel and handing out orders with all the panache of Auntie Mame in the Rosalind Russell movie my mother loves. But the moment I walked into that fine lobby and encountered the snooty gazes of hotel employees and guests (I couldn't tell which was which at first glance), nerves froze my face in a smile that probably made me look like I'd had major surgery without an anesthetic. I trailed after Alec, completely unable to say anything.

Luckily they must have known what to expect because the desk clerk began, in a solicitous voice, by asking how my mother was and then he offered me various things from drinks to some fresh fruit. When I got up to the two-room suite chosen for me, a chambermaid started a hot bath, my luggage appeared behind me, and a houseboy opened a bottle of champagne. While waiting for the elevator I had pulled out a cigarette for Alec to light, as much to give my hands something to do as anything, then I withdrew with it to a chair near the window that gave a splendid view of the greeny blue sea.

Whenever anyone came near I waved the cigarette at them, saying thinly, "Merci, merci."

They took it as instant dismissal and filed out. As soon as I was alone I poured half the champagne down the sink, pitched the cigarette after it, brushed my teeth, and retreated gratefully into the bath.

Dinner started out okay. We had a great table, great food, and after a few sips of Ruli's favorite drink, and no shock or horror from anyone around me I slowly relaxed into the Ruli role.

That left me intensely aware of my companion—who gave me that lovely smile, spoke with the silvery, intimate voice, and was doing his best to pretend I was someone else.

We hit two nightclubs in the hotel complex, one of which was also a casino. There was always a fresh drink at hand, so I kept sipping. Ruli's drinks were sweet and super-strong. I didn't intend to get drunk. I hate getting drunk—I hate the loss of control, and drinking and driving in LA is never a good idea. But I wasn't driving, I wasn't in LA, and I needed something to do with my eyes so I wouldn't be watching him. More, I needed a wall between *will* and *desire.*

At first the liquor seemed a good idea. You know, fuzziness, numbness, yadda yadda.

The floorshow in the second place began to revolve gently before my eyes; I don't remember leaving. What I do remember is the touch of Alec's fingers on my bare arm, cool and warm at the same time, the brush of his hair—as fine and soft as it looked—against my cheek when he bent to hear something I said, my awareness of his breathing, which I couldn't hear because the music was loud enough to reverberate through bones and teeth. But I noticed the pulse at his throat, and the slight rise and fall of his shirt over his chest, all this against the constantly changing kaleidoscope of color and noise in the background.

And so I drank more, trying to dull the effect, but what the alcohol did, as it usually does, is betray me by dissolving that wall between the bleak logic of will and revealing all the fire, charm, dazzle of desire.

My next memory is stumbling into my hotel room, cursing when my ankle twinged. Alec's arm went around me, and he took my weight with seemingly effortless strength. Feeling his body pressed against mine from shoulder to hip sent the blaze of promise through my sodden senses.

I stared up into his face. "You're cute. You *are* cute, you know . . . I hope I'm not helping the bad guys here. I mean, who is Black Michael?"

"Never mind, we're almost done," he murmured into my hair. "Will you be all right on your own?"

"You're leaving?" I croaked, falling backward onto the bed. And laughed when my feet, five miles away in another city, were tickled by my shoes being gently pulled off. I held out my arms as the world gently revolved. "A good night kiss?"

"Good night," he said, bent, and his lips brushed my forehead, his touch cool with pale fire.

"Oooh," I said intelligently.

His smile turned pensive as he moved out of my line of sight. I sighed as a counterpane dropped over me. "You're too much a gentleman to take advantage? Or do kings disdain the commoners?"

Way down, beneath the lake of booze, the sane part of my mind recognized that when I dried out I was going to regret making an ass of myself.

"I don't know," he responded, lightly enough. "I am not a king. And you are not in any sense common."

The light winked out and the door closed quietly.

THIRTEEN

WHEN I WOKE I felt like I'd been chewing the exhaust pipes on ancient buses. Worse, I remembered distinctly the pass I'd made at him, drunk, no doubt stinking of cigarettes and liquor and sweat, for this was the Mediterranean and it was the height of summer. Makeup probably smeared all over my face.

I groaned, wondering what monkey-butt my stupid remark about class had flown out of. Worst of all, there was no good answer. What was he supposed to say? *"No, you're not high class enough for a bash on my royal beauty rest."* Or *"No, class distinctions don't matter, I'm totally not into you."* Oh, that would make me feel so much better!

I glared at my scarlet nails, wondering why human nature was so perverse. He'd given me a graceful compliment in turning me down, implying that I was out of the ordinary—maybe he was practiced at turning down the various women who made passes at him, and it was a standard line—but it had been kindly said. And, I'm sure, kindly meant. He could so easily have done the aristo strut and sneered, but then I could have despised him for it.

And wouldn't *that* make the rest of the journey fun!

From now on we were drinking buddies, I resolved. Except I wouldn't drink. No more liquor slapped back by the gallon like the night before.

Having decided that, I sat up to face the day.

A thousand bowling balls promptly crashed through my skull. But get up I did, and moved to the window to throw it open. "Hell!" I snarled at the bright Dalmatian morning.

Steely sunlight and summer heat swatted me right back.

I took a hot bath and brushed my teeth twice. Then draped a towel over my head and bent over the sink with the hot water going full blast, trying to ease my smoke-dried sinuses by breathing steam.

I was in the midst of this when I heard a knock on the door. Tightening the belt on the rose dressing gown, I wandered slowly out.

"Who's there?"

"Breakfast," came Alec's voice, and I shivered with embarrassment. It would have been better had he just taken off, I thought, feeling like a worm.

No. It happened. I had to face him, as I'd faced the day. I opened the door, and a silent houseboy wheeled in one of those room service carts I'd only seen in movies. Alec looked alert and elegant, dark hair ordered. His fresh white shirt was unbuttoned at the neck and rolled to the elbows.

The sight of his throat, the edge of his collar bones, those strong forearms, and my knees threatened to give out. I turned away, making a business of smoothing the bedding and fluffing the—

Pillows! Bed!

I stalked to the window and shut it, then moved to the air-conditioning and jammed it on full blast. When I sidled a peek, Alec tipped the houseboy, and then sank down in the armchair, like he hadn't matched me drink for drink the night before. Do kings get superpowered livers? The thought both annoyed me and made me want to laugh.

"It's going to be warm today," he said. In the light from the window, I discovered his eyes were marked with tiredness underneath, his eyelids crimped underneath as if he had a headache. So maybe he did feel the effects. But *of course* he'd be cool and civilized in a force nine hurricane. "Tea?"

"Yes, thanks," I said, gulping another helping or two of the frigid air blowing out of the vent. Should I apologize for making that pass? He'd say something polite, and then what, a totally awkward breakfast?

Better take the coward's way out, and pretend it never happened.

"How do you feel?" he asked.

"Rotten. But if you are delicately referring to my beet-red face, I was snorting steam to ease my tortured breathing passages." I winced as I lowered myself into the opposite armchair and sipped at the tea he'd poured out. It helped. After a minute or two, I sighed. "Wodehouse was right. Tea does restore the tissues after a night on the tiles. As long as I don't move."

"Drink the liquids," he said, indicating the array of filtered water, OJ, and tea on that tray.

"Right. So, what next?"

"You continue down the coast with Emilio. We seem—"

His cell phone buzzed, and with a word of apology he took it out, checked the number, and a slight frown furrowed his brows. Geez, I thought, why couldn't he at least have a ring tone by some eighties boy band, *something* that would restore my sense of balance through sheer ridiculousness?

He excused himself and did not return.

So . . . he didn't want to be around me? Well, who could blame him? I'd totally blown it—but at least if he was gone I wouldn't have to sit here with my stomach boiling with regret. And in the sober light of day, with calming, civilized tea in me, I decided I was glad he'd turned me down. He was too high octane for me. It wasn't only the crown prince stuff, which I still found hard to believe. Marius Alexander Ysvorod the baseball player or the sous-chef would have been just as involved in his own world, leaving me hyperaware that I couldn't spend a hot weekend and then leave the next day, with no regrets, and no further interest.

I got dressed and went downstairs alone. As promised, Emilio was waiting with the Daimler for me.

The two of us cruised down the beautiful Dalmatian coast, slowed by an afternoon shower. Twice his cell phone went off, and both times he held short, low-voiced conversations in the language of Dobrenica.

We arrived at the next hotel well after dark, and I kept my promise to myself, holing up and doing a session with the major verbs of the Dobreni language. After that, for the first time in ages, I went to sleep with a sense of accomplishment.

In the morning my ankle felt well enough for me to work cautiously through a series of less strenuous ballet warm-ups, and a full set of push-ups, which left my body feeling much better than it had for days.

Alec was waiting for me when I came down to the balmy, sun-drenched terrace where they were serving breakfast. He closed the newspaper, then offered to share it with me.

I waved it away, saying, "No thanks. It's never anything but bad news, and that I can catch up with at home—"

I had only a few seconds' warning before a middle-aged couple arrowed between adjacent tables and descended on us, chattering away in French about what a surprise, and did we know you would be here my dears?

I shut my mouth and started fumbling in my bag to find the cigarettes as Alec stood and shook hands with them. The man reached down to take my hand and kiss it, his compliments on my beauty fatuous but also the words of a non-intimate.

Then it was the woman's turn; she was horribly thin, with too many jewels glittering hard against her skeletal frame, her overtanned skin like a well-basted Thanksgiving turkey's. Her mouth creased in a thin smile, her lips hardly moving a millimeter as she mooed in French, "Aurelia chérie! But how is your darling mother?"

At that my mind blanked, then Alec's instruction *When in doubt look bored* saved me. Pouting, I said, "Bored."

She gave a false trill. "You must remind her! We insist you come to us in Mykonos. But soon!"

"I'll tell her," I said.

They took their leave, the woman giving me air kisses. As soon as they were gone I muttered out of the side of my mouth, "Who were those people?"

He gave me a rueful smile. "Gaston and Tuti Laszlo-Salazar are their names. Does it matter beyond that?"

"They couldn't possibly have anything to do with—with Ruli's being missing."

"Right. Part of your moth—part of Aunt Sisi's crowd." He chuckled softly. "'Bored.' Brilliantly apt."

That chuckle zapped through my nerves, but I waited it out. *Drinking buddies.* "Brainstorm, eh?" I polished my nails casually on my sleeve. "So now what?"

"I think we'd better move on today, but you'll be glad to know that we are nearly done with this masquerade."

"Has it had any effect?"

"Possibly."

I started humming the theme from *Jaws.* As he got up and came round to the back of my chair, there was the faintest twitch of his lips to show he'd heard it.

Half an hour later he was gone.

When I came down from brushing my teeth, it was to see Kilber and Emilio finishing a conference—both of them with cell phones in hand. Kilber rumbled something gravelly about *Durchlaucht,* gave me an unsmiling nod of greeting, almost a bow, then went silently to take my bags from the bellboy.

Durchlaucht—I'd heard that before, but never so clearly. An outmoded title in German, but there was no irony in Kilber's face or voice. Roughly translated, it meant "*your highness.*"

Emilio handed me into the car as Kilber loaded my bags into the trunk. Then, to my relief, Emilio climbed in behind the wheel and started the engine, leaving Kilber to stride away across the parking lot.

I had the evening to myself, which I spent working with the Dobreni dictionary.

The next morning I rose, sober and brimming with intellectual triumph and, after a light breakfast, again worked through my ballet and fencing warm-ups—this time more strenuously, to smooth out the stiffness from the stretches the day before.

After that I ran downstairs and took a vigorous hike along the beach, enjoying the beauty of the coast and the oddity of seeing and smelling sand, sea, seaweed, and crying gulls on a southwest facing beach, all the while knowing I was thousands of miles from these familiar things in Southern California.

I'd almost made it back to the hotel when Alec, in slacks and shirt-sleeves, strolled out from the hotel terrace to meet me. After a speculative glance he asked, "How's your ankle?"

"Totally fine. I felt if I didn't get some exercise my legs would wither up like the wicked witch's in Oz."

I gave him a speculative scan of my own. He didn't seem to have slept at all.

He met my gaze blandly. "Shall we go turn up our noses at a couple of the shops, then get some lunch?"

I hesitated, aware of the dull colors and lines of exhaustion in the fine skin around his eyes. *He's not your business, Kim. He's the real Ruli's.*

"Okay." I shrugged. "Lead me to it."

We cruised some of the nicer stores, lingering over handmade Russian mosaics, Turkish rugs, and Greek artifacts, guessing if they were real or fake and trying to convince the other with patently fake scholarship. Nothing serious—nothing intimate. Just easy fun.

At noon we had a long lunch out on the beach terrace. Again we shared some wine. I remembered my vow and sipped, so it wasn't wine but the good food, the bright sun, and the reflective blue gaze across the table from me that made me heady, particularly when we made a foray into our respective childhoods, specifically reminiscing over pranks we pulled as kids. I felt this sudden, almost paralyzing wish that the moment—the day, the breeze, the company—would never end.

But it did. And when we got up to go, I forgot Ruli's high heels and tumbled. My hands scrabbled to clutch at the table but Alec was there first, righting me with hands that moved with remarkable swiftness to each of my arms.

"Thanks. Forgot the spikes," I said breathlessly, looking away from him and making a business of searching over the table for the clutch purse.

His hands lifted and he stepped away. "All right?"

"Whoa, I don't know when I've laughed so much." I grinned, trying to recapture the earlier mirth. "But you said Ruli doesn't laugh. I hope I haven't blown my character."

He smiled back, and his ring flashed blue fire as his fingers flicked to the single dimple in my cheek in the lightest and briefest of touches. "Not with that."

No time for a reaction; he went on to talk about the next resort on the list.

But the gesture stayed with me. My grandmother used to touch that dimple on my cheek with her forefinger when I was little, and call it her kiss-spot. The memory was poignant, from living gesture to remembered. But it made me uneasy.

The sense I was missing something strengthened as we drove about Split, looking at the beautiful light stone buildings with the grand archways, and the palm trees. Palm trees! Stupid to think I'd only find them in LA where they weren't even native.

Everything seemed off-kilter from those innocent trees to the crowded city drenched in the strong Mediterranean sun, so like that at home. The car insulated us from the crowd yet bound us into intimate space. I kept myself busy looking at ancient cathedrals and the boats floating out on the sea, anywhere but at the guy who would soon be out of my life forever.

We stopped for dinner at a hilltop Greek restaurant from which the aromas of roast lamb and spices like cardamom and ginger and saffron drifted all the way to the road, free but powerful advertising.

We didn't talk much. He seemed even more tired than I was, and he was definitely preoccupied, stilling every time his cell phone burred, and it burred a lot. He was too polite to take calls while we were dining (or too private) but when I came out of the restroom, he was talking fast, his expression tense.

He clapped the phone shut as soon as I rejoined him.

Afterward we went to an exclusive hilltop night spot, packed with a crowd in designer clothes, the guys with burnished tan-framed white grins in Hollywood Hustler duds: flowered silk shirts open to Gucci belts, ultra-tight pants, folds of high-denomination bills in gold or platinum money clips slid snugly into flat pockets. Some of the guys wore super baggy gangsta threads. The women were thin, with brittle movements like angry butterflies, and dark-painted eyes and blood-colored lips.

I felt like I was on Mars in the disguise of a Martian. Disorientation unsettled me as we passed a mirror and a strange woman glared back at me, cold-faced in chic makeup, clothed in an uncompromisingly high-fashion dress, and wary-stepping in strappy high-heeled shoes and a tiny, matching bag.

Alec looked remarkably self-possessed and stylishly unobtrusive against this backdrop. He found us a table with his usual magic (I'm sure it was the magic of money, it's only that I never saw him do it), ordered drinks, and was lighting my cigarette for me as I breathed, "Curtain up," when we got our first visitor.

Three guys in a row swooped down and kissed me, but none (after exchanging greetings with Alec who sat smiling and unmoved) tried sitting with us. The last one, a rakishly handsome Italian, was the most caressing. He shot Alec a smiling glance of challenge, then pressed me to dance with him.

This was a first. I shot my own look at Alec, but he sat there drinking, giving me no clues. Surely Ruli danced. Anyway, I never turn down a chance to dance, and hadn't for ages, and so I got up.

The band was playing an irresistible reggae blood-pounder, and with initial pleasure I saw my partner knew what he was doing. Hips and shoulders moving in slow, controlled circles, we prowled around each other, then he took hold of me in a cross between swing and tango. When he pulled me in close I spun away on my toes, my dark green silky skirt flaring about me.

Ah, it was good to be dancing again; my partner was no more

than an adjunct, like the band. Eyes turned to watch, but I did not care, and nothing punctured my fun until a soft kiss pressed, warm and moist, behind my ear. Startled, I turned to see my partner's face inches away, surprise mixed with a possessive smirk. *Does Ruli dance differently?*

Well, too late. We whirled and twirled and swayed, then once again my enjoyment chilled when he started touching me, longer and longer caresses, his body heat, his breathing, closing me in a cage of smothering lust. I stared up into suggestive dark eyes.

What if she likes him? I couldn't shove him away, but I could dance away.

Turning with practiced ease, he stepped close. Hands explored my back as he breathed into the hair above my ear, "You move as if inspired, sweet Ruli." His hand slid with skill under my arm to brush my breast as he whispered intimately into my ear, "You were always so stiff. So cold, when we danced. Now you are . . . *hot.*" On that last word he shifted from French to Italian, breathing the syllables into my ear. I tried to ease out of his grip, but he was like an octopus, tentacles wandering over my body. "When do you leave the formidable Alexander?" And then he tongued my ear.

Ruli. The urge to smack him turned into panic. This guy was one of Ruli's *lovers.* I shrugged his tentacle off my boob and tried for neutrality, since I couldn't manage friendliness: "Haven't decided yet."

"Can I convince you to come tonight?" He pressed against me again, but with a twist of my hips I twirled under his arm and away. And smiled.

"If I change my mind I'll know where you are, won't I?" I said, hoping it was true enough (and yet ambiguous enough) to keep him at bay.

He gave me a smug grin that made my palm burn to smack it off his face. This guy was her sweetie. She liked him. I kept my own face strictly bland, and my hands at my sides, and contented myself with keeping free of his grasp for the minute or two remaining of the dance.

At the end he took me back to Alec, who gave me a mildly considering glance and said, "You all right?"

"Another minute and you would have had to ask if he'd be all right," I stated through smiling lips.

Simmering annoyance made me breathe hard, then Alec added softly, "He never doubted your identity."

I nodded, the last of my annoyance vanishing. That guy had zero interest in Aurelia Kim Murray, which meant I was convincing as Aurelia-who-likes-to-be-called-Ruli, right up close and personal.

Alec shifted his chair slightly toward mine, his posture subtly intimate. I sensed at once that he was not closing me in so much as closing everyone else out. For his hands stayed where they were, and his eyes gave no clue to the thoughts behind them.

He said in English, "I think we're done. We'll go on to Dubrovnik in the morning. You've earned that cruise, twice over. Where would you like to go?" He lifted his head to glance around. In French, "Another drink?"

A cruise—the reward to the good sport. Thank you and good-bye.

It was straightforward, it was exactly what we had agreed on, and I'd known it was coming. But that didn't stop me from feeling truly horrible.

He was waiting for an answer.

I shrugged. "Yes. No. I hate this place," I muttered like a sulky teenager, and I struggled to get a grip.

"Shall we stroll through the casino?"

"Sure."

He put a hand on my arm, protective rather than possessive. No one else came near us as we descended into the thickly carpeted gambling room.

Watching the intensity of people's focus on the turn of cards, the flash of wheels, was no longer any fun. I excused myself to go to the restroom.

I stood at the mirror repairing the lipstick and glared at my mouth to see if the red line was even. As I grimaced that shadow in my left cheek winked in and out. Alec's touch that morning burned my flesh in memory, a palimpsest over the memory of my grandmother . . .

Oh God. Oh God.

Who did not have the dimple.

I bared my teeth at the mirror. My mother had the dimple, the same lopsided smile as I had, which transformed her round and serene face into unexpected charm and whimsy . . .

Ruli has the dimple.

"Grandfather," I said to the mirror. How long had I managed to go without seeing the obvious connection? Because Gran had said of the dimple, *"It's a family characteristic."*

She had never said which family.

Pressing my fingers into my eyes, I tried to remember—anything—I'd been told about my grandfather, Daniel Atelier. I heard scraps and snippets of voices . . . Gran's . . . Mama's . . . Alec's.

My focus broke when two matrons armored in silk and pearls flanked me determinedly, spearing me with glares of disapproval for hogging the mirror. I fumbled around lighting a cigarette, hoping they would leave, but they stood there, obviously outwaiting me, so I walked out.

Alec leaned on a rail gazing down into the gambling pits. At my approach he straightened up, and said quietly, "What is it?"

I jabbed my painted forefinger into my cheek. "You said Ruli has it, too. From whom did she get it?"

The curve of his mouth tightened slightly, though his eyes did not change. "From her mother."

"And she from—?"

"From her father."

"Her father. What did the wicked Count Armandros look like?"

When Alec first told the story I'd pictured some tall, cold guy with slick dark hair and a monocle, a villain in a melodrama. Despite all the obvious evidence surrounding me.

And so I was heartsick but not surprised when Alec said, gently, "He was tall. Blond. Slim. Athletic. Light brown eyes, and a distinctive smile, with a long dimple on one side. He was photographed in the traditional uniform when he came of age."

"*He* was Daniel Atelier? But he couldn't be!"

He plucked the forgotten Ruli cigarette out of my fingers, and flicked it spinning into an ashtray stand before it could burn me. "Let's get out of here."

FOURTEEN

HE DROVE UP to the palisades overlooking the sea, pulled over to the side of the road, and parked. We were alone there along the barren road, us and the rocky plateau. Below us the sea, above the clear night sky.

"You have a right to know the whole story, but I did not want to be the one to tell you," he said.

"Why not?"

"Because, under the circumstances, everything I tell you seems to worsen the personal consequences."

I shot back with instant hostility, "My mother and I can handle the consequences of the truth. And it's no one else's business."

Alec showed no reaction at all. He was staring out through the windshield at the bright stars glimmering peacefully in the sky, the distant fairylike twinkle of boats and buildings along the shore.

I got a grip on my temper. "I'm sorry I snapped. It's so—so disturbing. My grandmother's life—so awful. So . . . Please go on."

He was silent a few seconds longer, then said, "When Princess Lily renounced her title she told her father if she could not marry the man she had chosen she would not marry anyone, and she stayed true to her promise."

As usual, all the implications were slow to hit me. I said, "So he followed her to Vienna, is that it?"

"He took her there, and found her a place to live. He visited her in secret afterward, though not often, as the war made it increasingly difficult to travel."

"But what about Princess Rose, Gran's twin?"

"He married her. No difficulties, as far as Lily was concerned: when she left the country she told Armandros henceforth to leave mention of Dobrenica, its affairs, and its people back in Dobrenica. She intended to make a new life, which meant severing the old. This gave him carte blanche to do what he wanted."

"And so he did, and didn't get caught. What a sleazebag," I fumed. "I take it the old—ah, the king gave Rose permission to marry him?"

"No. They married first, then came to the king begging for forgiveness. It was well managed by her family."

"And *she* wasn't disinherited?"

"From the title, yes. That was passed to my father, as I told you."

"So Rose had a daughter, who was not a crown princess."

"Elisabeth Aurelia. Her nickname is Sisi—"

"Which is the nickname of Emperor Franz Joseph's wife. I know that."

"The nickname was chosen to remind the world that Sisi was, or so they thought, the last descendent of the twin princesses."

"Yeah, a political boost there, eh? But she's a von Mecklundburg, not a Dsaret. And I suppose Sisi's son, Ruli's brother, what's his name again, is another Armandros—"

"No. The von Mecklundburg heir always has a double first name, beginning with Karl, in honor of the emperor who first granted them their title. He was born Karl-Anton, but he's Tony to everyone except his mother, who is a stickler for formality."

"Okay, got that."

"Armandros was a second son, heir to his brother, who had no sons. They both died in the war. Sisi married the second cousin who inherited the title, so she is now the Duchess of Riev Dhiavilyi. Her son Tony is now heir, which makes him Count Karl-Anton."

"Okay. And you two Ysvorods—there are only two of you?—are both Marius Alexander, but senior is Milo and junior is Alec. Got it."

"Right. I should mention that Princess Rose, your grandmother's twin, died three months after my Aunt Sisi's birth."

I gasped. "How awful! What happened?"

"It was winter, she was ill, and rumor had it she became terribly thin by refusing to eat so she could resume court life at Christmas in a new Chanel gown. As soon as Sisi was born, Rose had her packed off to the Eyrie on Devil's Mountain, where she remained until the family decamped to England. In the people's eyes, this cemented the fact that Sisi was a von Mecklundburg, not a Dsaret."

"So she was definitely not a princess."

"Right. Not long after he abdicated, the king died. My father never had an official coronation, because by then the Germans held the country, but he's generally regarded as king."

"Generally. Not universally?"

"Can you guess which family doesn't?"

He had turned to face me, his right arm stretched along the back of the seat, the signet glinting with cool blue light inches from my tense arm, his palm turned politely away. "That portrait you described was taken of Armandros in the old Dobreni uniform, as I said. There's a bigger portrait hanging in the family castle on Devil's Mountain. The print that your grandmother has was probably made from the photograph hanging in the memorial museum in Riev. Armandros was one of the leaders of the Dobreni freedom fighters, young as he was."

"So he ran back and forth between Gran and Rose?"

"Flew back and forth. He'd learned to pilot after he won a small plane in a card game. He ran a series of bombing raids against the Germans, desperately and brilliantly risky, considering how little we had in the way of materiel and trained men. But in the last days when the Germans had been beaten back, it seemed our world was about to end and the coup de grace was to be delivered by the advancing Russians—with the collusion of the Allies. Much as he hated the Third Reich, he felt that the Nazis were finished. At that point Germany was fighting for its existence. He joined an offshoot of the Ostlegionen under the name Mecklund, in hopes of slowing the Russian advance, until he was shot down."

"So I was right about the Ostlegionen."

"But wrong about his name. It was right before he made this desperate gesture that he finally communicated with my father, telling him that your grandmother had parted with him, and gave him her address. He knew he'd never come back alive. Maybe he didn't intend to."

"*She* dumped him? *Gran?* I don't believe it!"

"They disagreed on ideological grounds. He saw a distinction between Germany and Nazism, and further that the Soviets under Stalin were now the biggest threat to all of Europe, not only to Dobrenica. After Rose died, he couldn't get back across Europe to Paris. So he went to the one person he knew could be relied on to take care of Lily. Four months later Armandros was dead."

"I see," I said, but I didn't yet, not at all. "And so, by the time your father got around to checking—"

The even voice did not increase in volume or sharpen in tone, nevertheless Alec cut across my sarcasm. "He was in the midst of the battle at home, and by the time he made it across the ruins of Europe to look for her, he found the rue de l'Atelier had been bombed, and the people were beginning to deal with the aftermath."

The facts began to make sense, puzzle pieces drawing slowly together. But the reasons, the motivations still were a mystery.

"He tracked down a few dazed former inhabitants, none of whom could account for Madam von Mecklundburg and her daughter. People shrugged, said that they must have been among the casualties, if there was no sign of them. He searched for several weeks, until forced to return to his work at home. There were no leads whatsoever, and so he was forced to accept that she was dead."

"That kinda goes with what Mom remembers about Paris," I said, feeling chilled to the bone as images fled through my mind, memories of photographs I'd seen of Europe in ruins—followed by memory of Gran's quiet face. "So, my grandmother never knew about Rose dying?"

"All I can tell you is that she never communicated with anyone in Dobrenica again."

"But what about the name Daniel Atelier? She would not have made that up. It doesn't sound like her at all."

"The flat your grandmother first moved to was on the rue de l'Atelier. She must have adopted the name when she fled France, which helps explain how they disappeared. They had lived in Vienna, then in Paris, under the name von Mecklundburg." The light, careful voice finished, "The name Daniel probably was adapted from Danilov, Armandros's second name."

"I wonder how she managed to get on the refugee ship," I said.

"I suspect the pearl gown your mother was photographed in as a baby was the Dsaret baptismal dress," Alec said slowly. Like he was feeling his way. "For two or three generations the heir had been baptized in it. It vanished when your grandmother did—she must have felt it was hers, but sold it to fund the journey to the United States." Again that tone, like he was waiting for a clue from me.

I took a deep breath. "So he was a bigamist and never got caught. Poor Gran!"

"There was no legal marriage," he said, so carefully his tone had flattened. Like he was hiding his emotions. Judgment? Against Gran? "Armandros confessed as much before he went off to be killed."

"I don't believe it." I smacked the dashboard. "I can't. She wouldn't have. Not Gran, not in those days—not at *any* time. Even if the guy she married was a louse and a slimebag, Gran is too old-fashioned. She'd never do one thing and preach another. I have no proof, obviously—" I faltered as something flickered in my mind, too quick to catch. I shook my head, fighting a tide of grief. "Not Gran. Never."

Alec was still and silent. The roof of the car cast a shadow over his face so I could not see his expression; starlight glowing softly on his shirt showed not even the shifting of breathing. He could have been a statue.

And he believes himself right, and me wrong.

Hot rage replaced the cold, sickening sense of grief. I have never cared who is with whom or how many, when, or how, but Gran's honor had become my honor. I said through gritted teeth, "At least she had the courage of her convictions."

Leaning forward to start the engine, he answered, "A quality to be admired." His tone was mild. "I think we're done."

Because he knew he was right, and I was wrong. *Gran* was wrong.

I swept on rudely, "It's something you'd do well to learn."

And as he did not respond, I added angrily, "All this stuff today, yesterday . . . not that I didn't have fun, but it means nothing to me. But it's disgusting because it doesn't mean anything to you, either. You're not into Ruli, you're into politics. She's a thing to you, a marker on your royal chessboard. Even if all Gran's high and mighty relations call my mother a bastard, at least Gran chose love over rank or wealth or titles!"

Alec drove in silence, his hands steady on the wheel.

"At least you could admit that I'm right," I said at last.

"But you're not right," he replied, still in that flat, even voice. "Unlike you, I acknowledge the existence of other points of view. And I don't want to argue."

"Points of view? How can you say there's another point of view besides honesty? And living up to one's convictions?"

"Because, if you will have it, 'honesty' for one person is 'selfishness' for another."

"Selfishness?"

"I'm glad your grandmother found a life of contentment with your mother and father and you. Glad you admire her excellent qualities. But under no circumstances would I want to adopt her convictions for my own."

"Honor? Being true to her vows?"

"I've no desire to emulate someone who in a time of impending crisis, when strength and unity were especially required, put personal inclination above duty."

I said slowly, "Even if you say politics are stupid, you put it—them, I mean—above everything."

"I put Dobrenica above everything," he said, "and therefore I get trapped in politics. Have you decided whether you would like to visit the Greek isles, or Italy, or perhaps a Mediterranean cruise?" Invincibly polite as usual.

"Any of 'em," I said, my mind two exchanges back and floundering, as I struggled to fight back the anger.

"I think an early and quiet departure tomorrow will finish the business, then," he said pleasantly. "And I wish to thank you for—"

"You don't have to take me to Dubrovnik." Hearing how rude my words came out I stuttered, "I mean, you must have stuff to do with whatever you planned next, and I am used to taking care of myself."

He stated quietly, "Emilio will take you there, and he will see you comfortably established on the ship you choose."

I was too upset to argue.

As he pulled into the parking lot, he said, "Since it is unlikely that we'll meet again, I want to thank you for your help, and I'm sorry I handled things so badly in telling you about—"

Hot tears blurred my vision. I fumbled in the handbag and pulled out the gold case and lighter. "Here," I cut in, and slapped the smoking stuff down onto the seat between us. "Give that to Ruli as a wedding present from me."

I pulled open my car door, slid out, and went straight up to my room.

I cried hard, washed my face, then dropped flat on the bed, exhausted, bewildered, angry, sad. Sleep was beyond me. My thoughts had splintered like a jigsaw puzzle, and the wherewithal to identify the pieces and fit them together had disappeared.

I finally got up and turned on the light. First I busied myself with removing Ruli's favorite color from my nails. That was quickly done. Okay, what to do next? My little pile of books lay on the nightstand, the Dobreni dictionary on top with the paper on which I had been taking notes stuck between its leaves.

Dobreni.

The print blurred before my aching eyes. Bright images of the pictures on Gran's night table, of Alec's face, his words, his ring glinting in the starlight, all drifted through my mind in a montage of vivid images. Gone was the cool air-conditioning and the stars over the beautiful Dalmatian coast and the compelling light-toned voice in the Daimler's darkness. I saw my grandmother's face again on those long-ago days in our house in Santa Monica.

There were days when she would sit down silently at the piano and play and play, sometimes for hours. Her action had seemed unfathomable to me as a child but I had welcomed the interludes because they were an invitation to put on the dated full-skirted chiffon evening dress my mother had given me to play dress up with, and dance to the enchanting melodies of Brahms, Glazunov, Bach, Glinka, Britten. The entrancing glissades made me dance out stories, fantasies. Responding in childlike fashion to half-sensed emotions, I was driven by the joy and sorrow and yearning captured in the music that flowed through the sunny dancing dust-mote afternoons.

There were her distant-seeing blue eyes, the certain set to the small, firmly closed mouth. When mind-filling memory had threatened to brim over she had channeled it into those shimmering rivers of sound.

And what memories! I relived the first time she had played an arrangement of Mom's favorite opera, Puccini's *Madama Butterfly*. The aria "Un bel di" had so taken me I couldn't move at first and stood by her side and stared down at her drifting hands—the sure fingers—

My breath caught sharply. *And on her left hand the glint of a plain gold wedding band.*

I knew it! I knew it.

I opened my eyes, stood up and began methodically to stack my books, and then pack the suitcases. The puzzle pieces had dropped back into place, and I smiled again as calm settled through my system like snow on a burned field. I knew what I had to do.

Emilio knocked at my door at six, but his apologetic air disappeared when he saw me smiling and ready. We descended by a back staircase and took a taxi to a side street a few miles distant, where we stopped and shifted selves and baggage to a waiting Citroen.

Conversation was intermittent, but I persisted with extreme care, and ascertained to my considerable relief that Alec had left earlier for Vienna.

Nodding, smiling, I pronounced everything lovely, from the food at the restaurant we stopped at to the luxurious arrangements on board the ship that they had reserved a berth on. They had reserved places on three ships; I picked the next one leaving the dock. To Emilio, as he carried my bags of Ruli clothes aboard and deposited them securely in the stateroom, I chattered on about the glories of the Greek Isles.

I walked back out with him, shook hands and thanked him, and waved as he descended the gangplank.

As soon as he was out of sight I returned to the attractive stateroom, removed all the ID from the suitcases, then picked up the small overnight bag, which held all my own stuff, plus a couple of things closer to what I would normally wear.

The trains were easy to find, tickets easy to buy, and when darkness descended I tranquilly closed my eyes as the *klank-klank, lunk-lunk* soothed me to sleep: I had begun my pilgrimage to my grandmother's homeland, to find out the truth.

FIFTEEN

TWICE I HAD to change trains, the last being a small one with only three cars and that had to date back a hundred years. Apparently it ran once a week—less frequently in winter—but I lucked out with only a half-day's wait.

As the train climbed slowly and steadily into the mountains, I thought about my grandmother. My mind ranged back in memory as the twisting tracks seemed to lead the train back through time: among the sudden, breathtaking views of rocky crags, dark and mysterious forest-cloaked valleys, and occasional mountain-hugging towns and villages were the few mundane signs of modern civilization. Several hours before we began the descent toward our last destination, someone pointed out the window across from me, exclaiming something in that language that sounded vaguely familiar.

I looked out at a mighty castle on a peak so high it was partially obscured by clouds. The three other people in that train car also stared up at that castle, which seemed partly medieval and partly Baroque. They talked quietly among themselves, then one grizzled old man shook his head slowly.

When the castle was obscured from view by a towering cliff, I turned my attention the other way, and was surprised by a spectacular view. Dobrenica was bordered by three chains of intersecting mountains that created a long valley roughly in the shape of a comma. The tail of the comma was a high plateau covered with ancient forest; the rounded part of the comma was a glacier-carved river valley whose winding banks were rich-soiled for farming. Summer seemed to find the land at its best. Everywhere were crops, long green grasses, and wildflowers of varieties I'd never seen before.

The weird giddiness came and went, leaving the even weirder sensation of having stepped back in time. No, that's not quite it. It left me with an eerie sense that time is mutable.

When the train rolled at last into Riev, Dobrenica's capital, I pressed my face eagerly to the window; a fair-sized town, mostly old slant-roofed buildings, lay on the gentle lower slope of a high mountain tucked into the northwestern corner of the kingdom.

An official dressed in a blue uniform with red piping down the side walked through the train, checking tickets. He'd passed me with a smile and a tip of his pillbox cap before I figured out that he represented the entirety of the Dobreni customs check.

Talk about a totally different interpretation of "homeland security," I thought as I disembarked and eyeballed the scene. The transit vehicles available to take one from the station into the heart of the town were two ancient cars, their vintage about 1930, and a plain black sulky drawn by a huge, hairy-footed horse in blinders.

Some ten or twelve people got off altogether. All but one were promptly greeted by relatives and friends. The lone man heaved his bags straight into the nearest of the cars; a party of happy relatives took the other, so I turned to the sulky.

A black-haired man around my age leaned comfortably on the iron rail dividing off the station house, watching the people. He had a snub nose and squinting dark eyes, wore a Cossack-style belted tunic over loose trousers stuffed in boots. I was to discover this was the way most men dressed here. As soon as he saw my tentative approach, he straightened up and gave me a quaint bow.

I spoke one of the sentences in Dobreni that I'd prepared during the last hour of the ride: "Can you recommend a comfortable inn in the center of town?"

The man's smile widened, and as he took my bag and tossed it up behind the seat he burst into a long, rapid speech punctuated by grand gestures. He ended with a question as he handed me up onto the seat, and I delivered my second sentence: "Please talk more slowly!"

He nodded four or five times, clucked to the horse, then said slowly and loudly, "Inn good . . . my mother [something] cousin—"

I plunged through the dictionary to track down the verb, but by the time I found it I'd lost the rest of his sentence. He smiled with goodwill, taking charge.

The ride through town was short, mostly uphill. I obtained swift impressions of tall stone houses, cobblestone streets with no traffic lights, and the weird sense of having stepped back in time was reinforced by the traffic, which was primarily pedestrian or horse-drawn. Here and there chugged old cars, mostly from the 1940s, their engines obviously much repaired.

The inn he brought me to was built on a corner where two streets joined and intersected another, the resulting triangle forming a courtyard fenced by beautifully tended rose trellises. The wide end of the triangle was formed by one wall of the inn, a three-storied building with a steep roof, green shutters, and flower boxes in all the lower windows.

The sulky stopped before the front door. A few people were out on the street, carrying baskets or pulling carts. One boy rode a rusty bicycle. Clothing from the entire range of the twentieth century seemed to be worn here, and no one paid any attention to it any more than they did the sulky pulling up behind a car that I think had been made in the 1950s; the few passersby seemed more interested in me than in the nineteenth-century mode of my travel.

The cab driver accepted my euros—though it took him a moment to calculate his fee in them—and I went inside, where I found a huge dining room with wooden furniture, white tablecloths embroidered with red flowers and blue birds in a pattern, brass fixtures behind the counter, everything scrupulously clean.

The sulky driver carried my bag inside, then knocked on the glass-paned door next to the counter. A short, sharp-featured woman approximately my mother's age emerged, conducted a rapid exchange with the driver, who gave me a friendly wave and departed.

The innkeeper brought out an old-fashioned ledger, and as she did not ask for a credit card or my passport, I registered myself as *Kim Atelier—Paris, France.* She asked in bad French how long was I staying. I told her a week, she said something that I assumed was the price in local currency, then I found myself guided up to a small but cozily charming room looking out over the courtyard from leaded windows.

A tray of coffee appeared on the side table next to the high bed with its carved wood headboards, curtains, and brightly colored handmade quilt that would be worth a fortune at home. The only other furniture was a table next to the window, a straight-backed wooden chair next to the table, and a tall wardrobe set in a corner, the top half for hanging clothes, and the bottom half divided into two large drawers. Madam shooed me to the table to sit down and sip coffee while she tackled my bit of luggage.

My few clothes were soon hung neatly or folded away in the wardrobe. Madam Waleska was like a force of nature, impossible to stop. Such people have only to move through a chaotic room and order results, sometimes despite the wills of others in the whirlwind's path.

Madam's husband—

I'd better clue you in on Dobreni forms of address. I didn't figure these out at once, but I'm going to throw in the explanation and get it out of the way.

Long-stratified Dobreni society has eight basic types of address. The aristocratic forms have close enough equivalents in English, which I'll use and don't need to describe.

The male head of a family is called either by his job title, or simply by his last name. The equivalent of Mister is Domnu, and their wives are Madam. They adopted the French Mademoiselle as a title of respect for unmarried ladies. The Dobreni have equivalents of Master and Miss for young people, and older, retired people are given the title of Grandfather or Grandmother, or Great-aunt and Great-uncle, which are all honorifics.

Finally there were the peculiar terms *salfmatta* and *salfpatra. Matta* and *patra* were *mother* and *father,* and *salf* the dictionary translated as *good*—though the word for *good* was altogether different.

But I'll get to that later.

So. The innkeeper, Domnu Waleska, was a silent man who ran the restaurant. The three daughters helped out when they were around.

It was the youngest of these daughters whom Madam presented to me as I sipped the strong, thick coffee.

"My daughter, Theresa—she learns French and German in Gymnasium," Madam said in slow and loud Dobreni, thrusting forward a shrinking girl of about fifteen who was clad in a severely practical and old-fashioned blouse and jumper that had to be a school uniform. She had thick dark hair worn in braids, a high forehead, and sharp features like her mother's.

Theresa blushed awkwardly, and as her mother prodded her further into the room she murmured in soft, stilted and alarmingly archaic French, "Mademoiselle does not speak our language? I am to aid you as best I can. Please forgive the poorness of my diction—"

"But it's good," I said, speaking slowly. "Can you tell me where to exchange my euro bills for the local money?"

Theresa said, "There is the national bank on the Royal Square, but if you do not wish to exchange great sums, the post office will do. It is at the top of our street."

Madam beamed in triumph as her daughter spoke, arms folded across the front of her white apron. After I thanked Theresa, Madam gave her daughter rapid instructions in her booming voice. Then nodded, almost a curtsey, and backed out of the room, shutting the door with a firm snap. I heard her heavy tread bustle back down the well-scrubbed and waxed floorboards toward the stairs.

Theresa stood where she was, hands clasped behind her as if she were about to recite before a school assembly. "Mama said to tell you, Mademoiselle, please, if you wish to eat with the family, being the only lady guest, and alone," her eyes widened slightly on the word, "it is at seven, thank you, and if you want a bath in the morning please say."

"Yes to both, thank you, Theresa." And, in an effort to ease the girl's obvious tension, "How do you come to speak such excellent French?"

A dark flush of pleasure crimsoned her thin face, and she said with much less frozen formality (and much more fluency), "I wish to study pedagogy, and Sister Anna promises me a place at the school in five years. I shall teach the languages French and English, and the literature of—"

She stopped then, her expression dismayed. Her thoughts were clear: she was afraid she had spoken too much and bored the sophisticated French visitor. Before I could say anything she gave me a schoolgirl's bobbing curtsey and fled in clattering haste from the room.

I took a couple steps toward the door to call her back, then stopped, remembering myself at that age, the windstorm of emotions. Heck, I'd been indulging my own adolescent windstorms far more recently. Best give her space and start all over again next time I saw her.

Meanwhile, time to make a scouting foray.

I pulled open the wardrobe to get out my straw sun hat, then caught sight of myself in the long mirror inside the wardrobe door. The dress I wore—soft blue cotton, the skirt reaching mid-calf—was the plainest of the Ruli clothes, the one I'd thought most inconspicuous, but it still reminded me of Ruli. The question then was, who else might be reminded of Ruli?

Then I remembered Alec saying that she rarely visited this country, and when she did go anywhere, she confined herself exclusively to her own set uptown. Meanwhile, my grandmother had been gone for well over half a century, my mother had never been here, so who could possibly recognize me?

Reassured, I plunked the straw hat on my head, grabbed my wallet, and left to explore.

The post office was small and cramped, but busy. From the cost of the inn (cheap by LA standards) I figured out how many euros I'd need for a week's stay. Because I hadn't had to pay for my pensione in Vienna, I was ahead. Not a lot, because of that pretty dress sitting in a field somewhere with the rest of my clothes. But a week would leave me enough to get me to Britain and my Scottish expedition before the flight home.

The short, elderly proprietor glanced from my euros to my face and back two or three times, making me wonder if she thought I was a counterfeiter, but she changed the money politely.

I lingered, thinking about writing a postcard home, but decided against it. Let them think I was still sightseeing somewhere in Western Europe until I got Gran's whole story.

So I left with a handful of mostly silver coinage, with a heavy gold piece and a scattering of coppers. The coins were curiously old-fashioned—not as sharp and shallow as modern, mechanically made coins. I wondered if these were produced by the knuckle-joint or lever presses of the mid-nineteenth century.

As I dropped the coins into my purse, feeling their unaccustomed weight, I walked uphill, which I soon discovered was the local version of uptown. In this case, literally. The avenues broadened, the shops of the corbelled buildings with their tall Baroque windows appeared somewhat newer. Older streets seemed to form spokes leading to circular pocket parks. The grander streets were more square, framing geometric eighteenth-century parks. About two miles or so up the street the spire of a huge Gothic cathedral loomed above the roofs, and maybe half a mile beyond that I spotted the towers of what turned out to be the royal palace.

Surely there was a royal archive.

No, it couldn't possibly be that easy.

Still, my heart thumped expectantly, and I walked faster. The street emptied into a grand traffic circle with a huge fountain in the center of a brick-bordered flowering garden. The central statue was of a girl of maybe thirteen or so, one hand toward the sky, the other reaching down in benediction over the heads of tumbling children and small animals of various sorts. The sprays curved over the heads of these figures, an umbrella of water, obscuring their details, but it looked like there might be some mythological creatures among them: I was pretty sure I saw goat legs below a human back, but the figure was twisted away, obscured by the water. Nearby a wolfish or canine limb ended in fingers instead of a paw.

The streets farther uphill afforded glimpses of grand houses, most built in the Baroque style so much seen all over the Danube regions, except that many of the newer ones had mansard roofs, like in Paris.

Some of the older houses bore damage to decorative corbels and statues, testimony to the parsimonious years under the Soviets. A number of these were fronted by rickety scaffolding as repair work was done on the stone. Others looked subdivided into smaller apartments, judging from doors in odd places and added stairways, but all houses, poor and grand alike, sported well-tended flower boxes in the lower windows.

Closer to the cathedral the houses were more impressive, most with walled-off gardens before them, the shops evoking an Enlightenment-era feel. Beyond these the road led to the great cathedral. I took in the decorated buttresses and six huge stained glass windows with an apostle depicted in each. Then I passed under a memorial arch with Roman numerals reading 1813 and emerged from it onto a main square.

The afternoon was warm, and I had walked so briskly I could feel my head damp all around my hat's brim, but when I gazed at the royal palace on the other side of the square with its impressive mosaic a chill roughened the skin on my arms.

It seemed impossible that my grandmother, who had played the piano while I danced around in my mother's cast-off high school prom dress, had been born and raised here.

I moved to one of the benches set at intervals along the perimeter of the square and took in details: old people sitting in the sun on the benches, feeding pigeons or reading papers or talking; people coming and going from the four imposing columned buildings on either side of the square perpendicular to the cathedral and the palace.

What I could see of the palace beyond those huge iron gates seemed deserted. Not so the cathedral at my left hand. Two lines of uniformed school kids came walking out, their sedate pace belied by little bounces, furtive nudges and grins, like kids everywhere. Adults flowed around them, going in and out.

I debated whether or not to go in. I'd thought to ask to see church records, but as I stared at that large and imposing edifice I thought that surely someone had done that long ago.

Of course someone had done that long ago. So why was I here?

I turned back to the great square. A huge pinkish circle next to the fountain marred the brick patterns—a gigantic red hammer and sickle. Part of it had been laboriously scrubbed into an inoffensive pale red, and the rest had been unsuccessfully painted over by pinkish gray.

At the other end of the square, the palace sat royally behind its fancy gate. Statuary-topped columns marked each end, one of the statues being a man with sword upraised and the other looked like some sort of huge bird. I'd thought the place deserted, but I made out flickers of movement between the iron bars and severely trimmed hedges.

At the far edge of the grand gate, I'd missed a small iron door. "Small" comparatively—it was about the size of a garage door. It was guarded by a soldier in a blue uniform like the ones worn by the customs fellow I'd seen on the train.

I hauled the dictionary from my pocket, constructed a sentence, hunted up possible words I might hear in answer, then I crossed the square.

The soldier was a young man, his uniform a more military version of the trim blue tunic with red piping edging the high collar and cuffs, and a red stripe down the outer seam of his trousers above shiny black boots. His brown eyes were bored until he saw me approach him. Then he stiffened slightly. The shape on the front of his dark blue helmet resolved into a brass crest in the form of a stylized falcon.

"Good day." I smiled. "Are there tours of the palace?"

"Sunday afternoons, when the Stadthalter is not in residence," he replied, his brown gaze blank. "Two o'clock, here at the gate."

"Will there be a tour this Sunday?"

He assented. I turned away, thrilled with my first real conversation in Dobreni.

Okay, I could do this.

Whether the records had been gone over a million times or not, I was going to see them for myself. Gran's strange mutterings about a breach might mean Armandros, but it was more likely it meant her family. As for the "them" needing help, there wasn't anyone here who needed rescue by me, except maybe Ruli, but Alec was busy with that. So, one thing for sure. I would find out as much as I could about Gran's family through firsthand research, then take it all home to Mom.

My first move was to find a place to start.

Begin with the most obvious, the place royal weddings had to have happened: the cathedral. But the shadows had lengthened. More people were leaving the annex beside the cathedral than going in. Closing time.

Okay, bright and early the next day I'd be first in line. Go from there.

I returned to the inn, stopping to buy a newspaper—I loved the fact that it came out once a week—so I could get a better idea of word order, grammar, and modern terms than was afforded by the century-plus out-of-date preface to the dictionary.

At seven I joined Madam and her family. They ate in a pretty dining room off the kitchen. High on the walls, a couple feet below the ceiling, a running motif of flowers and birds had been painted between thin borders about two feet apart; this proved to be characteristic of many Dobreni houses.

The family was all shortish, dark-haired, sharp-boned. I was introduced to the two remaining daughters. Tania seemed to be a couple years younger than me. Anna, the oldest, Madam announced proudly—but with an expressive roll of the eyes indicating much labor ahead—was to be married Saturday.

Madam's husband ate placidly without speaking. And Madam's father, called Grandfather Kezh, sat at the head of the table. He greeted me gravely with a few gargled words of unintelligible French.

As I watched them passing dishes of good, pepper-seasoned freshwater fish, I thought, offices aren't the only places for info. What about people?

I could tell Madam was avidly curious about me. She had to be wondering what could bring a young woman alone to Dobrenica, but she was too polite to ask outright. After two or three broad hints, while I in turn was trying to figure out how to ask the questions I wanted to ask, the perfect excuse came.

As Theresa politely asked me what I'd seen that day and how I like it, I leaned forward and said with a big smile, "Oh, I saw the square—very handsome—and the cathedral and the palace. Only the fronts, of course. I'll go into them soon as I can. Bringing me to my purpose. I'm doing a study for my professor at the Sorbonne on the Dsaret family."

I listened as Theresa translated this, following which the entire family—except the father, who merely gave a grunt of mild interest—burst into amazed and delighted commentary.

"And so—" I beamed round at them "—I wondered what is the best way to find anyone, anyone at all, who might have known the last Dsaret king and queen . . . or the twin princesses."

Score.

Grandfather Kezh pursed his lips, and after some heavy, knit-browed thought he rumbled a sentence, stopped himself, and addressed me in careful but clear German, "You must then be able to read the old tongue?" And when I nodded, he smiled. "Good, good. In those days, the people of rank, they all spoke German. I was in the stables. In those days they kept many horses. Sometimes I was in charge of the hunters up at Sedania, that was the royal lodge in winter. I had to learn German for the guests."

Madam clicked her tongue at this tangent, but Grandfather Kezh paused to take a sip of the dark liquid in his painted ceramic cup, then he went on imperturbably, "My good friend in those days was Tomasi Borescu. We worked together in the stables. Tomasi's sister Stasja—ah, she was pretty! But I was promised to my good Adela. Stasja used to bring us sweet-cakes in the cold mornings—"

"Papa," Madam coaxed, with a look my way. "She does not want to hear about good Tomasi Borescu—"

"No, no, Daughter, my point comes. Das Fräulein wishes for information about life then. I tell it." He gave a nod of stately dignity. "As I say, Stasja, Tomasi's sister, worked in the palace until she married Josip Ivaniev. She worked in the nursery, and she saw the princesses each day."

Madam threw up her hands and gave a gasp of pleasure. "Bless you, Papa! That is the truth." She added something in rapid-fire Dobreni to her daughters, gesturing with enthusiastic goodwill.

Anna turned then to me, and with a blushing, shy gravity that rather matched her grandfather's, she said in heavily accented German, "My wedding, it is Saturday. You will honor us with your company?"

Theresa added, "Old Grandmother Ziglieri, that was her name after her second marriage, she will come down from the mountain with the family. She will be there, and she likes to talk about the old days."

Madam chimed in with names of more people (some of whose connections with the Waleska family were tortuous in the extreme) who had in some way been associated with the royal palace, but there was no mention of the princesses. I pretended to take note of all these, and before we parted—me to go upstairs to work on the language—I accepted their invitation to attend Anna's wedding on Saturday.

That gave me a day to explore.

After a good ballet workout the next morning, I set out. The sky was a jumble of layered clouds, some long and flat, some puffy. In LA it never rains, so I didn't know what those meant. I armed myself with a sun hat, a sweater, and my dictionary before I set out on my exploration.

Yesterday's impressions resolved into more detail. I could see the different strata of history, the Baroque buildings built under the Hapsburgs juxtaposed with medieval ones, and with grand nineteenth-century edifices that presaged Art Nouveau. They all showed a curious blend of eastern and western motifs that was distinctly Dobreni.

There was still war damage, left for decades, and the evidence of King Milo's recent projects—big projects, like sewer expansion, and in some areas, electricity for what was obviously the first time.

Here's the weird thing. I sensed Alec's presence everywhere.

I kept thinking, *only your imagination, Murray,* but the atmosphere of the city reminded me of him—distinctive, even elegant in an understated way. It was Alec's space.

But not Gran's. Oh, I believed the stories—at least, everything but Gran running off with the Wicked Armandros without benefit of marriage. I believed it intellectually, but I couldn't get her into focus walking these streets, looking on these buildings.

I walked to the cathedral, just to discover it was still closed. Then I wandered around the city center in search of a hall of records or some equivalent, and not finding that, I headed for the cathedral for my second try. Right about then—like in Vienna—I got that feeling that I was being watched.

Last time it had turned out to be true.

I turned away from the cathedral. Since I didn't know who was following me, I wouldn't know if they got up close enough to hear my questions if I went into the cathedral. I didn't have Jason Bourne's savvy at spotting tails, but one thing for sure: I didn't want anyone hearing my business.

So I slowed down, looking around, ho hum, see the boring tourist gawking, nothing else going on, nosiree Bob!

The open marketplace in the old section of town and many of the tall, narrow, three- and four-story houses under their slanting roofs looked the same as they must have for the last eight hundred years. I wandered through several stores offering exquisite handwoven rugs and embroidered clothes and beautiful, complicated wind-up clocks that would have gotten my dad's mouth watering. Most everything in those shops seemed handmade, or at most made by simpler machines—no tech toys.

As I strolled around totally without purpose, I sneaked peeks over my shoulder from time to time.

Nothing. No sinister minions in mirror-shades, no Emilio or Kilber.

No Alec.

Most of the traffic was on foot. I wandered the streets alongside soberly clad Hasidic Jews doing Friday marketing preparatory for Sabbath meals, and smocked shepherds and cowherds whose clothing had probably altered little in style since 1300. I had to be careful where I stepped because these latter were often driving small flocks down the streets to or from market. They were interspersed with people in much more modern clothes. There were Slavic-boned faces, and here and there the unmistakable imprint of the Mongolian nomads in wide cheeks and tilted eyes. Most of the people were dark, but not all; the pale-headed and light-eyed evidence of long-ago Northern incursions also went about their business, wearing combinations of modern and local dress.

What I didn't see was a cell phone. Not a single one. Even the young teens—a few boys wearing jeans, others in the Cossack tunics, girls in skirts of varying lengths, colors, and designs—walked along with hands free, talking to each other and not on the ubiquitous cell of the West.

I'd reached a flower-filled park that fronted the Jewish temple when I felt that "watched" feeling again. I turned around sharply as the bells from the cathedral half a mile west started ringing a carillon that echoed from the towering mountainside above and back.

Nothing.

Just people hastening on their way, some casting appraising glances skyward.

It couldn't be the Ruli business again. The only people who knew her would either know where she was, or were all over Europe searching for her.

And it couldn't be Alec—if for some wild reason he'd zoomed back home to Dobrenica, I couldn't believe he'd slink around spying on me, especially after the whole Vienna mess. He'd come right up and ask me why I was there.

I stepped inside a corner bakery, breathing in the vanilla-tinged aroma of fresh-baked bread. I bought a nut-studded apple tart and sat at a table hardly bigger than a Frisbee as outside, a brief but violent thunderstorm sent rain hissing into the street. The squall was over before I finished the pastry and licked the dusting of cinnamon from my fingers. When I left, the cobblestones steamed in the pale afternoon sunlight.

I returned to the inn, feeling as if every step I took was marked by an unseen someone; on my arrival, I discovered the place was packed, mostly with relatives from the mountain heights come for the wedding. The common room was a roar of voices and clattering dishes; not until I made my way past them all did I feel safely lost in the numbers.

When I tried right after lunch—the cathedral annex was closed again. I made it back to the inn just ahead of a sudden, violent thunder-storm that made it impossible to go out for a third time. I had to give up for the day.

SIXTEEN

SATURDAY MORNING, the Ziglieri family arrived among an impressive cavalcade of relatives. The men got to work shifting tables and benches about. Boys were sent to deal with pony traps and ancient cars. Girls helped Theresa and Tania to decorate the inn outside and inside with fragrant bunches of flowers and ribbon-tied boughs. Older women turned their hands to last-stage preparation of enormous quantities of food.

I stayed out of the way, watching from the vantage of my window overlooking the courtyard and gardens until Theresa knocked on my door and shyly informed me that Grandmother Ziglieri wished to speak to me.

Had *consented* to speak to me, I realized with a spurt of humor as I followed Theresa to where three elderly women in widows' black sat enthroned on a sunny bench. They were overseeing the flurry of activity with the keen-eyed determination of conferring field marshals.

Theresa led me to the oldest of them, a diminutive woman with a snowy embroidered headdress on her small gray head. With a respect ordering on reverence, Theresa introduced me to Grandmother Ziglieri first, and then to the widows on either side of her, whose names I didn't register. I was too busy trying to figure out what to say.

The three widows peered up at me, the one on the left nodding, the one on the right squinting nearsightedly. Grandmother Ziglieri regarded me, her wrinkled face impossible to read.

The widow on the right said in a thin voice, "Yes? Yes? You come from Paris, the child says?"

The nodding widow's voice was dry, her German slow but clear. "Come! Sit with us. Talk a little."

"Thank you." I sat on the stool that Theresa set before their bench. Though she hadn't spoken yet, I addressed Grandmother Ziglieri. "Theresa tells me you worked at the palace under the old king, and that you knew the princesses."

The ancient woman's face creased into a thousand new lines as she pursed her lips.

The nodding widow said, "Yes, yes. So many pranks, Princess Rose! But so sweet . . . and Princess Lily . . . such a good child, always busy with her piano. But, oh, she could ride on her pony. Fearless, the both. And so pretty. Hair the color of yours . . . no, lighter . . ."

Grandmother Ziglieri leaned toward me, her dark eyes intent as she spoke for the first time. "It was the Swedish blood, that yellow hair. You have it, too." It wasn't a question.

"Yes," I said, uneasy before that steady gaze. I hoped she wouldn't ask me questions; I did not want to lie to her. I had this feeling those old eyes of hers could x-ray the inside of my skull. "Did you know the princesses as young women?"

The nodding widow was almost bowing as her head dipped slowly forward and back; her headdress was embroidered with cherry clusters and birds. "No . . . no . . . we worked as chambermaids in the nursery. When Their Highnesses left the nursery—Grandmother Ziglieri was married by then, to her good Ivaniev—I went to the bakery to work because it was closer to my two little girls."

She went on in a meditative voice to talk about raising two girls, losing a third, then losing her husband during the war, all while working in the bakery. She reminisced over the formidable preparations they had made for royal dinners, and how impressive these affairs had been.

I did not interrupt. When at last she paused I said, "Is there anyone alive today who knew the princesses when they were young ladies? Anyone who . . ." I braced myself. "Might have known Princess Lily before she disappeared?"

"Ahhh . . . how sad that was . . . how sad." She nodded gently, her eyes gazing long past the ever-shifting scene of frenetic activity going on around us. Finally she *tsked* two or three times. "Terrible sadness, to leave, and us open to—"

"Tsh," the right-hand widow hissed.

The left-hand widow stopped rocking and blinked earnestly at me, her withered cheeks mottled with color. "You're from Paris?"

The abrupt shift in subject startled me.

"I was there a couple of weeks ago. But please, what were you going to say?"

Grandmother Ziglieri muttered something in Dobreni.

The nodding widow raised a gnarled, work-worn hand, then said, "After, many years after—we found out that Princess Lily had died in the war, in Paris. So far from home, and no one to know and be with her. You knew this?" She touched my sleeve.

"I know what happened to her," I said with care. "But when she left Dobrenica—"

"Ah." The small, heavy-knuckled hand came up, palm toward me. "A bad business. She went alone, in the night. Quick-quick." She whisked her hands across her lap. "Like that. She took none of her own people!"

"Did you know any of them?"

"No relations of mine were in that wing, you see. We'd mostly to do with the food, our family. Two uncles, bakers, and a great grandfather, a pastry-maker. He was trained in Vienna. But Princess Lily . . . oh, the scandal when she left, and none knew where she had gone. Everyone questioned by the king himself . . ." She shook her head. "Those were bad days. And not long after, the king died, and then the German soldiers came. Terrible, terrible days."

"So no one is alive who knew the princess then?"

"But yes, some do live. I, myself!" She smiled, as if making a joke.

Grandmother Ziglieri spoke in Dobreni again, but this time I understood most of the words. I think she meant me to. "Tell her about the Eyrie governess."

"Mina Hajyos." The widow on the left rocked gently back and forth on her bench. "She said she knew nothing of the princess' plans. But her family lives on Devil's Mountain. She was . . ." A quick look.

The nearsighted one cut in, her voice urgent. "Many said afterward that Mina Hajyos served the count all along. Paid in secret. She went back to the mountain and married. When the new duke went to England she stayed in Dorike on Riev Dhiavilyi." I recognized that as Dobreni for Devil's Mountain. "Where she became Salfmatta Mina."

"Salfmatta?" I repeated. I still didn't understand that title yet.

The nodding widow spoke up. "My niece's two sons worked in the mines for a time. They were caught by an October snowstorm once . . . oh, four years back. Five. They took refuge in Dorike. They said Salfmatta Mina yet lives. She has a cottage near her grandson's house."

Grandmother Ziglieri leaned toward me. "Her family's roses always grow," she said slowly. "They are from English slips. The only rose garden in the village." Her gaze was intent, as if she waited for some word or sign—as if her words, so simple, carried some extra meaning.

Madam Waleska approached, giving the old women a quick bob. "Are you finished, grandmothers? We must not be late to Mass."

"No," Grandmother Ziglieri said, but when I rose, she put out her hand to halt me. Then she said in slow, heavily accented German, "You have the sight."

I stared at her, probably showing the perplexity I felt. I was certain I hadn't been squinting like the widow on the right, who was being helped away by a patient daughter. "Sight?" I repeated.

A tall, strong-looking middle-aged woman stood by, waiting.

Grandmother Ziglieri said in Dobreni, "You have the—"

But I did not know the word she used—and it wasn't the noun in the dictionary for "seeing." It couldn't be something like Second Sight—I had an idea from stories I'd read as a kid that those superstitions went with crystal balls and chicken entrails, or whatever.

"You will ask Salfmatta Mina." She hobbled slowly away.

I raced upstairs to put on a nice dress, hoping I could talk to the grandmothers later. But if I couldn't, at least I had a name and a location: Mina Hajyos, in the village Dorike, on a mountain called Riev Dhiavilyi.

The wedding was held in a medieval church as strange-eyed Byzantine saints gazed down with lovingly detailed expressions of benediction, their gold leaf halos glinting in the light of many candles. Incense spun slowly upward in the air, making me giddy again; my eyes stung from the smoke so that Anna's ancient veil, with buds embroidered along the heel-length hem, and her white gown with pearls worked across the bodice, blurred until I seemed to see a simpler gown with no train, then an elaborate one with a long train, flanked by garlanded girls in high-waisted gowns, their arms full of flowers; I felt a sense of falling slowly down and down, as if I descended gently through the years, the centuries, past kneeling brides and grooms beyond count.

The weird reverie broke abruptly when Anna and her tall, thin, and equally shy-faced husband faced us and walked arm in arm down the center aisle. The dizziness was stronger this time, making me grip the wooden back of the pew in front of me until I regained my balance.

When I get home, maybe it's time for a CAT scan, I thought unhappily as I followed the others out.

But first, Gran's quest.

We rode the short way back to the Waleskas' inn in flower-decorated wagons. People along the steep-roofed houses cheered or waved handkerchiefs, and a few girls and women threw bright blossoms down on us—mostly violet iris and rose-colored amaranth, but other flora as well, in every color except yellow.

Almost all the guests wore festive costume. Everywhere were flashes of glorious color; crimson, emerald, turquoise blue vests, all embroidered with contrasting colors. Dyed petticoats of contrasting shades peeped from under lace-hemmed skirts, trousers sported dashing weavings of color down the outside seam before disappearing into boots polished for the occasion.

Little kids ran shrieking around and around the perimeter of the patio at the inn as the guests crowded in, laughing and talking. The color, joy, the mixture of familiar and of strange customs was interesting, but the intensity of their happiness made me feel isolated and lonely.

I thought of Alec, and then tried not to think of Alec, which made me think about not thinking about him.

So I got up from the bench where I'd been sitting by myself. I forced a smile as the crowds parted instantly to make way for me, and helped myself to more of the spiced wine punch. Then I sat back down on my bench, my polite smile making my jaw ache.

I concentrated on picking out words and phrases in the flow of chatter around me, trying to gauge the minute I could sneak upstairs without being noticed. Madam was too distracted to pay any attention to me, but Theresa did, and the middle sister Tania, so when I saw them eyeing me anxiously, I gave them a wave and smile, and watched relief ease their faces as they turned to the rest of their unending hostess chores.

Supper was served before the long, golden sunbeams vanished behind the tall mountain above us. There was a variety of highly seasoned dishes, mostly pork- or mutton-based, with saffron-yellow rice, and then trays of Viennese-style pastry made with liberal quantities of cream or layered with the delicate sweet-sour flavor of *topfen* custard, and bread filled with nut- and rum-flavored layers of jam, dusted with cinnamon or powdered sugar.

The light began to fade, leaving a clear night. My mood lifted as musicians emerged from the welter of celebrants and began to play. Most of the food was gone; at Madam Waleska's gesture a number of the women descended on the long tables and cleared them off, following which the men carried the tables back inside the inn's dining room.

In the cleared space, the dancing began.

First Anna and her Josip, followed by close family members on both sides. That was the signal for general dancing. The guys went first, stamping and leaping and shouting. Then the women got out there with their own dances, full of swinging skirts, twirling and clapping and flirting poses.

There were also dances for couples, but the teens and young adults my age seemed to go for the sex-separate dances as often as the mixed, judging from the way they watched each other. Seeing those guys leap and twirl and rap their heels down in counterpoint to the galloping beat made me feel less isolated. I love to watch dancers as much as I love to dance.

Wine and laughter and good food and the slow intimacy of twilight's deepening to darkness charged the atmosphere with expectation. Grins flashed, glances met across the crowded courtyard as the accordions, mandolins, pipes, and banduras bound everyone together with the complicated melodies of Dobreni music.

Then torches were lit and brought out. As the perimeter of the courtyard leaped back in yellow flickering light I noticed two men standing beyond the open gate beyond the pointy end of the terrace, where the two streets branched off at either side of the inn. These were shadowy figures, in workaday clothes and boots, and the angle of both faces zapped my nerves: they were watching me.

I'm merely a tourist, I thought, and blinked hard to clear the punch-fuzziness from my eyes. I peered over dancers' shoulders, trying to find otherwhere-focus in those shadowy sockets, but the smoke and haze around me were too strong.

Anna appeared before me, breathing hard in her pearl-glistening white dress. "Come! Dance with us," she invited, shyness banished by triumph and joy and wine.

She took my hand and drew me into the crowd of women milling in the center of the courtyard. Everything else disappeared from my mind as the music started up, gay and tinkling with a clash and tap of tambourines.

I turned to Anna, who put her hands on her hips. Resting my own fists on my hips, I mirrored everything she did.

We danced face-to-face, laughing as I mastered some steps and missed others. We were the center of a circle; the music lifted us, twirled us in a flourish of belling skirts . . . and inspired to recklessness by wine, and torchlight, and the others' happiness surrounding my own ambivalence, impulse sparked me to improvise. Music skirled, torchlight flickered and streamed; light as autumn leaves chased by wind, I began to chassée.

Anna gave a crow of pleasure. Her friends clapped in time to the music. So I whipped into the steps of a tarantella, finishing with a twirling set of fouettés as they clapped in time. Then the music ended and a roar of approval sent a flock of pigeons clattering skyward from the eaves. I whirled in a double pirouette and came to rest in a dancer's bow before Anna.

At once I was surrounded by smiling and admiring women. Anna laughed and exclaimed in excited Dobreni, clapping her hands. I straightened up, grinning—until I caught sight of those two men beyond her shoulder.

They'd come a few steps nearer, standing right at the gate. A third had joined them.

I was in the peculiar position of being the only one who noticed them; the group of women dancers all faced the bride and me, and the wedding guests near the gate were either talking to one another or watching the women.

The way the third man stood signaled threat. He wore a khaki military jacket hanging loose over a white shirt, dark pants and boots, and a cigarette dangled from his mouth. He returned my gaze with an insolent scrutiny for a few seconds.

I turned to Anna to ask who that was—but as I raised my hand, pointing, he threw down his cigarette, leaving it smoldering in the street as he walked beyond the gate, the other two following. Anna and a few turned to look in the direction I pointed, but the men were already out of view.

So Anna and her friends begged me to dance again, but I was afraid that while one might be a compliment to the bride, two would be overdoing it. When the music started again and I recognized the piece as one of the earthy stamping dances I'd watched a while ago, I took Anna's hands and began it. As soon as she and the others had formed their circle I faded with practiced skill back into the group.

Half an hour later I slipped upstairs and got into bed.

And couldn't sleep.

Those men. Were they watching the dancing, or were they spying on *me?* Not for any good reason, whatever they were doing, I thought as I recalled that one with the insolent leer.

"Sometimes," I groaned, throwing back the covers and getting up without turning on my light again, "having an active imagination is a royal pain in the butt."

Royal.

I had been watched, and followed, in Vienna because of my resemblance to Ruli. I'd assumed that all Alec's people were out of the country searching, and that Ruli's people didn't have to search. Yeah, and what if I was wrong?

I peered through a crack in the curtains. No one in the shadows surrounding the courtyard wall, as far as I could see. Directly below me the party was going strong, but I did not see the work clothes or the khaki of the three watchers among them.

I frowned, looking around my dark room. The wardrobe! I hated the thought of someone getting at my passport and wallet again. The clothes I didn't care about, but the papers . . .

I opened the wardrobe, felt inside my travel bag, and pulled out the roll of my jeans and blouse, with the ID and wallet with my euros wrapped inside like a hot dog in its bun. Two choices here: either I ask Madam Waleska to keep the stuff, which would raise all kinds of speculation, or I hide it.

The wardrobe was topped by a narrow ridge of carved wooden decoration. I yanked a chair over then climbed up and felt above the carving. Behind the far side, between the back of the wardrobe and the wall, there was a few inches of space. The rolled cloth fit back there snugly and was completely invisible. Even a hand patting the top of the wardrobe would miss it. The rest of the few Ruli clothes I'd kept remained right in view inside the wardrobe.

After that I was able to sleep.

Next morning I did my warm-ups, dressed, and went downstairs, passing Theresa and Tania, who were cleaning dispiritedly in between serving the mostly subdued guests. Even Madam had less than her usual bustle, but she greeted me with customary warmth. Her husband looked pale as he polished and stacked glasses. It was nearly noon, and the relatives were beginning a slow exodus.

I found a corner table to sit at, where the Waleskas' relations scrupulously left me in splendid isolation. I studied my Dobreni dictionary as I ate cold leftovers for breakfast, then left.

It being Sunday there was no chance of finding anything official open. That had to remain for Monday. This day's exploration would be the palace tour. When the big cathedral bells rang a quarter to two I crossed the main square and joined the group of people lined up at the fence.

As I had suspected, the tour was to be conducted in Dobreni. The people in line, all middle-aged, were citizens from the mountain reaches, except for two Romanians. They glanced my way with covert interest as they exchanged comments, but no one addressed me directly.

The blue-uniformed guard chatted idly with the first man in line. As he lifted his arm to glance at his watch another guard came running out from the building visible inside the palace compound.

This man slowed about thirty feet from the gate, walked with military correctness to the guard near us, then bent toward him to mumble a message.

My idle interest sharpened into apprehension as they both looked my way and gave me a fast scan. One of the guards met my gaze and smiled timidly. The other looked . . . shocked.

The second guard said to the line of waiting tourists, "Come with me please?"

I didn't like that staring business, but I hadn't done anything wrong, and it wasn't as if any of them could possibly know me or what I was there for. So I shuffled along at the back of the group as the guard began his spiel.

The palace was built along customary palatial lines, the likes of which are to be seen all over Europe. This one had more of an air of Fischer von Erlach than anything I'd seen in France. It was shaped like an E, or perhaps more like an O and E put together; the semicircular main structure was built around a central garden, with three parallel wings extending into it, the outer two abutting the wide natural park that stretched up the slope of the mountain. The palace was about the same size as Schönbrunn.

At first I followed only bits of the history the guard reeled out. There were occasional references to Sweden, Russia, Poland, and the Holy Roman and Ottoman empires. There was something about Sobieski Square—the main square was built in honor of John Sobieski?—and a lot about the Russians and the Stadthalter.

The old and unwanted giddiness stole over me, at first without my being aware. I was too busy trying to fit my grandmother in this palace as I concentrated on picking familiar words out of the flow.

We toured through large, airy rooms with paneled walls, vaulted ceilings, and mosaic-tiled or marble or parquet floors. The most beautiful room was a rococo ballroom; its decorations had been stripped away by the various invaders, but the spectacular crystal chandeliers had survived (hidden by household staff), and the walls had been replastered with graceful molding.

I followed enough of the explanation to understand that the most valuable treasures had been removed by the palace staff right before the Germans swarmed over the border and were hidden in the mazes of caves and mines high in the mountains. But they couldn't save everything.

The various occupiers had lived *en prince*. When they left, they dismantled, rolled up, and shipped back home every panel, lamp, carpet, and fixture that they could pry loose.

We walked upstairs to the residential wing. In spite of the flickering at the edge of my vision and the mild throbbing in my head, I thought, wow, my dictionary work is paying off. I was beginning to pick up context; the more the guard talked, the easier it was to understand him.

We walked through the long line of splendidly furnished sitting rooms, libraries, and chambers with tall canopied beds as he talked about past kings, customs, and events.

I was totally unready for what happened next.

We left the museumlike grand residence and began shuffling down a long gallery of royal portraits, restored fifteen years ago from their hiding places in the ancient, abandoned mines in Mount Tanazca. The crowd gazed up at the gold-framed faces as the tour guide reeled out names and dates.

I followed along at the tail end, and that's when I walked smack into the woo-woo zone: I found myself face to painted face with the actor I'd seen twirling her parasol at the Hofburg and then again on the Glorietta.

No, really.

It was *exactly* the same woman. Right down to the sky blue sacque dress, the diamond drops in her ears, and the fine golden embroidery along the lace edging of her gown's square neck.

And here she was again, framed in gold, and below, a brass plate reading:

MARIA SOFIA ALEXANDRIA ELISABETH VASA DSARET

1721–1811

SEVENTEEN

I RUBBED MY EYES, then my temples, as I grasped for logic, for the calm of facts. The woman in the picture had to have been a Vasa from Sweden—a minor cousin of the Swedish royal family, packed off to central Europe to make a dynastic marriage. I glared up at her, willing her to be somebody else. There were the honey-brown eyes, a roguish smile—with two dimples. Her snowy wig was piled high under the charming flat hat with its ribbons and plumes.

A scrape of a shoe made me jump and look guiltily around.

The entire tour had halted at the other end of the gallery, and they were all staring at me. Some at the portrait and then back at me, others at the tour guide and then back at me, the rest goggling just at me.

My neck burned. I slunk past the eternal gazes of the remaining royal portraits and took my place at the end of the tour line, my attention firmly on my dusty toes in my sandals.

The tour guide cleared his throat and resumed his patter. The feet began shuffling again, and I slunk after them, determined to draw no more attention as I tried to figure out what had just happened.

Either someone was masquerading all around Vienna as this woman, or she had a common face. Or . . . could she be Ruli tripping around Vienna in a costume for some weird reason?

Except that traipsing around Vienna in costume didn't sound at all like the Ruli that Alec had described. He'd been definite about that—her only interest in the past being whose jewels she would inherit. Not that she'd ever sell them; it was a status thing.

As I struggled to make sense of something that I was afraid would never make sense, our tour group passed out of the portrait gallery and into a sunlit curved hall lined with windows down both sides. This hall formed the spine of the E—it lay above the state rooms.

Through the windows on my right, the tidy eighteenth-century maze abutted the grand front gate and beyond it the great square; the windows on my left overlooked the back garden, which opened onto sloping lawns with scattered chestnut and linden trees.

We reached the other main wing, and the tour guide said, "At this end is the chapel, the kitchens, and service rooms, and upstairs is the royal nursery."

The tour dutifully snaked its way through the suite of wide, sunny-windowed, plain rooms . . . and this time the zap hit me right in the heart.

The furniture was from the days of the twin princesses, gaily painted tables and chairs and a cradle, all somewhat battered. The curtains had butterflies embroidered on them. Later I'd find out that all these things had been smuggled into hiding, along with all the moveable furnishings and decorations of the palace, ahead of the German blitzkrieg. The furnishings had been restored by grandchildren of those servants, after the Soviet Empire fell.

But that wasn't what zapped me. The lightning bolt was the mural painted across the entirety of one broad wall, a stylized late-Victorian mural of flowers with fairies and folktale figures parading toward a castle built of shells.

I stared at that mural, recognizing in every single figure some story from my childhood.

From the time I was barely able to talk, every night Gran had told me stories about Fyadar and Xanpia, his female companion, and their band of orphans and special animals, including a werewolf, having adventures on the mysterious mountains that had spirits of their own. Stories she had stopped telling me when, at age eight, I started asking all kinds of questions about where the stories had come from and why couldn't I find any books in the library about Fyadar and his friends.

After that she read classics to me, but I never forgot those tales—and in every library I encountered afterward, I'd looked for them. I'd even decided recently to change majors back to German, so I could do research and find where those stories had been recorded, because Gran was not the sort to make things up.

My nerves tingled as I gazed at the flaking, faded mural in that long-empty room. Gran's having been born and raised here was no longer hypothetical. Nothing—my resemblance to this missing cousin—the portrait of Maria Sofia—the coinciding dates and names, *nothing* was as real as that mural.

I saw her, as clear as if I could reach and touch her tousled blond curls as she rocked on the wooden horse under streaming sunlight so strong she faded to shadow . . .

And vanished.

The tightness in my throat threatened to thaw into tears, and I turned away quickly.

I have always hated tears. I grew up believing them a sign of weakness, of defeat. If something hurts you, you either learn from it, fight it, or negotiate with it, and finally you move on. You never cry.

But here I was with stinging eyes and a lump the size of a basketball in my throat. I backed away from the wooden horse until I stumbled against a small chair wooden chair with flowers painted on it as the tour vanished down the stairs.

I rubbed my eyes fiercely and hustled to rejoin the crowd, pretending not to notice when everyone, including the guard, swiveled to stare at me, then turned away hastily.

In a self-conscious voice the tour guide told us that the last inside site would be the family chapel, then the tour would proceed outdoors to the stables, gardens, and fountain.

I was so overwhelmed I did not even question why I now understood everything he said, even though a lot of those words I would swear I never hunted down in the dictionary: seeing the mural had unlocked something in my brain. Maybe it was only memory. The language was there, though simple in vocabulary: a child's vocabulary.

I stepped inside the chapel and took in the cool, diffuse light over the smooth-carved marble that had been stripped of anything even remotely valuable. The altar had been swept clean, leaving only the walls, floor, and the high-backed benches on which the royal family had sat; even the gilding from the carvings of the royal crest had been scraped away, and the gold-embroidered velvet cushions taken. The guide's tone was affronted, as if the vandalism had happened a week ago instead of more than half a century.

The others followed the guide out and into the bright, revealing light of day. Sinking onto a centuries-old marble bench, I pressed my thumbs against my eyelids.

A rustle of silk, a whiff of vanilla and musk reminded me of the most expensive shops in Paris.

I opened my eyes. A tall, slim female silhouette stood framed in the doorway. "My dear, why haven't you contacted me—" She began in mellifluous French, then she gave a gasp, raised a thin hand to her lips, and stepped into the dim chapel.

And I stared witlessly into the face of my Aunt Sisi.

EIGHTEEN

SHE LOOKED SO much like my mother it was as if Mom walked in wearing a raw silk skirt and jacket expensive and tasteful enough for calling on a queen. Much as they looked alike, my mother and this woman could not have been more different. Mom, practically the poster girl for the flower child, did not walk with this deliberate straight-backed, governess-trained poise.

My mother's familiar round, sweetly smiling face on the duchess was refined into smooth, well-bred composure; my mother's serene eyebrows on this woman were groomed into arched sophistication. The resemblances and contrasts were so jarring on top of the headache and the giddiness and above all the emotional whammy that my brain went on strike, leaving me staring mutely.

She said with breathless graciousness, "I am not dreaming. You are not my daughter."

"No," I squeaked.

"Is it possible? You must be my—my missing cousin's child . . . are you?"

A diamond flashed with sun-fire as she pressed trembling fingers to her temple. Her blond hair, the same shade as my own, was drawn up into a perfect chignon that showed off a perfect hairline.

Your missing cousin? Try your missing half-sister's child. "I believe I am," I said after drawing my own trembling breath. "My name is Kim."

"My dear child—I, *hein!,* I—I hardly know what to say. To do. So Tante Lily did not die in Paris?"

"No."

"Does she live still?"

"Yes," I whispered, thinking of Gran sitting in her rocker facing east, the light from the window reflecting in her eyes with all the expression of glass. "With my parents."

"Your mother." Her voice was even lower, barely a breath as she stared at me in wonderment. "You are quite young," she observed, and I felt . . . not suspicion, more like a question.

Question as in doubt. She didn't believe me? Maybe it was fair. Wouldn't I feel the same if someone came up to me at UCLA or somewhere and claimed to be my long-lost whatever?

So I smiled determinedly and said, "My mother didn't marry until she turned forty. I came along a couple of years later."

She made a visible effort to collect her thoughts and said, "No one knew. We heard nothing. You were in Paris all this time, until you came here?"

"How did you know that?" It was out before I could stop it, and she turned her thin fingers out toward me in a gesture of plea.

"My dear, I received a message this morning that my daughter had been found. Did you know she had been missing? Did you know I have a daughter? You were seen at an inn not far from here, and it was discovered that you were registered under what was thought an assumed name, that you represented yourself as a French citizen. You look so much like my daughter, you must realize. For the Vigilzhi to have seen a young woman they thought was my daughter Aurelia—"

"Vigilzhi?"

Her hands made a Gallic gesture of helplessness. "The police and army combined. They maintain order in our little country."

"And they did not think to come up and ask me? They stalked me, thinking that was preferable?"

"You must realize that some of the old ways prevail here. No one would want to interfere if for some reason you did not want to become known. But you were always safe. You must not be angry with the Vigilzhi, who merely do their duty. They did not disturb you, but summoned me." She smiled, eyes wide.

I made an effort to pull my own thoughts together, to banish the curly haired girl from my imagination and to respond to this woman—the first blood relative I met—who was obviously shaken herself. The hand with the ring pressed tightly against the other.

"I'm sorry," I said. "This is a total shock."

"Yes. For us both, *hein?*" She breathed out in a well-bred, soundless sigh. "Come. Out into the sunlight. May I have a look at you? Can you tell me what brought you to Dobrenica?"

She led the way outside, into the neatly trimmed flower maze. My tour group was nowhere in sight.

"I came to see my grandmother's birthplace," I said. "I'll be gone again in a few days."

"You're not thinking of leaving, now that we've found you again?"

"I can't afford a long visit," I countered, trying to sort through my emotional whirlwind. Too many things too fast, too hard-hitting.

"But my dear! I thought it would be immediately evident. Please, you must come to me at once. To my house here in the city. It's close by. And there's a charming guest room next to my daughter's suite." The offer was instant, and gracious—so instant and gracious that my discomfort spiked.

"Oh, that's not necessary," I hedged, laboring to avoid being rude. I just needed a few minutes to take everything in. "I'm okay where I am. I already paid for a week," I said inanely as her chin lifted fractionally, though her smile never faltered. I added even more inanely, "Really. I really like it there."

"But a public inn? It cannot be *convenable.* You would be no trouble at all, three permanent servants in the house, plus my own staff, and I am so seldom there! I'd be delighted to have you come."

She had used the French word, *convenable,* which not only meant adequate, but connoted respectable or appropriate, and when I thought of Madam Waleska's scrupulously clean rooms, her bright, handmade curtains and quilts, Theresa's earnest face and shy enthusiasm, I felt a spurt of irritation, though I knew it was not fair. Aunt Sisi was not deliberately insulting these people—she didn't even know them. To her, a proper hotel probably had to be at least three hundred years old, staffed with an army of haughty liveried servants used to the ways of royalty, where meals were served on porcelain and the bathroom fixtures were real gold. It was the way she'd been raised.

I shook my head firmly. "Thanks. I appreciate your offer, but I won't trouble you."

She regarded me, but did not seem angry. More like surprised. I wondered if she'd expected me to start hinting for handouts. Again I felt a spurt of irritation and scolded myself for projecting. She said quickly, "Then you must agree to a family party, in your honor, or I shall not give up. It would be so charming for your relations to meet you."

Okay, that I could get behind. Newfound relatives! But . . . "I don't have a suitable dress for formal parties," I hedged. "I'm traveling light."

"Then we shall avoid the gala. A simple gathering for after-dinner drinks. As for party clothes . . ." A crooked smile like my mother's brought out the dimple. "What could be easier? I shall send over a frock of my daughter's. It is bound to fit. Please, my dear. I shall beg until you give in—"

"I'd be honored," I said awkwardly, feeling like a boor. "And as for the dress, don't put yourself out. I'll make do with what I have, since it's not formal or anything."

"Ah, thank you, dear child. Here is my address, should you change your mind and decide to come to me." She reached into her Hèrmes handbag, pulled out a sheet of folded notepaper, and handed it to me.

The address was engraved at the top, under a coronet. "So. Will you come to lunch with me, my dear? There is so much I wish to ask you. Your—your grandmother, how I shall enjoy meeting her. Once we have found my poor daughter, and her wedding is concluded. So tiresome! The details must be arranged, and the bride not here—pardon me, my dear, here I rattle on and you have no idea what it is I'm talking about, have you?"

I am so not going there. "She's getting married," I responded blithely. "That's easy to understand. As for lunch, I wish I could, but I did have something else going—"

It was the shock that caused me to lie. Thrilled as I was at the idea of finding my family at last, I desperately needed some time alone. I wasn't ready for this sophisticated woman who so weirdly resembled Mom but whose handbag probably cost more than our mortgage.

"Of course. Tomorrow evening, then. I shall tell you all about it when you come to me. Shall I send someone for you?"

"That would be nice." At least that didn't sound like I was begging for handouts, so I nodded like a dashboard doll. "Thanks."

"Gaspard will call for you at a quarter to eight, then. I hold tomorrow evening a treasured promise."

She had led us to the maze garden, which bordered the long curved sweep of a drive from the huge gate to somewhere on the other side of the palace. Directly in front of the palace waited a new Volvo with flags mounted on the front bumper. Seeing us, a chauffeur emerged from the car and opened the back door, where he stood at attention.

Aunt Sisi pressed my hands between hers. "Au revoir, my dear. Remember the address if you change your mind."

"Thank you." I turned away and marched briskly to the gate. The guard there gave me a salute. I gave him a rather strained smile in return.

When I got back to the inn I was met by a sharp change in atmosphere. Though the charming downstairs restaurant had always been tidy, it was even more clean than it had been for the wedding. Madam bustled out, calling urgently for Theresa, and this time she curtseyed before asking what my pleasure would be for dinner tonight? No mention of dining with the family. I stared down into her solemn face and slowly began to realize what Aunt Sisi's words had meant.

The local police had come here and asked about me. They—and the Waleskas—assumed I was Ruli, using a false name. Aunt Sisi had rushed to meet me . . . and now she was the only person who knew I wasn't her daughter.

I was about to straighten Madam out, but my reluctance to go into my background, my purpose for being here, made me hesitate.

If it didn't harm Ruli to have a double prancing around the Adriatic, it won't hurt her here, I decided. I'd let Aunt Sisi do the talking, when and if she wanted. Until that time, easiest to leave things as they were.

I turned to Madam, who had not asked why I suddenly understood their language. The giddiness had abated, but my emotions still roiled.

The Waleskas' faces showed concern, so I forced a smile and said to Theresa, "Anything's fine for dinner. There are two things I would like to do . . ."

I hesitated. I had been about to ask if they knew the hours to the business side of the cathedral, which had to be where they kept records, but everything Aunt Sisi had told me froze me up. I'd lost my anonymity. Was that a bad thing or a good thing? Bad in that everyone who might recognize me would want to know what I was doing, but good because if they thought I was Ruli I'd be wafted past red tape, but then there'd be even more questions . . .

So ask Aunt Sisi, right?

And I skipped to my second thing. "I would like to hire a vehicle to take me up into the mountains tomorrow, for a day trip."

Madam spread her hands as if to say "Anything—anything!" And since all friendly intercourse seemed to have been frozen by the awesome intrusion of Rank, I decamped to my room.

By morning, when I woke up to the roar of thunder announcing a major storm, I knew there'd be no trip to find Mina Hajyos.

But I was not upset. I wanted to spend time on the language—try to figure out what was going on in my brain. I could track down Mina the governess the day after Aunt Sisi's party.

It was early, so I did a set of ballet exercises, even using the empty hallway for some combinations, leaps, and turns. It felt great, except that I wished I could get in some fencing. My arms needed the work, or I'd lose my speed and flexibility. I settled for a double set of push-ups.

I was going to head downstairs to breakfast when Theresa came to my door in her old-fashioned school uniform. Surprised, I forestalled her shy questions by asking, "Do you have school in summer?"

"Yes, we have festival in spring, and mid-August to early September.

It is winter when we take our long break. The snow is sometimes too heavy for many students to come." Then back to business, "Mama wishes me to say that the rain might prevent a journey into the mountains, unless it is urgent."

I said, "It can wait a day. Meanwhile, I have a question, but it can also wait, if you've got to get to school."

"It is early. I helped mother get the bread in an hour ago." Her serious mouth lifted at the corners. "Please ask."

"It's about Fyadar. I saw a mural in the royal palace. Is he a Dobreni figure? I—I know a few of the stories, and I have loved them all my life. I'd love to find out more. Fyadar, and his friend Xanpia. She's either an angel or a witch, I guess, since she's got some kind of power. Fyadar seems to be a boy in some stories, and in some he's half-animal."

"You know about Fyadar?" Her expressive was odd, interested yet wary. Then she smiled. "Fyadar is a figure of legend." She spoke formally, with the practice of presenting a report before a class. "The stories about him and his friends are ancient . . ." She went on to describe how the teachers during the Soviet years explained that he was borrowed from the Greek Pan, because he was half-goat. Fyadar, with his band of other magical mountain-forest denizens such as a good werewolf and a young vampire—

"Vampire?" I yelped, almost adding, *Gran never mentioned any vampires!*

Theresa flushed. "Yes," she said in a low but firm voice. "It is true that they are cursed. As some say are the were-creatures. But many children, ah, it is not their fault, and Saint Xanpia is friend to all." Her voice hitched on a gasp. Her face flooded crimson, and she added, "So it says in the legends. Fyadar and friends, they roam the mountains."

"I wonder if the legends are the same ones I heard. Have they changed in the last few years?"

You know how people will give you an answer, but not to the question you asked? "The legends are old. Fyadar and his friends were allied with the animals and birds."

"Except for evil ones, like wolf packs," I said, hoping to get her past the obvious details to whatever made her hesitate, as if thinking out each sentence, innocuous as they sounded. "And evil fey." Since we were speaking French, I used the word *fée.* Her eyelids flickered, as if the word had extra meaning. Different meaning. As if it was a cue, or a code. "I never heard anything about weres. Or vampires."

She stood there, looking at the floor.

Somewhat exasperated, I went on, "In the stories I was told, Fyadar and his friends often appeared and helped lost children, starving children, mistreated children. I got the feeling that the Fyadar legends were myths centered around the mystery, and well, what with bears and wolves, the savagery of mountain life."

"The Soviet instructors called them escapism for children," Theresa said, still in that school recitation voice. "All religion, and stories about—about the mountains—were forbidden. The older generation, during the war, could only study German things. "

"But your parents and grandparents told them anyway?" I prompted. Because how else would she know them?

She gave me a quick, fleeting smile, before her dark gaze earnestly read my face again. "The adults, when young. In school. They . . . they had their own resistance. They wrote stories." When I didn't throw up my hands and run away in horror, she offered with less timidity, "My sister's generation. And older. Inherited them. And wrote more."

"They resisted by writing stories?" I repeated and laughed. "That is *awesome!*" The word came out in English. I hastened to clarify, to win an answering grin from her, all over her face.

As if a cork had been pulled from a bottle, Theresa explained in a stream of enthusiasm, her thin hands gesturing.

The secrets began with the hiding of the Jews when the Germans invaded. They vanished—in plain sight. It was a countrywide conspiracy. Later, under the Soviets, the suppression of all religion caused a similar urge to secret resistance.

The children included the secret hidings in their stories, to the extent of publishing them, usually by what used to be called jellygraph. This labor-intensive method of publication involved writing in copy-ink on a tray of gelatin, and pressing papers on the ink until the ink slowly sank to the bottom of the tray. Then you had to write it all out again.

"Anna joined a Fyadar secret society when she was ten." Theresa laughed. She was sitting on my chair, her feet together and her back straight. "They had signals, and passwords, and the little books were passed from hand to hand. Many had been recopied. I have collected some of these," she added self-deprecatingly. "They are rare and fragile."

"May I see some?" I asked.

Her cheeks pinked. "I will show you, but they are not, well, literature. Some are badly spelled as well, and have crude drawings not proper. Of the Gestapo, when they came to oversee the German soldiers, and of the Soviets. But," she tipped her head, "Sister Magdalene once told me Fyadar societies did more for making children remember their heritage than the combined efforts of the overlords."

"So the local Jewish children were part of this?"

"Yes." She smiled. "The Gestapo could not take away people who were not there. They dressed like us, and learned and worshipped in secret, and our parents and grandparents saw nothing, heard nothing. They had their own schools, in secret. But the children met to trade books, at certain places."

"Wow. How could that happen? I mean, the rest of Europe sure wasn't as enlightened. I wish they had been."

Theresa gave me a troubled glance. "I know. But here, early, we had to learn to live with one another, because . . ." She turned her gaze toward the window, and the wariness was back. "Because peace is good," she finished firmly, in that tone people use when they're trying to cover over for something they'd meant to say. "The people told the Germans that the Jews were sent out of the country two hundred years ago. There are no Jews anymore, that's what they told the Germans, and the Soviets."

"And it worked?"

"Dobrenica is small," she said, hands out.

"So tell me about the secret societies. You belonged to one?"

"By the time I was old enough to join, the societies were already small. The Soviets were gone, and it did not matter so much to be secret anymore. I loved to read the stories, and I began to collect them." She ducked her head and buried her hands in her skirt.

I said gently, guessing, "And you wrote a few, perhaps?"

She blushed, and there was the fleeting grin again.

"I'd love to see those."

"They are written in Dobreni." She was barely audible. "And are not very good. I was young when I wrote them. Now I am too busy with studies."

"I would enjoy seeing them, if you would enjoy sharing them. That's the story I grew up loving. And as for not very good Dobreni, I'm trying hard to learn, and the best way to learn is by practice."

So that's how I spent the day.

As soon as I began to read, the rhythms of sentences were so familiar I began to suspect that during those early years, when Gran had babysat me while Mom and Dad worked, she'd told me those stories in Dobreni. That had to be why the language surfaced in my mind like a reverse of the sinking of Atlantis—no sign of it at first, then suddenly it's all there, though in simple form.

Once I figured out the orthography and the spelling, reading was easy. Some of the stories were handwritten and drawn in battered old composition books, others blurrily reproduced by jellygraph. Most were what we'd today call graphic novels—drawings connected by dialogue. In the sixties someone must have discovered comics, because the dialogue began to appear in balloons like the comics I grew up with, as opposed to the early books with the dialogue written in tiny letters beside each drawing.

As had happened at the palace, the language became easier to read—partly because the vocabulary was simple. Kids wrote for each other, so there wasn't much attempt at sophisticated structure or poetic flights.

By lunchtime I'd worked through most of the books. The stories gave me a strong sense of spirit, a determination by independent-minded people striving to maintain independence. In the earlier books (two dated 1940 and 1942), the violent drawings and the gruesome ends to the conquerors expressed rage. On some pages, grade-school-scurrilous additions had been cramped into the margins by hands other than the original writer or copier, much of it fading. I wondered if school ink was thinned to make it last.

After I'd read through the stack, I sat cross-legged on my bed as rain washed down the windows. I had this weird sense that these little books were a gateway to some mystery. Maybe it was the way Theresa had been wary, had picked her words so carefully for no reason I could discern. But there was also that powerful, vivid experience of staring at the mural in the palace, the forest and mountains filled with detail that was almost Mannerist in form. One thing I knew about the Mannerists: every symbol was important, freighted with meaning.

I began to read more slowly, looking up every word I did not know. The storylines were pretty much the same thing over and over— Fyadar and his friends, or sometimes a friend had a solo adventure, fighting the invaders and defeating them. I began looking at the details, comparing Gran's stories to these.

Most of the details matched my memory, except for the mysterious Xanpia, who was sometimes called Shanzana, especially when she appeared on certain mountains. She was occasionally called an angel in a few stories—I couldn't tell if those were older or newer ones. My grandmother had never described what she looked like, so I'd pictured her like Tinkerbell in the Disney version of *Peter Pan.*

As I thought back, I had a persistent image of it being a question about Xanpia that had resulted in an end to the stories: after that, Gran said I was a big girl, and she would read aloud to me from real books— George Macdonald and Andrew Lang and in French, *La Fontaine Contes.* They were all fiction, unrelated to real life. Responsible people never mixed fiction with real life.

Two things hit me on that second read. One, brief references to Saint Xanpia's Blessing. It was so buried among mostly Roman Catholic talk (which you'd expect among mostly Roman Catholic people) and terse references to the different mountains that I nearly went past it. This Blessing was teamed up with the word *Vrajhus,* which was not defined in the dictionary. From the context, it seemed to translate as magic—except that they also used the word Magus.

Not for the first time I longed for access to the Internet. But there was no computer in the house. From what I could see, electricity of any kind was a relatively new thing—like hot and cold running water, from how the fixtures seemed to be jerry-rigged in the bathrooms, not matching the enormous, ancient porcelain tub on feet that probably had been filled by buckets lugged up from the kitchen until relatively recently.

I prowled around the room once, struggling against a strong wish to ask Alec. I wished he was there, but I didn't wish he was there. I wished he would show up after I'd proved him wrong about Gran, and everything would be . . . would be . . . would be what?

I flopped onto the bed and picked up the next book.

By late afternoon the difficult Germanic handwritings began to look like *wmwmwmwmwm.* I kept at it, hoping to crack the mystery, until I heard running feet on the stairs.

Theresa knocked, and on my shouting "Entre!" she burst in, face red and sweat beading her hairline.

"Did you read them?" she asked.

"Wonderful!" I enthused. She beamed with delight, so I said, "But what's Saint Xanpia's Blessing?"

Her smile vanished. Both hands flew to her mouth.

Totally bewildered, I waited until she said slowly, in that wary voice again, "It is an old thing. Mere superstition, many say. Please. Do not trouble yourself over such things."

She scooped up the books and fled.

NINETEEN

WELL, THAT WAS WEIRD, I thought as I looked at the now empty desk. But it was time to get ready for Aunt Sisi's party, so I couldn't track Theresa down and ask for an explanation.

Like I said, I'd grown up with a serious shortage of relatives. Mom and Gran had been alone ever since their arrival in the United States, and Dad's parents, who'd been even older when they had him than my parents had been when they had me, had passed away before I was born. If Dad had cousins, he'd never met them; his parents had come out to California after the war. So I was excited to meet my first relatives, but a little apprehensive as well.

I bathed, then took out the floral print dress that I'd worn to the wedding. As I brushed out my hair and pinned it up in a chignon I thought back over the day, wondering why that "Blessing" would upset Theresa. Should I pretend our conversation about the Fyadar stories had never happened? I'd take her behavior as a clue next time I saw her.

It was tall, sober-faced Tania, and not Theresa, who knocked on my door to say that the car was here for me. As I went downstairs, I looked around for Theresa. Nowhere in sight.

"Mam'zelle," the chauffeur said, opening the car door.

We didn't drive all that far—a couple miles of winding streets along which the houses got grander and grander. We pulled up in front of a handsome, fresh-painted house built along Roman villa lines, complete to the Corinthian columns. Remembering what Alec had said about Ruli's habits, I waited where I was. Sure enough, the chauffeur came around to open the car door for me.

I was halfway up the tiled steps when the double doors to the house opened. The man who greeted me at a Proper Distance was an honest-to-Jeeves butler, right down to white gloves.

"Mam'zelle. By what name shall you wish to be announced?"

"Kim . . . Atelier."

As soon as it was out, I grimaced. Stupid—the impulse had been to hide my last name so Alec wouldn't find out I was here, but he was going to find out anyway, wasn't he? The people I was about to meet were connected to him politically, and maybe by blood, and were supposed to be by marriage soon. The point being, one thing I'd learned through watching my friends who have large families—relatives talk.

But Jeeves was too intimidating for me to try a "No, wait, call me Murray." So I figured, go with it. In a way, the Atelier thing was legit, and I could always explain later once I'd found a sympathetic new cousin or two.

Jeeves led me inside a handsome hall with gilt molding and eighteenth-century decorative motifs in ovals high under the ceiling, instead of the folk art patterns I'd seen in more humble houses, when glancing in windows.

The stairway was lined with portraits. Coroneted ancestors in silks and velvets with ribbons and medallions and diamonds gazed into eternity over my head as I trod up the stairs behind Jeeves. One fellow in handsome eighteenth-century garb was tall and blond, another in a military tunic and medals was tall and dark of hair; there was a third, a gorgeous woman brown of skin, her tilted dark eyes smiling, her black hair curling charmingly in Directoire ringlets. She was dressed magnificently in early nineteenth-century velvets; she and the ones whose dates came after her all had the single dimple.

When we reached the top of the landing, with great ceremony Jeeves opened doors carved in ancient acanthi, discreetly gilt. When I got to the threshold, he announced in a hieratic voice, "Mademoiselle Atelier."

My first impression was of light and grace in fine eighteenth-century cabriole furniture. A crystal chandelier—with real candles—graced the rococo ceiling, and one wall comprised an exquisite eighteenth-century trompe l'oeil depicting a sylvan scene with elegantly brocaded and bewigged ladies and gentleman frolicking in sedate groups on an island among Nature's delights.

Aunt Sisi's guests—my relatives, I mentally tested the idea—wore the elegant modern version of high fashion as they stood in sedate groups near the white marble fireplace. A few sat on delicate chairs with embroidered silk cushions that would have been kept behind museum ropes at home in LA.

Aunt Sisi stepped forward with her hands outstretched, and folded her fingers around my hand for a brief clasp. She was wearing a beautiful raw silk evening gown of sea green, and emeralds glittered around her neck. "My dear child. May I present to you your family?"

Silk and emeralds. My pretty floral print day dress—ostensibly something her own daughter would wear—was completely wrong for this gathering. Obviously what she considered informal was my major formal. *What's formal to her? Wigs and brocade?* I thought as she made kind, set-the-girl-at-ease compliments on my appearance. *I should have let her send me a dress.*

In the background a quick susurrus of whispers, and an audible "Good God! I don't believe it!" was followed by a hasty "Hush, Percy!"

With a guiding hand on my elbow, Aunt Sisi took me around and introduced me. Most of them were von Mecklundburgs, but not all.

Robert von M. was a bulky middle-aged man who flashed a big smile as his manicured hand closed around mine. I gathered he was younger brother to the current duke, who was not there. "Quite a miracle, your popping up," he said in upper-crust English.

His wife put out a languid hand and murmured, "How charming," in Gran's French accent.

Parsifal ("We call him Percy") von M. was an awkward redheaded beanpole around my age with an enormous chin that hinted at Hapsburg connections. He seemed too stunned to speak after his earlier outburst.

I went around the circle, shaking hands when offered, nodding and smiling at those who didn't put out a hand. The names began to blend, especially as everybody said some variation on "charming" or "miraculous."

By the time I had made the circuit of the room, that "miraculous" began to tweak at the back of my neck. As a kid I was the skinny bookworm nobody noticed. My after-school hours were taken up with books and ballet, so I reached junior high pretty much oblivious to the complicated signals of in-crowds and out-crowds.

My initiation happened in eighth grade, after I was picked to dance the lead in a school production over a popular girl who had expected to be picked because she was popular. Her posse acted super-friendly.

I was thrilled to find myself one of the in-crowd until I finally started cluing in to the extra edge to smiles, the extra meaning to compliments, to quick looks when I wasn't supposed to notice. Then suddenly I was supposed to notice—that's when they started in on me with the word needles about my dorky clothes, my dorky hair, my dorky books falling out of my backpack, my dorky house and dorky dad with a beard and my dorky life, until I was emotionally bleeding.

They fed off that, like a bunch of thirteen-year-old vampires. Their enjoyment of my humiliation hurt far worse than their insults about my dorky everything. Mom made my favorite foods and said they must not have happy lives at home to want to make my life unhappy; Dad told me that the less I showed of the hurt, the sooner they'd leave me alone; and Gran had assured me that living well, and with grace, was the best answer. All of which was sensible, but life isn't sensible at thirteen.

Right before they went for blood—when I was wondering if I'd imagined those looks, the extra in voices and smiles and gestures—my neck got tight with warning.

I felt the same grip of warning now.

Supermodel-skinny Cerisette von M. gave me a long up and down. You know how usually when you catch people staring they look away, or smile, or at least blink, but she didn't do any of those things. She gave my print dress—which had been expensive, by the way—a look like I'd been caught Dumpster diving, and then asked what I'd seen so far in Riev. Her tone was polite—barely.

Honoré de Vauban (not a von M.) was tall and slender, with slicked-back black hair and elegant clothes—he looked to me like a cross between Christopher Lee and Bertie Wooster. He wanted to know how I thought the city compared to Paris. They seemed to find that question funny, for there were quick exchanges of looks, and a politely fake chuckle or two.

Then Morvil Danilov drawled, his pale blond eyebrows lifted, "Was it amusing, to take the public tour?"

"Yes." I fought the urge to back away from them. What had I done wrong? Was it against the law to wear a day dress at a fancy shindig?

Danilov's version of the dimple quirked the corner of his lopsided smile so that it seemed more sneer than smile. His voice was soft, his drawl cultured. "And Paris? What amusements did you find there?"

"Whom do we know in common?" Cerisette asked, leaning against Danilov as she blew cigarette smoke past my shoulder.

"Atelier," Robert's wife repeated. "I don't believe I've met the name in Paris. How odd it is, that we never knew about one another. You did say you live in Paris, Mademoiselle?"

A servant passed by with drinks on a silver tray with a coat of arms worked into its elaborate frame. I reached somewhat blindly for a drink that I didn't want as I fumbled mentally. I'd been two seconds from asking their advice—from telling them about my experience in the palace, and winding up with my question about Saint Xanpia. After all, these were my cousins. I'd thought they'd be thrilled to discover that Gran wasn't killed in the war.

A fast glance; no, the soignée Cerisette did not look glad, or even welcoming. When I met her gaze she stared back with a hostility I sensed, even if I couldn't quite see how she did it.

My question dried up: I could not see her, or any of them, eagerly reading handmade comic books, though maybe they had as kids.

Meanwhile, there were *their* questions.

"Paris," I repeated, after a couple of pretend sips of whatever it was in that goblet. The fumes were extremely strong.

Cerisette's eyes widened. "Pahr-r-r-eee," she said slowly. "City on the Seine? In France?"

Robert's wife made an arch motion toward Cerisette's diamond-braceleted wrist, a play slap. "Naughty!" She used the French word, then added, "Cerisette has always been naughty. She never believed in miracles even as a child."

Robert laughed, and Cerisette pouted in her mother's direction. Then she turned back to me, and this time she, too, spoke French. "You lived in Paris?"

I got it then—these people, apparently my only living blood relatives, thought I was a fake. No, that was wrong. They thought of me as a skeleton in a closet, popping out to . . . what?

I could have reacted a number of ways. Polite and vapid monosyllables—a sickly grin as I pretended to have fun—fear and a hasty retreat. The decision took no more than a heartbeat: I was glad I hadn't given them my last name, or anything at all about my life. I was not going to expose to their oh-so-well-bred disdain my easygoing, cake-decorating hippie mother or my wild-haired father and his clocks and Roman miniatures.

I felt my spine lengthen and my shoulders brace as all my years of ballet plus Gran's training gave me the sort of weapons-grade deportment we assume for the stage. For I *was* on stage. "No. My first visit was recently." I took a single sip from the fragile cut crystal. "I've been living in more exotic climes. Think of Rio, or Istanbul, or Florence. Or Venice. Quite inspiring to the artistic soul, is Venice."

"Rio?" Robert's wife repeated, perfectly plucked brows arched.

So far I hadn't—quite—lied. Then Cerisette drawled, "Most extraordinary, none of us ever encountered you at *our* schools."

Oh, why not lie. I was never going to see any of them again, that much was clear.

"I didn't attend school." I gave a tinkly laugh twin to hers—even tinklier, and plunked the crystal down on a passing tray. "I had tutors." I said it in my best French.

"Tutors?" She repeated as if she'd never heard the word before, then exchanged looks with Danilov. I sensed her taking aim again.

"Yes . . . they let anyone into these schools, these days." I matched her drawl. "Maman says we simply cannot be too careful."

"But . . ." A blonde about my own age in a black Valentino dress slid her arm into Danilov's as she cooed, her lips barely moving a millimeter, "Dear Elisabeth has hinted your circumstances are sadly reduced."

"You mean, we don't have any money?" I waved an airy hand. "Ah, too true! We gambled away a fortune in Monaco. Lost another when Hong Kong reverted to China. And a third vanished into the trunks of multinational corporate pirates. Ah, well, easy come, easy go! After all, what is money for but to be spent?"

"Yes, what else?" Percy said eagerly, echoed by Honoré de Vauban.

Waving my hands languidly in the manner I had adopted when pretending to be their missing Ruli, I spun ever-more glorious tales about my bohemian life. Lisa and my other fencing partner Kara would have been staggered to discover that the one wintered in Morocco and spent the rest of the year in her Scottish castle painting miniatures, and the other made her living shooting documentaries in the African wilds so that she could earn enough for her real vocation, which was breeding and training Lipizzaner horses for international dressage.

The sheer magnitude of my snow job made my reckless temper fade and I began to truly enjoy myself. And they swallowed it right down, as if the wilder I got, the more plausible it all was.

Robert had begun on my father (who I was about to reveal was a mad scientist genius with secret labs under half the Rocky Mountains, because I knew how much Dad would love it when I got home and told this story) when the door opened on a late arrival. I was finishing up about a bogus paternal cousin, "Yes, she lives in utter seclusion when she composes scores for films . . . pardon? No no, she is forbidden by contract to reveal—" when a male voice, laughing, cut through the well-bred hubbub, "Maman, what did you—"

Attention snapped to the door. I gazed across the room into slanted black eyes. I comprehended a tall man, a bit taller than Alec and about his age, with wildly curly light hair drifting down onto his shoulders and a rakishly crooked smile.

Unlike the formal guests he was dressed in a loose shirt, open at the neck, and baggy old slacks. He entered the room with an unhurried, careless step; it was obvious his lack of correct wear didn't disturb him in the least.

He exclaimed, "Good God, Maman, surprise is right."

Taking no further notice of his other relatives, he strode forward to clasp my hands in his. His long hands were warm and his squeeze firm as he carried my hands to his lips, one then the other. "You must be the missing Marie's daughter, are you?" He glanced past me to his mother, smiling. "Where did you find her? Or did she find you?"

"I found her," Aunt Sisi said, face and tone cool, her hands—long, like her son's, but thin—posed calmly. "Taking the Sunday tour of the palace grounds."

I turned back to the son. He was still smiling, but I noticed a vein in his high temple pulsing. He dashed back the lock of hair that had drifted down on his forehead when he kissed my fingers.

"Yes." My heart was pounding, too. "And you're . . ." *The Evil Count.* "Karl-Anton?"

The rakish grin flashed again. "Hell. Where are my manners! You'll have to forgive me. Yes, that's my name, but it's a damned curse. Tony is the best I can make of it. Do you speak English? I was raised in England, unlike Maman and Ruli—damn." He studied me closely from those slanty, Byzantine eyes. Laughter narrowed them as he added in a provocatively low voice, "Tell me, would it be incestuous to say you're quite a—"

"Anton, do not embarrass the child five seconds after being introduced," Aunt Sisi interrupted humorously. "May I get you something to drink?"

"Anything, Maman. Does Alec know?"

"I sent a note around to Ysvorod House," she said tranquilly. "I have no idea whether he is even in the country to receive it—"

As if on cue the butler opened the far door and enunciated sonorously, "His Excellency the Stadthalter."

"My dear boy, this *is* a day for surprises." Aunt Sisi's well-modulated voice broke through the elegant chatter without her lifting it at all. She moved forward with outstretched hands as Alec walked in, giving a polite smile at everyone, his cool blue gaze coming to rest on me.

TWENTY

THE PARTY NOISE started up again immediately: polite laughter, chiming crystal glasses, Robert von M.'s bluff male voice exclaiming in hearty welcome, as the entire party rearranged itself. Aunt Sisi touched the sleeve of Alec's beautifully tailored coat sleeve and guided him to the older generation, who circled big, cigar-smoking Robert. At my end of the room, Tony was the center of attention.

Tony asked in a lazy drawl who among them had attended the latest horse races in England, and what came of that recent drinking trip through the Bordeaux section of France in search of a new source for good wine? I saw no sign of evil, or even of political ambition in his breezy manner; he didn't act the snob like the rest, though his conversation was entirely leisure-oriented.

Twice he tried to disentangle himself from his relations in order to talk to me. The woman in the Valentino sheath leaned closer, pouting as she tried to tease out of him whether or not he was going to the Mediterranean for the rest of the summer. Tony's attention strayed my way, his smile as lazy as his half-shut eyes.

More drinks were brought around. I passed, as I'd begun to feel the effects of being in a small, tense room with too much smoke and noise; my temples twinged warningly and I wondered how long a stay would be considered polite.

Without any difficulty I picked out Alec's quiet voice from among the louder ones of the other guests on the other side of the room. Waiting for him to confront me was like waiting for an ax to fall: I could *feel* he was furious at finding me there, and I ached to inform him that these were my relatives, not his, and furthermore, I was free to go where I pleased and do what I pleased.

But he did not come. In fact, judging from the light murmur between the well-bred titters and chuckles, he was moving farther away.

Resisting the temptation to peek at him, I clamped my jaw against a huge yawn.

"Tired?" Tony had freed himself from the knot of relations. I found him next to me, brows raised.

I stepped back a pace. "Headache."

He made a careless gesture toward the door. "Come along, I'll see you off. No, you needn't pry Maman out. I'll stand host."

He gave a casual farewell to the group, and I followed him to the door.

Aunt Sisi exclaimed, "What, leaving, dear child?"

"Yes, thank you, but I—"

She smiled kindly. "I am so glad you were able to come. I shall hope to see you again before you decide to leave our little city."

Voices were raised in farewells; homely Percy, flushed with liquor, elbowed his way forward and planted a smacking kiss on my hand.

Alec lifted his glass in salute, his smile enigmatic. I zapped him with my forefinger, then got out of the room.

Tony spoke a few low-voiced words to the butler, then turned my way. "Car will be outside in a second. Here—" He reached behind me and shut the parlor door as he made a comical face. "Why Maman thought to call out the hounds of hell is beyond me. Must have been pretty fierce." He grinned engagingly, then waved a lazy hand for me to precede him downstairs.

I said, "Maybe she didn't want to raise false hopes. About your sister, I mean, and them thinking I'm Ruli. I guess gossip is going out all over to that effect."

"Do you care?"

I hadn't expected this question, but I shrugged and went for the casual. "Nope. I'll be gone soon. But hey, maybe hearing about me here might get your sister to show up. Do you think so?"

"Oh, hell, don't ask me. Everyone will tell you I don't take anything seriously. Including my sister. Who, everyone says, is probably off shagging the sort of tosser Alec will expect her to chuck when he does marry her." He laughed. "Here's what I think: do what amuses you most. How long are you staying?" he asked, opening the front door then lounging back against the car, arms crossed.

"Haven't decided," I said firmly. "I'm here to see the sights."

"Would you like a look at the best sites?" he asked as the Volvo pulled up. "Free tomorrow?"

"Well, I did have plans."

"Somewhere or someone?"

"Huh?"

Gesturing toward the car, he said, "If it's somewhere, I'd like nothing better than to give a new cousin a personal tour of our famous sights. All three or four of 'em."

"A tour?" I repeated, hesitating.

"It's free!" He smiled with easy humor. "And I know all the stories. Even the ones," his sudden, rakishly lopsided grin invited me to share a joke, "we don't tell the old parties who take the official tours."

I gave him the expected laugh, but I was thinking fast. Alec had told me this guy was a game player, and hinted that he was a troublemaker. I could blow off Alec's opinion of Tony for various reasons, including our argument about whether or not Gran had married my grandfather before leaving the country. But it seemed stupid to totally discount Alec's words when pretty much everything else he'd told me made sense.

So . . . what to do? I looked at Tony, who leaned against the Volvo waiting, without making any further effort to coax, urge, or bully me into agreeing to his offer.

He was a relative. So far, the only one beside his mother who seemed willing to accept me as a Long Lost. The worst I had observed about him was that he sounded like a typical rich slacker. So, if I go with him, what's the worst that can happen? He drones on about local politics, or brags about how much he wins at horse races?

I could sit through that, and smile, and nod, and after his tour was over, ask him to use his family influence to get me past the red tape so I could check the archives.

It was the red tape that decided me.

"That would be nice. Especially the juicy stories. What time?"

"You choose." He opened the car door with a flourish. "Earlier is better. If we get rain, the roads can turn into rivers."

"How's eight?" I ventured, thinking of my other errand. Also, eight in the morning might show how serious his friendly intent was.

He surprised me. "Eight it is."

"Got it." I gave him the forefinger.

He stilled, his gaze flicking from my hand to my face, then he grinned, and returned the gesture, with a whole lot more panache. "Good night."

Right before eight the next morning, I was trying to choose between my jeans—which would be practical—and my third dress, a full-skirted summer print with subtle patterns of leaves and twigs in shades of russet and gray. It was fine cotton, suitable for an interview, if I was able to get Tony to drive me to find Mina Hajyos. It was also comfortable, and anyway, I had no walking shoes.

I was still dithering when a horn beeped a couple times out front. That had to be Tony a couple minutes early. I'd half expected him to blow me off.

But a brief glance through an upper window revealed a sporty open red car and a tall blond guy, so I threw on the russet dress, jammed my feet into my sandals—and almost ran down Theresa, who had obviously been hovering outside my room.

I caught myself up short.

"Mam'zelle. I wish to apologize." She wrung her hands. "For my rudeness yesterday."

"It's all right." For the first time I recognized how carefully she'd avoided ever using my name. Was gossip zinging around that I was Ruli von Mecklundburg in a disguise?

I caught hold of her shoulders. "Theresa. It's okay. Hey, I've got my own stuff I'm not talking about. Not anything against you or your family, it's . . . sometimes, some things have to wait for the right moment. Seems you've got things, same as me."

She ducked her head, her cheeks flooding with color. "The right moment. Yes. Yes. Thank you."

"No thanks—" Another beep. "I have to run. Au revoir!"

When I got to the bottom of the stairs I found Tony leaning against his car, tossing the keys on his hand as he chatted with Madam Waleska.

Madam stood stiffly on her doorstep. In the daylight Tony looked even less like my idea of a count, with his tousled curly hair (that I bet his sister had wished she'd gotten, if hers was as straight as mine) and the eccentric clothes—a beautifully made shirt worn open over a black T-shirt and old jeans, the pants legs outside of what appeared to be handmade single-seamed riding boots. But the way Madam Waleska bowed each time he spoke reminded me of those invisible boundaries of rank that had nothing to do with personal worth.

As soon as I appeared he broke off what he was saying and addressed me in French. "Good morning, Cousin! We've an excellent day for touring."

"Bon." To Madam, I said in Dobreni, "I plan to be back in time for dinner."

This was as much to Tony as it was to her, if nothing else to establish limits to the day, but he didn't respond as he opened the door of the sporty British Austin. Candy apple red, right-hand drive, convertible.

As I settled into the left-hand seat, I pulled the ribbons of my hat down and tied them under my chin. Tony dropped into his seat without bothering to open the door and started the car. Soon we were bumping through the city at a brisk pace, the cobblestones rattling us thoroughly. The noise of that and of the engine prevented us from conversing much until we were beyond the limits of the city. A road wound up into the mountains past the quarry, and the car started the climb.

The high cliffs and dramatic forested mountain folds were breathtaking to my Los Angeles eye, the air pleasant. I was glad I'd worn the long-sleeved dress instead of a T-shirt; despite the bright sun the shadows were cool.

Almost at once we were enclosed in thick forest, but occasionally we broke free and were afforded spectacular views of the valley floor dropping away steadily below us. Tony drove carelessly, with one hand, and not very smoothly, but after a couple white-knuckled turns on my part he slowed down.

"Sorry," he called over the noise of the engine. "I'm so used to driving up and down these damned hills I don't think about a flatland passenger's nerves."

The remainder of the long steep climb up was done at a more sedate pace, punctuated by occasionally yelled identifications of buildings as we passed them. Finally the road leveled out enough for him to shift gear and reduce the grinding noise.

"Problem with this car." He smiled, tipping his head toward the engine as the wind whipped his hair across his face.

"I've always loved convertibles." *At home, I— no.* "Oh, it's gorgeous up here. Where are we going?"

"We'll go by the Capuchin monastery. It's quite old, and visitors always want to see it. The ruined Ysvorod castle as well. Then, not too far from there is the hunting lodge that used to belong to your family. Came to us through my mother, who made it over into a summer villa. We can have a picnic lunch on the grounds, if you're hungry by then. From there, let's see, shall we?"

"Sounds great." I settled back happily.

There were no personal questions at all from him during the early part of the tour. We did not stop at the Capuchin monastery (which is still in use, and people wanting to see it usually make appointments ahead of time, Tony explained) but he drove me around it so I could see the ancient carved stone walls while he told me some stories about medieval Dobrenica.

The ruined castle was mostly rubble, located near a poor village that was picturesque from a distance but up close reminded me of that farm

I found on my wanderings after jumping off the train. Like plumbing and electricity were decades from arrival. We poked about the fallen castle walls, and Tony told me about the cache of arrows and grapeshot discovered there early in World War II, which had been promptly used against the Germans.

"The arrows, too?"

"Yes." He gazed at the distant line of mountains that marked the western border of Dobrenica. "We hadn't been invaded since the Thirty Years' War. We used everything, old matchlocks and carbines, crossbows—those are actually quite lethal—to try to resist the Germans. Everything but boiling pitch. At the last, we blew up our own bridges and roads, but the Germans came anyway, and then forced our people to put up much better ones to their design. Which made it easier for the Russkis when they came from the other direction." He jerked a careless thumb eastward.

"Well, the Russians are gone, aren't they?"

"Not quite," he said, smiling, but I sensed an undercurrent to his words. Before I could identify it he went on again, the undercurrent completely absent. "Ready? From ruins abandoned centuries ago to the modern luxury of Sedania."

"What's that? Oh. The name of your summer villa."

"It was a hunting lodge, even if not much hunting was done there. Or hunting in the usual sense. Do you recognize the word? Corrupted Russian for *zhelanie,* desire—"

"I thought it meant wish," I interrupted.

He laughed and addressed me briefly in Russian.

"Not half as well as you do." *At school I—*

His indolent gaze crinkled with humor. "Wretched tongue, isn't it? No wonder most of 'em are crazy. Anyway, the word became an idiom for 'freedom' for us. Damnedest irony in the fifties. When the lodge was built, the name meant easing the inhibitions, one might say."

"Tell me about 'not quite.' Aren't the Russians gone?"

"The Soviets are gone, but the Russians aren't." He smiled sideways and jammed the car into gear.

For a time we climbed higher into the rocky crags, the engine roaring again. Then we crested a magnificent cliff like a rim of the world, and he slowed. "See that peak there, the squared one?" He pointed eastward.

"Yes—I think so," I squinted into the bright sunlight.

"Mother Russia can be seen from that height."

He took off again. We were going mostly downhill. He continued to drive with his left hand, leaning his right elbow on the car door and his hand on his forehead to keep the sun and the wind-tossed hair off his eyes, so it was hard to see his face. He commented idly, "So you've an interest in Dobrenica, have you?"

This was the perfect opportunity to broach my quest . . . but it was too perfect. I hesitated. He was friendly, but what did that mean? He didn't seem too concerned about his missing sister as far as I could see. But I knew that appearances could be deceiving.

I tried to match his careless tone, "Well, enough to visit it once."

The road abruptly narrowed. Spots of it were not paved and the turns, potholes, and dips into muddy water were frequent. But he drove it with undisturbed familiarity, and I gazed off into the distance, wishing I could have afforded a video camera to shoot these spectacular views.

Presently he turned onto an old paved road lined with two rows of venerable chestnut trees for two or three miles, then we rounded a hill. A succession of flowering shrubs opened onto a square building with numerous tall, narrow windows and a mellow limestone front. The windows had carvings over them, and corbels at each corner.

The drive was circular; the car rolled right up to the front, kicking up mud and gravel from the puddles left from yesterday's rain, and then we stopped.

"We're here," Tony said cheerfully, turning the engine off and leaving the keys in the ignition. "Ready for the grand tour? Oh, perhaps I should tell you, don't mind old Madam Coriescu, the caretaker. The Gestapo was rather rough with her when she was a kid—thought she was running messages for the resistance. Which she was. She's got a glass eye that's pretty frightful."

"No problemo," I said—belatedly noticing that we'd been speaking in English, not French. If he'd been testing me, I'd failed: I'd answered in my usual flat LA American.

No reaction from Tony. "This way. Ah! Good afternoon, Nonni." He went on in Dobreni to the old woman in the long black dress who peered out the front door.

The elderly woman's face was thin and lined, her short gray hair a bird's nest. She grinned in delight at Tony, obviously glad to see him; the glass eye had yellowed with age. When we reached the doorway he leaned down to kiss the top of her untidy head. "Dear Nonni, this is Mademoiselle Atelier. We're going to look through the house, then we'll eat out in the courtyard. No, I brought food. Pedro packed a basket. We shan't disturb your restful slumbers."

Madam cackled, bowed to me and to Tony, reached a gnarled hand up and patted him on the cheek, then vanished.

Tony said, "She's an old dear, but it's her son who keeps the place up. And his boys, when they're around. Now! The grand tour. The gallery lies directly through here, the scene of countless Dsaret drunken orgies—"

"And von Mecklundburg orgies?" I added as we entered a high-ceilinged room with a huge marble fireplace at one end with a pair of splendid crossed swords mounted high. The white ceiling was edged all round with scrollwork and stylized floral patterns that seemed vaguely Byzantine. Directly below was a huge polished oak refectory table surrounded by high-backed wooden chairs. Satin pillows cushioned the hand-carved chairs, a crest carved high on each chair back.

"Not here." He lifted a shoulder. "This is Maman's lair."

Tony pushed open the discreet wooden door at the back. We traversed a short hall and then walked into a gleaming white and copper kitchen. "Fairly modern kitchen, Pedro insists on that. He's my mother's chef. Trained in Paris." He gave me a wry look over his shoulder. "Be sure to ask her if her chef trained at Le Cordon Bleu if you want points with my mother. Pedro goes with her everywhere. Breakfast room in here—"

We entered an east-facing room with flowering plants in pots set in the corners. The ceiling here was lower, with a floral pattern all round the top of the walls.

"Note the private entrance." He lifted a brow in exaggerated suggestiveness as he opened a narrow door on the other side of the room, the door having been discreetly painted the same eggshell blue as the walls.

We trod up a narrow staircase. All the rooms upstairs had wide windows, balconies, and the floral stripe around the walls. The huge main bedchamber was bordered with laurel leaves; I was beginning to see symbolic patterns. Laurel leaves—royal. No, imperial.

The room itself was modern, the color a tasteful pale mauve. That, and the elusive vanilla scent of Jicky, an extremely expensive French perfume, brought Aunt Sisi to mind.

There was a library, a music room, and more salons. Everything fully furnished.

"Lovely," I said as we walked down the mosaic-tiled front stairs.

"Hungry?" was his reply.

"Starved. What time is it?"

"Midday."

"No wonder."

Tony brought from the car a wicker hamper covered with a pretty linen cloth and led me around the back of the villa to a blooming garden. Two low stone benches were shaded by an ancient oak. Here we sat down.

"You needn't be overly careful about crumbs," he said, setting out linen-covered, wax-paper wrapped packages. "The storks like the critters that forage on Pedro's bread crumbs."

"Storks?" I repeated, biting back the urge to say, *I've never seen one.*

"That sounds strange?" He cocked a questioning glance at me.

I shrugged. "Didn't expect them here—oh." I breathed as he unrolled a thin loaf of French bread that must have come out of the oven seconds before it was packed up.

"Pedro gave me enough for ten stout-hearted men." Tony extracted a slim wine bottle and a corkscrew. "I hope you're not like Cerisette and Phaedra, existing entirely on salad greens and an occasional olive for indulgence."

"I like food," I replied as he poured out a red Italian wine and handed me a glass. "I eat it up and work it off." I thought with regret of how long it had been since I'd had a good bout with the blades. Doing ballet stretches and lunges each morning didn't count as a workout. But I wasn't going to talk about that, either.

"Cheers!" He tipped his glass against mine, sipped. "Excellent." He smiled broadly. "Let's see what Pedro's given us . . ."

We had three or four cheeses for the bread, and two kinds of pastry with spiced meat filling, and several kinds of fruit. Then slices of a fragrant, moist lemon cake for dessert.

Tony asked me about Paris as we ate, and I easily described what pictures had been playing, what plays I had seen written up in the papers; after his encouragement I admitted how plodding and dreary I'd found a critically acclaimed postmodern play currently running in Paris, though I didn't tell him I'd seen it put on by students at UCLA. "Not that it was bad. Just the opposite. But so smug! How do you get moral superiority out of saying there is no point to anything?"

"Don't tell Ruli." He laughed, then finished his wine with a flourish. "Those plays never fail to send me to sleep when she or Cerisette bully me into going along."

I leaned back on my stone bench to stare upward through the interlaced green leaves and the mild blue sky beyond, while he started to pack up the remains. High above me an unseen bird warbled its song; bees hovered about nodding blossoms, their sound a krummhorn below the bird's soprano recorder.

It was time for a test or two of my own. "I'm sorry your sister's missing. I hope she's okay."

"Mmm." He smiled absently as he folded the picnic cloth.

"Must be hard on your mother. Especially with this wedding stuff coming up. She mentioned it the other day. Weird, to be planning a wedding without a bride around."

"Most of the planning she's doing would serve as well for a state funeral." His brows quirked. "They pegged you as a wild bohemian, the family wolves. So you've never met my sister?"

"No."

"Where'd you meet Alec?"

TWENTY-ONE

I BLINKED AT HIM. "How'd you know we met?"

"Give me credit for some observation." Tony lounged back on his bench, eyes half shut. "They said everyone else jumped like a row of electrified crows on a wire when first they saw you. As did I. Alec not only did not react, but there was no uncertainty as to your identity. It's never easy to sort out what he's thinking, but that much was obvious. He knew you right off, and could have been forgiven for some doubt. Unlike me, he's largely been spared Ruli's company in recent years. Also," he smiled as if telling a rare joke, "you knew him. And weren't exactly chuffed to find him there."

"All true," I said, still wary, though there was nothing threatening about Tony. So far.

"So, you met where?"

"In Vienna."

"Vienna," Tony repeated. "You were enjoying the sights? And . . . met up? By chance?"

"Yep. He thought I was your sister."

"Of course. He's been dashing around Europe on her trail for weeks. So you went to Split with him?"

I sat up. "You knew about that?"

"Wasn't that the purpose?" he countered, lifting a shoulder in a slight shrug, as if the whole subject was not to be taken seriously.

"Yes," I said slowly, wondering how he'd found out if he'd been in England attending horse races, or traveling around Bordeaux looking for wine. Oh yes, he was notorious for losing cell phones . . . but he certainly didn't sound out of the loop. And for that matter, why hadn't he asked me before? The questions, so sensible, seemed odd coming now. "Alec thought if she was hiding and sulking, if she heard about me pretending to be her, she'd come out of hiding. Or whatever. I did it because it was fun and a free trip, and it didn't seem as if it would do any harm."

"It didn't strike you as peculiar, the whole business?"

"Yep. Very." I stood up to shake out my skirt, which had gotten crumpled and covered with bread crumbs. "But he said the reasons were political, which meant ridiculous."

He flashed a quick smile. "So you didn't ask for any of these ridiculous political reasons?"

"Nope. None of my business."

"Then you parted on bad terms?"

"Why are you so interested?" I crossed my arms.

"Wouldn't you be?" He looked surprised. "Sister gone, intended in-law—incidentally the, ah, current guiding hand, politically speaking—looking for her, at the moment a mysterious cousin pops up. So Alec didn't find you, you were sprung on him by capricious fate."

"That's it, though I'd reverse the pronouns."

"And you exchanged family histories . . . ?"

"More or less."

"And secrets?"

"Like what?" I asked militantly, daring him to throw Gran's questioned marriage in my face.

"Well, for one, the Dsaret treasure, which you might legally lay claim to. You, no doubt, have been asking him where he's keeping it?" Tony's elbow leaned on the stone armrest, his cheek on his hand.

"A treasure? Never heard of it."

"Oh, naughty Alec." He chuckled as a gentle breeze stirred through his hair.

"You did say *treasure*? Tell me more."

"When it became clear the Germans were going to overrun us, a number of our former leaders put some effort into a secret project that

I guess had been going on for some time: consolidating some holdings, liquidating others, usually those in distant, troubled areas of Europe." He lifted a shoulder in a lazy shrug. "All our families were doing it, to some extent. Alec's father was particularly long-sighted—or his advisers were—in the matter of what to do with the cash when he got it. He invested everything. My family was not so keen in business. The king, before he transferred the reins of government to Milo, apparently converted his family's wealth as well as the major portion of the treasury to some liquid form, and it was hidden. Only old Milo—young Milo then—was told its whereabouts."

"It still exists?"

"Apparently. The Germans never found it, nor did the Russkis. It's possible they never knew about it. At any rate when my mother married, she was given her portion. Or, so she was told."

"There weren't papers, executors, that sort of thing?"

"We are sometimes medieval in these parts." He grinned, the long dimple flashing. "The lawyers don't yet control everything. So you might well have a claim. I've no idea what the laws say about descendents of natural children and inheritance. The point is moot since, at present, Alec *is* the government."

"My parents are married," I said slowly.

I trusted Alec to a degree. I liked Tony, but that didn't mean I trusted him, certainly not more than Alec . . . yet that stuff about the treasure was disturbing. If Tony was telling the truth, and there was a Dsaret treasure, and Alec knew Gran was the missing Dsaret . . . then why hadn't he told me?

What would Tony get out of a lie?

Maybe it was time to give him some info. A fair trade.

I said, "My grandmother was also married."

"What?" He paused, then continued to put the last of the items in the basket. "She married someone in Paris?"

"No. That's why I'm here—besides the look around. Gran never would have left this country with that man. Your—*our* grandfather. I'm the evidence she was with him, right? I know her. Have all my life. She would not have gone off with him unless they'd been married. So I'm here to find the record."

"There was no record," he said as he fit the cork into the wine bottle.

I shook my head. "Are you sure? Anything could have happened to it, what with the traveling and the war. They might even have married in Vienna, but I don't think she would have gone with him then. Not Gran. Anyway, she wears a wedding band to this day."

I glanced away from my hands to meet his slack-lidded, indolent gaze narrowed to intent. His voice was still casual. "I take it you're looking for proof?"

"Yep. But I'm on the trail. Several trails. I was hoping you might get me past the gatekeepers to look at official records, for one of my trails. Are we going?" I added as he packed the wine bottle in the hamper.

"Yes, but first, why don't we give these to Nonni? She loves Pedro's French tidbits, and her grandsons do also—" He stopped.

A fall of sweet sound, silvery laughing music, echoed up the hill through the thick fir trees as if from another world.

At first I thought it was from some fantastic bird. I ran to the low stone wall, ignoring the moss, and peered into the tangle of standing birch and wild climbing roses left for a century to ramble, twining up and over an ancient, freestanding stone portal. Golden light poured through in slanting rays between young trees, among which faces peered back at me. Not birds, but strange faces blended of green and brown, with tangled curls of bark for hair, and feral catlike eyes.

The giddiness gripped me so hard every cell in my body seemed to shift, as if I rode through a silent earthquake. Then footsteps broke the weird spell, slamming me back a step or two. Sight: an old ruined door with medieval carving on it, blurred by moss and time, standing a way down a slope; sounds: the complicated arrangement of a violin concerto of Ernst Bloch's, played on a wind instrument, and Tony's leisurely step crunching grass and gravel as he joined me at the wall.

"Sounds like Nonni's grandson is home." Tony smiled.

"He's—he's good," I said numbly, peering at the ancient door. No faces, only the dappled sunlight on leaves tossing in a gentle breeze. *Fanciful.*

"He studies music at the temple school. Practices up here, usually when his father's not around to complain about how little he works and how much he plays."

"That's not play, that's art."

"As you say, he's good." Tony cocked his head in the direction of Riev. "But we have a remarkable number of good musicians in our corner of the world, and his father feels that a steady paycheck as a carpenter is a better future. What were you looking at so intently? There are a lot of folktales about that old door."

"Like?"

"Nonni told us stories about its being a magical portal. Ruli and I used to run back and forth through it when we were small. Trying to get to the Nasdrafus."

"You mean to Fyadar and his friends?"

He laughed. "So you heard those old stories, too? Of course—your grandmother must have told you."

"What did you find?" I asked.

"Nuts, insects, and leaves, exactly what you see now. Ruli got bored pretty fast, but I didn't give it up as a bad job until Alec joined us the next summer, bringing Milo's sensible rationalism to answer such questions as, if magic worked, why couldn't it do something useful like save Nonni from the Gestapo?"

As the unseen musician began again on the transcendently soaring piece, Tony remained by my side as we stared at the tangled wood; I was intensely aware of the slow rise and fall of his breathing below the white shirt, the fine scars, like knife cuts, on his long hands. His still profile as he gazed down at that stone doorway—no portal, only an old abandoned arch, its walls long rotted or tumbled down. This time I didn't imagine any bizarro faces, but enjoyed the brilliantly played music accompanied by the sough of wind in fir branches, and by the far-off cry of birds.

At the end he said, "Shall we go on your errand?"

As we trod around the hunting lodge to the front where the car was parked, I sensed his gaze from time to time, though he kept an arm's length away, out of my personal zone.

Except my personal zone had widened, and I was aware of all the clues that add up to covert interest: he was watching me, and not idly.

I shifted my focus to the wooded mountains all around, so thickly wooded they were blue. I glanced skyward, appreciating the clear air, the complicated woods scents, and the crunch of our feet in the gravel.

Tony said casually, "What was it, ballet?"

"What?" I felt that zap of nerves I get when I think someone is looking at me and it proves to be true.

He lifted his hand in an arc. "The way you move. You studied ballet?"

"Yes." Without shifting one inch closer to me, he'd crossed from personal space to intimate space.

I was *so* not going to go there with him.

So I said the obvious, "There's the car." And the subject dropped as he politely held my door open for me.

He vaulted over into his seat, fingers tapping lightly on the dangling key chain as I tied on my hat. Then he said, "Who've you discussed your search with?"

"Mmm? No one. You're the first."

"I'm honored, and I promise I shall give you whatever aid you desire." He flicked my knee with his fingers—casual, even impersonal. The way he would to a kid, or an old friend. "How's that?"

"Great." I sighed. "Thank you." And, as we started back down the avenue of trees, I remembered Mina and her village. Maybe I could get Tony to take me, instead of finding my own ride. But how far away was it, and was it too late to descend on her unannounced?

Tony rolled onto the road and began to accelerate.

"It's time to head back," I said, as the afternoon rays began flash in slanting beams between the branches sheltering the road. "I do have my errand."

"I thought I'd show you one more thing."

"What's that?" Surely he'd know where Dorike was. Wasn't his castle on Devil's Mountain?

"The Eyrie. First built in 1210, everyone always says it's a fascinating old pile. And the view from the towers is the best in the entire country."

"Oh! Sounds wonderful." How perfect was that? Straight to his castle—and maybe we could stop at Mina's on the way to it, or on the way back. "How long a drive is it?"

"Not very."

As the road wound ever higher, the scenery opened into sudden vistas overlooking lacy waterfalls, plunging valleys that vanished into shadowy mystery, and striated cliffs that hinted at dramatic tectonic shifts millions of years before.

Before I brought up Mina, time for a last test. "I know it's none of my business, but how exactly do you and Alec disagree?"

He shrugged. "Thought you weren't interested in politics."

"No, but I am in people."

Shading his eyes with a long hand and driving with the other, he said, "Alexander and I have . . . let us say . . . two different plans for regaining our autonomy. He arses around without doing anything, like his old dad."

"Anything what? You mean social and fiscal change?"

"No, I mean getting rid of potential trouble."

"Fighting? You can't take on Russia—that's like a gnat going after an elephant."

He laughed. "A gnat can bring down an elephant if he does it right," he said. "Never mind. You're interested in people, not politics, and I am interested in both. Tell me, did Alec send you here to make your search?"

"No. He thought I went to Greece. I didn't tell anyone I was coming. It was no one's business. Certainly not his."

"What? Even your people?"

"Pe—oh, family. No, I'm not telling 'em until I know everything. How would you like to tell your mother that her brand new relatives all think she's a ba—" I choked off the word and stared at Tony in total dismay.

He flashed that rakish smile. “Bastard? No, I would not like to tell my mother she is a bastard.”

“Dude! I’m sorry.” I grimaced. “I didn’t think about what it would mean. To your family. If he did marry Gran first.”

“A proper cock-up, eh? Though it might be worth it, to see the expression on my mother’s face.” He laughed, hair tangling in the wind as he downshifted, and the car jetted up the narrow road.

TWENTY-TWO

I'D FINALLY MET Rupert of Hentzau.

"It's your timing," he went on, pleasantly and kindly. As if we shared a big joke together. "If accident really landed you here just now—this month, this week, even—it almost makes me believe in cosmic forces, or at least in cosmic humor."

"I'm not here to cause trouble for anyone," I stated.

"But you already have." His tone was unaccusing, even friendly.

"Then I'll make amends. On my own."

"I salute you for being so cooperative." He flashed a grin at me, his teeth white and even, a reflected sun glinting in those black eyes which made them not lazy at all, but acutely direct.

My danger sense—obviously hibernating until now in the Clueless Tent—finally woke up. Except there'd been no threats, no dire hints, not even any anger. We'd had a lovely picnic and pleasant conversation . . . but I was not on my way back to the Waleskas.

So far I'd agreed to everything. On the surface, no trouble. Maybe it was time to make it clear I wanted to go back.

He was driving faster, in spite of those lengthening shadows, accelerating hard on the straightaways, and taking corners with tight control and scarcely a touch of the brakes. The lowering sun's rays slanted between lichen-boughed trees, splashing molten light in speckled patterns here and there in the deepening shadows. The grass at the verge blurred at our speed; the farther scenery changed like a fast-forwarded video.

"How much farther is this Eyrie?" I asked.

"Another half hour or so."

"It's getting late, and Madam Waleska expects me. And I'd hoped to get my errand done before we returned."

"What is your errand?" he asked. "We'll make time for it. I promise."

No way was I mentioning Mina until we were safely on the road back to town. "Tell me about the Eyrie?" I asked.

"It's built in four layers on top of the highest mountain in the country, which is called Riev Dhiavilyi. Oldest part of the castle laid down in 1210, with sections added every three or four centuries afterward. Portions of it are comfortable, I assure you. All the amenities—except, unfortunately, a phone. The cables, which aren't reliable even at the best of times, were destroyed by some enterprising Russkis on a raid a few years back, and between one thing and another we haven't been able to restore them."

"So is this a sightseeing tour, or—"

"An extended visit to the home . . . lair . . . seat, depending upon your partisanship, of the blackguardly von Mecklundburg family. Full of history and scenic as bedamned. You'll like it, I assure you."

"*If* this is an invitation," I began.

"Hey. Bear with me! I'm trying to make it sound like one," he returned, flashing another grin—all in fun, utterly without threat.

But the wheel was in his hands, and his foot on the accelerator.

Okay, I walked right into this one. I gripped my hands in my lap. *Let's see if I can walk right out again.*

". . . a stream-fed pool, though the weather's rarely warm enough for outdoor bathing," he was going on. "And not long ago, to get ready for a visit from my whingeing sister, we hauled a DVD player and a few boxes of films and shows up there. Were you born in the States? I rather wondered if all that wank I heard repeated last night after you left was a payment in kind. Not that I blame you a bit, you understand. I think I would have done the same myself."

I said numbly, "I take it you've had your sister up there all along. No wonder you weren't searching."

Alec, you were so right.

"I get away whenever I can. Large as the place is, sometimes I need to put a country between myself and her bleating or I might have to, as my stiff-arsed British cousins say, extend the patio." He grinned, taking the seriousness out of the threat.

"Why stick her up there at all, since you don't like her company?"

"There we return to your detested politics, Cousin Kim. I would so hate to bore you."

"I wonder how you can look your poor mother in the face!" I remembered her reaction to me in the chapel: the shaking hands, the tense eyes. "What a crappy thing to do."

"She should be grateful to me for taking Ruli off her hands. You'll give Ruli sympathy and company, and she'll use you as a handmaid. And maybe—with any luck—you'll help her discover a sense of humor. I do appreciate the lack of hysterical invective, by the way."

I kept my hands in my lap and my head averted, face as calm as I could manage, though I was furious. One thing for certain: if he was holding his sister, then having both of us would give him an edge over Alec that I did not intend he should have.

So I had half an hour to think of an escape. When I did act, I couldn't give him the slightest clue beforehand.

Tony took the corners at enough speed to cause the car to lean. I hated the idea of jumping out and maybe falling down a cliff. But even if I didn't fall, a sprint along the road wouldn't do any good. He could stop the car and be after me in about five seconds flat. If he could run as fast as I could.

A quick glance at Tony. He drove with one hand on the wheel, the other hand shading his eyes as we moved in and out of deepening shadows. Despite the idle pose we were racing at a dangerous speed for these mountains roads; his open shirt rippled in the wind, revealing the black T-shirt that showed the contours of his arms and the outline of six-pack abs. Tony might act like Mr. Laid-Back but he was in shape. He was also at least half a foot taller than me. Considering the fact that we shared a lot of athletic genes, there wasn't much chance I'd win a fistfight or a foot race.

I squashed a strong wish to be back at Sedania, where I could grab one of those swords from over the mantel. Too late for that. I'd have to watch for another chance.

First, hide my intention. I sighed. "Madam Waleska will be looking for me if I don't show up soon."

"She knows you're with me," he replied. "Since she believes you're my sister—using a fake identity for some reason—she won't question your giving it up to go home. The family will talk for years to come about the night Ruli von Mecklundburg danced at her daughter's wedding. You are a mystery, Cousin Kim. What is your name? Is it Atelier?"

"If it will annoy you, I'd be happy to change it to Dsaret," I said sweetly.

"Don't be angry! Think about the serenity of a mountain retreat. Everyone gasses on about how healthy the air is—I suspect that's because it's too cold up there for germs. I'll keep my promise to help you to discover your proof that Grandfather Armandros was a bigamist. And with twin sisters! My respect for him grows daily. Have you any clues to go on?"

"Nothing." To bolster my image of meek acceptance, I added, "I was hoping you might get me past the red tape so I can check the official records."

"Which official records?"

"Any of them."

"For church records, you'd go to the bishop in Riev. All of the royal funerals, coronations, baptisms, and most of the marriages—except the hasty ones—were conducted right there in the cathedral. You didn't ask?"

"No. At first I didn't speak the language well enough, and then, well, things started happening too fast."

"What makes you think these records haven't been gone over thoroughly, at least once?"

"I want to see them for myself," I stated, glad the engine-noise hid the sudden slamming of my heart as I spotted dust ahead in the trees. Someone coming?

"I'll get an interview for you, though I suspect this is familiar ground."

"Thank you." I tried not to sound excited as I saw my chance ahead.

Tony had slowed to drive onto an old wooden bridge which spanned a rushing river some thirty feet below. As he passed the center, with a noise of bleating and more dust rising in clouds, a flock of sheep converged on us from the other side. They had surrounded the car within seconds, and Tony was forced to slow to a stop. He leaned back, muttering an unheated curse. He kept the car in gear, one foot on the clutch, other on the brake; one hand on the wheel, the other gripping the gear shift—

I pulled my feet up and flung a leg over the car door.

Tony reacted with startling swiftness, jamming the gear into neutral and reaching for me. He managed to grasp my right ankle with his fingertips.

I had enough presence of mind to restrain the urge to kick out at him, which would have enabled him to better his grip. Jerking my ankle against his thumb, I snapped free and whirled out of the car.

"Shit." He laughed. "Don't be a fool."

The car was closer to the left side of the bridge than the right. So I only had a few sheep to dodge around—stumbling as one butted against me in silent protest—before I reached the rail of the bridge and could run along beside it.

Tony rammed the hand brake on, jumped out and came after me, and despite the sheep, he was beginning to close the gap with such speed it was time for desperate action.

So I vaulted over the bridge rail and stood on the outer edge, clinging tightly to the rail with my fingers. Below was a sheer thirty foot drop to the rushing water.

He stood in the center of the bridge with sheep swarming around him and lifted his hands. "Kim," he said with some exasperation, "come back here. Please."

"I don't want to go to your damn castle," I snarled through gritted teeth.

"Right." He took a slow step toward me, and I slid away along the rail. He stopped. "I'll take you back to town."

I needed to go about six more feet before I would be over the middle of the river. A quick glance down showed that depth could not be judged, and too close to the sides was the white water indicating rocks.

Tony held his hands out wide. "Truce?"

"What is it," I demanded, ignoring his offer, "about the guys from this place? Do you always pull the pirate shtick on women? No wonder they run off."

He laughed. And took another step.

I slid away, watching him unwaveringly—and knocked against a stanchion. I clutched feverishly at the rail to steady myself.

Tony bit off an exclamation. Then said with care, "You didn't have trouble with Alec, did you?"

"If being knocked out and stuck on a train qualifies as trouble, yes."

He had reached the rail about eight feet from me. Leaning idly against it, he gave a crow of laughter. "*Alec?* I'd love to've seen that."

"I wish you had been in the starring role," I retorted.

"So that's how he got your cooperation in Split."

"No," I said loftily. "I jumped out the window on the train."

His eyes widened briefly. "I wish I'd known that," he said, leaning the other elbow on the bridge rail. "What happened them?"

"Nothing more to tell. He got my cooperation by *asking* for it." No need to ruin the effect by mentioning that my escape had been short-lived.

"Poor Kim! Ill-used by us damned Dobreni." He took a slow, cautious step. "Please get off that thing, you're scaring me." Another step. "I'll take you anywhere you like."

We stared at each other for a long moment. He was smiling, wind blowing in his blond hair, the long hands so much like my own leaning carelessly on the rail. I glared back, clutching the rail.

"I don't believe you." And, bracing myself: "So I guess I'll have to—"

He lunged.

If I hadn't decided to jump, he would have got me, too. As I'd suspected, he could move fast when he wanted to, but so could I.

A brief, panicky moment as his fingers snatched inches from my wrists—I yipped—and fell away through the cold, breezy air.

I barely had time to wrap myself up into the cannonball dive we'd used as kids, high diving at the municipal pool. Cannonball jumps make an almighty splash but don't hurt, and one doesn't go down too deep.

I hit the water like a rock. My breath smashed from my body as cold water closed over my head. I fought my way to the surface, propelled by an uncompromisingly strong current. Kicking and gasping for air, I fought my dragging skirt, then turned over to see if Tony had come after me.

He was still up on the bridge. I caught a glimpse of the last of the sheep milling past him as he leaned on the rail watching me, his head bright in the afternoon sunlight.

Watching to see where I climb out, I thought.

Cold as it was, not to mention fast moving, I couldn't resist sticking a hand out of the water and giving him the point-and-shoot. He grinned and twiddled his fingers as the white water swept me into the center of the current. I struck out, swimming hard to stay with the current, keeping a close watch for rocks as the river swept me along.

The next time I risked a glance back I'd already been swept completely beyond sight of the bridge. At least the water was rain runoff, rather than snowmelt, or I wouldn't be writing this now. It was chilly enough, and I was moving fast downstream as the river bent and twisted. Remembering those waterfalls glimpsed from the drive, I worked hard to swim to the side, hampered by my skirt, which acted like an anchor or drag sail.

Water splashed in my face—I paddled hard to avoid rocks that seemed to come at me at freeway speeds—then I nearly choked when I caught sight of a strange, barky face peering beneath the limbs of a willow. Splashing hard I lunged up, trying to blink water out of my eyes. My foot encountered a rock long enough for me to shove against it.

I fell with another splash, but when I came up, I was within a few arm's lengths of the bank. I'd passed that rocky point—I risked a look back—nothing. *Of course* nothing!

When I faced forward again I almost missed it—a long branch reaching into the water, somehow caught between a couple of huge boulders. I caught the strongest twigs in a death grip. The water tried hard to suck me past, but I pulled myself hand over hand along the branch, grimacing at pricks and scrapes.

As soon as my feet touched ground I surged out, panting and shivering, falling heavily onto a mossy stretch of rock-strewn mud. It was slimy, too; my feet slipped out from under me when I tried to stand so I crawled up until I reached a tangle of thick shrubs. I grasped a branch and pulled myself up onto the higher bank, then collapsed on the long thick grass. At once flies and gnats came to investigate. Slapping at them, I sat up again. A tug on my scalp made me realize I'd lost my hair clip, and my braid hung in a sodden rope around my shoulders, bits of twig, leaf, grass, and mud caught in it. My hat had also disappeared down the river. The late afternoon breeze ruffled briskly over my scalp, making me shiver.

As soon as I stood up the brisk wind caressed me with all the balmy warmth of an industrial refrigerator. I knew the only remedy was to dry out and walk fast, so I started slogging my way up the steep, overgrown slope, wringing out my clothes as best as I could.

Okay, what next? I tried not to think about freezing night temperatures, or wild hills full of bears, lynx, chamois . . . are chamois carnivores?

The ethereal sound of a wooden flute echoed through the trees. Was it possible I was below Sedania? No, we'd driven too far for that, and the river had taken me farther south, not north. But the quick, butterfly melody, light and magical, reminded me of that unseen player at the hunting lodge.

I turned around slowly. Music is fine, but what I wanted was a human being to point to the road. If I could find the player, I could ask directions.

The melody changed to something vaguely familiar. Had my grandmother once played that? Memory carried images of our back porch in Los Angeles, and the breeze-tossed jacarandas sifting the westering light as my grandmother played songs on the piano that I never heard again after I began pestering her about titles and composers.

I lunged up the hill in the direction of the music, mentally forming questions with my nascent Dobreni vocabulary.

After trudging determinedly up the long, pine-covered slope I found a narrow goat or sheep track. I was no closer to the musician, but at least my climb got easier.

The track was fairly easy to follow, even in slippery, squashy sandals—my second ruined pair since I'd met up with my noble relations.

Anyway the spongy moss and pine needle–strewn ground was clear and firm along this narrow track, and it wound around treacherous rockfalls and impenetrable underbrush. I got my breath back despite my swinging pace.

The occasional low rays of sunlight had deepened to amber. I paused to catch my breath, peering through the towering blue-green spruce that soughed peacefully overhead, almost drowning out that breathy flute.

The player was moving away.

I hustled up the trail. I was totally lost, but somehow the idea of being lost within earshot of another human (except Tony, I amended mentally) was bearable. Totally lost without anyone for miles around wasn't, especially with dark fast descending.

When I topped a small rise bare of foliage, I stopped for breath, turning slowly as I listened. The view was sensational. The last rays of ruddy gold-tinged light flooded the valley. Above the rim of the distant line of mountains behind Riev, the reddish sun rested. Far below ribboned the dark blue gleam of the river as it crossed the farmland.

Behind me, smoke drifted gracefully up from beyond a mysterious close of forest. I no longer heard the pipes, or flute, or whatever it was, but smoke? That had to mean a house. Or even a camp. Or *something* with humans around.

I swung about, examining the slope. In the fast-gathering shadows I'd almost missed the narrow dirt road almost directly below me some two hundred feet.

And, in a loop lower than that, a turnoff.

Next to that, a sign.

For the second time, I started slip-sliding down a mountainside.

When I reached the halfway point the sun disappeared, the sudden shadow investing the forest around me with a sinister darkness. But I kept my sights on that sign: I didn't care what it said, I was going to head for the nearest town or village and trust to luck that Tony wouldn't want to advertise his kidnapping attempt by having people go out and search for me.

Presently I crouched on a bluff some yards above the sign and squinted down at it. The letters were in Cyrillic, and there were arrows before each of the three choices, pointing off in three directions. I almost didn't bother sounding out the second and third villages listed, as the first had 3 km painted next to it. The second was 5 km and the third 11—but that third one . . . I puzzled out the worn, rough painting—dor . . ee . . keh . . .

Dorike. Governess Mina's village.

Or another Dorike? No. I remembered the widow at Anna's wedding. *On Riev Dhiavilyi.* Devil's Mountain . . .

And we'd been on the way to Tony's blasted castle, probably at the top of this same mountain.

So this was definitely his territory. I sat back on my heels. Good news and bad news. Good news, maybe an ally in Mina. Bad news: I knew enough about local custom to realize that, if this was the heart of his family's land, there was a good chance that Tony *would* have the right in local people's eyes to search for a blond female on the loose, reason unstated.

I wavered for half a second, then slid the rest of the way down, and started marching for Dorike.

Darkness fell rapidly, and with it the cold intensified. My hair was dry enough for me to spread over my shoulders in a forlorn hope it would act as a cape. I swung my arms vigorously as I strode along. When the road became hard to see, I told myself at least no one could see me, and to keep my spirits steady I sang Loreena McKennitt and Mediæval Bæbes ballads, and when I ran out of those, I reached back to the stuff my folks had played when I was growing up, beginning with the Beatles, working through Joan Baez and Bob Dylan.

I was on the second verse of "Jack of Hearts" when the tinny growl of an old Volkswagen engine cut through my lousy singing. I looked back down the road where twin beams twinkled between the trees.

I ducked out of sight behind a broad tree trunk as a fantastically decrepit VW bug on four mismatched, elderly tires rattled slowly by in second gear. Four men had stuffed themselves inside, two with long-barreled rifles poking out of the windows. Each man scanned the bushes and trees at the sides of the road: I glimpsed the blobs of their faces turning this way and that.

I thought of telltale prints leading to my tree—but the headlights only illuminated the road ahead of the car, which passed me and kept going. I waited until the engine noise had vanished beneath the rising sound of wind in the trees, then I resumed my trek—this time quietly.

Once a sudden thrashing upslope frightened me into scrambling behind some brush as a low, canine shape swarmed by, plumy tail lifted. It was only a fox. It vanished, going about its business, and I marched on.

It seemed a thousand hours later that I was wondering if I had somehow missed a turnoff, or a sign, when I smelled the sweet, unmistakable scent of roses in bloom.

Wondering if I'd gone around the bend mentally as well as on this endless road, I tried to walk faster. When I got past the last dark stand of silent fir, the weak glow of small, whitewashed buildings appeared in the light of the moon. The road widened into three paths, the main one going straight through the center of a village. I had to be in Dorike.

Most of the houses were dark. I walked as quietly as I could, examining each cottage for any sign of the rose bushes I could smell.

I was so expecting the pruned shrubs I was used to at home that I almost missed it. There, at the other end of the village up a steep slope, I could see a cottage through the arched opening of a trellis covered with some enormous shrub that rambled in tangles, forming a natural wall up and beyond the house, in some places as high as an oak. The perfume of rose on the cold air clued me in: a close look revealed a mighty rose tree, or combination of trees, winding up the walls and over the roof of a roadside shrine like the ones I'd seen all over the countryside. The shrine was sheltered by the thick boughs of ancient skyscraping fir—like Sleeping Beauty's century-old garden.

Leading down from the cottage were stone steps that had probably been set in by hands five hundred years ago, if not longer. The cottage was small and round, its roof also shaded by huge firs.

The windows were dark.

In my ruined, mud-caked sandals, I walked cautiously up the neat flagstones to the low door, my dress bedraggled, my hair hanging limply down—hoping Mina Hajyos was not gone, or living with one of Tony's most ardent partisans, I knocked.

"Madam Hajyos?" I whispered, my gaze on an open window a few paces from the door. "Salfmatta Hajyos?"

Muffled sounds inside, a scraping, slippers on a wooden floor and then golden light flared, swinging: an old-fashioned lantern.

The door was pulled open a crack. Weak light touched my face and the front of my disheveled clothing. I got to the first word of "May I talk to you?" when there was a sharp gasp as the door flung wide.

"Durchlaucht," an old voice cried. "Princess Lily?"

The lamp was set down with a crash, and taking my hand in her two old ones, Mina bowed over it and cried.

TWENTY-THREE

IT WAS SO LATE, and I was so tired (and relieved) that at first I didn't think anything of her mistaking my voice for my grandmother's, though more than half a century had passed since they had spoken last.

Tante Mina—she insisted I call her that—spoke German and French, though she had not used them for many years.

Despite the lateness of the hour she insisted on tucking me up into a hand-carved chair as old as the cottage, with a bright folk-patterned quilt around me, while my clothes boiled in a pot on the hearth. In my hands I held a cup of a fiercely strong liquor that smelled like the drink at Aunt Sisi's party, only harsher—unblended with more civilized liquids. Mina perched on a small bench nearby, wrapped in a shawl. She wept quietly from time to time as I told her everything.

We'd both intended to sleep, but she asked a question, then another, and tired as I was, I got a second wind as I launched into the story of my life, right down to Gran's long wordless concerts.

And the fairy tales, which she stopped telling me.

"Ah, Fyadar," Tante Mina murmured, and wiped her eyes. "Yes I understand. All had changed for her."

"What had changed? I keep feeling that there's something secret," I exclaimed.

"I will tell you everything you wish," Mina promised. "But please. What brought you here to us, after all this time?"

I told her about my trip, and about Alec and Aunt Sisi and Tony. She clucked once or twice when I got to my meeting with Alec but did not interrupt, and she smiled and shook her head and mopped at silent tears when I described my afternoon with Tony. Her reaction to my B-movie escapes was a shake of the head and a humorous crinkling of old, dark eyes that said *good for you* even as her mouth pursed up expressing *not ladylike.*

"And so," I ended, taking another sip of that eye-watering distilled liquor, "I heard somebody playing a flute. Or a panpipe. Or something. But I couldn't find whoever it was. But I did find that road sign, and so I walked here, hoping there wouldn't be any search. From Tony, I mean. I might get you into trouble if I'm seen here."

"Then we shall make certain you are not seen," she replied with a tranquil dignity. "Yes, you are right in understanding that here in Dorike your rumpled cousin Tony is Count Karl-Anton Danilov von Mecklundburg, the duke's heir, and on this mountain he has at least the authority that the Stadthalter has. Therefore we must be like mice for a time, and think, but this problem is not insurmountable. And first you must sleep."

"But he's got his sister a prisoner up in that castle! I *must* get into town and tell Aunt Sisi! And Alec."

"Yes, yes, but we want to do it quietly, without notice, yes? I already know a way, when my son goes to Friday market. So you lie in this bed, and sleep, and when you waken you will eat a good hot meal and we will talk more. I will tell you stories about my darling Princess Lily. So good she was, and you, her granddaughter, and so like! Ah, God is good, truly." She smiled.

"I can't take your bed."

"You must," she said firmly, pushing me to the narrow bed with the fresh-bleached white sheets and bolster. "A night's sleep missed is nothing. To know about my Lily, to meet her daughter's daughter, ah, my life is worth much to me. Perhaps we can redress terrible wrongs. You lie down and sleep, and I will clean this pretty frock, and in the morning I will walk to the bakery and gossip." She buffed her fingers against her thumb. "I will hear if the count searches for the missing sister—or for a new cousin—with noise and to-do, or quietly."

"Oh, thank you, Tante Mina." I sighed as I lay down. Then I popped up again like a jack-in-the-box. "Please, tell me one thing first. She did marry him, didn't she?"

"But yes." Mina smiled tenderly. "You knew her well, how could she do else? She married him in secret. I know, for I was there. I shall tell you all when you waken again."

"Oh, Mama," I breathed as I sank back into the bed. But it was not her face I saw as I drifted into sleep, it was Alec's. What a pleasure it would be confront him with Gran's vindication, and my mother's. And mine . . .

In Los Angeles, an eleven kilometer hike in good shoes, on flat ground, takes maybe four or five hours of easy rambling. Up in the mountains with those steep hairpin turns, on rotten roads, in high-heeled sandals, it had taken me at least twice that long.

I slept through most of the next day, then woke to find my clothes freshly ironed and waiting. The air was savory with a good rich stew that must have cost Mina a week's grocery money. I knew better than to protest. Instead, I ate until I thought I would not be hungry for a week, and then went back to sleep after Mina told me she would stay at her son's for the night.

The day after, I woke at noon feeling fine. Mina was not around. I didn't dare go outside until I knew I wouldn't get her into trouble, so I sat there reluctant to even stretch, the one room cottage was so small.

Her kitchen was tucked in a corner, organized around an iron stove that looked like it might have been new in 1890. It was the most modern item in the place.

There were a few fine Sevres pieces in a corner cupboard. Against that wall was Mina's narrow, curtained bed. Next to that, both in range of the hearth, sat the one big, upholstered chair with an exquisite hand-crocheted antimacassar on its back.

Her things were stored in a couple of ancient carved trunks, and in a golden oak drop-fronted Biedermeier desk that might have been homely in 1820, but was a museum piece now, smelling of beeswax polish. On it, between statues of a nymph and another folkloric figure, was a small collection of leather-bound books, printed no later than the French Revolution. Those books and the crystal prisms on the lamps were the only decorative things in the place; the ceiling was low, age-darkened beams, the walls rough-plastered, with a crucifix and a couple of old Scherrenschnitte, or silhouette-pictures, in oval frames.

I read an old book of poetry until Mina returned, and then we had another splendid meal of steamed and buttered cabbage picked right out of her garden, poached freshwater fish, and slices of the rolled sweet bread of the sort I'd tasted at the Waleskas'.

By the time she took the scraps out to the pigs, evening had fallen. Conversation was easy until then—the village, the roses, the weather—but at last she brought a serving tray and set it down on the table next to the hearth.

With a solemn air, she poured us each a glass of heavy cinnamon-spiced coffee lightened by thick cream, with a dollop of that strong distilled liquor in it, and said, "They have been searching. My grand-niece Katrina, whose house is at the crossroads, reported that twice yesterday and once today she saw automobiles carrying men from the castle. They stopped and asked people if they have seen a young blond lady wearing a brown-patterned frock. They have not given a name, but rumor is flying about that the Lady Ruli is lost in the mountains." She smiled. "No one is certain. They all preface the gossip with 'they say.'"

I laughed. "Not so different from home."

"Not so different from wherever people live," she responded, smiling. "My son Pavel drives the village lorry. He will take you into the city early when he goes to market," she continued. "From there, I do not know—"

"From there, I'll take care of myself," I said. "Easy enough. It's getting there that would be a trifle difficult. I hope you'll tell Pavel how grateful I am."

"Pavel knows my love for Lily. He is happy to help her granddaughter. As for the count, Pavel thinks he would do better to resolve his great affairs without the imprisoning of Lily's granddaughter."

I laughed. "I second that motion! Tante Mina, I insist you sit in your comfy chair, and I am going to toast myself on this hearth here while I tackle the mess I made of my hair." I picked up the carved comb she'd given me, and sat cross-legged on the hearth as Mina sank into her chair and sighed.

"I promised to tell you about the marriage of my dear Princess Lily, and so I shall, but you must forgive me if I weep. No one but my good Vasilo, and he has been dead many years, has ever heard what I know and saw." She squared herself in the chair and took a fortifying sip of coffee.

"First I must go back. Lily was fourteen when I first came to her. I was twenty, and fresh from training. I was to teach her, but she already had the grace of a lady twice her age, and oh, she could play so beautifully on her piano. Even the king, who rarely praised his daughters publicly, said once after she played for us at Christmas that she could have gone into any concert hall in Europe and held up her head. And knowledge! Oh, she read, and rode the trails behind the castle, usually with the young Marius. They all called him Young Milo. Their duets on the piano gave us all much pleasure."

Mina stared into the fire burning beside me and talked for a long time. Her voice was low and steady, and she rocked back and forth in her chair as she talked. I listened to anecdotes about the lives of the twin princesses Lily and Rose as I combed out my hair and then fixed it in two long braids.

". . . Rose was silly and vain but not cruel. I think she flirted only to show that she had the power to attract Count Armandros. He was so handsome, and skilled at flirtation. But I saw him with Lily, for in those days young ladies were seldom alone. He was quieter with her. Not serious. Never that! But they talked, they did not merely flirt. With other ladies, including Princess Rose, it was always the flirtation, the wicked count."

She paused to wipe her eyes with a faded, much-washed hankie.

“There was a night, directly after Christmas. The snow was deep. She came in dancing in joy, from a late night at someone’s villa. A masked ball for Epiphany, I think it was. She and Count Armandros had managed to get time to talk alone. He asked her to marry him. She made a vow to do so. She warned me the storm would soon break, and it did. That was a terrible year, the beginning of our troubles.”

“But why?” I burst out. “Why should it matter so much whom she married?”

“Because of the Blessing,” Tante Mina said simply.

“I saw a reference to it in a Fyadar story, but Theresa Waleska wouldn’t tell me what it was. Why not?”

“Our greatest secret.” She glanced upward. “Long ago, Saint Xanpia was saved in our valley from the hordes out of the east. She and the orphans she hid in the Roman temple on the mountain. She settled here, and many are the stories of her miracles of healing, and her aid to the young, to the helpless. She was friend to all—not only the young, but to the spirits of forest and water and air.”

“Spirits?” I repeated.

Tante Mina leaned forward. “Princess Lily did not tell you?”

“No—” I was about to add *of course not,* but changed it to, “She told me stories about Fyadar when I was small, but then she said I should leave babyish stories behind and read books. I was eight. She never told me stories again, though we always read together.”

Tante Mina wiped her eyes again. “Oh, she must have been so unhappy. So alone. Except for your dear mother. I am glad she had her music.”

I didn’t want to say how dreary she had found it to take the bus from house to house to teach the basics to kids for years and years—most of whom didn’t want lessons, or lost interest long before they were permitted to quit by their parents. Back then, the teacher went to the students, not like now, when the students go to the teacher. Not that Gran ever complained, but my mother had said once, *“I didn’t inherit Maman’s ear for performing, so I figured out when I was little the best thing I could do for her was to show no interest in piano. That’s when I got into opera.”*

Mina had paused, staring at the fire in reverie. Then she broke through my own memories by saying, "I must resume. It is said that Saint Xanpia never died, but walked through the gate to the . . . the *Nasdrafus,* we do not have that word in French, perhaps *pays de fée?*"

Fairyland?

"Do you believe that?" I asked,

"But yes," she said, so calmly I found it disturbing, like when someone you'd always regarded as sane comes out with something totally crazy.

"Before she left us, the saint made a promise that when our kingdom was under threat, if our people all came together in peace on her day, September 2, then Dobrenica would be protected from the world by a borderland of the Nasdrafus. If there was division, the protection would vanish and those causing trouble in our world would be able to enter freely again."

"Protected by what? What does Nasdrafus mean? Is it something like purgatory?"

She touched the rosary on the wall. "The Church teaches us that purgatory is where souls go after death. The Jews also teach about a purgatory in Gehenna, though I am told that they have differing beliefs about such things. But we all are told that in the Nasdrafus, the living walk among many beings, some of those being those we think of as dead."

"So does that place, whatever it is, have anything to do with this other word, *Vrajhus?*"

"That is the word for the old powers." She smiled. "You find it hard to believe, when you were shown the way to Schönbrunn by your own ancestor?"

"I what?"

She gazed at me with her eyes wide. "You told me. I remember. You saw the spirit of Queen Maria Sofia at the Hofburg, where once she visited, the year after she married the crown prince. In those days they always made their visit to the emperor or empress. You described her exactly! Maria Sofia was a friend to the great Maria Theresia, who understood both worlds. Later, after the great empress died, our queen tried to convince Emperor Joseph not to reject all the old ways at once, but he was so fierce, it was said."

"So . . . you're saying she was a ghost."

She studied me, then sighed. "I can see you are polite, but you do not believe this, or about the Blessing. The count did not either . . . and at the end," she whispered, "I fear that Princess Lily gave up her belief."

If she ever had any such belief, I thought. My childhood was proof of that.

"If you check the oldest records elsewhere around us, you will discover times when Dobrenica vanished from mention. Whisht! Alas, someone always began a feud, or a skirmish, and then enemies found their way over the border again."

Okay. Maybe she wasn't crazy—it was unfair to think that way. Tante Mina was simply old, and old folks tend to stick to old forms, even when outmoded. Especially when outmoded. And I could see Theresa Waleska falling for romantic notions of magic and ghosts and the like.

But did *Alec* believe in that?

I remembered what Tony reported about Alec and that stone portal at Sedania. I wanted to clock Tony with his own picnic basket the next time I saw him (which I hoped would be never), but I didn't think he'd lied.

"The ritual when we wished to invoke the Blessing was a royal marriage solemnified on Xanpia's Day—September 2, celebrated in church and temple," Salfmatta Mina went on.

"So they were holding this superstition over my grandmother's head when they wanted her to marry Milo, is that it?"

Mina looked at me sadly. "How can you judge so easily?"

"I'm sorry," I said. After all, it's one thing to be modern and rational, but I didn't need to be smug and superior right in her own home. "I can't get used to the idea of ghosts. I mean, it makes no sense that anyone could see something without material form. Sometimes. And the person next to them can't."

"It is always easier to close the mind to what we do not wish to understand," Mina said.

"I'm closed-minded?" I said, surprised.

She set her cup on the tray. "Some do not like the responsibility that comes with such knowledge."

"Okay, I have to think about that," I said.

"Good. As for denying the existence of the Blessing, and the Nasdrafus, many, such as Count Armandros, felt the same. They said that the old ways of seeing this world, and others, are outmoded. Or are mere legend. In these modern times, how can miracles exist? Count Armandros did his best to convince my dear Lily that this was a way the old folk used to force the young to marry where told."

Then I got it: Mina had thought I was Gran's ghost when I first showed up on her doorstep.

"Have you seen ghosts?" I asked.

"Yes. Rarely, but yes."

"Did my grandmother ever see them?" I asked.

Mina made a negative motion with her gnarled hands. "Rose said she did, but it turned out to be a pretence. To gain attention, which she had for a while. Lily was as shamed as Rose when the truth was known. More shamed than Rose." Her lined face creased with a wistful smile. "The count chided my Lily for setting aside their love for superstitious nonsense. He did not believe the Germans would bother with our kingdom—and if they did, we would throw them right out again."

"So those who believed, like the king, expected her to marry Milo on that special day? Then the entire kingdom would . . . vanish?" *Shades of Brigadoon.*

"She wavered. The king took her alone to Sedania for Easter Week. We stayed behind in the palace, on the king's orders. He included Lily in the secret councils. Duke Milo also. He was seen riding and talking with her, and even playing duets with her as they had when she was small. Not in coercion, you must understand. He said, in my hearing, that the choice must lie with her. When she came down Easter morning the whispers said that she would go ahead with the marriage to Duke Milo."

Mina straightened herself in her chair. Her eyes stayed distant as she said softly, "It was Rose who brought about what happened, I have always suspected. Never a word was spoken by Lily against her sister at any time, even as children. Lily shared the blame for infractions because she thought it hard that Rose had a mischievous nature and was always being chastised for it. Lily felt bad to always to be held up as an example, which was so unfortunate for Rose! Ah well. She never told me, but after, in the few days left, she did not again mention her sister's name. I sometimes think Rose listened to a sprite of jealousy and taunted Lily with the fact that she, at least, was free to marry Armandros. Lily went to see her father and gave him a paper she had written. I never saw that either. She had me lock the door while she wrote some letters, and she told me, calm as the sky on a summer's day, that she was leaving that night. Leaving Riev, I thought, but never the kingdom. 'You must call me Mademoiselle, Mina, for I have no title,' she said.

"I begged her to tell me where she was going, I would go, too, to take care of her, but all she said was, 'I do not yet know. If Count Armandros comes with a priest, let him in. And if he comes alone, I will not see him.'"

Mina rubbed her hands across her eyes. "How it all comes back! The weather was so chill that night. How I shivered—I thought I would never be warm again. The count did not come, but he sent a message, to say that he had arranged for the priest and for the necessary dispensations, and she was to meet them at St. Paul's chapel at the old school. She wanted me to come and stand up with her, which I did happily, and even though the count had brought two friends to serve as witnesses, she insisted I was to sign as bride's witness."

Mina sat back, gazing down into the fire, the light softening the lines in her face. Her expression was tender, a little sad. I curbed my impatience: she was getting to what I'd come all this way to hear.

Presently she continued. "The priest was from the Cistercian monks high in the northern mountains. I was surprised to see him, for they do not normally mix in the world, but I thought there must be a family connection. The priest, he was young, and stiff and performed the marriage awkwardly, but as I said they are monks up there, and I expect he had never presided at a wedding, only baptisms and funerals. But it was done, and the count put the ring on her finger. Oh, I was crying and could hardly sign my name to the paper! After I signed, the count took me aside and made me promise never to tell anyone what I had seen that night. I was to say that when I left the princess to go to bed, she was in her room writing letters. This surprised me but I had no time to ask any questions, for then Lily turned to me and took my hands, and ordered me to go back. I pleaded and begged, but she said she was going to make a new life, and she had no right to ask anyone to give up the old."

Mina sighed, and pressed the handkerchief to her eyes.

I leaned forward, my heartbeat loud in my ears. "What about the marriage papers you signed? What happened to them?"

She frowned at the glowing remains of the fire. "My mind was bound up with Lily's leaving me behind. All I recall is the priest rolling them up and sliding them into a pocket in his white cassock."

"Ahhh!" I sat back. "Do you remember his name?"

"It was Father Teodras." She lifted her hand toward the north. "From the Cistercians, as I said."

"So then what happened?"

"She left with her husband, and I never saw her again. The rumor got around that Lily had left Dobrenica. Ah, that broke her father's heart, I can tell you. May I grind you more coffee, my dear? That hearth is so hard."

"I'm fine," I said quickly. "So then what happened?"

"There is little else to tell." She lifted her hands. "The count returned. The king had dismissed me, but his heart was so sore I forgave him, especially as I knew I kept the truth from him. The count sent for me in secret, and told me Lily was living abroad and happily. He arranged for me to assume new duties up at the Eyrie, until I married and settled here." She leaned over and touched her rosary, which hung on a special hook below a holy picture. "I offered novenas for her every night—and asked forgiveness for not speaking about the count's bigamy, a terrible sin. But who would it help if I spoke, and without proof? The times were so bad." She shook her head. "In truth, I was a coward."

"So Armandros went and married Princess Rose?"

"On September 2 that year. But there was no Blessing. The Germans came the very next winter. When it was clear we could not force them out the king abdicated, and then died, many said of a broken heart. The troubles had begun. The baby came two winters later, and poor Rose died almost immediately. She had risen straight from childbed and went to parties every night. So nervous and strange she had become! Always flirting and laughing. I have always thought she was unhappy. So the count was no longer married to two women. I prayed for his soul, too, and for the baby. We cared for Sisi as we did the other children, but none of them were like my Lily. Afterward my Vasilo died fighting the Soviets at the mines, but I then had the comfort of my sons."

"So . . . what does it mean, to be called Salfmatta?"

"I protect Dorike," she said. Her brow wrinkled in perplexity. "You could say in German Schutzmutter, but *Schutz* has a different meaning, I think, and the French is also different. But I protect us through my novenas." She indicated the rosary again. "And through my roses, which keep the vampires away."

"Vampires!"

She raised a small hand. "Do not worry. The boundary is strong."

"Oh. Uh, good." I never expected to hear that word from an old lady—but after all, the whole vampire legend came from this part of the world.

So . . . did that make it true?

What is truth anymore?

I shoved that aside as she sighed tiredly and folded her hands across her lap. "I am happy that Lily lives. And a daughter! Happy in America, with a good home, and a good man, and contentment. God is good, God is good," she repeated, nodding, then she said something surprising. "It would be proper for you to tell King Marius. For now the wrongs can be righted again."

"I'm sure Alec will have told his father about us already," I said, stretching out my cramped legs. "And if Alec wants to do this marriage thing on the second—" *I put Dobrenica above everything therefore I get trapped in politics,* he'd once said. Even to pretending to believe in magic? "—he'll soon know where Ruli is."

She nodded slowly. "Yes, that is true."

"One last question. Why do you think Gran would tell my mother that her father's name was Daniel Atelier?"

"Perhaps she did it because to depart from France with a German name, von Mecklundburg, would be to earn opprobrium. You must know how much all Germans, even those who had not wanted Hitler's government, were hated in those days."

"Gran certainly hated them," I said. "Or she wouldn't have left him. So I was told."

"I can believe it happened," Mina said soberly, looking old and careworn as she stared back into the bloody history of her youth. "Such angry partings also happened here. You must understand the strife in Dobrenica in the last days of the war, when it was clear that Hitler would fall at last. Each report brought news of further advances by the western Allies deeper into Germany, and that Hitler was fighting against his own military leaders. They were trying to assassinate him. Yet Stalin, who was just as evil, was poised to take us from the other direction. When the duke his brother died, and Armandros became duke, he called all the men to him. Vasilo came down from the castle and told me Armandros promised them that the madman Hitler was finished. But Germany still had planes. It . . ." She looked away, into the fire, then straightened as if she had come to a decision. "He wanted to protect his home, finally." She rose. "You must sleep again. Pavel starts for the city soon after three, to be at market in time to set up. You must be ready to slip into the lorry. I will wake you."

"Mina, I can't thank you enough—"

She reached up and laid a finger against my lips. "If your grandmother decides to come home, you must bring her to me so I can see her face. It is soon enough that I will see my good Vasilo again in heaven," she added cheerfully.

She got up and went about finishing her day's labors. I sat where I was, staring into the fire. I knew my first duty was to tell Aunt Sisi where her daughter was. And then I'd better tell Alec. I remembered his face at Aunt Sisi's. Would he even listen to me?

Maybe if I found Father Teodras and recovered the marriage documents. Then I could give him all the truth at once.

TWENTY-FOUR

IT SEEMED A minute later Mina was shaking my shoulder. The cottage was dimly lit by a candle on the floor. Mina had prepared hot porridge sweetened with honey, and as we eased out into the chill night air she pressed a warm cloth-wrapped package into my hand.

"Bread and good cheese," she whispered as she walked down the stone steps to where a dilapidated World War I era truck waited. "Eat this at dawn. God bless you, child."

"And you," I said awkwardly, bending down to kiss her forehead. "Thanks a thousand times."

"Wrap up warm now, and stay under the blankets."

Pavel was nothing more than a silent, bulky shadow. Mina waited as I climbed onto the truck bed and wedged myself between baskets of produce and bales of sheep's wool, and other goods difficult to make out in the darkness. Pavel's job, besides blacksmith and mechanic, was trader for the whole village once a week in the open air market in lower Riev.

I settled on folded quilts, and someone laid a heavy rug over me. With a lumbering lurch, the truck began to move. Pavel killed the engine. Lulled by the slow bumping of the old tires as Pavel expertly coasted the vehicle down the winding mountain, I drifted into a drowsing sleep.

I woke when the engine kicked in. As it putt-putted us across the floor of the valley, I fell back asleep.

When I woke, darkness had barely lifted. There were the familiar mounds of the rock quarry: we were on the outskirts of the city.

The engine stopped when we reached the open market, where people were busy setting up stalls and chatting. I scrambled off the truck bed. Pavel wasn't in view, but I figured he'd prefer not to find me at all than to hear thanks from someone he didn't even know, so I slipped between the flimsy barriers of two booths. The city proper began on the other side of the row of wagons and ancient, decrepit vehicles, with a long horse picket beyond; farmers still drove wagons.

Now that I knew where I was, I had to figure out how to get to Aunt Sisi's safely—all the way at the other end of the city.

I chose the narrowest streets and alleys I could find, avoiding the main streets, which were full of people heading down to the market. I had no idea whether a search was going on in Riev as well as on Devil's Mountain, and if so, what the searchers looked like. I also did not know if the Vigilzhi were on Alec's side or Tony's. Or which side might mean trouble for Yours T.

As I slunk across a main street, I remembered those guys watching me at the wedding reception. If there was a search, that would be the first place they'd check. So I wasn't going anywhere near the inn.

At least I had something to eat.

I ducked into a narrow, inset doorway with a laughing gargoyle carved over the archway. I stared up at the weatherworn face, half-bird, half-human, the ropy, muscular arms clutched around bony knees, the long toes like bird talons curled over the arch. The gargoyle's wings arched up above the skinny shoulders, creating a heart shape.

I wondered what it would be like to live in a house guarded by a gargoyle—growing up reading Fyadar comics in secret, and watching for ghosts on windy nights.

Was it true that I saw ghosts? This was an entirely different paradigm—a way of understanding the world. All the rules had changed, at least in this country. Maybe here it made sense to expect Alec, as the distant crown prince, to protect the kingdom by marrying on a specific day.

Time to get moving. I had three things to do: get to Aunt Sisi and tell her the news, then ask her to send a servant over to the inn to collect my clothes and other things. Third, hire a ride to Father Teodras and the Cistercian monastery.

I did not want to toil all the way up hill to discover Tony's red car waiting outside his mother's house. Even if Aunt Sisi would tell her son to act civilized, I didn't know if he'd listen. Not if he had his own sister as prisoner up on that Devil's Mountain.

The cathedral bells rang, echoing from stone walls and streets. Voices penetrated as well. Children's voices. I remembered Theresa's uniform. Her school was next to the cathedral—

—three or four blocks from me now.

I slouched up the street, lurked behind a potted juniper, and peered up in the direction I thought she'd come. The school kids walked in groups, some wearing the thick navy and white uniforms, others in equally old-fashioned brown uniforms.

I spotted Theresa with two friends, one in navy and the other in brown. That was a setback. I had assumed she would be alone. I pressed back in the shadows as the girls got closer, faces earnest as they talked in low voices. The girl in brown was tall and thin, with thick glasses and dark red hair worn in braids to her hips. The other girl had a round face and dark braids like Theresa's.

Theresa looked up—our eyes met. I jerked away, but then oozed back as her sharp face lengthened in surprise. She whispered something to her friends and all three homed straight for me.

"I hoped you would think to look for me if you returned, Mam'zelle," Theresa greeted me without preamble.

The other two girls nodded, one firmly and the other with a furtive glance back at the street.

I recovered from my astonishment. "Tony's people came and got my stuff, did they?"

"Yes. And then yesterday—"

"Hst!" the dark-haired girl whispered, motioning violently toward some distant kids.

The four of us hustled around the side of a steep-roofed house to a brick alley. A cat sat like a meatloaf on a high stone wall, tail hanging; otherwise no one was in view.

"Look, I don't want to get you into trouble," I began.

The dark-haired girl said in heavily accented French, "It was only Xani, a girl with nose trouble. She went down Prinz Karl-Rafael Street without seeing us."

The redhead and Theresa then exchanged glances. Theresa said, "Let us go to the cloister garden. That is a quiet place, and we can talk. We have time before our schools begin."

The other two agreed, and the dark-haired girl, with a grin of excitement, led the way back along an alley and then unlatched an unmarked door in the featureless wall that bordered the back of the cathedral's grounds.

Inside was an enclosed courtyard, visible from two stories of windows on one side. Theresa led us to some grass beneath a drooping willow, adjacent to a statue of a saint. "The sisters are at the school now, and we can talk here. Oh! Katrin and Miriam are my friends. They know what has happened, but they have already promised not to say anything."

I sank down as the girls gathered around me. "What happened?"

"The evening of the day you went on the tour with the count, at dinnertime, two men came. They said they had been sent by Count Karl-Anton. He had called them on a telephone from somewhere. They said Lady Ruli had decided to go home to Riev Dhiavilyi, and they were to pay what you owed Mama and to bring away all your belongings."

"I was afraid of that."

"So Mama packed up your clothes and they took them away, and afterward I cleaned the room, which is my chore. Part of the work is to wash and polish the floor, if the guest has stayed longer than one night. And so when I moved the armoire out, a thing fell and hit my head. It was blue jeans, and a blouse, and papers! I discovered an *American* passport, but in it was your picture. And I thought, there must be a reason. I thought also, Mama would feel she must send a message at once to the count. That is her way. So I showed the things to Anna and Tania. Anna said, a thing is hidden for a reason. Tania felt we should continue to hide your blue jeans, and your papers, until you came for them. She took them to her shop, where she said she put them in the barrel where they store the old and broken spectacles. No one would ever look there." She grinned. "And Josip added, that to tell everyone about the passport is to make everyone laugh at us, for much envy has come to Anna that you were at her wedding! Everyone thinks—as we did, at first—that you are the Lady Aurelia von Mecklundburg, you see."

"Be sure to thank Tania for me," I said feelingly.

"That is not the end. Yesterday, again at the dinner hour, the count came to us himself. Mama was excited. He said your papers were missing from your suitcase, and had you given her anything to hold for you?"

"Argh. Was he a bully about it?"

"Oh no, he was polite and pleasant. Mama was upset that we might have had a thief, but nothing else was gone, and she told him that when she packed your case with her own hands she had found all your things exactly as you always left them. So he asked to see the room, and he looked around, and even felt on top of the wardrobe, but no one asked me anything. If they had," she added seriously, "I would have said, no one *gave* me anything to keep, for that is not a lie."

I said, "I don't want to get you into any trouble, political or moral."

She smiled. "Anna said, if the reason is good, a small lie can be confessed and is forgiven. Tania agreed. So Mama said you must have taken the papers in a handbag on your outing, and had forgotten it somewhere, and the count should ask you to mentally retrace your steps and he said he would. He left. Josip told Anna and me at night that a man seemed to be watching the inn. And another was there this morning when I left."

"You are totally made of win," I exclaimed. When they looked puzzled, I hastily translated.

Anna blushed in pleasure, and Miriam's eyes were crescents of magnified delight behind her glasses as she whispered over and over, "Madeuffween, madeuffween."

"What's going on, is this. I am not Aurelia von Mecklundburg, who has been missing for some weeks."

"Ah, there was a rumor," Miriam spoke up for the first time. "Now gone, since you came."

"Well, I said nothing to anyone because I wanted to achieve my purpose anonymously, but I am the granddaughter of Princess Aurelia Dsaret."

Katrin gave a sigh of pure felicity. Miriam grinned, hugging her thin arms to herself. Theresa said, "Better, oh, so much better."

"My name is Aurelia as well, but you can call me Kim. When the count tried to make me go up to his castle, I found out that he's already got his sister up there. Anyway, I escaped."

Miriam's glasses flashed as she sat up straighter. Interpreting her expression correctly, I said, "I jumped out of the car when it was stopped on a bridge by sheep, and then I dove off the bridge. I climbed up the mountain, following flute music. But instead I found a road sign, and that led me to a—a friend. I hid in a wagon this morning in order to get back into the city."

Katrin's hand covered her mouth. Theresa bit her lip.

Miriam breathed, "Vrajhus."

I said, "What was Vrajhus? I really did get help from a friend."

Theresa exchanged glances with the others, then Katrin's long face turned my way. She said seriously, "It is Vrajhus that brought you there. The music on the mountain."

"Not . . . ghosts?" I asked, old habit making me embarrassed to be speaking the word like I was serious.

All three shook their heads. Not a grin among them.

"You must have heard one of Them from the Nasdrafus," Miriam said with a firm nod. "Guiding you."

Okay, it was possible. Anything was possible. If I had to accept ghosts, what was one more step? Except it was clear that no beings ectoplasmic or otherwise nonhuman were stepping out to guide me now.

So I said, "I don't want you to get into any trouble. *I* don't want any trouble. My intention right now is to get to the duchess to tell her about her daughter. And the Stadthalter should be told as well," I added. Whatever Alec thought of me—and whatever lay behind his neglect to tell me about the Dsaret treasure (assuming Tony hadn't made that up)—he had the right to know. "He and Ruli's mother can decide what to do. It's their affair. As for my stuff, if Tania won't mind hanging onto it for a while longer, until I know my next step—"

Theresa nodded vigorously. "I will wait for you, or for a message."

"Great. So, the duchess. First, I don't know if the count is there. He was driving a red car. Second, if any of them ordered someone to search for me, well, they would have described this dress and my hair." I indicated my long braids.

As great bells began to ring, Miriam jumped to her feet. "Fifteen minutes."

"Do you think you could sneak me one of those uniforms?" I asked. "That would get me across town anonymously enough."

"No, it will not do," Miriam said decidedly. "Every busybody shopkeeper will call out, 'Girl! Why are you not at school?' I know a better thing . . ."

"You can't make it to your school in time," Katrin said in Dobreni.

"No, I will say I have the asthma again. I will, too, by the time I run home and back here and then to temple."

"Please! Wait here," Theresa said to me, and I barely had a chance to call "thanks!" after them before they were all gone.

I couldn't have sat on the grass longer than about twenty minutes before Miriam reappeared, crimson-faced, carrying a bulging plastic shopping bag.

She plumped down and gasped, "It is ugly, a dress my aunt meant to be cut up and made into cushion covers. No one will miss it."

"Great!" I said. "Good thinking."

She colored even more. "And this is my own scarf. If Mama notices, I will say I lost it."

"I'll get it back to you, even if I have to wait until things settle down." I stood up and shucked my dress. "Another thing, though you've done enough—"

"Please!" She gazed at me, wide-eyed with anticipation.

"It's the Stadthalter," I said. "He should know as soon as possible, I guess, and a verbal message sent now might be faster than my finding ink and pen to write to him, or trying to track him down."

"I know where Ysvorod House is. If he is not there, they will know where he is to be found," she said briskly, in spite of the heaving of her thin chest and the dark flush of overexertion in her cheeks. "What is the message?"

"The count admitted to me that he has his sister, and I've gone to tell the duchess. But please, Miriam, there's no need to run anymore. Take it easy, okay?"

As I spoke I wrestled into the horrible widow's dress, which was made out of some scratchy material, dyed a rusty black and laundered until the seams were a different shade than the rest. The aunt, I thought as I scowled down at myself, must have had even worse eyesight than Miriam to be able to wear that thing.

I frowned at her, uncertain. "Are you sure you will be all right?"

"I would go if I died, like the Angel Xanpia," Miriam declared passionately, then scrambled to her feet and hefted her schoolbag. "I will go now."

"Miriam—thanks."

She flashed a grin and slipped through the heavy gate.

Miriam's kerchief was a subdued gray-blue. I tucked my braids up into it, making a lopsided bulge, and stuffed my russet sundress into the bag. The sandals couldn't be helped.

Affecting a hunched walk, with my face down, I slipped out of the cloister garden and started into the street.

I felt like I was outlined in Day-Glo paint, and my shoulders twitched against the tap I expected at any second, followed by Tony's grinning face, but I kept my pace slow as I crossed town.

Once I made it to the handsome streets that marked the posh section of town I had some difficulty remembering which street was Aunt Sisi's. Eventually I found it, and the house, and at last I knocked on the door.

The butler opened it, took one look at my getup and addressed me from a height of about ninety feet of moral superiority. "What do you want?"

I straightened up and said in my most formal French, "I wish to speak with my Aunt Sisi. Er, the duchess."

His jowls quivered with shock, but he pulled the door open, then led me up the stairs to a charmingly decorated sitting room done mostly in white and soft greens with touches of gold. Aunt Sisi was seated at a dainty and ruinously expensive looking desk, but when she saw me she jumped up and exclaimed, "My dear child! What—what has happened? Are you alone?"

"Yes, I'm alone," I said. "The, uh, dress I can explain. My other stuff has gone up to the castle with your son. Ah . . . I don't know how to tell you in a nice way, but Ruli is safe. But she's a prisoner at the Eyrie. Has been all along." And, as she continued to stare wordlessly at me, "Ah, I didn't *see* her, understand. But Tony told me, and I don't think he was lying about that. Uh, I'm sorry."

Her brown eyes were wide and shocked as she said slowly, "I fear I don't understand. What has happened? Who brought you here?"

"No one," I said firmly. While I was crossing the town I had resolved that the fewer people who knew who had helped me the better. At least, until things got straightened out. If ever. "I walked. I felt you'd want to know right away. Also. . . .I was hoping I could maybe stay here, at least until I decide what to do next. You did offer."

"Yes. *Naturellement!* You are most welcome. I will have a room prepared this instant—and—and luncheon. You must be hungry. Have you eaten?"

"I could sure use a glass of water, thanks."

"I will get you some now, with my own hands," she stated, a quiver in her voice. Her eyes were still wide and shocked, her face pale. I winced, thinking maybe I could have broken the news more gently.

She crossed the room to the door, then stopped and turned back. "No one knows you are here?"

"Not yet—" I said, hesitant to elaborate.

Violent knocking on the front door below carried all the way upstairs. Poor Aunt Sisi flinched as if she'd been stabbed. She pulled open the door. Male voices echoed up the stairs, then we heard quick steps.

Alec entered, looking slightly disheveled and grim.

TWENTY-FIVE

AUNT SISI TURNED sharply to me. "You said—"

"I sent a message." I shrugged. "I didn't think he'd get it so fast. That was lucky."

"Lucky indeed." Alec's light voice was distinctly ironic. Then he spoke more mildly to Aunt Sisi. "You've heard the news?"

"About my daughter?" She looked dismayed, her hands open in elegant helplessness. "This moment. The child just sat down. I have not had time to turn around."

"Why don't you take some time to think it over. Come to my place tonight. We'll discuss how to handle this matter. I'll take Kim off your hands."

"Oh, no, no, please." She gazed earnestly up into his face. "It would be a pleasure—so comforting—to have her stay. I promised her luncheon."

"She can get that at Ysvorod House."

"I couldn't—"

He gave her a short sentence in Dobreni, his voice so quick and low and I did not catch the ending word. Only the beginning, "Consider it . . ."

Her hands fell to her sides and she sighed, giving me a rueful smile. My heart squeezed; I admired her for trying to be soignée despite the maternal distress she'd revealed. "Very well. You will send when you want me?"

"Yes. Thank you," he said, and to me, "Let's go, Kim, if you are ready."

"I can stay here," I started, but as an implacable determination tightened his mouth I sighed. *Why argue? I'll be gone soon anyway.* But I felt sick and irritable that he was still angry with me.

He bade Aunt Sisi au revoir and followed me down the stairs. At the bottom, in the hall, stone-faced Kilber waited with the equally stone-faced butler. No one said anything as we all filed out, and Kilber opened the door of a plain black Volvo that was waiting at the curb.

Alec got in beside me, and Kilber went around to the driver's seat. Alec smiled. "Did you order that gown in Paris?" he asked with mendacious admiration.

"Why, yes," I simpered, batting my eyelashes. "It's definitely *le dernier cri.*" Then sighed. "You could have let me stay with my aunt without making a big deal of it."

The amusement faded. "And how long do you think she'd be able to keep you from a second invitation should her son show up? Five seconds? Six?"

"As I was walking, I thought it over. He won't dare show up. He must know I'd tell his mother about Ruli first thing. Anyway, you can be sure if Tony did waltz in through the front door, *I'd* be out the back door in *four* seconds."

"And into his mates' waiting arms."

I snorted a laugh. "Okay, well, I did worry about that."

He went on, "I heard what happened on the other day. If Tony gets another chance, he won't be so careless. You might have thought of that before running to his mother for protection."

"I didn't run to *anyone* for protection," I retorted. "She's Ruli's mother, and a mother has a right to know where her missing daughter is. I was only going to stay there until I arranged my next, um, errand. That reminds me. What was it you said to her in Dobreni? I got part of it. 'Consider it'—?"

He sighed, leaning his head back. "Custody," he said reluctantly.

"What?" I squawked. "Custody? So I'm *under arrest?* What's the nature of my crime? Or can you arrest people when you feel like it, whether they committed a crime or not?"

"One crime would be wearing that thing in public." He pointed at the dress, his smile whimsical, attitude wary.

Wary. I expelled my breath and said more quietly, "And I was planning to order a hat to match. Why 'custody'?"

His blue eyes looked tired. "A warning—to Tony. Your reasoning is good, but I still think he will visit his mother. Probably on the way right now. If he does, he'll hear what I said, and the word *custody* reminds them who holds Riev. That will grant you some freedom in the city, at least. So. I would never dream of trying to direct your movements—" The irony was back. "I suggest you consider before going up Devil's Mountain again. Who was the girl in the temple school uniform?"

"A friend."

"That's what she said when Kilber questioned her. 'I am Lady Aurelia's friend,' like she'd go to the stake with that line. Eh, Kilber?" Alec lifted his chin.

"That is true, Durchlaucht." Kilber's voice was like the gravel at the bottom of a well, his English heavily accented.

Alec turned back to me. "You have a knack for finding partisans. I suppose you weren't lost on the mountainside the past couple days?"

"I was okay. That's all *you* need to know."

"That's what I thought." He gave a soft laugh.

"Miriam has a good heart, and I suspect a taste for adventure. I hope there will not be any trouble for her."

"From me?" His brows went up.

"You, or anyone. I mean, if Tony's evil minions saw her go to the palace. I was worried about that."

Alec said, "The girl came to my house, and even Reithermann is prudent enough to stay away from my house."

"Reithermann? Who's that?"

"The chief, you might say, of Tony's evil minions. If you decide to hare off into the hills again, you will no doubt have the pleasure of making his acquaintance."

I sighed again. There were so many questions raised by this I did not know where to begin. *Easiest first.* "Then you don't live at the palace? I remember the guard said no tours when the Stadthalter is in residence. You are the Stadthalter, right?"

"Right. I don't live there, but most of the bureaucracy is settled there, at least in summer. Plenty of space, though the place is a damned icehouse in winter and we can't afford yet to put in central heating and better plumbing."

"You're short of money?" I tried to hide my elation at nailing him. "What about the Dsaret treasure?"

He didn't start, or betray dismay or anger, only mild question. "What about it?"

The car stopped then. A distracted glance out the window showed us parked at the end of a street of modest narrow, two-storied houses with tall windows and vaguely Baroque-style facades that made me think of the 1700s. On one side of us was a small park beyond which could be seen more houses; I wondered if this was considered a "new" neighborhood, so much of the city was far older. "Not that I mean to change the subject, but where are we?"

"At a place," said Alec, "where I hoped we could talk uninterrupted while I try to find out what you want to do next. We're in the northwest part of the city of Riev, called the Khonzhinya District, in case you feel the urge to slam out of the car and sprint off. I can take you to the train station—the train leaves for the Danube cities in less than two hours—or even to the airstrip if you want to get out of Dobrenica. You can fly to Belgrade, or Bucharest, even to Berlin. Or if you decide you have to stay for more of your . . . sightseeing—"

"You mean troublemaking."

"—I didn't say that. You did." He was obviously trying not to laugh. "Anyway, there's a quiet flat a few meters from us which you are welcome to use; as I say, you're perfectly safe in Riev, but there's the possibility you might want to grant the Waleskas a few days of peace."

"All right, cut the sarcasm," I said sarcastically, feeling more uncomfortable by the second. "So I've turned out to be a Joe Btflspk, or however it was said—"

"What?" He was still trying not to laugh.

"*Li'l Abner.* Or was it *Dick Tracy?* Never mind. A comic book character of years ago. My father collected comics when he was young, and I read them all when I was about ten. Anyway, Joe B. was a walking disaster area, through no fault of his own. And it's not my fault about any of this stuff. I was minding my own business. I'll even get out of town, if you want, as soon as my business is completed."

His expression had gone blank.

"Look," I said sharply, fighting the urge to flush like a teenager. "I admit I was an idiot to think no one would notice me if I came here. Okay. But I feel I had the right to come. And I promise I'll take myself off as soon as I'm done with my . . . my research. But until then, well, I'd like to know what's going on."

Alec's palm came down flat on the door-handle and sprang the mechanism with a clunk. "Then let's go into Nat's place, shall we? Kilber." He addressed the silent man in the front seat, "I'm here until the appointment with the bishop. Kim, where are your clothes? Kilber can get—"

"No he can't. Tony's got 'em."

"Ah, I should have thought of that. You do have problems with your wardrobe, don't you?"

"But at least I get my hotel bills paid," I gloated as we got out of the car.

Kilber took off at once, and Alec and I walked at a leisurely pace past the corner of the park and up the narrow street of quiet houses.

I gave him a scan. He was wearing a good shirt and slacks, much in his usual style. I tried to picture him in jeans and a black T-shirt, then realized what I was doing, and shook my head, hard, to dismiss the image of Tony that had blipped unexpectedly into my head. "So, whose place are we going to?"

"Belongs to a friend. Out of town at present, due back any day. Don't worry, you're welcome either way. Here." He stopped at the corner house abutting onto an intersection, pulled an old-fashioned key from his pocket and unlocked a narrow, whitewashed door. "She lives at the end because she gets calls day and night. Mostly night."

"She?" I repeated.

"Her name is Nat. That is, Natalie Miller, but she prefers Nat. Comes from the States. Wisconsin, I think. A doctor in obstetrics. The locals think of her as a remarkably adept midwife. She's got a thriving practice," he went on as he shut the front door and we trod down a narrow hall to a jumbled, small living area. "Surgery is in there." He pointed to the other door off the hall. "Living quarters here. Have a seat."

He was evidently at home in the cramped apartment; he lifted the Venetian blinds at the tall front windows, left the sheers drawn, and pointed toward a couch lined with unmatched pillows that I suspected served as a bed at night, with a minute table between it and an old chair covered with handmade pillows. The two side walls were stacked high with books and boxes. In back of the couch was a curtained off area.

I wondered if this Nat was one of his sweeties—or did he only date those with coroneted pedigrees?

"Something wrong?" he asked.

"Tired. And thirsty. I had to hide in a truck bed to come into town, and it started out at three AM."

He smiled. "I won't ask, I know you won't tell me. Want some tea?" He rummaged on a cluttered round end table beside the couch and came up with an enameled metal cup.

"No. Thanks. Not right now."

He set the cup down and dropped into the chair. "The water tap's in the surgery, and though it only runs cold she's rigged a clever way of heating and sterilizing water quickly."

"So, your friend is an American?"

"Born and trained there. She's been here for nearly ten years, and I met her in London before that. She was beginning a practice in an abysmally poor borough. When I found out she was trained in obstetrics and looking for a challenge, I brought her here. She adapted to the peculiar situation almost immediately. She was my first success."

"Peculiar situation?"

He smiled. "The sixteenth-century practices and beliefs, among other things. Older, even. I think you'll like her. Dresses like the most pious matron, and her modern technique is cloaked in archaic language that has won over a remarkable number of old diehards."

Among other things. Like Vrajhus, maybe? At Mina's, or talking to Theresa and her friends I could almost accept it, but here in this crowded apartment full of medical books and modern paraphernalia, in the light of day, I fell right back into the old rules. The comfortable rules. *Don't let your imagination get away with you, Aurelia Kim . . . People won't believe you if pretend your little stories are true.*

He went on, "Nat loves Dobrenica. Says it's the challenge she always dreamed of. Yet I think these trips to London to stockpile supplies are also trips to enjoy the benefits of modern civilization, while . . ." He lifted a shoulder.

"While?"

"While we resolve our difficulties. Anyway, when I spoke to her by phone yesterday, she offered her place for you, should you turn up again and need it. It's free."

"Free." I rubbed my gritty eyes and rolled my neck to ease tense muscles. "Crouching in an ancient truck does have its downside. Back to the Dsaret treasure. Why didn't you mention it before?"

"I didn't think of it until that last day in Split, and I decided I should consult my father before telling you. That was right before you dusted your hands of us."

I grimaced at the amusement in his voice. "I suppose Gran was disinherited from her share?"

"She wasn't disinherited from anything. You don't seem to understand yet that your grandmother was not cut off from us, it was she who cut Dobrenica out of her life."

He was right. But so was she. Feeling as if I was walking on a tightrope stretched over a windy canyon, I rubbed my eyes again, and shook my head. Even though I'd slept plenty at Mina's, exhaustion, or something, pressed on my brain like a stifling weight.

Too much has happened too fast.

"Shall I leave you to rest?"

"No. Thanks. Let's skip over my Gran for now. Tell me more about this treasure. So it does exist?"

"It does."

"And no one knows where? Except you and your dad?"

"That's not completely true."

"Tony thinks his family was cheated. That is, he didn't say it, but he sure implied it."

Alec said, "Tony's family got their share, and they know it. The question concerns the remainder. Part of that hoard is the old treasury, and part was to be kept in case your grandmother resurfaced. How long to wait was agreed between the old king and my father, but my father left things as they are for his own reasons. "

"Like?"

"Like he does not want the money to go toward financing Tony's private army."

"What? Private *army?*"

He leaned back, smiling tiredly. "Surprised he has one, or that it costs a king's ransom to equip one?"

"I want to know why. That, and how'd he get the troops? Advertise in *Soldier of Fortune?* Even today armed and trained minions have to come from somewhere."

"No need. Most of 'em are willing volunteers from his hills. Men our age who fretted under the Soviets as they grew up. He's also harvested a number of recruits from the valley. It's been a theory of mine that our crime rate is so low because the troublemakers skipped to the hills to play guerrilla with the rest of Tony's boys."

"That sounds like a solution." I laughed. "Send your criminals up to drill and clean weapons and war-game."

"Except," he said gently, "there's this problem with standing armies. You have to do something with them, or they get restless."

"I see. He said something about getting rid of the Russians."

"The von Mecklundburgs sustained a doubly hard blow under the Soviets," he said. "The 'trade agreement' the local authorities imposed on us as the grounds for their leaving is in reality little more than tribute. We send ore and silver, and we are supposed to get modern farm machinery in return. Equipment yet to materialize, except in token amounts—and it's old stuff needing repair—yet it's made fairly clear we must meet our quota. The von Mecklundburg mines provide most of it, and while I—that is, the rest of the country—subsidize the workers, you can see how it effectively makes us poorer. It's harder on Tony's family. The mines were their primary source of income."

I snorted. "So he gets a job."

"He's trying for a job. Mine." Alec glanced at his watch, then turned his attention back to me. "His other grievance also concerns land. That line of mountains is high, rough, and though the von Mecklundburg people despise the Russians they are the most Russian of all of us. Their dialect carries many Russian inflections. The higher villages keep traditional Russian mealtimes. Some of them use patronymic name forms, though that's partly because their clan structure is so complicated. A lot of them are Orthodox instead of Catholic, as their ancestors have been for over a thousand years. They are rabidly independent people. A certain portion of von Mecklundburg land—a few hundred square kilometers of the fiercest terrain—was kept by the Russians, and they are desperate to get it back."

"Ore?"

"Mainly."

"And Tony's gang aims to get it back any way they can."

"Yes."

"Maybe if you were to let them try, it would keep the pressure off here."

"Do you think a war would keep the pressure off?"

I shrugged. "No."

"You've got the idea. Right now this place is too much trouble for the returns the Russian consortiums get—a policy developed and fostered by my father."

"Which relates to the treasury being hidden?"

"Which relates to the treasury being hidden."

"And—" I hesitated, absurdity making me want to laugh, but there was nothing funny in this conversation. "—the Blessing?"

"So you found about that, did you?" His brows lifted.

"Yes. I also know you don't take it seriously. That's what Tony told me up at Sedania. Isn't that why he wants to fight, because guns and knives and the like are real? I mean, isn't it ridiculous to even *think* that if everyone huddles in your valley and you and Ruli get married on a particular date—"

"September second."

"—that the Russians, or whoever, won't be able to come in and zap you whenever they feel like it?"

Alec gave me a sardonic smile. "Ask Tony why he grabbed his sister," he said. "And if we do set her free—and she agrees to the marriage—see if he isn't right here on the second of September."

Agrees to the marriage. Here I was, enjoying the easy give and take, the way we seemed to be on the same wavelength. Then there's the Ruli thing, right in my face again.

There was also the other big question. "So you do believe in magic?"

"I will do whatever it takes to make peace. If the Blessing doesn't work—and I don't expect it to any more than it worked for your grandfather when he married Tony's grandmother, or for my father when he risked his life accompanying my mother back here under the guns of the Soviets, for a secret wedding on the right date in the right place—at least the people will see that we made the effort."

"Huh. How could Tony think he could win a fight against the Russians, unless he has a secret doomsday weapon? And is willing to use it."

"Tony would. Can't you picture that? Smiling, apologetic, he'd press the button and blow up their headquarters and then stroll out and watch a horse race."

I laughed. "I can totally see it. Not that he seems heartless. He was so nice to that poor old woman up at the villa. He was nice to me—even after he decided I was going to pay a visit to his castle, whether I wanted to or not. Though his laid-back attitude could be a front, and he's as mean as a rattlesnake."

"Tony is always laid-back. Life's too much of a game. But he does have a fairly individualized sense of ethics. How did you turn down his invitation, by the way?"

"Oh, I jumped off a bridge into a river when some sheep marooned his car."

Alec grinned. "I'd like to have seen that."

Wasn't that the same thing Tony had said, when I told him about the train? "At least he didn't jump after me."

"Not Tony. Too much effort. He'd count on catching up with you later, and then he'd congratulate you on your impressive efforts."

"To remind me they were unavailing. I won't go on any more tours with *him*. I wouldn't even go across the street with him. Though it was fun. Until the end. I appreciate your not gloating, by the way."

"Why should I gloat? You could have easily become his partisan. Might have become, if he hadn't been so premature with his efforts to get you up to the Eyrie."

I winced. "I guess I deserved that."

Alec's gaze was surprised, and direct. "Didn't intend any insult. Not all Tony's followers are like Reithermann. And Tony is reputed to be persuasive with women as well as men."

"Euch." I pulled off Miriam's kerchief and rubbed my fingers over my aching scalp.

Alec went on in the same reasonable tone, "Plus you're a blood relation. A good many of those up on Devil's Mountain feel that the duchess—and Tony—were cheated out of their birthright, and they support him without even knowing his politics."

"That's where the practical advantage of the marriage comes in, I suppose."

"Whether or not Nasdrafus exists, the marriage, and the treaty that we worked out among the leading families, would resolve some of the trouble we've inherited from the bad years. Marriage isn't always romantic, but it can be diplomatic."

"Certainly worked for the Hapsburgs," I offered.

He gave a quiet laugh. "And, as for your going off with Tony, I blame myself. If I hadn't been so quick to warn you off him when we first met—"

"I didn't go driving with him to spite you!"

"Did I misread you? I thought the face you showed me at Aunt Sisi's party was that of someone throwing down a war-gauntlet."

"I thought you were mad at *me*."

"No. Mad at the situation, yes. It would be stupid to blame you for wanting to meet your relations. I also didn't want to see you walk off with Tony into possible . . . trouble, but I knew an argument with you about that wouldn't accomplish anything beyond entertainment for the avid von Mecklundburg clan."

"Yeah, you called that right."

"In any case my honorary aunt and prospective mother-in-law worked so hard at keeping me away from you that I felt my part as bridegroom was to cooperate. Oh, yes. Loved the codswallop you gave them, and didn't deny any of it." He stood up. "Shall I leave you to a well-earned rest? First, do you want to meet with Aunt Sisi tonight?"

"I promised I'd cooperate." The last of the tension had drained out of me, taking the last of my energy with it. "I know I've caused trouble for everyone. I want to make amends, if I can, before I leave."

The tension had drained out of him as well, I could see it in the smile reaching his eyes at last, the open gesture of his hands.

. . . And now that we'd established détente, it was time for him to go. "Come to dinner. Nat's hot plate is less than optimal. Perhaps we can present Aunt Sisi with a brilliant plan."

"Okay. Sure. Where do you live?"

"I'll send Kilber with the car, as I think rain is on the way. Seven?"

"Okay. Fine."

"Nat would want me to encourage you to help yourself to anything. Oh, if anyone comes, if you wouldn't mind taking a message I know she would appreciate it."

"She's a doctor and doesn't have a phone?"

"Phones are unreliable up here." He gestured. "Cables sometimes work, sometimes don't. Even when the Germans, or the Soviets, weren't cutting them. Mobile phones never work, probably because of our distance from repeater stations."

"But there are satellites," I said.

He gestured toward the door, his ring glinting. "That is on the list of things to investigate, but investigation takes money, and so far, the governing council considers such things as mobiles frivolous. Most people don't even have telephones. I'm late—you'll be all right?"

I could feel the real question, *Will you stay here?*

"I'm okay. See ya later."

Again the smile, the real one. "Right."

The door shut behind him.

I'd see him again, and this time I didn't have to dread it. The thought made me feel better about everything than I had in days. What did it mean?

No speculation, I decided as I wandered past the examination room to the bathroom. Time enough to figure things out after I got my evidence from Father Teodras.

In the meantime, I'd look forward to dinner.

The cold water felt good when I washed my hands and face, but when I saw my ratty braids and the horrible widow's dress reflected in the round mirror nailed to the wall, I decided what I needed was a good, hot bath.

Nat's water-heating system was ingenious. I yanked on a cord that worked by pulley, connected to a pump in the basement. Gushes of water filled the cistern built over the tub.

I used the waiting sparker to light the propane tank below the cistern. While it was busy heating the water (which had a temperature gauge soldered on) I discovered a kettle set up on an electrical system behind the water heater.

She had rigged a converted kettle over the tub. You pulled the cord dangling from the cistern, and hot water poured into the punctured kettle, making a perfect shower.

While the water heated I prowled around aimlessly, looking at Nat's things. If people put things out, that's their public face, and it's okay to look. But I draw the line at opening drawers or cabinets.

She had an old mid-60s hippie "Welcome to Middle-Earth" poster, scenic snapshots (like Stonehenge at dawn) pasted on a wall; some framed, faded instamatic snapshots of smiling people in seventies and eighties clothes were stacked on a table in a corner. An abacus, a cloisonné jar, two jade luck-fish sat on crammed bookshelves. Lots of pretty embroidered cloth from Eastern European countries covered boxes, or hung on bits of exposed wall. A CD player, with tight-packed shelves of CDs ranging from 60's rock to old folksingers (mostly Dylan) to Alan Stivell and Dead Can Dance was plugged into an extension cord running to the back of the apartment.

I wondered what kind of creative wiring the house had—the bathroom had obviously been a pantry long ago, as the examination room had once been a sizable kitchen.

A battered pink toy box sat on the other side of the couch, serving double purpose as an end table. And in a corner, adjacent to an old metal bookcase packed with books, papers, and things stuffed untidily on top of the books, was a computer table.

Here I saw my first computer in this country—a sturdy, fairly new laptop, which I turned on. To my surprise it wasn't password protected, but all I looked at was the row of little icons down at the lower right-hand corner. Sure enough, the icon for Internet had a red X through it. No cable, no wi-fi, no Net.

The insistent *wheee!* of a whistle let me know the water was boiling. I shut down the computer and went to get rid of the last of Devil Mountain's mud. The russet dress was wrinkled after its ride in the trunk and being crammed into the bag, so I shook it out hard as I could before I put it back on.

Then I went back to the couch, sat down, crossed my arms, and said, "Ghosts? If you're real, come on out."

Nothing.

"Kommt sofort raus! Zeigt Euch!" I tried in German.

Nothing.

I tried French, Dobreni, and even a few words of Russian as I begged, pleaded, commanded, then finally accused. "Acting coy is not going to convince me you're anything but figments of my imagination. C'mon, you don't even have to do a full-on haunt. In fact, I'd rather not get all TMI with gore and skeletons rattling. Please flash a face. Or move a pencil. That's all you have to do."

Nothing.

"Okay, be like that."

Like Mina had said, it was easy to fall back on my old convictions. Were those convictions narrow-minded? If ghosts were real, I didn't seem have the vocabulary for talking to them, much less about them.

Was all that crystal ball and Ouija stuff the way to the ghost world? But if it worked, surely it would be a regular part of life, like bookstores selling *Computer-Ghost Interface for Dummies,* or a college class on the Etiquette of Post-Existence Family Relations 101. I didn't want to be closed-minded, but I was still not convinced.

I sank back on the couch, intending to rest my eyes for a minute, but I fell asleep. No dreams of doom or portent, no ghostly messages woke me; I slept until Emilio knocked to say he had the car waiting outside.

TWENTY-SIX

EMILIO WELCOMED ME as if our last parting had been on the best of terms. Well, it had—sort of. He'd dropped me at the cruise ship in good faith, sincerely wishing me a wonderful journey.

He left the car to a quiet teenage boy (who turned out to be his grandson), and took me inside himself. Ysvorod House was Georgian in design, not as large as Mecklundburg House, separated from the homes on either side by hedge-lined gardens. As I entered the old-fashioned hallway I felt as if I was trespassing into Alec's personal space. I'd looked forward to seeing him again, now that the misunderstandings were cleared up, but as I looked around the eighteenth-century entry hall, my heartbeat accelerated. At least there wasn't an intimidating Jeeves lying in wait.

Emilio took me upstairs to a library. It turned out that Emilio and his son-in-law traded off being Jeeves, spelled by his brother-in-law when Alec sent Emilio out of the country.

Alec got up from behind the walnut desk on the other side of the room, hanging up a thirties-style telephone receiver as he did so. I took in the three walls of books and handsome cabinetry set on either side of tall leaded-glass windows with cut crystal prisms set into them in geometric rose patterns. Opposite the door was a fireplace with exquisite ancient Chinese palm-pattern rugs hanging on either side.

He came forward to greet me. "Sit down. Relax. Something to drink?" he said, indicating the wing chairs set before the fireplace.

I discovered my hands laced together tightly. As I sat down Alec moved to a sideboard below one of the rugs and poured the same sort of liquor Mina had served me. Bringing these crystal glasses over, he smiled. "Kilber's potions are safely locked up in his flat, and you can choose your glass." He held them both out. "To set your mind at ease."

"Ha ha." I grabbed one and took a slug of the contents. My eyes burned and then teared as the stuff hit my insides like an incendiary bomb. "Aunt Sisi served this, but it was diluted with soda water and white wine. What is it?" I gasped.

"I should have warned you. It's local, a mountain product. Called *zhoumnyar*. The recipe varies from valley to valley, but raisins, pears, and certain herbs are constant ingredients. Take it easy; a pint of the well-aged, triple-distilled stuff would probably fuel a six-hour jet flight. Indispensable in winter."

"I like it! After the first gouge."

"Curiously," he said as he sat in the wing chair opposite mine and inspected the brightly leaping fire on the grate, "one of the best varieties is produced in a Cistercian monastery, high on Mt. Corbesc. Folklore attributes all manner of healthful properties to it. They sell it to the rest of us."

"Cistercian?" My heartbeat thumped as I said casually, "Are there many Cistercian monasteries around?"

"Not in Dobrenica."

"This one is high on . . . what was it, Mt. Corbesc?"

"Would you like to go there?"

I hesitated. The urge to tell him about Father Teodras was almost overwhelming, and it would be awesome to zoom up there in one of his fancy cars. But on the other hand, the urge to be alone whenever I found out the truth was even stronger.

It wasn't any lingering resentment from various misunderstandings. He'd explained, I'd explained, we were okay with each other. My problem was the opposite. Salfmatta Mina had never told anyone but her long-dead husband about the secret marriage, so now I had the inside scoop. I wanted to get the last bit of evidence in hand, and then deal with my reaction alone, because I didn't want to seem like I was gloating. Though

I needed to find the truth, I was beginning to see what an extreme hassle it was going to cause.

I gazed at the fire as if it was about to talk to me. "There are lots of things I'd like to see. Before I do," now I could face him, "I have a question."

"Fire away."

"If you suspected Tony had nabbed his sister, why didn't you search his place? Especially since you've got—you *are*—the long arm of the law."

Alec smiled. "If you'd seen the Eyrie, you wouldn't need to ask."

"What is it, a giant pile?"

"That doesn't begin to describe it. It's got so many secret passages that, even when the Russians held the castle, there was enough traffic moving through the place to make it sound like Friday market in Riev. Not to mention its reputation for being haunted."

"Whoa. I'm surprised they didn't blow it up."

"It made a great barracks." Alec leaned back and saluted me with his crystal glass, which glittered with shards of reflected firelight. "Also, I hear the last captain in charge up there rather liked Tony. In the way of enemies you love to hate. After all, the war of attrition was constant and successful but there was little actual bloodshed, and even a certain amount of humor in some of the actions they pulled off. At any rate I do know that the captain joined one of Tony's hunting parties over a winter—"

"What?"

"You can't imagine Tony making that gesture?" Alec flashed his quick grin. "Still, I suspect it was more in the nature of psychological warfare than friendliness. You've got to be half-mad to ride in those hills. The Devil's Mountain people are all half-mad, and Tony's the wildest of them all. The captain was, gossip reported gleefully all over the valley, much shaken; apparently his KGB training didn't include old-style Cossack field experience."

I gave a hoot of laughter.

"But back to Ruli. To search, I'd have to take half an army up there to hold the castle, because his people are loyal to Tony. Didn't want to unless forced to it. I did hear a rumor that a female was being entertained up in the castle's private quarters, called the sky suite, but she could have been a friend of Tony's. The most recent clue, gained the day you vanished, was that the volume of washing had increased enormously, which annoyed the servants."

"Washing—oh, you mean laundry. Ruli's infamous mega-wardrobe."

"She also likes bed linen and towels to be changed every day, and everything has to match. So your news didn't surprise me."

"Sounds like a bit of a princess, eh?"

He made a quick gesture. "She's fastidious. Always has been. Her father's the same way, I'm told; if a visitor hasn't sufficiently wiped his feet, he'll mop his own marble floor if the servants aren't fast enough."

"So how can I help? Or can I?"

"There's an obvious course—" He got up to poke at the fire with the tongs and stood back to watch a log fall with a shower of brilliant sparks. "But first we would need Aunt Sisi's cooperation. And the rest of the von Mecklundburgs as well." His smile was brief and humorless.

"Obvious—oh! A repeat of the Split plan? I pretend to be Ruli. To whom?"

"In the eyes of the people, you *are* Ruli. If we were to entertain Tony's family as the engaged couple, it would be an effective counter to Tony's hold on us. He can't call you a fake without the word getting out that his real sister is his prisoner. A delicate balance. Better than waiting for his next move."

He'd already finished his drink, and got up to pour out more. "Aunt Sisi will be arriving any time. If you have other questions, let's talk fast."

I could sense it; he was enjoying the conversation as much as I was. "Okay. First. Why all these moves and countermoves? What's Tony waiting for? He is planning to come in and take over, right? Well, why don't you take your Vigilzhi and go solve things once and for all?"

"Tony knows that I'll try to avoid civil war. I'm counting on the fact that he doesn't want the streets of Riev to run with blood any more than

I do. To pull off a painless coup means he has to get popular support after his mountain hotshots secure the centers of power. If they bungle and we slip away, the country will be divided into two warring camps, with my partisans hiding in the western hills, his in the east, and the valley a potential battleground. Everyone here knows their history, and every time that's happened, it hasn't ended well."

"I get it. And while you're busy hunting one another, the Russians step in to keep the peace."

He smiled, and finished off his drink. "You saw that, did you? Something to bear in mind when you consider Reithermann's background."

"Him again. Who is this guy? His name's German."

"German born, but by the time he left the country when he was around twenty there were warrants all over Germany waiting for him if he ever goes back. You name any illegal and violent splinter group over the past twenty-five years, and he's been connected in some way, especially in the States. He was living there in some remote locale for the last couple of decades, playing around with your American brand of gun-toting nutters. Until your Homeland Security flushed him out, and he ended up here, offering his services to Tony."

"Why'd Tony take him on?"

"Tony's idea seems to have been to weld the hill gangs into a modern and cohesive force, and Reithermann seems to have convinced Tony he could do that. Tony is astute enough to know that taking potshots at Soviet patrols and dismantling their outposts is simpler than taking control of a country. He apparently is not astute enough to know how to pick allies."

"So he's got organizational problems."

"That, and a desperate need for money." Alec got up and moved to the window. He glanced out without moving the curtains, then strolled back to his chair as I exclaimed, "The Dsaret treasure again!"

"More than that. If he could get his hands on it, he'd use it to fund his coup, which would make him more willing to gamble on future support here. Tony knows why my father and the old king hid the treasure years ago. They wanted to leave as little as possible for the conquerors, and if the time came when the conquerors pulled out, they knew stability would be established faster if we had the power of the purse."

"So the treasure isn't in a deep vault somewhere?"

"The bank on Sobieski Square is the only one with deep vaults. And it's used by maybe forty percent of the population."

"So where do people keep their money? In Germany or Switzerland?"

"No, right here. In trunks under their beds, or in wall hiding places, buried in fields, or stashed in old mines and caves."

So it would be there if the Blessing closed them off from the rest of the known world . . . I shook away the thought. "Who controls the treasure?"

"I do. With my father's advice and agreement."

"I can see how that's the best way to control power. But what's to stop someone like Tony from arranging an accident for you on some lonely byway? Your house of cards would collapse pretty fast."

"No, it wouldn't. I channel most of the budget through the Church—"

"What?"

"—so if I do meet my accident on the lonely byway they know my wishes, and my father's, and have the authority to act as they think best. I don't think Tony'd rank high in their plans. Nothing could prevent him from stepping forward to claim the crown, but if he tried to wrest the money from the Church he would shortly become only slightly more popular than the Soviets had been."

"But the *Church?*"

His brows went up. "What are you imagining, a sinkhole presided over by modern Borgias? If so, forget it. If there were any such left in the local diocese in the last sixty years, the enthusiastic persecution by the Soviets weeded them out." His tone was decidedly ironic, but not nasty. "In any case, Baron Ridotski watches over them—our own version of checks and balances. He was selected by the Jewish community, as they also have a vote in governing decisions. In addition there is a Russian Orthodox member on council. The rest of the council is secular, representing various interests."

"So that brings me to Ruli. And to me. By holding her, Tony is postponing the hatchet burying, which increases local pressure on you. I see that much. But why an interest in me when he knows who I am? I don't believe he's enough of an ass to think that by kidnapping me he will get closer to the Dsaret treasure."

"The symbolism works both ways, Kim. Supposing—" The door opened, and Emilio peeked in.

The tension was back. I could see it in Alec's forehead, and in the set of his shoulders as he walked to the door. They conferred quietly, then he returned. "Supposing someone should show up claiming to be a descendent of the long-lost crown princess," he said. "Someone who has the crown princess' face. And supposing this someone decides that the life of a princess might be nice. And so she agrees to marry the son descended from the other Dsaret princess."

I got a vivid image of Tony driving far too fast on the mountain road. "Aren't Tony and I cousins in some way?"

"Quarter cousins. Not only legal, but common enough in families concerned with protecting names and fortunes. I'd say this couple would present a picture of royal appeal, wouldn't you? Perhaps not in the eyes of his relations, but that doesn't matter since he already has their support. In the eyes of the people, yes."

And supposing the descendent with the crown princess' face claims legitimate birth for her mother—thus removing any claim her newfound family might have both to legitimacy and to inheritance. And supposing said descendent shoots off her big mouth to said quarter cousin?

The heat of embarrassment prickled all over me. "How stupid I was not to see it. But even if I were crazy enough to marry Tony on the second of September, your magic thing wouldn't work for us, would it? Supposing it works at all."

"I don't know," Alec said, and moved to the sideboard. "What I do know is that a wedding that day, according to the old tradition, would look damn good to a lot of people, especially to those on Devil's Mountain. Want another shot?"

"No. I've got a buzz on from this much, and I have to remember my formal manners, as I don't think Aunt Sisi is the TV tray and feet on the coffee table type."

He gestured to the door. "It turns out she's detained. Sends her regrets, and will join us for dessert. Shall we sit in the dining room or would you like to eat right here?"

"Anything's okay. Do you think Tony showed up and is harassing her?"

"I think he showed up, yes. Could be they both have a great deal to say to the other." He flashed a wry smile. "We'll eat here. The chairs are more comfortable, and it's warmer. When the duchess comes, we'll have to shift to the dining room for the dessert I ordered from her own cook." He got up, went to the door, and opened it. "Emilio? Why don't you bring the trays in."

"The famed Pedro provided the meal?" I asked.

"You've heard of him? She never travels without him and won't eat anything but Cordon Bleu-quality French food. Luckily her Pedro is not averse to earning extra money on the side by preparing dishes for others who might find themselves entertaining Aunt Sisi."

Emilio came in then and set up trays for us, then served *Marbré de poulet fermier au foie gras,* followed by *Longe de veau de Corrèze rôtie, légumes printaniers au jus*. I refused any wine; Aunt Sisi was due soon, and I wanted a clear head.

We chatted about food, as I inhaled that exquisite dinner. I found out that the porridge I'd eaten at Mina's was probably the local version of *mamaliga,* which was a corn-based staple popular in that corner of the world. I discovered that he had never eaten Mexican food, and I tried to convince him how much he was missing.

During this chat I was trying to rethink my position. I'd regarded myself as distanced from Dobrenica's problems, which I had no stake in. I was here on a private quest. But some of these people seemed to expect me to take on the identity my grandmother had abandoned. *And that means—*

I shivered.

"Are you cold? Would you like a wrap? Or something more to drink?" Alec asked.

"I'm fine."

When Emilio came in to remove the trays I rubbed my hands slowly, trying to press warmth into them. *So if I do find out that Gran's marriage was the legitimate one, what does that do to Ruli's status—and her marriage to Alec?*

I'd promised myself not to think about that until I had my evidence. But the longer I spent in Alec's company, the more I . . . tried not to think about Ruli and that marriage.

I said to the fire, "You told me the city's safe. Did you know someone's been watching the Waleskas' inn?"

Alec was over at the sideboard again. "I know." I heard his smile. "No problem."

"So . . ." I said slowly. "People turned to your father for guidance out of the misery, right? Because he inherited a crown?"

"Partly. My father's reputation was formidable. He was tireless in slipping in and out of the country, often one or two hours ahead of the Gestapo, and later the Russians. The Soviets were pretty heavy-handed in those early days, and though he was young he had a price on his head. Which only served to foster his hero-image."

"They would have done better to welcome him with open arms and mire him in petty bureaucracy." When Alec smiled, I went on. "So you grew up hearing about your father's exploits?"

"I read about them in his journal."

"His journal?"

"He kept one for many years, the idea being to pass it on to his successor to show what he had done and why. Some of it is damned harrowing. And some is—how did my father put it, about the writings of the classics—'a paean to the best of the human spirit persevering despite the worst of circumstances.'"

"I'd love to see it," I exclaimed impulsively, then began a hasty and embarrassed backtrack to cover for flagrant nosiness. "Not that it's any of my business, but my interest in history—"

"You can, if you like." He looked down at the drink he'd just poured, not quite frowning, more like he was thinking.

I said, "Not if it's in any way inappropriate."

That broke the spell. "No, not at all! If you're expecting the confessions of Henry the VIII it would be a vast disappointment." His expression was serious, but I knew he was joking as he deliberately set the drink down, and then returned to his chair. "My austere father has led the most blameless of existences. All things considered, it's probably a miracle I was born. You won't find any mention of mysterious powers, magic, spirits, or otherwise in the journal, either. He rarely discussed those things. If he did, he used the conditional. But as I told you, he did marry my mother on the right day, in the right place. And nothing happened. The Soviets were still there when they came out of the church."

"Okay," I said. "I still want to read it. Where is your father, by the way?"

"He's not here—yet. His health is uncertain, and his visits are always quiet. It's was one thing for an Ysvorod to waltz in and out of the country bearing a proper Socialist title, but it was another for a king, even uncrowned, to make a triumphal return. It's taken these many years to work things out, and his coronation was to be this year, after the wedding."

"The" wedding, not "my" wedding.

"I wondered about the Stadthalter business. The Soviets set that up?"

"I'll have you know I'm a duly elected official. Our first election, in fact. They put my name up against the Soviet Commissar, who hadn't been bad in his five years' rule. His border guards and I used to exchange gossip when I was entering and leaving the country. Anyway, though he was the only one permitted to run a campaign—a modest one, nothing like what I hear of your American circuses—the returns were still overwhelmingly in my favor. Not only virtually unanimous, but there's a good chance a lot of the population wanted to make *sure* their voices were heard in their first election by getting back into line and voting again—" His reminiscent smile faded as his head came up quickly; he stilled, listening.

I heard nothing. "What's wrong?"

"Aunt Sisi is here. A few minutes early." He got up again, moved to the door, and laid his hand on the knob. "I meant to ask you, purely for my peace of mind, if you'd promise not to leave the city unless either Emilio or Kilber or I go with you."

"I'm not the least worried about that jerk Tony—"

"It's not Tony I'm thinking of," he cut in.

"You're trying to tell me there's real danger?" I scoffed. "What if I say no?"

He shrugged. "You say no. But I did want to request this as a favor from you." Footsteps could be heard outside, but he did not move or lift his hand from the door.

And if I say no, I'll be watched and followed?

My irritation was tempered by wondering how much more was going on that I did not know about, and by his evident regret. "All right," I said. "But under protest."

"Acknowledged." He lifted a hand, giving me that transfiguring smile as Emilio opened the door.

Aunt Sisi walked in, her gaze shifting from Alec to me and back again. Then she smiled and stretched out her hands in greeting.

I scrambled to my feet, she kissed my cheek and I caught the vanilla note of Jicky perfume. She was elegant in a peach-colored suit of soft wool. A diamond brooch glittered in the snow-white folds of the lace cravat at her neck. Perfectly matched pumps, obviously made for her narrow feet, and faultlessly groomed hair finished the picture. "My dear children." She smiled graciously on us both. "Have you been putting your young heads together on my poor daughter's behalf?"

I'd expected her to be upset, or even anxious on her daughter's behalf, instead of smiling with sophisticated assurance and a hint of humor when her gaze took in my rumpled dress. She truly did come from a time when self-control was taught from the cradle.

I gave her an awkward greeting. With pleasant expertise Alec took over as he led us to the dining room, starting off easy talk about wines of various countries. The dining room was severely formal, the table and chairs old enough to have pleased Lord Chesterfield with their restrained cabriole curves and subdued Enlightenment pine green and white.

We were waited on by Emilio who had metamorphosed into a black-jacketed butler as we partook of white dessert wine in chilled goblets, light, puffy apricot *Pets de Nonnes,* and social chat, congenial but not relaxed. I didn't know if Aunt Sisi's straight back, her posed hands, her modulated voice signaled the upset I'd expected to see. I couldn't read her at all. But I did notice that Alec—smiling, suave, affable—watched her every move.

After dessert we withdrew to another formal salon, this one a harmonious whole made up of Baroque flourishes: tapestry-cushioned shield-backed chairs—blue with stylized snowflakes in white—and tables with mythical beings carved along the curved legs. A tapestry depicting warriors in various shades of brown and red and gold foundered in snow around a silvery central figure, an angel or a girl.

I was afraid to sit on the chairs—were they antiques meant to be looked at? Alec and Aunt Sisi sat down without a second thought, so I followed suit.

Emilio wheeled in a polished solid silver coffee service with a crest on each piece. The dishware was blue and gold Royal Doulton Harlow pattern coffee cups—in other words, heavy social artillery.

While we sipped at the excellent coffee, Alec brought up the subject of Ruli.

He was, I thought at the time, very direct. "Our idea is this, Aunt Sisi. We will embark on a public social life, entertaining your relations—with your cooperation, of course. To anyone else, Kim is Ruli; as it happens Aurelia is also her name, which makes things easier."

Aunt Sisi set her coffee cup down. "I shall be happy to do anything you think will resolve our . . . unusual dilemma . . . with as little awkwardness as possible. You will pardon the slowness of an old woman, but I do not see how this Machiavellian masquerade will inspire Anton to bring my daughter down from the Eyrie to proceed with our plans."

Alec sat back in his chair and laced his fingers on one knee, presenting an attitude of ease but I could see tension from the line of his shoulders to his hands. "Because he is beginning to feel enough pressure from within his organization that some added pressure from without might help to bring about a resolution fairly quickly. The pressure of time."

"Time? The wedding date approaching?"

"Yes," Alec replied. "And no talk of postponement."

Her brows went up and her eyelids dropped, which effectively shuttered her expression. Then she gave a nod. "Perhaps that will be profitable. The social portion will be entertaining! You leave that to me." She leaned her chin delicately on her fist and tipped her head to one side, which reminded me disconcertingly of Tony. "An idea has come to me. What could be more appropriate than a masked ball? At the palace. Everyone of any standing to come."

Alec gave her a look of mild surprise. "Do you think a party that size is necessary?"

"Why not? It would be most suitable. And you know, all questions of precedence are relaxed at a masquerade ball."

That went right by me. Not so Alec. His mild, steady gaze blended with hers, then she smiled my way. "I shall invite everyone of any importance, and you, my dear, will be the Queen Maria Sofia who was the mold for us all. As for a gown, I'm convinced you would fit into one I wore a number of years ago. Perhaps fresh lace and one or two alterations." She smiled at my enthusiasm, the dimple flashing in her cheek. "You would enjoy a masked ball, child?"

I gave a sigh of delight, but Alec said nothing.

Aunt Sisi smiled at him. "You do not like the idea, dear boy? May I ask why?"

He was in the middle of pouring more coffee all around. "It's rather a lot of trouble, isn't it?"

"No trouble at all." Aunt Sisi said humorously to me, "What man likes fancy-dress parties? Balls are purely for the ladies, and if the gentlemen wish to please their ladies, they attend."

I cut a fast glance from her to Alec, to find his gaze on me.

"Shall I leave the planning in your hands, then?" he asked.

"Please, dear boy. It will be no work, but a positive pleasure. I shall begin with a dinner party. It would be an appropriate gesture on my part." After a pause, "Speaking of appropriate, perhaps our Kim had better remove to Mecklundburg House."

"No, she'll stay here," Alec said equably.

Aunt Sisi's brows went up again, daintily creasing her high forehead. I couldn't help thinking of my mother's broad, clear, always serene brow. "My dear boy, you must remember we are not in Paris—"

Alec said with good humor that exactly matched hers, "There'll be a suitable—and visible—chaperone here by tomorrow, and Kilber and Emilio and his family to guard the door. And I will spend a great many nights at the residence wing, preparing it for a bride."

Aunt Sisi's gaze flicked to me then back as she said smoothly, "My daughter did indicate she wishes to live at the palace, did she not?" She gave a sigh of surrender. "Such a quick mind, dear Alexander. You are right. Well! I shall go, then. There is much to do."

"It's raining. I'll have the car brought round." Alec got up swiftly, went to the door, and said a few words in a low voice.

Aunt Sisi reached to pat my hand. "You will have quite a tale to take home, will you not, my dear?"

Not sure how to answer this, I said warmly, "The best thing will be a masquerade ball."

"You've never been to one?" she asked with pronounced amusement.

I remembered the lies I'd told at her party and said airily, "Sure I have." *If you count the Renaissance Pleasure Faire.* "But not in a royal palace that housed one set of my ancestors."

Alec spoke behind us, "Aunt Sisi? The car is downstairs."

We went out into the chilly night air, and Alec opened the door for her. "Good night, Aunt Sisi. Thank you for coming."

She responded graciously, and he shut the door, then followed me around to the other side. Aunt Sisi's face turned toward us; I climbed in. "Thanks for dinner," I said.

"Good night."

Kilber drove the two and a half blocks to Aunt Sisi's place. She gave me an affectionate good night as she got out. Kilber then took me to the other side of town in the same complete silence he'd brought me. I watched rain on the windshield.

When he stopped at Nat's, Kilber spoke. "I was to give you this."

He handed me a flat package.

"Thanks. And for the ride."

He gave me a short nod, then drove away.

Nat's place was chilly, the darkness strange. I climbed into the bed, opened the envelope, and pulled out an old-fashioned composition book.

In a clear, slanted fraktur hand—the handwriting of a young man—an inscription in German on the first page:

> *"Within half a year I, Marius Alexander Ysvorod of Domitrian, will be assuming the duties of governing our homeland Dobrenica. The times are strained on all levels, and appear to be worsening steadily. I begin this with the purpose of detailing for my successor the events I will live through, if it pleases Our Lord, my successes and mistakes, and my thoughts on all these matters. 14 December, 1939."*

Avidly, the cold room forgotten, I turned to the first entry. *The king had given me the task of coordinating the disguising of the temple as another cathedral. The Benedictines donated old vestments to this cause, so if the Gestapo does come, they will find Benedictine monks observing the medieval hours . . .*

It was a quarter to three by Nat's clock when the slanted hand began moving like an escalator before my eyes. I reluctantly laid the book down, turned out the lamp, and slept.

TWENTY-SEVEN

I READ THROUGH THE whole of the next day, pausing only to work through my ballet exercises.

Outside, rain tapped the windows with steadily increasing force as a storm moved in over the country. I lay sandwiched in Nat's cheery quilt on her couch, and absorbed the threatened days of Dobrenica at the start of World War II.

As Nat had nothing to eat, I made hot tea twice. I was nearly finished with Milo's book when Emilio came for me. He waited while I washed my teacup and put everything back where I'd found it.

As I locked Nat's door I said, "Is Alec at his house?"

"He is not in Riev today, Mam'zelle. I am instructed to arrange for your comfort at Ysvorod House."

"Did you know he gave me this to read?" I brandished the composition book, which I had carried tucked under my arm.

"Kilber told me last night, Mam'zelle. Exciting days, those." His smile was melancholy.

"I can see that. And I'm almost done with this one. I was wondering if I might see whatever comes after?"

"I will consult Kilber," he promised.

A hot lunch was waiting for me, also a note from Aunt Sisi on crested notepaper that carried a drift of Jicky. It begged me to let her know if she could do anything for me. I found notepaper in the library, and wrote, *Yes! Does the offer hold about borrowing Ruli's clothes, since mine seem to be residing at the Eyrie?*

I was curled up in the armchair, finishing the last pages of Milo's book, when Emilio entered. "Mam'zelle, a trunk has arrived from Mecklundburg House, from Madam la Duchesse. Also, Kilber requested me to show you this." He indicated a darkwood cabinet set in the far corner between two high bookshelves.

He turned the brass key in the lock, and lifted up the panel to reveal a row of old composition books. They were the rest of Milo's journal. "Please feel free to read these at your leisure."

And that's what I did, as soon as I'd unpacked the trunk in the pleasant, old-fashioned room they gave me. After which I sat down at the desk, used the good paper I found waiting, and as I wrote a proper thank-you note, I half wished they'd also left me a quill pen and iron-gall ink instead of the ordinary ballpoint.

Time passed. Steady rain kept me inside during the daylight hours, which I mostly spent in Alec's library, reading.

The library was pleasant, but about as personal as a museum room. Yet I felt Alec's presence there. Finally I went hunting for the source. Certainly not in the centuries-old bound books so carefully dusted in the shelves, or the fine cabinets. On the desk lay a platinum lighter with a fancy crest worked in gems on it. I couldn't imagine Alec carrying around something so gaudy. Probably why it sat there like all expensive but disliked presents. He also had a computer, an expensive, high tech model. I asked Emilio if they had Internet, and surprise! He said there was no connection this high, you had to go down the mountains and across the border. Maybe that explained why the computer looked like it was fresh out of the box.

I finally identified that sense of presence in the two small items on the table next to the reading chair. One was a Waterman pen like the ones I'd seen him use on our Adriatic jaunt, and the other was a much-read, leather-bound volume of Milton with a silk bookmark at "Lycidas."

So I lived in Alec's house, among his things, waited on by his servants, reading his father's private journal, but he was not there. Alec scrupulously observed "proper" etiquette. I refused to think about Ruli, the switch, or the future until I found Father Teodras.

Meanwhile I had a staggering quantity of expensive Parisian clothes and Italian shoes to wear for the nightly social events that Aunt Sisi arranged. Ruli was my height, and more or less my build, except she was either a size or two smaller or she wore her clothes tight. The sleeves were particularly constraining, which made me move with less freedom.

Wearing the clothes of someone whose taste was so different from mine, whom I had yet to meet—whom Alec was to marry—was unsettling. A subtle scent clung to them from having been stored in cedar wood with lavender sachets. I'll remember that scent for the rest of my life.

Her expensive shoes were all high heeled and way too small for my muscular ballet feet, so I stuck to the open-toed sandals and had to change my walk. Judging from the second glances when I met her relatives, we did not move alike, however much we resembled each other. But no one said a thing.

Another oddity was Aunt Sisi's attitude. Oh, she acted ever so gracious and kind. So did the relatives, as we met over and over in a series of beautiful homes for a series of dinners and cocktail parties all so alike they blend together in my mind. There were no more questions about my personal background. In fact, some of them acted so sweet and friendly—chérie this and that—I had a feeling they knew I'd scored off them with my scam that night, and they hated my guts for it.

But Aunt Sisi's attitude was rueful humor, as if she were an unwilling but good-natured participant in childish pranks. Her attitude toward me was gracious and kind, yet it was not until nearly the end of this period that I found out that she had subtly but thoroughly arranged it so that questions of precedence were kept vague.

In my LA circles nobody pays attention to that stuff. Unless there's some VIP or a poser who considers themselves a VIP, people go through doors from one room to another in any order, and if a hostess arranges seating, except for the guest of honor (if there is one) the idea is to put people with those they'll like talking to. Not so here. The hostesses managed so skillfully—and everyone cooperated by knowing his or her place—that I was completely unaware of what was going on until the night Alec gave a dinner party for them at Ysvorod House.

Alec was the host at his party, backed up by good old Emilio. The surprise was that this time I sat at a different seat in reference to the others. I wouldn't have noticed had I not caught a strange look pass between Aunt Sisi and Cerisette when we were seated. A strange, cool look; they were signaling each other. I couldn't pick up the message. But I felt it.

While the meal went on—and while I silently admired Alec's effortless skill at hosting—I wondered what the problem was. I finally figured out that I had been placed in the guest-of-honor spot all along, which did not put me in rank-order. Alec put his aunt there instead, and me in . . . I recalled the seating at the last two dinner parties.

He had put me where the hostess would go.

Where *Ruli* would go.

It was then I became aware that a silent conflict was going on. Alec seemed to be making a statement by his action. The von Mecklundburg posse behaved with perfect manners, but I so did not feel the love.

I asked Emilio how I could return Miriam's scarf. His son was ready and willing to be my messenger. I considered asking him to take me to Mt. Corbesc, but my instinct was too strong: I needed to make that trip on my own. Without anyone on either side knowing about it.

So I returned the scarf by messenger, with only a note expressing my thanks.

My plan was now to wait for a nice day, walk to the inn (making sure I wasn't followed), and hire someone to drive me to the Cistercians, paying with the money still hidden with my passport inside my jeans and T-shirt wherever Tania had stashed them.

My chaperone was a gentle, quiet woman named Madam Aradyinov. She was a maternal relation of Alec's who'd been widowed during the Russian mess, losing her livelihood as well. Madam A. spoke rusty French and English, and I sensed after sitting through two uncomfortable meals with her that the situation with Tony (what little she knew about it) disturbed her. She was religious, shy, went to Mass every day at an hour unlikely to discommode my "social schedule," and she loved Alec. When she saw him she brightened up considerably, and he called her aunt.

There's even less to say about the parties, which were pretty much limited to the von Mecklundburgs. I didn't meet any of Alec's friends or allies; a few council members were invited, all of them old. I was constrained against real conversation by having to pretend I was Ruli.

One evening I did forget to be Ruli; I'd just been introduced to a baroness connected to the number two man in the country, Baron Ridotski (who I'd read about in the journal, and longed to meet if he was still alive). The old woman turned out to be another ballet aficionado. In my delight at the prospect of an actual conversation, I began talking about the performance I'd seen in Vienna before I was interrupted in the smoothest way by Aunt Sisi.

I'd forgotten. No one could forget Ruli, Aunt Sisi made it clear.

And she was totally right. No one *should* forget Ruli—she was still a prisoner in this horrible stalemate.

The rain moved on. On the first nice day, I dressed for a walk. My plan was to tell Madam A. that I needed some exercise—I'd lunch somewhere, then do some window shopping and return by evening. I figured that would be enough time to get to the Waleska inn, hire someone to drive me to Mt. Corbesc, and get back again.

Madam A. clasped her hands anxiously. "Can you wait a moment, Mam'zelle, while I consult the watch captain?"

"Watch captain?" I repeated witlessly.

She lifted her hand in a circle, indicating the house—the street. "We are guarded at all times."

"Guarded? That is, the whole house?" I ran to the front window, but didn't see anything beside the quiet street beyond the orderly garden full of blooms.

"Yes, Mam'zelle."

"Then . . . the threat is more serious than I thought."

"Yes, Mam'zelle," the old lady said, in a low voice.

"Right. As my dad says, eighty-six the walk, then."

I contained my impatience until that evening, when Alec arrived to escort me to a party. When I asked, he said, "Tony's friends have already made two tries to seal off my street."

"Twice? But I didn't hear anything."

"No."

"Somehow that's creepier than sirens and yelling and noise."

"Tony doesn't want a body count any more than I do. I don't trust Reithermann. Anyway, if you wouldn't mind staying inside the perimeter? It's only a few more days."

"Right. I did say I'd cooperate. I take it they haven't given up."

Alec's smile was grim. "Not at all. I wish they'd make their move."

"Yeah. Me too. I think."

"I apologize for the lack of things to do, other than being seen with your relations."

"I'm good with your dad's journal. And you've plenty of other books here—though it doesn't look like your library has much written after 1810."

Alec smiled. "This is mostly my grandfather's library, which was hidden with the furniture right before the house began its long occupation. We finished restoring the place within the last decade. Most of the modern stuff is still in London. I've brought a few things over. Please help yourself to the CD player in the cabinet in the library. Didn't Emilio tell you? I have a reasonable selection of music that doesn't have 'composed by' as part of the title."

Madam A. appeared then, and we left for the de Vauban dinner party.

The evening was typical. The von M. gang spent the entire evening talking about amusing parties hosted by a bunch of people I'd never heard of. At the time, I thought if this is sophisticated conversation, then I've got no hope of ever becoming sophisticated because I am so bored. Later I began to wonder if they were being deliberately boring—which is kind of cool, in a twisty way. Paybacks for my big lies, which officially hadn't been proved one way or the other.

I didn't have a chance to speak aside from "please pass the . . ." and "thank you." When we got back, Alec hesitated at the front door. No more than a quick, questioning glance—meeting my own questioning glance.

There was no drama in how comfortable we'd become with one another. I could sense his effort to scrupulously stick to business, but I couldn't help tipping my head toward the library any more than he could help dropping his coat over the banister pole with a murmured "For a minute."

"I wanted to ask about some of this other stuff. What's here that I can occupy myself with," I said.

He led the way to a *dressoir* cabinet with *fenestrage* carving around the top, reflecting the stylized pictures you see in stained glass windows. There were three of them; those cabinets had to date back to the Mannerist period. "Here are the CDs I was telling you about. My ancestors, who appreciated music enough to keep musicians on the household payroll, would probably love what's in here now. Once they got over their surprise. Those two cabinets over there are full of LPs that my father collected. These I brought when I first became Stadthalter."

As he opened the cabinet doors, which had been carved in a relief scene of a man in Renaissance garb surrounded by books, I said, "Your ancestors would probably think CDs were magic. One of my dad's favorite quotes is by Arthur C. Clarke, who said, 'Any sufficiently advantaged technology is indistinguishable from magic.' If your people here get the modern stuff you're bringing, maybe the belief in magic will vanish."

Alec lifted his hand toward the stacks of CDs, and the player, inside the cabinet. "You'd think so." He leaned against the wing chair, watching me as I scanned the contents.

"But you don't know so? Is that what you're saying?" I said.

The top row of CDs was everything the Beatles ever did. From there the collection ranged from classical to classic rock, with representation from European bands, like Schandmaul, who combined metal with ancient folk music.

"Ask Tony about his vampire treaty," Alec said, his expression wry, as I propped my elbows on the other side of the wing chair.

"That's the third time I've heard about vampires. Tony laughed at the idea of magic when we were at Sedania. But he believes in *vampires?*"

The easy atmosphere had changed; I was aware of his arm lying along the back of the chair; his gaze dropped from my eyes to my hands. Changed and charged. Neither of us had said anything, or moved, but the quiet room had become intimate space.

He straightened up. "Claims to know at least one. If you ask him, he'll tell you that vampires and magic are two separate issues. I'd better go."

So on the surface, social frivolities. Underneath? The tension of so many pretenses. For me the tension was underlined—intensified—by Milo's journal during the years of World War II.

That whole week reminds me of Ravel's *Boléro,* steadily, inexorably, building toward a crescendo. I could feel the crescendo coming—in 1945, and in the present.

Alec kept to the path of virtue, though gradually staying longer and longer in the evenings after dropping me off. By tacit agreement we no longer went into the library. Instead we'd stand on the stairway, me two or three steps up, leaning on the banister, he at the foot with his head tipped back, his jacket slung over his shoulder.

One or the other of us would ask a question, and then another after that, shooting ideas back and forth, mixed with the same sort of ironic jokes. It was only chat, but these chats got longer each evening, and they were the best part of my day.

Rain caused Honoré de Vauban to cancel the picnic at the river down below the city, so I curled up to read more Milo. I closed the last page of November 1944 as the clock struck two AM.

I was curious to see what Milo would have to say in his own words about the search for my grandmother. So I got out of bed, where I had been reading since cold had driven me out of the library, picked up Ruli's dressing gown, and pulled it on. The pure silk felt wonderful against my skin.

The library was dark. The fire had burned down to a few redly glowing embers. I turned on a lamp and went to the cabinet. I replaced the old book and picked up the next. Then, feeling as if I was carrying a live grenade, I carried it to the lamp, flipped it open to find the date at the top: *June, 1948.*

I sprinted back to the cabinet, checked again, checked succeeding volumes to see if it had been placed out of order, but the rest of the books went on in steady jumps of years until the last page, which was addressed directly to Alec, apparently written right after his birth.

I was standing there holding June 1948 in my hand and curling my bare toes against the cold floor, when the door opened behind me. I jerked around to see Alec enter, dressed in black; the only color about him in the dim lamplight was cobalt flickers from his ring.

"You look like a ghost," he said with a soft laugh.

"No, *you* look like a ghost." Turning away to switch on another lamp I went on hastily, "I haven't slept yet, I was reading. Oh! A problem, and I promise it wasn't me, but there's a book missing. Maybe more than one."

"Nothing's missing." Alec closed the door behind him and advanced into the room. The stronger light touched his features as he leaned over to stir up the dying fire. He smiled in a way I'd rarely seen before.

"What is it? You're laughing at me. No, you're pleased about something!" And, quickly, "Tony?"

He shook his head. "I was having some fun tonight poking around where I had no business being. So you've still been reading the journals?" He took a hunk of wood from the holder and threw it into the fireplace, sending a firestorm of sparks whirling up the chimney.

"Yes. Steadily," I said, watching him kick the wood into place with the toe of his boot. He was dressed in a black thick-knit sweater, jeans, and boots. Completely uncharacteristic, but I liked him in that gear at least as much as I liked him in a tux or his Stadthalter clothes. "But what about 1945?"

"Isn't one."

"Did something happen to it?" I leaned on the back of a chair, balancing the journal for '48 between my hands as Alec moved to the desk and started looking through the drawers.

"Want to know what happened?"

"I can guess at some," I said. "The Russians came. And there was that business with Armandros. And his search for Gran," I added. "I guess I should have expected he wouldn't talk about it, seeing how he never mentioned Gran in the journal at all."

He used the poker to position the wood, then stared into the fire. "Bad years—everything he tried failed. Armandros shot down, your grandmother reported dead in Paris. Then the Russians came. Move up the years. He married my mother on September second, in Xanpia's sanctuary on Mt. Adeliad, like I told you before. And for whatever reason, the Blessing did not work."

"Were all Tony's family here for that as well?"

"All of them." Alec said. "Your Aunt Sisi's first introduction to Dobrenica was heralded by crowds lining the roads and throwing white roses at her."

The image was so intense, I got this fast, unsettling roar in my ears—the roar of a crowd, engines—a whiff of crushed roses and diesel smoke. I shut my eyes and held my breath, willing the giddiness away.

I reopened my eyes as Alec gestured toward the book in my lap. "Don't feel you have to read the rest, since it takes up after the events that directly concern you."

"I'm interested. In fact, some of it may be enjoyable, now that the war part is past."

"There's some heavy going in '49, '50, '51, when that first Soviet commander allowed his thugs open season on the decadent superstition-mongers of the Roman Catholic church, and of course the Jews. And I should probably warn you there's a fairly rough part in February of '52 with several nun-teachers, though my father and Kilber did successfully lead a rescue party."

"Thanks. I might do some skipping; I don't think I need to read any more evidence of inhumanity to other humans. It's the courage, the humor, the risk and skill I admire."

He laughed. "There's enough of both, because after all, people are people. But it gradually gets somewhat better, as the oppression lifts. The Jews began living openly again in the late sixties, and were largely ignored by the increasingly nominal government representatives. The last one, before the Soviet government collapsed, used to attend the concerts at the music school, which is connected to the temple *shul.*"

"That's cool."

"I have to be at a city council meeting in, ah." A quick glance at his watch. "Six hours, in order to listen to them squabble about the streetlamp issue. What's on the social schedule tomorrow? Today? I never can remember, and my calendar is back at the residence." He got slowly to his feet.

"Concert at the cathedral—my first public appearance. I believe the *canaille* will be at it, from the way Cerisette was sighing the other day. Though it could be she aimed that at me."

He paused in the act of picking up the papers he'd dropped on his desk and gave me a brief smile. "Cerisette only wishes you *canaille.*" Before I could figure out how to answer that, "Meanwhile you've been cooped up without getting to see anything. Shall I take you over to the palace and show you Queen Maria Sofia tomorrow afternoon?"

"So there's no sinister Tony minions lurking about?"

"Oh, they're out there, but not around the palace."

"I'd love to go. I've already seen Maria Sofia's portrait once," I said. "But I'd like to see her again. Take note of her hairdo, since I've got to figure out how to copy it myself, as my maids seem to have taken the year off."

He was still smiling, more than the dumb joke warranted, then said, "See you tomorrow."

TWENTY-EIGHT

I DON'T KNOW what I expected to find in Milo's journal after Gran's departure. Like Alec said, there was no more emotional drama than there was magic. I still kept at it. The journal changed considerably over the decades after the war. The human side of Milo—the shy, reserved, extremely well-read man devoted to duty, always thinking about the country even when running from the Russians (and Alec was right, Kilber *did* save his life several times)—vanished, replaced by a series of mission statements.

It was so detached it was nearly inhuman. By the time I reached the end, I wondered if hints of love or laughter, much less magic, were present by their absence. Milo didn't even mention anything as innocuous as music, though there was that enormous collection of LPs in the library, and Mina had said he was as good a piano player as Gran, and they'd played long duets together.

The last entry I read was a thoughtful, closely reasoned essay based on experience, addressed to "Marius." An adult Marius, though I knew he wrote it after Alec's birth. It began with the duties of a king then moved on to a list of Dobrenica's prioritized needs—with reflections on the state of the Soviet government and what he thought would be its future.

I was impressed with the farsightedness, but as I closed it, I wondered what it was like to grow up with such a person as a father. I had this vivid image of a smart, lonely boy with books as his constant companions. His dedicated, austere, universally admired father would be too busy with crucial governmental duties to ever take him to a soccer game or to a movie.

I was replacing that last journal when I heard the noise of an arrival, which was the delivery of the masquerade ball gown Aunt Sisi was loaning me, along with its accoutrements: silver high-heeled, jewel-buckled shoes à la Cinderella; a fantastically lovely petticoat with yards of stiff tulle and lace that could have been worn alone and been admired; a headdress of pearls and feathers; a brocade fan; the mask was a scrap of lace with seed pearls sewn on.

She included a note saying that if the gown needed alteration, she could send a seamstress over. The shoes would be too difficult to replace on such short notice, but if they did not fit I could wear Ruli's silver sandals.

The dress was a *Robe à l'Anglaise a la polonaise.* It was a struggle to deal with the zillion hook-and-eyes at the back of the tight, stiff bodice. I could understand how a maid had been indispensable.

When I got a look at myself in the mirror, I almost fainted.

The gown was ice-blue brocaded silk satin, with a cream-colored taffeta skirt beneath the huge polonaise swoops. Both were embroidered in silver. The elbow-length sleeves and the low square neckline were edged with pearls and heavy lace. The result was that I looked like Cinderella.

The shoes were tight, but with silk stockings they would be bearable for a night. They were too perfect with the gown.

I danced around the room, loving the whoosh of the wide skirt, until Madam A. tapped at my door to announce Alec's arrival.

"Tell him I'll be down in five!" I yelled.

I wrestled my way out of the dress, sat down and scribbled a note to Aunt Sisi, saying that the dress fit fine. Then I raced down the stairs, resetting my hair clip as I ran.

Alec was waiting in the hallway. "You know, you can sit down in your own house," I greeted him.

"Let's go," he replied, smiling.

"Aunt Sisi sent the gown for the masquerade ball tomorrow night." I sighed happily as we walked out into the hazy sunlight. The lawns and flowerbeds were all deep with color, and huge sky-reflecting puddles pooled in the streets. "I was trying it on."

"And? Does her gown meet with your approval?"

"It's gorgeous. I can hardly wait for tomorrow." I looked at the red Fiat waiting. "What happened to the green machine?"

"This car is easier to drive on the old back streets. And the mountain roads."

"Bright colors on purpose? So animals and people and the occasional other car can see 'em?"

"And hear them." He started the car.

"Thought so. Tony's ride is red, too. Do you know if Aunt Sisi ever wears costume jewelry?"

"Costume jewelry?"

"You know, fakes. Like, to wear with costumes. That Queen Maria Sofia dress is beautiful, but the broad expanse right here," I smacked my collarbone, "looks bare without any sparklies. Would she be insulted if I asked?"

He turned the car up a back lane into the palace complex, then shot me a humorous look. "She would," he said with conviction. "She'd be offended if a guest to her dinner table wore false jewelry in her presence. I've a collection of family jewelry, and no female relatives to use it. Would you like a necklace? I've got half a dozen of them. Two old. The rest newer. All very sparkly."

"The real McCoy?"

"Yes."

"No thanks." I shook my head. "Much as I'd enjoy putting something like that on, the thought of having to replace an irreplaceable heirloom would haunt me all evening, and *nothing* is allowed to spoil my night at a masquerade ball in a real, licensed and patented royal palace."

He pulled up behind a wing of the palace and parked. "So you took the palace tour?" He opened a discreet side door, which led into a plain white-plastered hallway.

We were in the servants' quarters—which we didn't get to see on the tour. It took a crown prince to gain access to them, a thought I found funny. "Sure. How else was I going to see this place?"

"You expected to move about inconspicuously, and to leave unremarked after your purpose was accomplished?"

He didn't say *visit,* he said *purpose.* Cravenly I overlooked it as we trod up a flight of stairs. "Yep. You'd said Ruli was rarely in the country, and when she was she only hung out with the blue bloods, and I thought it impossible anyone would associate me with Gran. I had doubts about the whole thing being connected with me in the first place. But that sure changed when I saw the portrait. And then the nursery. And five minutes after that, Aunt Sisi found me."

"Nursery? This way." He opened the door down another plain hall.

"The mural. Gran used to tell me Fyadar stories, and that was the scene of a lot of 'em. Did you ever read any of the Fyadar comics and stories made by schoolkids under the Germans and the Soviets?"

"Yes." He glanced at me with that expression of mild inquiry. "Milo brought me back a few children's stories in Dobreni when I was small, to encourage my learning of the language. And my first friends here showed me some of the smuggled books when I was around thirteen."

"Did you like the comic books?"

He shrugged. "They were part of home. I read a few. But after a dozen or so I was disgusted to discover that you could tell where the story was going by the mountain it was set on."

"The mountains," I breathed. "I wondered about that."

He opened an unmarked door and we stepped onto the parquet floor that stretched gracefully between two grand stairways. I remembered following the tour along the marble floor below, peeking in through the doors at the grand ballroom.

"Leaving aside the question of otherworld inhabitants, no matter how cynical and sophisticated he or she becomes, you will never completely convince a Dobreni that the mountains don't have distinct personalities. Certain valleys are believed to be better for herbs, others for the breeding of sheep. Makes for obscure jokes."

"Speaking of jokes, you once told me that Devil's Mountain got its name from bad weather. After what I've been through what I want to know is, what's it really known for? Devils?" I laughed.

"I already told you. Vampires."

I gave a snort of disbelief. "I don't believe it."

"All I can say is that I have never seen any. However." We had walked along the parquet past two high paneled doors. Alec opened the third door as he said, "My father thinks he might have. Here we are."

"What?" I squawked, staring around the high-ceilinged rococo gallery. "He never said anything about *that* in the journal."

"Only evidence of what he could see—what he could prove—went into the journal. He's deeply devout, but you never saw a reference to attending Mass, either. Faith is not proof, it is . . . faith." He opened a door to a familiar long gallery. "Here we are."

Down one side was a row of tall windows that overlooked the garden. Every available foot of wall space between and on the long wall across from them had been covered with various sizes of portraits.

Alec waited patiently, surrounded by the silent eyes of our ancestors as I took it all in.

Dsarets predominated, though twice in the nineteenth century the rulers were Ysvorods—and there, in a late-Renaissance frame was another Ysvorod king. Grigorian was his name. "Your family have a title when not throne-warming?" I asked over my shoulder.

Alec had opened a window and was sitting in it. "Domitrian. Dukes of."

"Ah." More Ysvorods; it appeared they'd had control for most of the Middle Ages. These portraits were so stylized, after the fashion of the time, that all one got a faithful impression of was the clothes.

The last of the early Ysvorod kings caught the eye partly because he was (despite the artist's valiant attempts to draw attention away from the fact) enormous, emphasized by a fondness for pink satin slashed with crimson puffs.

"That guy." I pointed. "Don't tell me he was a pious monk-type."

Alec laughed. "Good old Thaddeus was exactly what he looks like, a dedicated gourmand. He was the only ruling Ysvorod to marry a von Mecklundburg—you notice they are the only family who Germanized their names, back in the 1600s—but no children resulted, so the throne went to the Dsarets. It was after that marriage that the Swedes invaded us."

"So how—" I stopped.

Maria Sofia Alexandria Elisabeth Vasa Dsaret smiled benignly down at me.

"Where are her kids?"

"She had several daughters, and finally one son. Here—" He tipped his chin toward the opposite corner, where a ringletted lady reclined in a filmy white gown on a sylvan background. Curly black hair, slanty black eyes, Mediterranean coloring, arms plump and rounded after the Directoire fashion; she had the crooked smile, charming and insouciant. I'd seen her before, along the staircase at Aunt Sisi's.

"Daughter?"

"Daughter-in-law, Aurélie de Mascarenhas. She's the one who brought your name here, though it reverted to the Latin form, Aurelia. Many family stories about her. Beautiful, ambitious, opinionated. The crown prince wouldn't marry anyone else. Championed by the queen, despite some questions about her background. Sofia must have seen herself in young Aurélie, who came here straight from Napoleon's court, where some hinted the upstart went to meet another upstart."

"So her pedigree wasn't pure?" I asked, doing air quotes on the word 'pure.'

Alec opened a hand. "The queen vouched for her, so that was that. Family legend has it Napoleon made a pass at her. Perhaps he did. She was much sought after in Paris and Vienna. Some say England, too. That was painted when she married the crown prince. Her daughter married into the von Mecklundburgs, which is where they get the black eyes and that crooked smile."

"Wow," I said, staring slowly around the room. "My relatives. No wonder people pay a fortune to have their genealogies traced—it's amazing to look at them and see resemblances to one's self and one's relatives. Like this fellow. He's definitely got The Face."

I pointed up at a stiffly posed slender young man wearing a nineteenth-century military tunic with sashes and braid and epaulettes. He looked like a somber Tony, with the same pale hair, but with light brown eyes. No hint of the crooked smile.

"That's your great-great-grandfather. Painted a year after his twin was killed in a duel up in the eastern mountains. He married another of Old Sofia's descendents. It's their child who was your grandmother's mother."

I sighed. "I wish I'd been a good tourist and brought a camera. I'd love to show these to Mom."

"Why don't you let her come see for herself?"

I turned to face him, feeling this sense of doom. More like DOOM. It was that visit to Father Teodras hanging over my head.

"I guess we'll see," I said, knowing I sounded like a weasel.

He opened the door. "Shall we go?"

We drove up the mountain road behind Riev. He pointed out various old ruins, giving me quick histories. We stopped at a village Gasthaus to eat, and over a tasty meal we discussed his father's journal, going from there to the other major projects, like the newly finished hydroelectric dam and the new plan for building of wind turbines in mountain valleys where the winds howled down fiercely all winter long. Let the wind howl and make electricity.

It was a pleasant afternoon, and I was disappointed when we had to return. I must have shown my reaction because he said, "Bored with the social whirl?"

"Is any of this social whirl goosing Count Tony the Obnox a bit?"

Alec's grin flashed. "Tony was chased up a tree by your appearance," he said with satisfaction, "and now his branch is breaking."

"Because of me?"

"You're the catalyst."

"That means more trouble with that Reithermann bozo?"

"That's a good part of it."

"What's the other part?"

"There will be an end soon."

"Good." *Father Teodras, here I come.*

He was back by 6:30, in order to dine with Aunt Sisi and Madam A. and me. French food and French conversation, about classical music this time. Again he was a perfect host, and Madam A. was seated in the hostess spot, so Aunt Sisi and I faced one another. Two guests of honor. Afterward the four of us set out in amity for the cathedral.

The city was gearing up for Dobrenica's big two-week festival starting on August 15 and winding up on September 2. This year, the festival was to culminate in the wedding.

The cathedral was packed with Riev citizenry of every degree. We joined the rest of the von M. clan, who flanked us on either side, and a few of them behind us, as we were front row center. I felt cramped and itchy, but as soon as the music started my surroundings faded.

The three accompanying musicians were excellent, but the old Russian violin master was superlative playing adaptations from Rimsky-Korsakov's *Invisible City of Kitezh,* some Glinka, after an evocative melody from Mussorgski's *Khovantschina.* Possibly the arrangements were sublimely skillful but I think the artist—like Gran with her piano—could carry any piece.

Even in the shorter, lighter pieces he told stories without words, mixing poignancy with laughter, weaving a bright thread of—no, I was about to say magic, but I don't want to use that as a metaphor. The music made me think of the way emotion was absent in Milo's journal, making it omnipresent, which led to thinking about emotion in historical works . . . and somehow I was sitting among men with top hats and women with extravagant hats atop elaborately piled hair, the still summer air thick with musky perfume and candle wax as people listened to Mily Barakirev—

"No, but I believe Milo sent the girl on the cello to Moscow to study," Aunt Sisi's bored whisper arrowed into my images of an icy river in the Russian steppe gleaming in the low winter sun and splintered it.

I jumped. On my right was Aunt Sisi's profile, calm and enduring. On the other side of her, bulky Robert von Mecklundburg whispered to his wife behind his hand.

I became aware of my own hands clenched in my lap, and I relaxed them. Then I felt Alec's brief but considering regard.

I could not recapture the mood after that. Aunt Sisi's boredom sat like a weight in the air beside me. I became aware in an ever-widening circle of the restlessness of people packed on uncomfortable wooden benches; I heard coughs, sniffs, shoes scraping, whispers. A lighthearted piece from Borodin and it ended, and I was glad.

Alec said nothing to me until Aunt Sisi had been unloaded at her home and we pulled up in front of Ysvorod House. Then: "You all right?"

"I'm fine."

Madam A. preceded us in, bade us a grave good night, and disappeared. Alec hesitated at the bottom of the stairs, then followed me up the stairs to the library, as he said, "I didn't think you were white-knuckled from pain, or from ennui, particularly when I recalled a similar reaction to *Les Sylphides* in Vienna. But something pulled you out of whatever head space you were in."

"Aunt Sisi was bored." Images from the music danced in the flames. "No, it's not her fault. Some people aren't into music."

"Ruli doesn't like it, either," Alec said, his smile ironic. "When they said she left for her clothes shopping trip so she wouldn't have to attend the spring music festival in the valley, I didn't question it. Wasn't until she'd been gone for six weeks that I got suspicious."

"So Tony must have grabbed her as soon as she agreed to the marriage, huh?"

"I wonder."

My stomach muscles tensed as I tried to sound casual. "Do you happen to know if there is a musician named Mily Balakirev?"

"Ah . . . wasn't he a composer of one of the pieces we heard?"

I didn't know that. Or did I? "Of course. I must have overhead that without being aware." I was rubbing my hands up my arms, though the room was warm and even summery. I turned my back to the fire. "I always thought I had an overactive imagination."

"What did you see?"

The impulse was to scoff, to fall back into old patterns. But I wanted so badly to tell him the truth because I knew he would listen. Though he'd never seen ghosts, magic, Nasdrafus, or the tooth fairy, he was exerting all his effort to bring about a marriage on a specific day, just in case.

"This isn't like seeing ghosts. I don't think. I sat in the cathedral audience, hearing that music when it debuted. The people around me wore late Victorian dress. It—it even smelled different. Like a billion candles burning, so there was wax in the air. How could that be possible? I don't think it has anything to do with ghosts or blessings."

"No, it doesn't," he agreed. "What you are talking about—deuteroscopy—is rare, what is sometimes called the sight, or Second Sight."

"Gran told me, very firmly, that such things are merely imagination. No truth in them."

"Whether it exists or not I can't tell you. This isn't the first time." His tone was observation, but I felt the question.

"Not even. I've always had too much imagination. I never went to scary movies—why pay for it, when it was so easy to scare myself? That was part of the reason I picked the sport I did, so I could fight back, if any of those shady monsters ever . . . I know, me, me, me. Sorry about that."

"Kim." He flicked me a look, brows raised. "I don't think twenty seconds of answering my question meets the modern standard for 'me me me.' If you don't want to talk about it, then we'll drop it."

I sighed again, trying not to squirm. Fighting the instinct to get up and move away. "Yeah, I'm wussing out. It's . . . all these years. I thought . . ." I didn't want to say anything about Gran. "Okay, you know why I went out to Schönbrunn that day? Because I was following . . . a ghost. And not just any ghost. It was Maria Sofia. I recognized her the second I saw her face in the gallery. It's even the same gown. And down in the Kaisergruft, for a second, I saw . . . something beyond one of the crypts. Then the wall was there. And that day when I jumped off the train, I wandered onto this farm, and they gave me water. I drank it and everything. But then I could see through the woman, and when you drove me by there the next day, the buildings were modern. A tractor. The field patterns different."

He frowned down at his hands, then looked up. "There are some people I know who might be able to give you better information about that than I can. What I'm told is that Dobrenica possibly exists in a kind of liminal space. It would explain some of those anomalies, like the fact that the entire country seems to function as a natural jammer to electromagnetic radio frequencies. Most reliable are either shortwave or COFDM, but neither are reliable enough to depend on. Another unexplained anomaly is the increased instability of nitrocellulose in weapons—"

"Which is?"

"—smokeless gunpowder. Old-fashioned black powder is actually less unstable up here, though not by much. That's why you'll find old style rifles in gun closets."

"Got it."

"The Salfmattas and Salfpatras insist there is another form of energy that is present in places around the world, but it conflicts with EM. You might be one of those who can see, or sense, those mystery borders."

"But neither Gran nor my mom ever saw a ghost, or anything else."

He lifted a hand, then dropped it. "I'm out of my depth here. I've no experience of any of it. I can put you with people who seem to know more. Though maybe we should save this subject until we get the current problem sorted."

"Okay. I'm good with that."

"Want a nightcap?"

"Sure."

"We'll sit on the terrace. Take advantage of one of our rare balmy nights."

The terrace was a balcony with iron furniture. Alec left me there while he went to talk to Emilio. I stared up at the diamond-bright stars in the black sky. Music drifted on the summer air from a house on the hillside below, a series of plaintive folk melodies with a Russian feel. It was live music, not a stereo. I'd heard more live music in the past few days than I had in the past ten years.

Alec returned and handed me a mug of coffee with a big dollop of *zhoumnyar* in it.

"Why did he stop the journal when he did?" I asked.

"He left it behind after some trouble that kept him on the move until after the miners' strike in Romania. It was some years before he found where he'd left it, and he'd lost the habit by then. Then—this was the late eighties—he suffered a slight stroke, was ordered to take it easy for half a year. That's when I first assumed some of his duties. And when I didn't fail too spectacularly, the six months stretched into a longer time."

"You must have been super young! 'Fail too spectacularly.' Is that modesty, or did you make mistakes?"

"I made plenty of mistakes. I was an insufferably callow know-it-all in those days," he said calmly. "Impatient with what I considered the lumbering and superstitious trappings of the past, I was going to appear like a comet and brilliantly gift my backward country with modernity."

"Like Joseph II."

"Exactly like him. Except that I didn't have an entire empire to piss off. One small country was tough enough to handle. I learned fast. Had to."

"But . . . wait a sec. I hope this won't sound like he-said she-said, but Tony said you were, ah, conservative. Like your dad."

Alec's laugh was so soft it was more like a snort. "Tony wasn't around when I made those errors. Heh. I thought he would have heard about them." He leaned his head back and smiled skyward, obviously deep in thought.

From the hillside below came the sound of a wind instrument, and then another joined in, the melodies braiding in a dancy folk beat. We listened in silence; gradually I began to sense the question that lay between us.

My nerves began to send warning sparks through me. I was hyper-aware of sitting in the chair with soft, blossom-scented air caressing my face, Ruli's silky crepe dress cool against my skin. Alec gazed across the starlit valley, feet stretched out before him. He had rolled his sleeves back to his elbows; the white of his shirt glowed in the starlight but his forearms, throat at the open collar, and face were in darkness, his profile a silhouette against the stone wall.

I stared down at my hands. What was it he had said, when I demanded to know if Armandros was my grandfather? *"I did not want to be the one to tell you . . . multiply the personal consequences . . ."*

His hand came up with the drink, and his ring flashed a cool blue wink. "That ring," I spoke up randomly. "It's a signet, isn't it?"

He dropped his hand to the chair arm. "Yes. My great-grandfather had it made."

"Then it's comparatively new? So it wasn't used to seal secret letters in the good old days?"

"No. Disappointed?" I heard rather than saw him smile.

I turned my attention to the rooftops, and beyond them the palace crowning the hill, silvery in the summer moonlight. The air was charged with promise, but it was not for me, not for me. I'd made a pass at him once, and been turned down: he was marrying someone else. I looked like her, but I was not her.

Time for a joke. "First time I saw it," I said with a fair assumption of carelessness, "I had you pegged as a Regency rake."

"Regency? Oh, the Beau Brummell fellows—Hell! The ones who wore patches and rouge and ponced about on heels higher than yours?" he asked with mock affront.

"Think of Byron, then."

"Even worse," Alec stated, and I choked on my drink. "Though he wasn't the ass he appears in what they call Byronic fiction. I read his journals and letters the last year before I left school."

"I know, I've read 'em, too. He was good to a lot of people. Had a sense of humor about himself. Sad, at the end—reminds me of Oscar Wilde in 'Ballad of Reading Gaol' and not like the ranting Baron Wildenhaim at all."

He frowned, then turned my way. "Wilden—ah. *Lover's Vows* by way of *Mansfield Park*." His tone was difficult to define. Almost meditative.

"Right." I pictured a lounging figure with curly blond hair and wicked black eyes. "Maybe Tony should be Byron, then. But he's a far better Henry Crawford."

"He's Byronic enough galloping around with rifles and swords up in his hills," Alec said, getting to his feet. "I had better get back to work."

Leaving me wondering what I'd said wrong. Or rather, what my words had done inside his head. Because I hadn't said anything wrong. But something had sure changed the atmosphere.

TWENTY-NINE

I DID NOT EXPECT to see Alec again before the masquerade dinner.

I was standing in the library looking out the window, thinking about how best to reach Father Teodras (Josip, maybe? Only how could he help me fend off Reithermann or his minions if they jumped out from behind the bushes?) when the door opened behind me. Assuming it was Emilio with another of those notes from my aunt, I said, "Does it require an answer?"

"You haven't heard the question," Alec said.

I whirled around, every nerve flashing hot and then cold.

"How about another drive? The weather is perfect."

"Sure."

"I take it Aunt Sisi has been bombarding you with communiqués from the front?"

"Twelve so far today," I said. Each couched in affectionate terms, assuring me that she was only thinking of my comfort, but together the effect had been the opposite: intimidation. But she'd gone to a great deal of trouble to organize this masquerade for me, so I was determined to see everything in the best light possible. "I know she means to help. I don't know the etiquette up here, my pirate life in Rio and so forth aside."

He laughed as we got into his Fiat. "Do what you like, and forget the rest," he said. "There's nothing wrong with your manners, and at masquerades, nobody worries about precedence."

"Got it," I said, as he pulled away and drove slowly down the street. No Secret Service. No phalanx of sinister minions talking constantly into pin mikes—in view, anyway, making me wonder how much of "security" is visible intimidation?

We rolled slowly through the main streets of Riev. It was two o'clock, the traffic heavy as shops reopened for afternoon business. Alec occasionally nodded or smiled or lifted his hand at individuals in the crowded streets. Doing the Royal Appearance thing? If they thought I was Ruli, I could do my bit. I smiled and lifted a hand whenever I caught the eyes of staring citizens, feeling fake. Especially when some of the people bowed.

It was a relief when we passed the quarry at the edge of Riev. Abruptly the city ended in open road. He sped up the hairpins into the mountains westward. I asked over the engine-roar and wind, "Someplace in mind?"

He gave me a brief nod. Sunbeams flashed between tree branches to emphasize the rocky striations in cliffs and limn leaves and petals with glowing light. Alec put on sunglasses. This was the first time I regretted the loss of my hat down the river off Tony's mountain. I shaded my eyes as I took in the misty green scenery. The recent rain had caused cataracts of frothing water to hiss and thunder down under bridges and through canyons; the thick forest growth had deepened in color to a blue-green mystery, and the flowers to light-giving brilliance.

Alec slowed as we neared a sleepy-looking village near a roaring river. A rare sight caught my attention, a reasonably new vehicle—a Renault altered into a jeep. It was parked in front of a tavern. Two men leaned against it, both holding beer mugs. A third, older man sat on a bench in the sun. As we passed, all three raised their heads, and as Alec lifted his fingers in greeting, and a man wearing a scarlet-embroidered Dobreni tunic genially hefted his beer mug.

This happened about three times more. I finally said, "Is today the beginning of that holiday you were talking about?"

"The holiday begins the fifteenth. The Feast of the Assumption."

"Sounds religious."

"It is; for the Roman Catholics the holiday commemorates the Virgin Mary's assumption into Heaven. But it also marks the beginning of our national holiday as well. I'm taking you to where it all begins."

"There seem to be a lot of people lingering about. Is that because it's such a pretty day, after all that rain?"

"That's part of it," he said.

We were above the city now, on the steep eastern slope of Mt. Adeliad. Alec turned up a drive, then pulled out onto a wide promontory which afforded an unimpeded view of the northern portion of the river valley. Huge moss-barked spruce crowded the edges of the ledge, creating a natural frame. Behind us, set deep in the trees, was an old stone Romanesque church. And before it, spreading nearly the entire width of the ledge, was a mosaic of chipped and fitted stones of all colors and shapes. The mosaic was laid out in geometric patterns that suggested stars and planets. Except for the cross at the center and the Christian symbolism around the edges, it had a Roman feel.

"It's beautiful," I breathed. "And so's that." I jerked my thumb over my shoulder at the splendid view. "I don't know who's done better here, humans or nature."

"The site was originally a Roman temple. There's evidence that even older civilizations celebrated here. The stone ledge is the most modern addition, having been repaired in the mid-1300s on the old pattern, but with the religious symbolism added. After plague ripped through Dobrenica in the 1380s, this church was dedicated to Our Lady of the Assumption, and the Fourteen Holy Helpers were added for good measure. September second is St. Xanpia's feast day, and it often begins the Jewish High Holy Days; gradually all these holidays came to be connected into the national celebrative week, and it all begins here. Here, have a look."

We walked across the ledge to the edge. The mosaic under my feet was fitted together without any grout. Riev lay spread below us, vaguely circular in shape.

Southward below the city the patterns of farms spread straight to the river, which gleamed like molten metal in the sunlight. In the city center the cathedral spire reached heavenward, and around it lay splashes of green: the parks. We were too high to see individual cars or people, though there were flashes of the sun on metal or glass.

I wondered what Alec thought when he gazed down on the city like this. I sensed an undercurrent of excitement.

His head turned; he caught me staring. "Question?"

"Let's say the Blessing is real. Why bother with it now? I could see the Dobreni trying in 1939, or during the Iron Curtain days, when your dad married your mom. But things are pretty peaceful in this particular area now, or as much we humans ever seem to get."

"On the surface, yes." He looked away from me, at the hazy mountains on the other side of the valley, crowned by Devil's Mountain. "Historically, the five ruling families were known as guardians." He spoke slowly, choosing his words. "I think the easiest way to explain is to say that if we lose those mines, we lose the country. We need to be united to resist . . ."

"Economic pressure? The rampant black market extralegal shenanigans going on in Russia? Some jackbooted tyrant popping up from one of your neighboring countries to reclaim all this territory?"

"All those," he said.

"And more," I ventured, eyeing him.

He faced me. "I'm trying to stay with Realpolitik."

"I get it," I said. "Or maybe I don't, but I do get that there's way more going on than meets the eye."

"Yes."

"So tell me this. Is Xanpia a real historical figure?"

He clasped his hands behind him, staring down at the city. "The details of various legends differ, but certain facts are common to all versions: whether the people who saved her were traders, refugees from the Mongols, or Christians, and whether the chasers were bandits, Roman soldiers, or Mongols, she was a kid. A shepherdess. You know from your history that kids usually had jobs at a young age, or at least were apprenticed."

"Right. Some say they did not have any childhood."

"Certainly not in the modern sense, organized around the school year. She was roaming the mountainside with her sheep when she found a starving band of orphans from some war and took them in. Then they in turn were saved from the pursuers by the united efforts of the locals. When the pursuers tried to surround them a freak snowstorm hit, though this was late summer. The pursuers searched and searched but went around in circles before they found their way out of the mountains and back into the west. Meanwhile she and her band dedicated this site in thanksgiving."

He waved a hand back at the church behind us. "From there the legends get obscure—some saying the band split up and moved to other mountains, others that they passed into the Nasdrafus and remained there for a century before returning. The modern view is that they moved down the mountain into the trade village that eventually became Riev and took up life there."

Birds scolded from the trees lining the parking apron; I turned in time to see some kids chase each other around Alec's car and vanish into the church.

The sound of childish voices chanting drifted out moments later. "What happens during the festival?"

"Beginning early on August fifteenth, a crowd of girls, usually thirteen- and fourteen-year-olds but often brides-to-be as well, dress in white and gather here on the ledge. They march with lit tapers down the path beyond that stone archway. It's an old sheep path—never widened for vehicles. Leads directly down the mountain to Riev, through the palace grounds. Legend has it that Xanpia marches with them if their hearts are pure."

"Pure! The boys don't have to be 'pure'?"

"You know your history." He turned out his hands. "But purity is not always equated with virginity. That's been debated, if you look at certain records, especially when a number of Salfmattas claimed to see the saint marching along with a pregnant bride-to-be. I used to wonder if the Salfmattas were doing some social damage control when claiming to see their spirits, though a friend insists they were seers."

"Now that's interesting. So then what happens?"

"The girls go straight to either the cathedral, the Russian Orthodox church, or to the temple, which they reach at dawn. This signifies the beginning of the Lady Festival; she's a saint to the Catholics and an angelic figure to the Jews."

"I thought angels were a Christian thing."

"Some conservative Jews in the Hassidic tradition accept angels as delineated in the works of the scholar Maimonides."

"Okay. Go on."

"The streets and houses of the city are decorated with green boughs for the duration. On the fifteenth and again on the second white flowers appear, mostly worn by girls. A side note." He smiled, his eyes narrowed, reflecting pinpoints of light from the sun. "The white was not only a symbol of purity, but of magic, the white of the mysterious snow. During times of occupation—including the last war—the conquerors were bemused by the white flowers that young women wore in their hair and on their clothes during those two weeks. Flowers that the young ladies would smilingly toss at them."

"In hopes that the magic would work again and get rid of them? I don't know if that's sad or cool!"

Will you be here? I heard the question in my mind, but when he spoke, it was different words: "Shall we go into the church?"

"If the kids are done," I said, distracted.

"Kids?"

"A minute ago. While you were telling me about the festival. Chanting. I thought they were doing a church service."

"I wasn't aware—but then I was talking. Probably too much," he added ruefully.

"No, I find it interesting."

"You didn't have a religious upbringing?" he asked as we crunched across the well-raked gravel.

"Dad calls himself a neo-Platonic syncretist, which means he's open to anything, he says. Mom wasn't raised with anything. She told me once she vaguely remembered attending Mass, but by the time they reached California, Gran had stopped going. About ten years ago, Gran went missing Sunday mornings, and Mom said she was going to Mass again.

Gran didn't say anything. Kinda weird, isn't it, though I didn't think anything of it at the time."

He said mildly as we entered the nave, "Seems there was a lot she didn't tell you."

Cool air smelling of incense bathed our faces. The church was lit by lamps on two levels: down the outer two aisles, and high above in the triforium. Candles burned as well, but the massive stone of the chevron-carved drum piers overshadowed the flickering tongues with impassive patience.

The children had left by some other exit. I turned toward the apse and was startled by vivid color and human figures. What I took at first to be a crowd of people moving about the altar proved to be statues. But so lifelike!

Central, up high over the altar, was the Virgin Mary, garbed in white, eyes and a hand lifted ecstatically heavenward. The other hand stretched protectively toward one of the six male figures crowded at the side. He had a hand out, and from it dangled a length of blue fabric, which blended harmoniously with the figures around.

Near Mary stood a strong, white-robed male who had to be an angel. He carried in both hands a container. Each figure was individual, expressing through its pose a different mood, or mode of faith, was my guess. The statues, the utter quiet, the cool air blended with the echo of childish voices rising and falling, the treble chant floating high overhead. The children had to be in the gallery—no doubt they were a choir.

"So those are the Fourteen Holy Helpers with Mary?"

Alec had stopped behind me so as not to limit my view; his heels rang on the ancient stones as he rejoined me. The chanting ceased.

"Those are the twelve Apostles and the Archangel Michael." There was an odd quality to his voice. "The statues were replaced half a century ago. These new ones are in roughly the same grouping as the old."

"Were the old ones this beautiful? These seemed alive when I first came in." My eyes rested on Mary the Virgin's upturned face, which was lit by two high lamps. Even from this distance, her expression was exalted.

"No. That is, not from what I've heard. The old ones were stiff medieval figures, carved from wood and painted and repainted. They were rotten by the turn of the century, so the process of change was begun. These things take time in churches, you know." He smiled.

As I got closer, I discovered that the figures were larger than life-size. I peered more closely, appalled to discover bits of plaster gleaming spottily in the figures' robes. Chips and hairline cracks marred faces and hands; on some, the paint had discolored from smoke, weather, or from being poor quality paint in the first place. In others the paint had puckered and peeled. "I guess it's a poor church?"

Alec's soft laugh this time was more like a sigh.

"The art that went into making those figures deserves decent materials. Plaster, in this climate? Why not chop down one of those trees outside? A whole army of saints could be carved from a single tree."

Alec did not immediately answer, but stared up at the figures for a time. Then he said, "The Germans and Soviets thought so, too. They left this church alone. In fact, its being out of the way to almost everyone, as well as unprepossessing in appearance, made it one of the few allowed to function during the antireligious period."

"This is where the Blessing is supposed to be invoked?"

"Right. This is it."

"What happens exactly?"

"According to the records, it has happened three times. All five leading families were present, the occasion a royal marriage and a vow of peace. Afterward no one could get in, or out, of the country for the duration of whatever war was going on. Until the Dobreni began fighting among themselves."

"Exactly what constitutes this mysterious Nasdrafus? Walls that miraculously appear? Mysterious beams of light?"

He brushed his fingers over the back of a pew in a restless gesture, then started up the aisle. "From the outside? Snowstorms. Fog. Travelers always seem to find their way right back to where they began. Go in circles. Nothing miraculous or mysterious. From the inside? In modern terms, the country shifts to what we call liminal space, out of reach of the dimension in which we stand now. In historical terms, otherworld beings exist side-by-side with humans. Notice I do not say 'live' as life and death are defined differently."

I paused to look back into the empty sanctuary to discover that it wasn't empty. One of the choir kids stood before the altar, looking up at the silent figures. She whirled around, her tangled yellow hair flopping. She wore the same sort of smock I'd seen on kids running around on Riev's streets, her skinny legs sticking out below like twigs. Her face lifted in a sudden smile, and she waved at me, a quick twinkle of fingers. I waved back, and she dashed into the shadows and vanished.

"Whatever happened, your history seems bound up in this church, this site, this mountain," I said.

Alec halted on the mosaic and took in the church, the valley, and the mountains beyond with a sweep of his hand. "Our history is bound up here," he said as we passed into the afternoon sun.

I threw back my head, my eyes tearing as they readjusted to the streaming light, and took in the rustle of breeze high in the trees and the chirp and caw of unseen birds. "Someone ought to have those figures recast before they disintegrate."

"I will. Soon," Alec promised, smiling.

THIRTY

WE PASSED SEVERAL more groups of men sitting out in the sun chatting and drinking beer. Alec exchanged waves with them, everyone genial; I wondered if the women were inside working while their menfolk took advantage of the lovely weather, but I didn't say anything. Why destroy the good mood? It wasn't as if my opinion was going to change anything.

When we reached Ysvorod House I remembered the ball, and I clapped my hands and rubbed them. Alec gave me a peculiar grimace which I understood immediately. "Don't tell me you're one of those dull guys who moan about having to wear a costume?"

"I like them very much—at certain times. This isn't one of them."

"Politics again?"

"Yes."

"What are you going as? Herod the Horrific? Or Ivan the Terrible, with pointed shoes and a bearskin cap?"

"My fallback is King Alexander, whose wife was a Ysvorod. Then I only have to put on a ribbon and a few of his medals over my Vigilzhi uniform. The most formal uniform has altered little in a hundred and fifty years."

"Then that's not a costume at all."

"True. But so much easier to manage while dancing. Would you like your ankles impaled by pointed shoes?"

"No, and I wouldn't want to give up waltzing for medieval verisimilitude—there will be waltzing, won't there?" I had a sudden terrible thought. "Not stuff like the cha cha or two-step? Though those are better than the prom shuffle."

"Aunt Sisi shuffle at a formal masquerade ball? Aurelia Kim, where are your wits?" he teased, leaning on the banister and laughing up at me as I started slowly up the stairs.

I heaved a loud sigh of relief.

Alec added, "We'll leave for Mecklundburg House at twenty after six. If you need a hand before then, holler for help."

"One of Aunt Sisi's notes promised honest-to-princess maid service. If they don't show, send up the Vigilzhi. I'm gonna need 'em to lace that waist over my abs of steel."

The phone rang in the library. He laughed, waved a hand, and vanished.

True to her word, Aunt Sisi sent a pair of women to do my makeup and hair. The women were quiet and efficient; my hair was piled up in eighteenth-century loops and swirls. The headdress, a faux coronet made of pearls attached to feathers and bits of lace, fitted securely into the complicated hairdo. Even without powder, I looked unnervingly like the portrait of Queen Maria Sofia.

I turned reluctantly from my own image in the mirror, which I'd been staring at, wishing I could get into the minds of my long-ago ancestors before they attended their first ball. You'd think with all those weird imaginings I could have a fun one—but no, my brain remained stubbornly fixed on my own image in the mirror.

At 6:15 Alec knocked on my door. "Kim?"

"I'm ready," I called.

"I've got something for you," Alec called back.

I tore myself from the mirror and tripped in my buckled shoes to the door, glorying in the rustle and hiss of my skirts. I knew I looked my absolute best, but what I was not prepared for was how hot Alec appeared in that uniform.

Those tight-chested, high-collared tunics were designed to set off male bodies, and as he already had a good basic structure he was magnificent—his fine, dark hair combed back so it fell in waves at either side of his temples, his straight shoulders emphasized by the epaulettes and the baldric with the loops of gold braid, the blue of the tunic's fabric reflected in his eyes and echoed the sapphire glow on his signet ring. He carried his gloves in one hand. The other rested on the graceful hilt of a dress sword.

I met his eyes—he was clearly enjoying my astonishment. "Pretty spiffy," I managed finally.

"May I return the compliment?" He lifted his hand. Under the gloves he carried a flat black case.

"Oh no." I backed up, covering my throat. "Not if that's your mother's stuff."

"She had no daughter and her sister had no children. There's no one to care whether her jewelry gets lost or not. Any child of mine will inherit such a quantity the parts will never be distinguished from the sum. Please."

"If Tony were a Regency fellow he'd have known to get his mother's jewels copied," I said nervously. "Then he could finance anything—" I stopped gabbling when Alex opened the case. "Ack."

I stared down at a diamond necklace of the sort Florence Ziegfield chorus girls got from machine-gun toting gangsters in the Damon Runyon days. It was a *string* of diamonds. Any of them would have made a killer ring. From the center three delicate diamond pendants hung, the middle pendant the longest, with a teardrop shaped stone the size of my littlest toe. It glittered and winked on its black velvet bed as if it were alive—*sentient.* "No way!"

"Throw it off a cliff at the end of the evening if you've not lost it," he said recklessly, lifting it out.

"Oh, be serious. I couldn't." But I stood, frozen, as he stepped behind me and clasped it around my neck.

The unfamiliar weight settled about my collarbones, but my attention radared backward as his fingers lightly brushed the nape of my neck. A shiver ran through my body, and as I could not suppress it, to hide it I bustled to the mirror.

No doubt about it. I had been happy with my appearance before, but the necklace made the costume.

"Your mother's family must have been the local Rockefellers," I said nervously, putting a finger up to touch the largest stone, which flashed and glowed with my breathing. The brilliance didn't just reflect and refract light, it seemed to gather it; barely audible was the high, pure tinkle of the crystal prisms hanging on my lamp. Had I left my window open?

"This particular necklace is an Ysvorod heirloom. Goes to the brides. No one will recognize it, except perhaps Aunt Sisi. Heirloom jewels seem to be a hobby with her. She knows everyone's—that's how Ruli got into it."

He had taken a step forward, so I could see him reflected behind me in the mirror. The room seemed filled with light as our eyes met in the glass, and held—

And there it was again, the sudden awareness of him, and I could feel in the change in his breathing, the contracting of his pupils that he felt it, too.

My nerves flared with expectation, and for the first time I saw past the surface of his cool, competent mask, sensing the electric flow from me to him—from him to me. We stood there, not touching, our gazes met and blended in the reflection of the glass, until expectation fluoresced into desire, and I found it difficult to breathe.

It is not the right time.

My thought or his, it didn't matter. Time—responsibility—the world broke the spell enclosing us, crowding with other demands.

Someone knocked at the door.

"We gotta go." I drew a deep breath. Okay, that sounded pretty normal. I touched the necklace. "Thanks. It's too pretty for cliffs. I'll do my best to see that it lives through the evening. Um, don't you have a mask?" I asked, seeing that he held only his gloves.

"Not everyone wears them anymore, though all the old traditions are still observed. Watch the feathers," he added with a smile as we left the bedroom, and I ducked down so my headdress would not get knocked askew.

I paused in the door way to check that I hadn't left anything behind; I noticed the prisms were still.

Aunt Sisi's face blanked when she saw the necklace, but after a glance at Alec her usual composure returned and she gave me the most gracious of compliments on my appearance.

Phaedra was gorgeous in a high-waisted Directoire gown à la Josephine Beauharnais, but when I complimented her she thanked me in a kitten-mew of a voice, so cold it was as if I'd thrown mud on her. I didn't dare compliment Madam Robert in her (probably vintage) Worth gown, with ropes of pearls and an Art Nouveau headdress of pearls and diamonds fitted around her narrow head. From the way her angry gaze touched me and shifted, I knew I'd chosen right.

Oh, it was going to be a charming dinner, I could tell already. But I was determined not to let them spoil my evening.

It didn't help that I caught the first note of sincerity in Robert's voice when he complimented me on my looks. Tall, heavy-chinned Percy did not attempt to hide his admiration. Cerisette, who reminded me of a black widow spider—an elegant one—in her vintage Chanel gown and jeweled cloche hat from the twenties, had absolutely nothing to say. I could see by the bitter compression of her lips that she was working hard to fix that.

Aunt Sisi was statuesque and elegant in her soft Edwardian-style gown, with her silvering blond hair piled high and curled gracefully. On it rested a gold and pearl coronet with three graceful arches. No, a tiara; those were diamonds at the peak of each arch.

When I complimented her she touched the pearls at her neck in an uncharacteristically quick gesture and said, "Thank you, dear, but tonight is for you young people." And she led us in to dinner immediately thereafter.

Dinner was . . . weird. Not the food. P. G. Wodehouse's great Anatole could not have surpassed the superb offerings Pedro sent up for Aunt Sisi's guests. I was seated between Percy and Robert, who looked like a Russian emperor in his fur-edged velvet tunic and elaborate bearskin cap. Both men seemed to have made liberal inroads into Aunt Sisi's liquor supply before we had arrived, and during the dinner they kept Aunt Sisi's butler on the hop with demands for refills.

The butler topped my nearly untouched goblet so many times I felt a silent reproach, as if my manners were lacking because I wasn't downing wine like most of the rest of them. And they shouldn't have. Robert kept patting my hand every time his wife and Alec, who were dinner partners, were exchanging small talk, and his pouchy dark gaze rested frequently on the low neck of my gown. I longed for his former rudeness.

The von M's ignored Madam A so I leaned over and talked to her until I noticed Robert leaning out to look down my dress. Ew ew *ew*.

On my other side, Percy seemed nervous. I wondered if this was his first masquerade, too, the way he chortled and rambled on about the clever mask he had ordered. He was costumed as a buccaneer, in a black velvet pirate coat with huge gold-edged cuffs. Under that was a front-laced white shirt, tied with a crimson sash through which he'd thrust a long-barreled toy pistol. Black velvet loose pants were stuffed into wide-cuffed buccaneer boots with high square heels and dashing buckles on the uppers.

Three or four times toward the end of the dinner he pulled the pistol from his sash and waved it around growling "Arrrr!" until Aunt Sisi finally asked him, in the nicest way, to zip it.

We seemed to have fifty courses before that horrible dinner was *finally* over. As soon as everyone rose from the table to adjourn for coffee Alec promptly excused himself.

"You're leaving me here?" I sidled up. "Tell me you're not."

"Have to," he said, sending a flick of a glance toward Aunt Sisi that revealed suppressed anger. "I'm already late."

So, more of the subtle game playing—the dinner had been deliberately dragged out? Talk about grade-school, I thought, but I kept my social smile firmly in place. Nothing was going to ruin my night, I vowed. "You rat," I muttered to Alec out of the side of my mouth. "Cowardly rat."

Alec flushed and hid a laugh behind a cough.

Aunt Sisi turned, clasping her thin hands in consternation. "I fear I was not prepared for you to leave alone like this. I already have five to be fitted into my car." She indicated my miles of puffy skirt. "We do not have the space."

"I thought we arranged this," Alec said to her, smiling and polite, but I sensed every line of him radiating tension. "I must get there early. The council is waiting for me right now."

"My dear." She met his steady gaze with hand-folded composure, "I did offer to convey your ladies to the ball, but when I discovered you were bringing them here yourself I assumed you had arranged to transport them from here as well."

So Alec had to send for Kilber; as soon as he got hold of him through Aunt Sisi's telephone, he took off. I hadn't known she had a phone—all her messages to me had been written on scented notepaper. I wondered what she used the phone for as Alec picked up his gloves and departed.

This was a matter of maybe ten blocks they were talking about, on a pretty night; I would have loved nothing better than to walk, without any more von M company than necessary, but I knew Madam A would not wish to walk, and my buckle shoes were tight. So I kept quiet.

Percy touched my arm. "What do you think of my mask, eh? Isn't it handsome?" He slipped it over his face, clapped his hat on, and posed. "Savvy?"

The Captain Jack Sparrow reference made me like him a lot more, even if he'd obviously drunk too much. I smiled at his mask, which was full face, with leering pirate features. Over the back he wore a long black wig, and on top a tricorn hat with plumes held in place by a rhinestone buckle. "Like the feathers?" His voice was muffled. "They were my own idea."

His cousins stood around and smiled and uttered fake variations of, "Oh how clever!" as he postured and flourished.

When he caught his cutlass in the curtains, Cerisette and Honoré (who looked more like a sinister Bertie Wooster than ever in his elegant Oscar Wilde evening dress) rushed to help, Cerisette disentangling the brocade from the steel, and Honoré thrusting his cousin's sword back into the baldric, then muscling Percy in the direction of the coffee service.

After all those parties, I still didn't know any of them—but the way they cooed over Percy, who'd obviously had about a gallon too much of whatever had been in those crystal glasses, I wondered if he was the richest of them, as he wasn't the most titled. Or the smartest, I added mentally when he staggered and nearly trashed a cloisonné lamp on an ancient Chinese table.

Aunt Sisi joined Honoré. "Coffee, Parsifal?" was the last thing I heard before the butler announced, "The automobile is here for Madam and Mademoiselle."

By which were to understand that Kilber had arrived at last.

I couldn't get out of that house fast enough. Madam A looked like an escapee from a gulag as we climbed into the Daimler.

I'd scarcely settled my billowing skirts across three quarters of the back seat when we pulled up at the palace in front of a rolled out red carpet.

There was no announcing, not at a masquerade. But an army of liveried servants came out to take wraps, offer drinks, and escort us inside the ballroom. We blended into the arriving guests; Madam A found some old friends and seemed to relax.

After some self-conscious or laughing introductions ("Queen Maria Sofia, may I present Queen Eleanor of Aquitaine?") and smiles all around, I excused myself to walk about and see the sights. Madam A seemed to think that was all right, so I took off, feeling like a ship under full sail in my miles of tulle, brocade, and satin, the diamonds bobbing gently against my collarbone.

The ballroom had four huge doors, all thrown open as the air was balmy; the vast chamber was made of white marble, the fixtures of gold, which scintillated with the brilliance of a zillion candles in sconces and chandeliers. That much candlelight has a silvery sheen, flattering people with golden warmth as they strolled up and down the marble hallways.

I cruised the entire perimeter, but didn't see Alec anywhere. His secret meeting had to be in an antechamber, probably behind closed doors.

To my surprise (and relief) it was a good twenty minutes later that Aunt Sisi and co. crossed the mile or so that lay between Mecklundburg House and the palace. I assumed that the time had been spent in attempting to sober Percy up, for he walked a lot straighter. I zipped around a corner before they spotted me.

People dressed in historical costume thronged the ballroom in graceful groupings, chattering and laughing. Jewels flashed and glittered, brocades and velvets hushed by in graceful swirls. I was tickled by a glimpse of two young guys who, resplendent in barbaric Cossack garb, were practicing clicking their heels and bowing before the long mirrors set into the paneling of a small anteroom.

I had slipped on my mask, but everyone seemed to know who "Queen Sofia" was: I heard a few muted "Lady Aurelias" and everywhere I went crowds parted, deferring with bows, smiles, nods, and "good evenings."

Then the orchestra in the overhead gallery struck up. A footman in eighteenth-century livery, complete to white wig, rapped on the marble floor three times and announced sonorously, *"Avec la permission de sa Majesté, la bal commence! Promenade royale!"* Interesting that German had been replaced as the language of government, but French lingered on at events such as these.

Alec appeared with Aunt Sisi on his arm. As they took their positions, people converged into partnerships; I was paired with an eighteen-year-old scion of the House of Trasyemova who peered at me with such shy and awkward admiration that I spent most of that first dance cracking jokes in French-laced Dobreni to get him to relax. This dance, the royal promenade, was a simplified minuet. The slow, dignified steps and the poses and bows were easy to pick up.

With the second piece of music the rococo gave way to the nineteenth century. As the orchestra began an introduction in waltz time, Aunt Sisi guided Alec toward Phaedra. Alec bowed slightly, said something polite, and left them. They watched as he crossed the room to my side.

My young partner backed away, eyes wide, making me smother a laugh. Alec bowed to me, his face solemn, except for his eyes.

I smothered a laugh behind my fan. As I placed my gloved fingertips on his gloved wrist, I muttered, "This is political, isn't it?"

"A reminder to Aunt Sisi that though she can manage the masquerade, it's best not to attempt managing me. Do you mind?"

"Not a bit. The sooner I get to waltz in this dress, the better."

The betraying smile in his eyes intensified, then his expression smoothed as he guided me to the center of the room.

I minced on my toes so that my wide skirts floated and did not swing like a bell. As we took up waltz position other couples formed up and joined us, the floor soon so crowded that when the music began we were hardly dancing so much as moving in a circle. After we'd been bumped two or three times, and my hem nearly stepped on, I took my hand off his shoulder and scooped up the back part of my skirts.

Alec was no more romantic than the dance—he seemed absent, his gaze flicking about the room over my head.

After a round of the entire room, he smiled apologetically. "Sorry. Didn't mean to ignore you—thought you wouldn't mind while I do a reconnaissance."

"No problemo. You're managing real well with that pig-sticker. No livers cut out yet, and in this crowd that's a feat. You said once you know how to fence. Did you compete?"

"I had a few bouts here and there." A hint of grin. "It's my grandfather's blade. Family legend has it he fought a couple of duels with it."

"I wouldn't mind trying a few passes with it."

"Oh yes. The trophies—I take it those are real?"

"Real," I repeated in mock horror. "I'll have you know I was picked to try out for the Olympics, but Gran's illness intervened, cutting short what surely would have been a gold medal career."

He laughed.

I told him about Percy, the cutlass, and the curtains. Alec enjoyed that, and as a space momentarily opened up he maneuvered us deftly into it. His clasp was light and his leading seemed effortless—but my following was effortless as well. That physical awareness was there again, but less intimate in these surroundings, and therefore less demanding. I know how trite it sounds, but I truly did feel as light as a feather, and we whirled and turned as if we had practiced together all our lives.

Then the music ended and I was besieged by hopeful partners. I didn't sit down for a long time, and never noticed the need. The shoes had stretched, or my feet decided to cooperate.

Not that it was all joy. Far too frequently for my taste I found my hand summarily claimed by von M's, mostly Robert and Percy. Rank was supposedly relaxed, but when any of that gang approached me, would-be partners always deferred. I was determined to be polite—but Robert gave me no chance for a polite "no." He'd take hold of me and start dancing, sticking me with another long session of cigar breath and his clammy hands getting chummy, especially during what I decided would be our last waltz, when his alcohol fumes were almost as strong as the cigar.

Then there was drunken Percy, who wasn't a letch, but they hadn't been able to sober him up completely. Liquor made him even more awkward than usual, and his pirate boots threatened to smash my feet until I started dancing with my toes turned outward in first position.

After a couple of hours the white-wigged, liveried servants opened up a punch room, serving iced wine punch out of cut crystal bowls, along with coffee and tea. Percy thanked me sweetly for the latest dance and wandered over to take up a station there. Relief!

But I would have rather had him as a partner than Robert, who bulled aside a nice-looking fellow my age coming toward me. I pointed meaningfully at the restroom, from which I peered out until Robert got tired of waiting and vanished into the punch room.

The ballroom had gotten warm by then. The footmen threw open the doors to the terrace that aproned out into the garden, which was lit by hanging paper lanterns. With almost a collective sigh the guests began spilling out into the cool night air. People danced on the terrace, from which the orchestra could be heard splendidly, and others strolled out into the balmy darkness along the ordered paths.

Safe from Robert, I had slipped out again and was claimed for the last of that dance by my eighteen-year-old Sergei. Shyness now banished, he began telling me eagerly about engineering studies, and how if the Stadthalter got his way over the old dodderers on the council, the wind turbines plus the hydroelectric plant would soon guarantee even the meanest Dobreni house would have electrical lights, if they wanted them. Many didn't, he explained. So many of the old folks thought electricity mere foolery—

He stuttered to a stop, his gaze riveted over my shoulder. His head moved as he tracked someone, and I noticed two young and only superficially demure Victorian ladies strolling close by, bustles undulating either side of cinched-in waists. Languishing looks were cast at my partner, followed by giggles; one of the girls was fanning herself so hard her friend's hair was blowing. The advantages of modern electricity? Gone with the wind.

I used my trusty restroom excuse, freeing him up to join a friend his age. From the safety of the inner door I watched in amusement as he gestured briefly and violently, then both young men started off in the direction the girls had taken.

It wasn't until he was gone that I wondered if Ruli would have handled the encounter the same way.

The orchestra next played a local dance, which I recognized as a refined version of one played at Anna's wedding. In the garden three or four young ladies partnered one another, splitting and reforming, to an admiring circle. The second verse had begun when a short, elderly Napoleon presented himself to me, asking with old world charm if her majesty Queen Maria Sofia would consent to dance with a mere upstart of a Bonaparte. I laughed and held out my hands, enthusiastic when I discovered that he was light on his feet, his grip gentle and impersonal.

Eleven o'clock came and went; when I spotted Robert on the prowl, I asked Napoleon for the next dance, though etiquette seemed to be that you didn't dance with the same person twice in a row.

He hesitated—glanced at Robert bearing down on us—and then

with a cordial smile held out his hand again. I relaxed and enjoyed the dance.

His French was good, his conversation centering on the delicate and peril-fraught hobby of growing orchids. He talked about kinds, colors, et cetera, as I listened politely, grateful that he'd rescued me from Emperor Octopus Hands. His politeness had extended into the detail of the enthusiast as I gazed past his shoulder for Alec, who I hadn't seen for some time.

My gaze crossed Aunt Sisi's once, and she nodded and smiled at me. Elegant and queenly, she was surrounded by a group of men who had to be Council Staff, wearing swallowtail coats and baldric-type sashes with medals pinned on that seemed impressively authentic.

As the next piece of music began—and Napoleon stayed with me—Alec reappeared in the ballroom. He moved at an unhurried pace among the guests, exchanging comments and salutations. He tapped my partner on the shoulder, and Napoleon gave way with a smile and an airy gesture.

Alec held out his hand, and I laid mine in his. Light, music, and air swept us into the center of the floor. Once again attraction flared between us, strong and bright as flame. I fought for equilibrium—grasped at humor. "Don't tell me. You've been hiding in the card-room Aunt Sisi had opened up," I said with fake asperity. "If so, better watch out for your feet."

"All I've been playing is political pundit," he returned—and paused, looking past my shoulder. I sneaked a look. A guy in livery waited a respectful distance away, but his body language was broadcasting loud and clear: Urgent Message Alert!

Alec shifted his attention back. "Don't cripple me, please, at least not before I find out if you'll save the Midnight Waltz for me. Unless someone's beat me to it?"

"Midnight—oh, unmasking?"

"Unmasking," he repeated, giving the word an entirely different meaning. Then I remembered old novels, and how unmasking at midnight had often meant a kiss.

"I'll be waiting," I said, and I was scarcely prepared for the power of the response. He said nothing, but I felt his reaction through his hands.

The music ended, and, with an unhurried gravity Alec raised my hands and kissed them, sending through me an anticipatory frisson. Then he bowed and walked away toward that side door, where not one but two of those messengers closed in around him.

THIRTY-ONE

I WATCHED UNTIL he vanished into an anteroom, then turned toward the kaleidoscopic whirl of guests beginning another waltz. At the edge of the crowd was a still figure: I was caught by Aunt Sisi's gaze.

She stood by the door to the punch room. The chandelier light reflected in her wide eyes. I wondered if I should go over to her and say something polite about how much fun I was having at her masquerade, or thank her yet again for the loan of the gown. Her steady gaze was unnerving. That and the stillness of her stance made me wonder if Alec's gesture, so public, so deliberate, had made her angry.

Oh, right, Murray. He's engaged to *her daughter.*

But he didn't mean it—it's the night, the dance, the costumes—All these excuses streamed through my mind, to vanish again into the night. He did mean it. I didn't know what it meant for *me.*

Then she smiled, her chin lifting. It was a triumphant smile, and she raised her hand in salute, the queen's gesture. I flashed a smile back, relieved nothing was wrong, and glad she could enjoy the achievement of a successful ball. She'd certainly worked hard enough to bring it off.

She tapped her fan on the arm of one of those swallowtailed men, and included his buddies in her smile. I had to admire her skill in group management—in ten seconds flat, she was the center of their circle and had them all talking and laughing.

I turned away, spreading my fan and flapping it slowly. Bad news: I discovered that I was surrounded by von M's. Good news: they were at a safe distance, each busy with a partner. Including Robert, actually dancing with his wife.

I wandered in the direction of the terrace, seeking cooler air—glad to have a breathing space—then spotted a familiar plume-hatted pirate making his way directly for me.

"Percy." Cursing inwardly, I headed for the restroom. At least he appeared to have sobered up again, enough to walk straight—his stride increased and he neatly cut me off.

With a leisurely bow and a flourish of those ridiculous gauntlets, Percy reached for me.

"Pardon," I began as he took my hand. His grip was firm; resisting the urge to yank my hand free (and cause everyone in the room to stare) I said, "I was on my way to the restroom."

Percy didn't answer this obvious lie. He slid the other hand around me and moved gently in place—step-two-three, step-two-three—the waltz time was irresistible, and he seemed to have lost his clumsiness. Maybe he'd switched to swigging coffee. Since the dance was half over, I shrugged and gave up—and with a sweep he whirled us out onto the floor.

How do you tell a guy you don't know that when he's sobered up he dances a thousand times better? Not only expertly, but with panache.

Percy headed straight down the middle, and everyone gave way before us. I became aware of his altered grip, his hand on my waist drifted up my back in a caress.

I looked up sharply—to meet the leering pirate mask, and to hear his breathing. He stepped neatly aside as the music dipped and he handed me in a twirl under his arm. Long years of training made my feet and body respond automatically, my skirts flaring. He promptly sped up.

I danced on my toes, my feet almost leaving the floor. A silent challenge had been issued, and I met it by matching his pace. When we reached the other side of the floor he whirled me into another turn, and when I came out of it, locked me against his lean body with unexpected strength. The stupid toy pistol jutted uncomfortably against my ribs as we spun into a series of tight turns.

Waltzing with Alec had been friendly, then romantic, then sexy. This dance wasn't the least friendly, it zoomed past romance straight to sexy. Now I understood why people had spent all night waltzing a hundred years ago. If a drunken fumbler could exude this much firepower, maybe waltzing should be outlawed, I thought hazily as the world spun past. Gran must have danced right here with Armandros when she was sixteen—

I gave myself up to the giddiness this time, enjoying the melding of colors as the background whizzed past and we danced out onto the terrace, and into the cool night air. The music wound down to a close; Percy slowed. I blinked as the torchlit garden revolved gently. "Dizzy," I murmured. "I think I'd better sit down."

Percy took my elbow and guided me down a garden path. "Where are the benches?" I was glad to be outside. Not only was the air cooler, but I needed to make a quick adjustment to my gown before I experienced a serious costume malfunction.

He passed a couple of benches that had flirting couples on them, even though there was plenty of room. While he was looking around I gave my bodice a couple of surreptitious yanks and tugs.

We passed an empty bench, golden-lit through the window panes in the palace on the other side of the garden. And then the lit windows came to an end. We'd reached the side building, where plain doors opened onto modest parterres.

I was about to protest when he opened the first door we came to, leading into a dimly lit servants' hall. My feathers brushed the low ceiling, and I clasped at them quickly, but too late: the waltz had loosened them, and they came off the headdress altogether. By then Percy had found the door he was looking for, and opened it. Assuming this was a lounge, I walked in.

To find an empty room.

"Hey," I began.

"Hey what?" a laughing English voice answered.

I knew that voice, and it did not belong to Percy.

"Tony! What scam is this?"

The room was a parlor with a window giving onto a courtyard garden. As I glared at Tony, he gave a sigh of relief, yanked off the plumed tricorn, mask, and wig, and tossed them negligently onto the table. "Damn mask is hotter than hell. But it was worth it." His smiling face was flushed.

"I'm so glad for you. Not." I waved my feathers at the door. "Now, if you'll kindly step aside . . ."

"I could listen to that accent of yours forever," he replied, thumping his back to the door. "To answer your question: I wanted to dance with you."

"All right, so you did. Let's go back."

Tony, convulsed with laughter, took a casual step toward me.

Gliding backward, I snapped, "What'd you do to poor Percy, mug him in the men's room and pinch his costume?"

"Admit that you preferred me as a partner." He spread his hands.

"Okay." I shrugged. "Much. And now, if you don't mind stepping out of the way so I can return to the ballroom—"

He pulled off one of his gauntlets. As he thrust it into a huge pocket of his pirate coat, I swept my skirts aside and ducked around him.

Or tried to. He stretched out an arm to block my way. "I did want to dance with you. I couldn't resist. But I also had in mind some conversation."

"About what?" I snapped with hostility, retreating into the room.

He slid back a lace-wristed pirate sleeve to look at his watch, then smiled at me. "I wondered if you have found your proof yet? I did promise to help you look, and I'd hate to duplicate efforts."

"Haven't had the time to finish." I shrugged as I tossed the feathers onto the table beside his wig and mask. Instinct demanded I keep my hands free.

"Have you had the time to tell anyone of your search?"

Remembering my earlier mistake with him, I said promptly, "Sure! I blabbed about it to everyone. Um, except your relatives, on account of that bastard business. But I totally spread the word, because I knew my search would be quicker if I had lots of help."

"Ah. Wise." He grinned, and I couldn't tell if he'd swallowed it. Once again he took a leisurely step into the room, between me and the door. "I wondered as well if, during your cozy moments alone with Cousin Alec in Ysvorod House, you taxed him with his keeping the Dsaret hoard to himself?" He sauntered toward me, one step, two.

"If you mean have we talked about it, sure," I said coldly, backing away. "What about it? Did you want me to recite its history according to the Ysvorod School of Thought, as compared to the Revisionist von Mecklundburg version?"

"No, I want you to recite its location." He pulled off the other glove, looked at it with his brows raised as if he could not believe he had been wearing such a thing, and thrust it into the pocket containing its mate. Then he took another step toward me.

"I can only tell you where it's not, which is in the bank vault."

"Everyone knows that. It's also not at the palace, or the cathedral. Or in one of the old castle dungeons."

"Probably not. But boxes and boxes of gold bars have to be hard to hide, and even harder to transport around without people asking what's inside them and blabbing, so my guess would be they were taken to a Swiss bank, maybe before the war hit."

"It's in the country," he said, unheated as always. "You'll naturally be forming plans for a treasure-funded future—to which you are entitled. So am I! But if you do happen to find out where it is, there would be the problem of removal. I can help with that. So I propose that you and I split the proceeds equally."

"But I don't know where it is," I repeated. "You have to be stupider than I thought to believe that Alec would blab it to me when—if—he's kept his lip zipped all these years."

"So Alec didn't even give you a hint? No . . . ah, gloats? Say . . . offers?" He loomed over me, smiling quizzically.

"Offers?" His tone implied less of business dealings than of boudoir wheedlings. "I suggest you ask him."

"I will, at the right moment," he promised. "Soon, I trust. But I did want to give you the opportunity first. Because of your claim."

"Meaning you won't give me a share if I don't spill the beans? Well, since I wouldn't believe you even if I did know, it's not exactly a loss."

"But I'd keep my word. I always do. If I give it. Then there's the alternative, you combine forces with me. We can talk more of that later, when you've had time to realize the many advantages—"

"No-double-thanks!" I snarled as the back of my skirts rustled against the paneling of the wall. "Now, if you don't mind—"

"Unfortunately, my friends are late, and—" He grinned. "—your expression of virtuous outrage is as charming as that American twang. Let's try an experiment."

With three long strides he closed the distance between us. My enormous skirts kept me from vaulting over the table as I would have if I'd been in my normal clothes. I tried to wrench free, but he was much stronger.

"I wonder if this'll seem like incest? So far it doesn't," he murmured, eyes nearly closed, and pulled me against him with one of my hands clipped against the small of my back. He brought his head down and kissed me.

No, it didn't feel like incest. Would it have if we'd grown up together? I can't answer that. All I can say is that I wasn't fighting, or he'd have had a tough time getting anywhere near my face. Angry as I was, there was also that attraction, hot and bright. Denying grace, honor, friendship, even respect. I did not feel the kinship of blood, but even more important, there was no kinship of the mind, of the spirit—but damn, was there chemistry.

The kiss was incredibly hot, but I was still mad. Since the poufy skirts kept me from effective resistance, and he had one arm pinioned, I leaned into him so my satin-and-lace bosom brushed his chest. And I felt his grip falter.

We broke for breath, he laughed, and pressed soft kisses against my lips, my eyes, even the tip of my nose as I groped blindly at the side of his waist, where I knew from the too many times I'd seen Percy's costume that the butt of the toy pistol stuck up from his sash. There it was. As Tony zeroed in for another lip-lock I grasped the gun handle, yanked, and poked him hard in the chest with the barrel.

I meant to use it to clock him if he grabbed me again, but he freed me at once, taking a couple of steps back, palms out. Cold air rushed between us as I realized this heavy pistol was not a toy.

So I brought it up and leveled it past his right ear, hoping it looked like I was about to drill him between the eyes. He dropped back another step or two, shaking with silent laughter.

After scrubbing my free hand across my mouth, I said with hearty loathing, "YUCK!"

"Hey! And I got so much pleasure out of it, too."

"And you've been drinking. Ugh! No, don't move, I'm mad enough to shoot you now and dance on the remains." I kept my eyes and the pistol trained on him as I edged sideways toward the window.

His eyes were wide as they flicked to the window and back; that glance gave me an idea where it was.

He stepped forward, palms toward me. I straightened my arm as if taking aim, and he halted as I groped with my free hand, found the curtains . . . the curtain edges . . . the window—

"Could you shoot an unarmed man in cold blood?" he asked, smiling ruefully, gazing straight into my eyes as he advanced—unhurried but deliberate.

Grinding my teeth together, I pawed for the handle to the window. He took another step, another—

"No," I shouted as the window swung free. And, knowing I had maybe a second before he reached me, I flung the pistol out the window, then started after it. The million yards of fabric stuck me tight in the window.

We both heard the mighty splash as the pistol hit an unseen pond, then his hands closed on my shoulders.

I twisted away with an angry wrench and stumbled against a straight-backed chair, my skirts swooshing all over the place. As I kicked at them in disgust—I'm here to say you *cannot* adventure successfully in a ball dress—Tony dissolved into helpless laughter.

"Oh, God, a fishpond! How'll I explain that to Dieter?" he said unsteadily. "He was so insistent about my taking this antique, though it only fires a single shot at a time, and it's a bastard to reload."

"I'm so glad one of us is amused. So I'll leave you to it—"

"No, no, you're far too much fun." He leaned against the window, still laughing.

To deflect his attention as I began edging my way toward the door I said sweetly, "Would *you* be able to use that thing on an unarmed person, in cold blood?"

"No," he said. "But I wouldn't chuck it into a fishpond, either."

"Maybe I should have kept it," I said, as he advanced on me.

"You wanted that kiss as much as I did," he retorted.

"True." My voice shook. "But it's over."

"And I can't tell the difference?" He pushed back the blond lock hanging in his eyes. "I'm glad we'll have the time to explore this matter; I wonder if part of what's going on between us is how alike we are."

"That's an insult if I ever heard one," I shot back.

He laughed. "We're very much alike. The strange thing is, my sister couldn't be less like either of us—"

I whirled and sprinted for the door.

It was a good try. But when Tony caught up with me the door opened and three men entered.

I recognized the first man's hard-lined, angry face—the man in khaki at Anna's wedding. Behind him came a cute guy with curly black hair. He gave Tony a rueful grimace over the first man's shoulder; I felt Tony shrug slightly and his chin lift in a private signal, or private message.

The guy in khaki gave me a nasty smile, and raised the back of his hand to strike me. Tony pulled me back against him, snapping in a voice completely unlike his usual, "Dieter! Back off."

The man dropped his hand. In the other he held a pistol—not an old-fashioned one, but a heavy caliber handgun. And as I struggled against Tony's grip I smelled a thick, cloying odor that made me shudder instinctively as the third man, blond like Tony, fumbled with a cloth and a small silver bottle; the guy with the curly hair grabbed it.

Over my head Tony gasped, "Hurry, Niklos. Damn, that stuff reeks."

Despite my desperate efforts to free myself the wad of cloth was bumped up against my face. A brain-numbing sweet stink scoured its way through my sinuses into my lungs. I coughed violently, but it was too late; darkness settled gently over my vision. I sagged in Tony's arms and drifted into oblivion.

Another awful smell, trailing eddies of nausea, hauled my brain from its well of velvet darkness into light, with an unavoidable sense of urgency.

"Nooo . . ." I moaned, turning my head.

Once again the smell pinched at my nostrils. I jerked away and opened my eyes. Aunt Sisi bent over me, holding a bottle of nail polish remover. Nausea clawed up my throat. When I gagged she capped the bottle.

I fought against nausea, and won, then stared at her, trying to comprehend her presence. My head ached and my sinuses felt like they had been packed with dried chili beans.

Aunt Sisi gazed back at me, eyes wide and intense, mouth pressed into a line. "Anton's in trouble."

I was in a room I'd never seen before. Stretched on a bed. My skirts lay in a softly glistening mountain over my legs.

Gone were the pearls and tiara. She was dressed in a severely plain navy blue pants suit.

"He drugged me," I croaked.

She twitched her head, dismissing this irrelevant detail. "My son is in serious trouble and cannot help me." Her voice was trembling, and even more uncharacteristic, she spoke in English. "My daughter is still a prisoner at the Eyrie, and apparently this Dieter Reithermann wishes to use her life to bargain with."

"What?" I was breathing slowly and deeply, trying to clear my head and conquer the residue of nausea.

"You must help me get her out."

Adrenalin burned along my nerves. I forced myself to sit up on my elbows. "Where am I?"

"You are in my house," she replied in that same quick voice. "My Gaspard found you in a palace anteroom and brought you here to safety."

"Where's Alec?"

"I do not know. Someone at the palace said he was out chasing after some of this Reithermann's gutter-scum. Someone else thinks he is busy pursuing my son."

"How can I help? Isn't the Eyrie guarded?"

"There is a way into it only known to my son and me. Even if Reithermann has people watching up there, we should be able to find Aurelia and get her out before anyone can interfere. But the passage is steep and narrow, and I would have extreme difficulty with it. I have no one left whom I can trust. Will you come?"

I didn't even ask where the von M's were. Of course they'd be worthless as aid. My biggest worry was the necklace—which, I was relieved to discover, was still around my neck. Tony was a villain and ten kinds of a jerk but at least he wasn't a thief.

"Sure," I said, struggling to sit all the way up. "Let me go back and change and then I'm yours."

"I've things here—"

"No," I croaked. "Argh. May I have some water? Ysvorod House first. With my own hands I am going to put this blasted necklace in Alec's room."

Her brows rose. She cut a fast look over her shoulder; my gaze followed, but too slowly. All I caught was a flicker of movement as someone left the doorway.

"I'll get you some water." She walked out.

I got to my feet. Other than feeling like my body was made out of stone, I was all right. The gown was rumpled, the headdress completely gone, and my hair was coming loose from the pins.

Aunt Sisi returned quickly; I drained the water as she said, "I believe we should go now, and in haste."

"What about the ball?"

"C'est fini, tout à fait." She led the way out front, to where Tony's Austin was parked.

"Tony's car?" I said blankly, also switching to French.

Her head twitched again. "It's mine. He borrows it when he's in the city."

We got in (me having to stuff those skirts around me, no small feat) and she started it up. Her hands trembled as she turned the keys.

In silence she drove to Ysvorod House. The ground floor was ablaze with light. She studied it silently, her mouth grim. Then Emilio's wife, the housekeeper, appeared in the doorway, followed by Madam A, who at the sight of us clasped her hands prayerfully.

Aunt Sisi said to me, "I'll talk to Alexander's people. You change as rapidly as you can."

Her tension sent adrenaline shooting through me again. I bustled in, giving Madam A a breathless, "Hi. I'm all right. I have to help Aunt Sisi."

I whizzed into my room before she could protest.

All right, first thing. No ball gowns for castle breaking-and-entering. I squirmed and hopped and struggled, but finally freed myself from that gown. Breathing freely for the first time all evening, I ripped clothes out of drawers, and found a pair of brand-new, never worn designer jeans. They were tighter than I like, but they'd do. For a shirt I took down an expensive full-sleeved black silk, thinking of protective coloration. Next was the elaborate hairstyle; I ripped the pins out, wound my hair up on my head and secured it with my hairclip.

I only slowed down when I unclasped the diamonds that Alec had touched several hours ago. I turned to my mirror. Even in the dimness of my room with only one lamp lit the diamonds flashed with celestial fire as I lifted them away from the V neck of the black shirt.

Then, after jamming my feet into my old flat sandals, I carried the glittering necklace down the hall to Alec's room.

The door opened under my hand; the air inside was cool and still in the way of rooms long unused.

Consumed with curiosity, I forgot my haste and turned on a lamp.

The furniture was plain dark wood, the bed covered by a pale gray wool comforter that matched the gray rug. I saw only two hints of personality in the room. On one wall was a beautifully framed oil painting of a young man seated stiffly next to a table. One hand lay on the cover of a book, the other rested on the arm of the chair, a familiar sapphire ring on the ring finger. The uniform I also recognized, and the sash: Alec had worn replicas of them and the sword at the man's side earlier tonight. Or maybe he had worn the same items. The face was long and solemn, with heavy brows, a high-bridged hawk-nose and a spade chin. The mouth was well cut, completely expressionless, the eyes wide-set and gray in color, but the shape and the heavy dark lashes were Alec's. *Milo.*

On the opposite wall, framed under glass, was a battered copy of a rare Beatles poster from 1963. Not the Official Beatles Poster, but the more interesting and casual shot of the Fab Four that was depicted on the *Meet the Beatles* album. This poster had not been sold to fans, having been used for advertising in record stores—during the days when such things existed. I stared silently up at George with his bowl haircut, his ridiculous suit with no lapels, hand on Ringo's shoulder, whose arms were crossed, Paul laughing, John . . .

I'd grown up hearing Beatles music. Dad and Mom had convinced me how exciting it was to hear the Beatles when they were young; how with music four guys could change the world, making anything seem possible. Now they seemed the ultimate in romance—and I wondered if Alec saw them that way, too.

A rainbow flash over the poster, echoed in the prisms hanging from the lampshades reminded me of the necklace dangling in my hand. I laid the diamonds on top of the bureau, then I shot my forefinger at the Fab Four.

"Better run for your life if you can," I said, and left.

THIRTY-TWO

AUNT SISI WAITED at the foot of the stairs, her face set in a mask of determined calm completely belied by the tension in the fine skin around her eyes. Behind her, Madam Emilio stood silently, her face unhappy as we walked out; Madam A was not there, but I heard her quiet voice in the alcove where they kept the downstairs telephone.

Outside, Aunt Sisi said, "Can you drive, chérie? I don't trust myself at the speed I think we should make."

I gave the right-hand steering wheel the hairy eyeball, having never driven this type of car before. But her request put me on my mettle. *And it's not like I'll be dealing with LA traffic.*

By driving in the exact center of the road, I accustomed myself to the strange balance of right-hand drive. We soon passed the few cars on the road that cut across the valley to the mountains on the other side. There, I opened up the speed until the needle jammed to max.

I don't know how long I drove; the moon seemed to hang in the sky above us, and the world spun beneath the Austin's wheels. The gradual curves got tighter, and the road steeper.

We'd reached Devil's Mountain. I began to slow.

Aunt Sisi murmured a distressed comment about her poor daughter, and I smacked the accelerator down again. I was driving faster than I felt was safe, so I concentrated on the curving strip of road ahead, winding ever upward, trees flashing by.

After a long nightmare of hairpin turns and ghost-lit branches flashing low overhead, as we played hide-and-seek with the sinking moon,

Aunt Sisi said, "Soon you will cut the engine and coast down a short hill."

"The lights'll drain the battery fast," I warned.

"This will only be for seconds. The road is almost directly below the castle. It's unlikely they would hear the engine even if we were to drive directly to it, but we will use this precaution. We will also hide the car in case anyone comes up or down."

"Give me the word," I said.

Another mile or so along she said, "Now," as we rounded the crest of a particularly sharp hairpin turn. I cut the engine at once and shifted into neutral. The car rolled heavily and bumpily downward, the tires' rumbling sounding loud and sinister.

"Prepare to turn hard to the right . . . here." She pointed into a black space between some shrubs. We bumped sickeningly through looming branches, then at last she said, "Stop."

I hit the lights, and utter blackness slammed down on us.

"Leave the keys." Her tense voice sounded loud in the silence.

My neck was stiff with tension, and my hands and arms ached from the effort of driving. Aunt Sisi climbed out. Her feet crunched on pine needles. She opened something, and pulled a bulky thing out that crackled like a plastic tarp. "We must make haste."

"What are you doing?"

"Setting a tarpaulin against the back of the car so the lights won't reflect if someone passes."

"That's clever. So you've used this spot a lot?"

"During the days of Russian control."

I climbed out of the car and swung my arms in wide circles, trying to loosen the stiff muscles. I stumbled on the uneven ground, but once we were past the shelter of the overhanging trees, the brilliant canopy of stars overhead revealed the pale oval of Aunt Sisi's face, the narrow track of the road hugging the sheer granite cliff, and beyond another long drop into a shadowy valley. Somewhere below was the muted thunder of a waterfall, and night birds sang, heedless of the human drama intruding on their world.

Aunt Sisi walked close to the face of the cliff with quick, sure steps. The straight section of road we walked on would have been a few seconds' relief from the hairpins if we'd driven it; now it seemed as long as Highway 5 back home.

Our feet crunched steadily. The fresh air was waking me up, clearing my head more thoroughly all the time.

The road swung away from the granite cliff as the slope widened. We stayed next to the cliff face, though, Aunt Sisi pushing her way through shrubs with hands that looked even more fragile in the starlight.

Beneath the cover of a tall fir, she stopped. "This is it."

She slid a hand into a pocket of her jacket, and extracted a medieval-looking key with six or seven teeth. "The stairs are steep for a long way, then there is a sharp right-hand turn. More stairs. You'll feel two wooden doorways on the left. Pass those. They open onto the wrong levels—the kitchens and the main library. The last opens into the sky-suite bedrooms, which is where my daughter is being kept. The first room is probably where my son sleeps, but no one should be there now. The intervening door can be opened with this." She pressed what felt like a regular door key into my hand. "It opens all the sky-suite doors. The passage door has a latch on this side, and on the other side a button hidden in the paneling. You would do best to leave the passage door propped open."

"Ruli doesn't know how to trigger the passage? In case?"

"I don't believe she does. She has not been at the castle except for brief visits since she was little, and I do not think Anton would teach her the passageways now."

"She's definitely in that room? How'd you find that out?" I asked.

"One of the house servants sought me out this evening, in order to tell me." She pushed aside a heavy bough, and felt along the rock of the cliff. Then she inserted the medieval key into a lichen-choked crack. I heard several metallic clunks, then a graunching sound, as part of the cliff swung out. It was a disguised door, and beyond it was a lightless hole.

"Do you have a flashlight?" I could not help asking.

"I do not. There will be spiderwebs, but nothing else. No one has ever been hurt in there. Please, be hasty. And when you find her, warn her what to expect in this passage. She has a horror of spiders. Send her down before you, so she won't panic and run back up if she encounters one."

"Okay. Back as soon as I can."

I ducked past the fir bough and marched into the pit.

Immediately I saw why Aunt Sisi did not attempt it. Felt, rather, as sight was completely impossible. The steps were rough-hewn from stone so each was a different size and shape, and *steep* was an understatement bordering on euphemism. The only thing these steps had in common, besides being nearly on top of one another, was their thick covering of moss. Slimy moss. With a phosphorescent glow in patches, light enough to make one think one was seeing spots before one's eyes, but not light enough to be the least use in navigating steps.

I had to crawl on hands and knees, therefore, and I patted with my right hand at the growth-smeared wall every few feet, hoping for that turnoff. There seemed to be a slight but persistent veering to the right as I climbed upward for what was probably no more than five minutes, but seemed ages. Soft things brushed my hands and face and I frequently stopped and flung myself flat on the steps when taken by violent sneezes. I was terrified of jerking over backward. I didn't think I could recover from a fall down those stairs, either physically or mentally.

Once I had to clench my teeth on a scream when something with a lot of legs dropped onto my head, skittered to my neck and then fell off. I shuddered so violently I nearly lost my balance, but this heartening episode provided the burst of adrenalin I needed to send me scrambling top speed the rest of the way.

Encountering the sharp right encouraged me further; also, the incline leveled abruptly about fifteen degrees which enabled me—cautiously—to stand up. The webs overhead here were fewer. A more traveled passage? What lay in the direction she had not told me about?

I was not about to explore.

It seemed a long way to the first door because I expected it at any moment. But I found it, passed it, then found the second and the third. I heard muffled voices behind the second and passed on quickly, my heart banging up near my throat.

I listened for a full minute at the third before I brushed my fingers over it in search of the latch.

The door opened soundlessly. I peered into a huge, chilly room. The windows were clerestory style, high in the opposite wall. The starlight was weak, but after the Stygian totality of that passageway the pale light greeted my eyes with the strength of a 100-watt bulb. There was a grand, canopied bed, a hand-carved teak rolltop desk most of the people I knew would have to pay a year's income to buy, and some other handsome antique furniture. I propped the panel open with a footstool and walked cautiously in.

Then I saw doors on the adjacent walls. Both had yellow lines of light at the bottom. I picked one, put my ear to it, then jumped back: music! Over voices!

D'oh! A *television!*

Once again my heart thudded painfully as I shakily inserted Aunt Sisi's key into the lock. The door opened, whapping me with the sharp scent of fingernail polish remover.

Curled up asleep on a big bed was someone enough like my mirror image to seriously weird me out. She wore a dressing gown over wool slacks and a matching sweater. On a side table lay neat rows of cosmetic items, including fingernail polish lined up according to shade. The only open bottle was the polish remover.

Clothes were piled everywhere, but in a kind of desperate order: slacks draped neatly over chairs, blouses folded and stacked on the bureau, sweaters on the floor. Next to the TV sat a couple towers of videocassettes and DVDs, perfectly squared. A quick glance showed an amazing array—from sophisticated French films to all seven seasons of *Buffy the Vampire Slayer.* Stacked below the TV table was a mixture of glossy-covered fashion magazines, French, English, and American titles.

The persistent stink of the polish remover clobbered my senses into awareness, echoing that horrible stuff I'd been drugged with earlier. I breathed out sharply, then moved to the bedside and reached to cap the bottle. Why would she leave that open? She couldn't possibly find the smell pleasant. Maybe antiseptic?

The loudness of the television masked my movements; I thought I recognized Fellini's *Amarcord*. I pressed the off button.

Then I turned back to my twin.

The light came from electrical bulbs in wall sconces. I stepped toward the bed and studied Ruli's profile. This time I looked for differences between us. She had high arched brows, beautifully plucked like her mother's. Her lower lip had a suggestion of a pucker.

Her eyes opened. She saw me and sat up, staring. Despite the shoulder-length hair, the makeup smudges below red-rimmed eyes, and the subtle differences I'd already marked, it was enough my own face to give me a sickening second or two of vertigo.

What did Alec think when I did not show at midnight? Now I will never know.

I drew in a shaky breath and said in French, "Your mother is waiting at the other end of a secret passage. I think we had better hurry. There's something weird going on."

Neither of us stopped studying the other's face. Even as I spoke I was noting further subtle differences between us: her forehead was slightly higher and more narrow at the temples than mine; a hint of point to her chin. She was fashionably thin, with no muscle tone.

She cleared her throat. Her voice sounded higher than mine to my ears. "Are you Kim?"

"Yes." And as she had not moved, I added, "Best hurry."

She got up then, and stood beside the bed, looking about wildly. "Oh, God . . . It's been so horrible . . . Where's Anton?"

"Somewhere in Riev, according to your mother."

She winced. "I thought you'd be Dieter. He's been threat—oh, I'll never get over this. Never." Her voice rose at the end.

"I think you should wait to talk about it until we get out," I suggested nervously.

She pressed her lips together. "Yes. Please."

I locked her door behind me. In Tony's starlit room she stood right at my shoulder, looking back frequently toward the other door.

At the black passage door, she stopped. "I can't go in there." Her whisper was tremulous with terror.

I said, "I came up that way, and nothing happened to me. You go first. I'll be right behind you. If someone comes after us, I'll deal. You go, and think to yourself, *Cousin Kim was here, so there won't be any spiders.* Can you handle it that way?"

She stilled, except for the tremble, her eyes closed. Then, "To get away from Dieter. I will. Do anything."

"Great. Then the faster you get down, the sooner it's over. It's steep, and you'll have to be careful, but think about the end—and freedom." I was going to have to talk her through it. "Remember, I was there a minute ago. Repeat, freedom, freedom, freedom."

"I'll be free when I'm home again," she said softly. It was clear *home* was not here in this castle.

She said nothing more, but I heard the harsh breathing of effort and fear, so I kept on gabbling encouragements and jokes, interspersed with warnings of what to expect ahead.

When we got to the super-steep down-drop she whimpered once, then began her descent. Hesitant at first, from the sound. "Not far," I called. "And your mother is waiting. And at Mecklundburg House a nice hot bath . . . tea or coffee or whatever you like to drink . . ."

It was far worse going down. I caught myself nearly slipping on the moss, so rather than risk crashing into her if I fell, I let her get well ahead. When it sounded like she was about fifteen feet below me I started down again little-kid style, that is, bumping down gently, heels then butt.

"Oh, I see the door," Ruli cried happily, at long last. Then, "Yes! Maman?"

"Aurelia?" Aunt Sisi's voice was faint, cautious.

"Yes!" Ruli laughed on a high, thankful note.

I spotted the top of the door, and began bumping my way down more quickly.

Ruli stumbled through the open door into the silver-glowing night, arms outstretched and her dressing gown flapping behind her. Then, with a graunching sound that seared from my heels to my teeth, the door swung shut.

And—*click-click-click*—locked.

THIRTY-THREE

"AUNT SISI!" I SCREAMED. "Please, Aunt Sisi, please open the door!"

I stumbled the rest of the way down, tripped, and caught myself against the door. It did not budge. I dug my nails in, trying to find a way to open it, and I have to admit I panicked there for a while, screaming and begging.

Finally it occurred to me to shut up and listen—she might be out there trying to tell me something, or worse, some enemy must have appeared. *Some*thing had to have happened. It made no sense for her to lock me in after asking for my help. And getting it.

So I pressed my ear against the wood, laboring to quiet my shaky breathing, but heard nothing.

"If they were caught, it's up to me to rescue them," I whispered, my cheek grinding against the granite-hard wood of the door. "Right. It's up to me."

I pushed away from the door with both hands, and swung wearily about, doing my best to ignore my own trembling until two things with a lot of wiggly legs dropped on me. I batted at myself crazily, knocking them off. One crunched as it hit the step. The result? A five minutes' climb was done in about two minutes flat.

When I reached the platform, panting like a marathon runner, I felt at the two adjacent doors and found cold metal keyholes on both. I tried my key as quietly as I could, but it fit neither. So I turned up the right-hand passage again, and this time listened at each door.

The kitchen sounded like a hub of activity, so I passed on.

The library had at least three men talking in it. I pressed my ear hard against the door, heard Dobreni words . . . and finally deciphered enough to realize what was going on in there was not a secret war conference but a card game peppered with reminiscences that made it clear it had been a looooong time since some of those guys had had a date.

So I toiled on to the third door and listened. Like before, no sound. So I opened the door, and for a second I was so glad to see light that I forgot about danger.

Not that it mattered. Tony saw the passage door open the second I lifted the latch, and even if I'd caught on quickly, where would I have gone? Still, it was a shock to have the door pulled out of my fingers and to find myself face-to-shirtfront with Tony.

I recoiled back into the darkness of the passage but his hand snapped out and closed around my upper arm. He pulled me into the room. I flung his hand off violently as he shut the passage door beside my head. The edges disappeared seamlessly among the jointures of the wood panels. I stared at the now invisible door for a few seconds, rubbed my stinging eyes, then turned around.

Tony was on the other side of the room, pouring water from a pitcher onto a white cloth.

"Here," he said conversationally as he came back toward me. "That passage is vilely filthy." He held out a dampened hand towel.

I rubbed the cool wetness over my face. When I pulled it down the hand towel was grayish black with grime, but my face felt better. I started cleaning my fingers as he smiled at me and leaned against his bureau.

"Charming," he went on, his indolent, slack-lidded glance moving slowly down my body. "Strange, you have my sister's features but you don't look at all like her. Not at all," he added, his gaze drifting back to my jeans, and when I scowled, he smiled. "What can I do for you?" And with an ironic echo of the point-and-shoot, "I'm at your service, my dear Kim."

Despite the cold of the room he was wearing only the frilly white pirate shirt, half-unbuttoned, and the black trousers of his costume. Bare feet, even. I had interrupted him in the homely and everyday task of getting ready for bed. Which might be expected at . . . what was it, two? three? in the morning. But common sense did not prevent me from flushing neon-red right up to my itching scalp.

Tony had been watching comprehension work its way into my brain, and now his amusement intensified in proportion to the crimson in my face. "A couple minutes more and I would have been very much at your service." He laughed at my embarrassment.

"If you want to help me," I said sourly, "you'll show me the quickest way out of this dump."

"I noticed Ruli's taken off," he commented. "As yet I'm the only one who knows. What happened? She's not in the passage, is she? Did you lose the base-door key on the stair?"

"No, she's safe. With your mother. The door shut in my face," I said reluctantly. "I thought maybe they were caught by some of your goons lurking out on the road."

"The door shut?" he repeated with mild interest.

I finished wiping my hands, and put the filthy towel down on an exquisite side table. "Yes. When I had only a few steps to go."

"Ruli went first?"

"Yes. Which suggests to me there might have been trouble . . ." I began. He seemed disposed to stand around and chat. Fine. I would respond, but my mind was on the door on the other side of the room.

"At—my mother's request, perhaps?"

"Yup," I said agreeably, hooking my thumbs in my belt loops and sauntering a step. Another step. "Sure wish I knew what happened. Everything had gone so well until that point, too." I shrugged as carelessly as I could while gripping the key against my palm. "So, if you want to help me, you might point me toward the front door in this pile so I can be on my way."

"No, because that won't—"

As soon as I heard *no* I snapped out a side kick, sending the marquetry table crashing toward his knees, and vaulted over a hassock.

Tony laughed.

I grabbed a bedpost, propelled myself around the corner, and lunged toward the door. One step, two, key outstretched—

And as usual the difference between 5 foot 8 and 6 foot 3 worked out to 5 foot 8's disadvantage. When he grabbed me, I whirled around and began to fight.

The struggle was short. I thrashed wildly, which almost worked only because Tony was trying to gain control without hurting me. I nearly wrenched free once, then he increased his efforts, catching hold of my wrist. I yipped in anger and kicked him. His grip shifted, and I flew through the air to land with a splat on the bed.

A second later he was on me. A second or two after that he had me pinned down by a knee across my thighs, a hand over my mouth, and his other pressing my wrists over my head against the mattress.

He grinned down through his drifting blond hair into my (no doubt) richly purple face and said, "My, this is tempting—"

I gave an almighty heave with my middle that bounced the entire bed. He laughed, like a grammar school kid playing a game. "—but maybe we'd better postpone the fun." He got that out with some difficulty because of my enthusiastic efforts to fling him off, then he paused, studying my face to see if I understood.

I did: truce. So I lay still.

He continued, "I think I'd better catch you up."

I tried to nod, which was difficult with that palm holding my head firmly against the mattress.

"No screeching? The wicked count is supposed to be asleep, and I'd as soon not shatter that illusion. The crashing of furniture might not raise any interest, but shrieking would."

I nodded again, and he lifted his hands.

"Jerk," I snarled. "Let me up."

"No more kung fu?"

"Unless you try to harass me again."

"I promise. With extreme reluctance." He laughed and freed me.

I promptly rolled away and landed on my feet on the other side of the bed, straightening my clothes as I did so. Tony remained sitting on the bed. Next to him, where I had been lying, was a big smear of gray grime.

Pointing at it in triumph, I said, "Hah. I hope you have to sleep in it."

"Dieter will never believe you are Ruli," Tony responded reflectively. "Never."

"She's gone, and I'd prefer not to meet any of your minions. So, if you'll tell me whatever it is you have on your furry little mind, I'll be about my business."

Instead Tony leaned back against the pillows, crossing his hands behind his head, the ridiculous lacy sleeves of his pirate shirt draping over his hands. He was chuckling as he repeated *minions,* then he stretched his legs out comfortably on the bed, ankles crossed. "Where did you wake up?"

"At your mother's."

"Ah. And she told you . . . ?"

"You were in trouble, and this Reithermann scumbag—was that the guy waving the gun?—wanted to kill Ruli, and she had only me to help her get Ruli out. So we drove up, and I got her out."

The light from the wall sconce reflected in his black eyes as he gazed upward. "You had better understand first that my mother was right, I *am* in trouble. In fact, I'm a prisoner in my own house." His light tone and lopsided smile made light of the words: if it was true, he wasn't any too worried about it. "Which is why I retired. To figure out my next step."

"You mean, that Reithermann fellow everyone says is such a creep has pulled a palace coup on you? So tonight you did, in fact, try to pull a palace coup on Alec while the masquerade was going on. Right? And that bombed, and so Reithermann has pulled a coup on *you?*"

"Well, he has the gun, as you say, while mine ended up in a fishpond. More important right now, he has the keys."

"If that doesn't serve you right," I chortled.

"Perhaps," he said with no diminishment of his usual good humor. "But it makes your position rather precarious. Neither of us has a key to the stair door, so you have the option of remaining here and continuing to impersonate my sister, or continuing on in your efforts to get out of the castle. The first would be the safer course, I suspect. Ruli is too effective a block to any retaliatory moves on Alec's part for Dieter to want to harm her, ah, permanently."

"Ugh." I frowned, contemplating this last.

He nodded slowly, his smile mordant. "That's why I had her moved up here."

"So, that would mean I sit in that locked room until someone bothers to let me out."

"I expect that would be the safest course," he agreed.

"No thanks." I shuddered. "Any other passages? They all lock? And this jerk Reithermann has the keys?"

"The important passages are at present inaccessible, though Dieter does not yet know it. He thinks some of those keys are for the flat in Paris, the house in England, and so forth."

"Does he know about the passages?" I asked, intrigued despite myself.

"Only about one or two," he returned conspiratorially.

"You've got no one to help you? Or—"

He lifted a shoulder. "Our return was in disorder, and in glum spirits, and Dieter—being a professional—was ready. There's a lesson in all this."

I knew he would not say the obvious or the moral. "What, not to mix mercenaries with masquerades?"

He shut his eyes and gave himself up to laughter. "Ah, Kim! What can I give you to throw in with me?"

It's not a what, it's a who, I thought and grimaced.

Meanwhile Tony was silent, his eyes open again, and intent. "Shades of our fathers," he said in slow, appreciative Dobreni. Then back to English. "Don't tell me—"

I cut in rather rudely, "So this Dieter clown has all your people under lock and key, is that it?"

"I'd say merely under guard. No one is locked up except my sister. Supposedly. You have a key to these rooms?"

"Yes. I did." I hunted over the floor, bent down, and picked it up from where it had fallen beside the bed. "Does it work anywhere else?"

"No. If you decide to risk the house, your best last resort is to pretend you are Ruli and that you nicked my key while I was asleep. I'll back you up, and you'll be safe enough here."

"What will you get out of it if I 'risk the house' as you say? Since you aren't threatening to lock me up now."

He lifted his hands and lounged to his feet. "But I wish you all the best in the world, Kim! Despite my plans being knackered ever since you turned up. I sympathize with your wish to take what you can get out of this cock-up. I certainly will."

"I'm not taking anything," I stated. "There's nothing here that belongs to me. I don't count your stupid treasure, wherever that is. I'd rather live under a freeway overpass than fight over it or steal it."

Tony sighed, and stopped right in front of me. "Can I change your mind, I wonder? We'll see. For now, if you run through the house it'll rouse 'em, which should allow my people—if they aren't asleep, or drunk—to make a try at altering the balance of power. That's to your advantage. If you're quick, and use your wits, you might even reach the gate. But I think you'd best go for the garden wall," he added, giving me a considering look. "I suspect you've no objections to scaling an eight-foot fence made of granite?"

"What's on the other side?"

"Filled-in moat all along the old walls." He laughed. "Heh. The idea of Ruli even thinking of jumping a wall—"

"She did pretty well in that lovely strollway," I interrupted, jerking my thumb over my shoulder at the paneling behind me. The way he kept comparing me to Ruli was beginning to irritate me. "Let's hear the layout of the house."

"So you're going to try a run?" he asked, studying me intently. "I ought to remind you that you're safe only as long as they think you're my sister. You've no value at all against my mother, and your value against Alec would be doubtful, though I'm beginning to suspect—"

"We've been through that," I said with acid exasperation.

"We haven't been through it," he countered. "What I'm trying to tell you is if Dieter's men do retain the whip hold—"

"They might not be civilized," I said fiercely. "Look. Spare me the good news, all right? My insides are a pit of boiling snakes right now, and you aren't helping. I'm not going to sit in your sister's room and wait for you idiots to decide my fate. The house, please."

My voice went a trifle uneven at the end, but he refrained from comment about it. Without any further attempts to dissuade me, Tony gave me a precise description of the castle, which was laid out in a step pattern, the highest point being right where I was standing now, ending in gardens on a gradual slope that was bordered by thick forest. It was this forest I was to aim for.

And then—

Well. I had a lot to do before I needed to worry about *and then.*

Tony finished, giving me a whimsical smile. "Want a kiss for luck?" he offered, reaching lazily for me.

"If I wanted bad luck I'd break a mirror," I said, ducking around him and jamming my key in the lock.

"Kisses," he said reflectively. "You know we've unfinished business, you and I. Whatever you claim about hating me."

Gritting my teeth, I yanked open the door, then I whirled around. "I said I enjoyed it. But next time, *I* choose the time—and the place. Now can I get on with my escape?"

"I'm going to remind you of that one day."

"Fine. Whatever. Good-bye, have a nice life."

He laughed softly and shook his head, moving toward a bureau.

"What are you going to be doing?" I asked unwillingly.

"Since it seems the night's entertainment is not yet over . . ." He brandished the riding boots I'd seen him wear the day of our picnic. "I thought I'd get dressed again."

I shut the door and ventured onto the landing beyond, scanning the area warily.

The sky suite was a square tower at the highest end of the gigandor castle called the Eyrie. Solid granite walls, heavy staircases, and huge marble slabs on the floors would have made the place seem like a dungeon but for the high arched ceilings, the pillars with Corinthian fluting round the tops, and the airy multistory square around which each main stairway formed.

As Tony had explained, the castle was built on the mountaintop in a series of four huge steps. The sky suite was highest, on Devil Mountain's crown. Each "step" was a building formed around a central square stairwell. The ground floor of the highest "step" connected to the upper level of the next by a long hallway, and so on down.

He had given me a precise explanation, but I had no idea what it meant until I got outside his bedroom door and took in the landing like a picture frame around the stairwell, with a circle of arched clerestory windows up under the domed roof. On three sides of the stairwell, opening off the landings, were a series of heavy carved doors to match Tony's.

This was the smallest of the four buildings.

Ooooo-kay.

My eyes soon adjusted, aided by the silvery-blue moon- and starlight glowing on the marble from the high windows.

Across from Tony's door, the first stair started down.

My heart thundered as I slunk along the cool marble, my sandals hissing. When I reached the top of the stairway and paused to look down into the square, I saw four or five stories below me—a sizable journey for someone trying to escape. And this sky suite was only the first "step."

For a second or two my nerve failed. I turned my attention back to Tony's door, beyond which lay relative safety. I didn't trust him much—but I didn't trust Reithermann at all, from the brief glimpses I'd gotten.

The thought of being parked somewhere for my own good while these guys played out their games infuriated me. Better to make my run for freedom.

I was about to put my foot on the first step when movement caught my eye on the other side of the balcony.

Someone was there.

Fear make me snap up my head—

And I stared straight into the honey-brown eyes of my ancestor Maria Sofia Vasa.

THIRTY-FOUR

IT WAS LIKE all the moon and starlight coalesced into the figure of a young woman with high-piled silvery hair wearing a 1760s robe à la française of blue the color of dawn. I can't tell you how I saw the color of her eyes across fifty feet of airy, moonlit space, but I did. Yet I could see through her, too: the latch to Tony's still-closed door was visible through her graceful bodice.

"I'm seeing you, right?" I whispered. "Can you talk to me?"

She gazed past me into some other dimension, slowly fading out until all I saw was the wall and door.

Okay, that was weird. But I had a castle to escape from.

I slipped down the shallow steps. At intervals I edged close to the marble balustrade and peered quickly at the lower levels, moving when I saw no one.

First landing.

I tiptoed along the perpendicular hall, nearing an open door. Bright light beyond. Stiffening my toes against my sandals to keep them quiet, I moved to the edge of the balustrade and swiftly glided by—one step, two—three! No noise, no alarms. I skipped on down to the next landing.

So far so good. But now the danger would increase—I could see electric light sending dramatic slants between columns into the stairwell.

Two more floors down, then the staircase broadened to a spacious, brightly lit landing off which two sets of carved wood doors opened, just as Tony described. Now I was at the second step, the old medieval keep, which had been modernized in the 1700s, with electricity added by the Russian occupiers. An ancient tapestry hung between the doors. Strange Byzantine eyes stared out of stylized figures, the tapestry greenish-dark with age. The eyes seemed to move with me as I passed—a chill gripped the back of my neck, and I almost ran into another ghost.

I scrambled back, nearly tripping over a dark blue rug as a young man walked through the shut door. He wore a tunic not unlike Alec's costume, down to the high boots and the sword. He was tall and thin, with a somber face that tweaked at me—I knew I recognized it, even if I couldn't remember where or how. He passed within about six feet of me, glowing silvery, though I could see through him. But his details were extraordinarily clear, from the spurs at the heels of his boots to a lock of curly blond hair falling on his forehead.

When I saw the dueling pistol he carried in one hand, I remembered him. One of the Dsaret twins, the one who died in a duel? Prickles tingled across my shoulder blades as he drifted through the balcony into the air above the stairwell—and faded.

I listened at the door he'd come through, sure it must have some significance. No sound. Hoping I wasn't making the mistake of my far too short life, I eased the door open.

The room was empty of people *and* ghosts. A lamp burned on a massive oak table before an equally massive fireplace. Under my feet lay a thirty-foot Persian carpet with riotous patterns and color. On a wall hung two Renaissance paintings of hunting scenes. Between those was a battered tournament shield with two heavy swords crossed behind it.

Swords.

Maybe this was the von M dueling chamber or weapons room, which might explain the ghost—if ghosts can ever be explained. Duels, I had no interest in.

But what about self defense?

I looked down at my empty hands, then up at the wall. Those heavy late-medieval weapons would be tough for me to lift, much less swing, if I had to defend myself.

I whirled around. A crossed pair of nineteenth-century curved cavalry sabers had been set on a far wall, mounted behind an ornamented horn, and ahhh! On the short wall next to the fireplace? A pair of dueling rapiers.

Set directly below was a small case containing several gold-inlay and chased *main gauche* blades.

I hopped up onto the case and freed a rapier from its mounting. It rang softly with a metallic shear, and I shivered.

I did a few lunges to stretch my legs, and swung the sword to warm up my arms.

The rapier was heavier than our fencing sabers back at UCLA, and there was no button on the end. I brought the point up and tested it with my thumb. Sharp.

The door I had come through opened, and a man walked in. We stared at one another, equally startled. He was big, and heavy, wore half-boots and a Dobreni tunic and loose trousers. I wondered whose flunky he was—and whether it would make any difference to my position at all.

He demanded in Russian-accented Dobreni, "What are you doing here?"

"Practice," I said, trying to lower my voice.

He advanced on me and I lifted the sword point to halt him. He checked for a second, looking at it impatiently. "The Captain will want to know why you are walking around down here."

"The Captain," eh? Not Tony's minion, then.

"Tell him I'm getting some fresh air." I smiled—it felt like a grimace. "I'll move right along now." My voice shook a little.

I might as well not have even tried. He ignored the excuse and stomped toward me, hands out to make the grab.

Moment of truth.

I fought the urge to plead, back away, reason, be civilized, because there was no civilization in his expression, only fury-driven intent. So I whipped a tight bind round his arm and smacked the blade sharply across the back of his hand. He jumped back, cursing harshly.

"Why don't you go on your way?" My voice came out high and sharp, but clear. *I'm good at this. I can do this.*

Two angry red spots marked his fleshy cheeks. He snatched at the rapier. I twitched the point away, zipped it back, and dealt him a stinging blow to the upper arm.

Baring his teeth, he lunged straight at me, and I wove the point between his extended arms and crooked fingers, and—clamping my teeth to brace myself—I let his own momentum run him into the sword. I shuddered as the point sank deep into his upper arm, then ripped the blade free. He recoiled, his breath gasping in shock.

My mouth dried, a reaction to the horrible feeling of steel entering real, living flesh. The man staggered backward, blood flowering brightly and terribly around the wound and down his tunic. He clapped his other hand to his arm as his boots got tangled in the rug-fringe.

He fell heavily, his head thumping against a carved leg of the display case—which toppled slowly toward him. I spun on my toes and fled.

For a heartbeat I wished I was safe in Ruli's room watching the television, then I heard the case crash, glass splintering.

There's no turning back.

I closed the door behind me, jammed a fragile chair under the latch because it always seemed to work in the movies, then ran into the hallway and started down the second set of stairs. The wall sconces on this step were brilliant. The fourth step belonged to the staff and was mostly storage; it had its exits, but Tony had said that I could get out through the third, which was the main building, with the light and dark checkerboard marble floor.

Male laughter echoed up from somewhere; behind me, the door latch rattled violently. Holding the blade at the ready, I ran down the next set of stairs, and the next after that . . . I was halfway down the following stair when back at the top level my victim slammed open the door of the dueling room and bellowed, "Hallo! Paolo! Yussef! The bitch is out." His voice echoed, running the words together.

I muttered, "A little farther, a little farther . . ." and leaped down several steps at a time.

Directly below me, a man yelled in Russian, "No one down here!"

I skidded around the bottom of the stairwell, trying to keep to the far side, and pounded down the hallway to the next "step."

Now I'd reached the biggest building in the castle, with the guest suites and function rooms and salons, and at least two grand ballrooms. *Against you is a rather long run,* Tony had said. *For you is how far Reithermann's sods have scattered, the fact that they still aren't used to their pin mikes not working—and how long they've been drinking their victory.*

As I started down the first set of stairs of the top story, two men dashed out from the third story hallway below. Both caught themselves up short, staring at me. Too many above—no retreat. My heartbeat was as loud as a thrash metal band as I leaped down the rest of the stairs, swinging the sword. One man froze, and the other started sliding a hand into a bulky jacket.

I whipped the rapier across the man's wrist with a crack that dropped him to his knees. Then, as his partner lunged at me, I smacked both his hands away and stabbed him in his right arm. I leaped between them and ran.

Next set of stairs. Noise and shouting echoed from the rooms above. As I rounded the landing corner I risked a glance upward—and almost stumbled in shock. Maria Sofia hovered at the top level, bright as day—

"There she is!" someone shouted in French-accented English.

Footsteps thundered along the upper hall and up the stairs to the sky suite, where the ghost had glowed.

I shoved away from the balcony and vaulted down six steps. My teeth jarred as I bounced down, my sandals sliding on the smooth marble. If only Ruli had owned a pair of running shoes!

The balustrades were elaborately carved now, with patterns of leaves and winged lions at the corners—I caught hold of the jutting wings of the lions to help propel me along. As I passed halls leading from the landings, I glanced down them. Everything was lit, and the halls seemed to be as long as those in giant hotels, though the mirrored insets in the archways confused the eye.

I'd reached the halfway point when another pair of men dashed from a hallway with a vaulted ceiling. From above, footsteps clattered down the stairs. Gritting my teeth, I sliced the last man across his collarbone—he raised a length of pipe to hit me—I scored him across the forehead so blood ran into his eyes. He stumbled, howling curses and clutching at his face. I ducked around him, then ran at flat-out speed for the next flight of stairs. *Two flights to go.*

Footsteps ahead.

I stopped to scan, back to a pillar. Above: shouts, curses, the sounds of an altercation. And then another outburst of angry shouting and noise, this time from below. Cursing in several languages. Tony's men were fighting Reithermann's?

I leaned out over the balustrade, peered up—and froze eye to eye with the dark gray metal of a shotgun barrel. It was leveled across the balustrade up one flight, pointing straight at me.

Then, floating humorously from farther above, came Tony's voice. "Surely, Stefanos, you can manage to stop a girl without splattering her brains all over the walls?"

The man's head jerked skyward—Tony leaned on the balcony two stories up. Footsteps behind—I whipped around to the other side of the pillar as another pair of men topped a grand stairway.

One brandished a fireplace poker, the other a wooden cudgel. The landing was a vast polished space with several sets of high doors set in exquisitely painted walls, with fanciful flourishes above each, centering around a gleaming gilt coronet: I'd reached the ballrooms.

A shout echoed up and down the airy, echoing stairwell, "She's got a blade!"

The guy with the poker loomed up, feet planted well apart. He wore paramilitary cammies.

"Drop it, bitch." His accent was flat Midwestern American.

I kept my focus on the poker, and let my peripheral vision take care of the other guy, who was slowly edging to one side.

The poker arced toward my blade, the casual swing; the guy's grin made it clear he expected me either to squeal and drop my sword, or he'd knock it out of my hand. I lifted my point enough so that the poker swung under it, and then as the second guy tensed to make a lunge I flashed the rapier horizontally and scored the point low across his forehead. He jumped back, cursing as blood ran into his eyes; the cudgel clattered to the marble floor. The first man swung the poker at my head, this time with grunting, murderous intent. I whipped my blade up in a block. The poker smashed into the rapier guard, sending a painful shock up my arm.

He swung around and jabbed at me.

I can do this.

"Hah!" I parried, then feinted toward his face.

I shifted my weight as the second fellow rushed me, arms out to envelop me in a bear hug. Stepping aside to keep him between me and Poker Guy, I whirled my point to his shoulder and let his momentum decide the depth of the thrust. He staggered, twisted away, hand clasped to the wound.

Poker Guy used all the weight of his body to try for a home run on my skull. I braced myself, and *wha-a-a-a-ang!* The poker glanced off the rapier guard and whooshed a couple inches over my head.

Ridiculously exhilarated, I snapped the blade under his arm and stabbed him in the shoulder . . . and couldn't resist quoting breathlessly, "As I parry the best lunge of all—"

He bellowed a curse, slapped the poker into his other hand, and swung at me again.

"—I thrust as I end the refrain!"

I zapped his other shoulder. The poker fell ringing to the marble—he threw himself at me—I leaped aside and pinked him hard in the knee. He shouted in pain as I yanked the blade free.

I ran past and leaped down the grand stairway.

A pistol cracked somewhere overhead, the shot smacking echoes off the stone. The angry voices increased.

One . . . more . . . stair—

I reached the landing so fast I bounced into a column, then whirled around. They were coming at me from both sides, slow and wary. From the sounds, more on down the stairs—and a party hustling up from the service level below.

To my left, several carved doors. These had to be the salons and anterooms to the big public chambers. Trying the doors one at a time with frantic fingers, I found one open, flung myself in, and slammed it shut behind me. High on the door was a brass latch, and I flicked it into lock position a bare two seconds before hands started rattling the door handle.

Bodies crashed against the heavy door; men cursed and bellowed. A louder voice than the rest roared in French, "Open this door!"

"Yeah, *right.*" Dashing across the opulent sitting room, I wondered what the electric bill in this place would be with every one of the bazillion rooms lit. I got a swift impression of cherubic frescos and Directoire furniture, then I reached the nearest of two huge windows. Yanking one open, I found a balcony outside, and I stumbled out.

I was one story above the gardens, but it was a thirty foot story. I leaned over the edge of the balcony and peered down into the darkness below. I couldn't jump it. Not when I could not see the ground.

"Bloody hell," someone shouted in English. "What *is* that?"

More shouts, then someone else yelled in Russian, "It went through the wall!"

You guys seeing ghosts, too? Guess I'm not so special after all.

I leaned farther as the door began splintering. If I could spot a patch of grass, a pond even! All I saw was a jumble of dark greenery, a few branches side-lit from adjacent windows—and a rose trellis.

Tucking the sword under my arm, I climbed hastily over the balcony, a hand reaching to catch hold of the latticework.

Rose thorns caught at my clothes and hands, but I scarcely noticed. The sweet scent of crushed blooms was heavy on the cool air as I fought my way down.

I had made it about three-quarters of the way down when another pistol shot banged loudly from behind the windows several rooms away. The shots did not sound like they do on TV; there was a loud report and sharp cracks and pops. Then shouts, more cracks and pops and crashes from higher up in the castle: the fight was spreading.

One foot tangled in the thick vines. I kicked free, and jumped.

I landed hard on soggy cool grass, fell on my forearm, and scrambled up. I didn't realize I'd lost my clip until my hair rolled down my back. I glanced around, but there was no chance of finding the clip in that darkness. *So much for pretending to be Ruli.*

Yellow light gleamed palely on the blade of the rapier a few feet away. As I grabbed it, a window above me crashed, glass tinkling on the marble as a man shouted, "The garden! Comb the garden! The bitch is loose, and armed! *Find her.*"

The voice was loud, harsh, angry. My stomach knotted as I crouched and ran away from the windows into the woods—where I nearly crashed into a still figure. I jolted to a stop, blade out, then realized the figure wasn't moving.

The golden glow from the million castle windows sharply highlighted the contours of a statue, the details so fine it seemed real. The statue was a man in elegant late-nineteenth-century evening dress, one hand out, the other raised as if to block a blow from overhead.

I ducked around it and ran full out.

The wall. Where was the wall?

A pale face loomed at me—this time a living man, breathing hard. I recoiled, then slashed at him with the rapier. It laid his cheek open. He shouted and spun away as a cudgel sliced the air a few centimeters from my own face. I blocked, thrust, blocked, punctured the guy's wrist, then plunged past, the sharp tang of pine stinging my nose as I broke through small branches.

The trees cleared ahead, circling another of those statues, its outline medieval, weather-blurred, and mossy. I caught its bony wrist—carved so realistically—to propel myself around, then ran crazily, leaping over low shrubbery. The thud of feet on both sides bolted fire down my back and gave me the strength for faster speed.

I'm not going to make it . . .

My breath burned the back of my throat but I pushed myself faster as footsteps pounded closer.

I nearly stumbled. Glanced down: herbal border. I leaped over.

Beyond another pair of those odd statues I spotted the wall, about a hundred yards away. Eighty. Fifty. Thirty . . .

Five runners reached it when I had maybe twenty feet to go, and whipped round to face me, spreading out at the ready.

"Back off," I yelled, waving my blade in a circle. "Back off!"

"Halt! Right there," someone ordered in Dobreni.

A man planted himself squarely in my path, his hands at chin-height, leveling something dark. It was the handsome guy with the curly hair from the palace, and he was pointing a pistol at me.

A distance of maybe ten, twelve feet lay between us as the others closed in slowly behind.

"Stop," he said to me, closing both hands around the pistol. "Drop it."

I closed my eyes briefly. *I have to try.*

I lunged at him, the sword whistling in a downward stroke.

Flash!

I don't remember any sound. I was flat on the grass, the quiet stars overhead blocked by a football huddle of faces, the dark, pitted eyes of one of those statues beyond.

Okay, this is weird. If they'd only let me lie here a minute, I could get hold of my thoughts. But I was being carried by hard hands at a jolting gait, voices around me talking too fast to follow. Light burned, vivid yellow and painfully glaring. I squeezed my eyes shut and tried to turn my head away. *Why are they jabbing a red hot nail into my shoulder?*

I wanted to say "Lay off," but my lips felt rubbery and numb.

A rasping man's voice echoed weirdly ". . . find the sister! Now! And you'd better . . ."

I dropped with a splat. It knocked my breath out.

It also doused the lights.

THIRTY-FIVE

I MUST HAVE FADED completely out of consciousness and then in again, because when I opened my eyes there was Tony's face.

He smiled ruefully. "Here. Take a sip."

"I saw ghosts." My voice came out like a frog's croak.

"They do appear to be interested." He pressed something pungent smelling to my lips.

Obediently I sipped, swallowed, and gasped as a pleasant warmth eased its way down into my numb, cold body and up into my foggy head.

I gasped again, then said, "You know about the ghosts?"

"Castle's full of 'em. Never seen so many at once, though. Something's got 'em stirred."

"But you told me. You don't believe. In magic."

"Ghosts have nothing to do with magic. Drink a bit more. It will help for a time."

I swallowed again, and the gray murk behind Tony resolved into a brightly lit chamber. Yellow light gleamed in Tony's pale hair and glittered in his black eyes. Beyond him was a wall with floor to ceiling bookshelves filled with leather-bound tomes. An oval portrait hung on another wall in a gold frame, a woman with powdered hair dressed high. Her hands were posed gracefully . . . the image blurred, was she real? . . .

"Big sip," Tony encouraged.

I swallowed, gasped, and once again my head cleared. "Vampires."

Tony's brows twitched upward. "Don't tell me they spoke to you. I hope not," he added.

I tried to struggle up, but I couldn't move—and the effort hurt. "They're *real?* You've *seen* one? Up close and personal?" It took a few breaths to get that out.

His long fingers lifted in a sign too brief to catch. "I don't recommend the experience."

"I'm dreaming," I muttered. "That's it. I'm dreaming. Except. I thought you don't. Feel pain. In dreams."

"Save your strength," he murmured, almost too low to hear, sending a meditative glance somewhere up behind me.

I was still struggling to figure out why I couldn't move, what had happened. I glared at my hair lying in waves across the front of my black shirt. When did my hair get loose? Wasn't I supposed to be Ruli? Beyond my shirt, my legs stretched out, feeling about ninety feet long . . . And they were tied together at the ankles with something silky.

Alarm pushed back more of the fog. I was propped up on a couch against a wall of embroidered pillows. One shoulder was tightly wrapped by cloth, though it throbbed with glowing insistence. But I couldn't touch my shoulder because . . . because my hands were squashed into the pillows behind me, uncomfortably squashed there.

I couldn't move them—somebody had tied my wrists together, and then put me on this Directoire recliner.

And that throbbing in my shoulder, oh yeah, that guy with the pistol, and then the flash—

I'm tied up, and someone *shot* me!

As Bertie Wooster says, I was definitely knee-deep in the mulligatawny.

Tony sat on a piano stool next to me, forearms propped on his knees, hands clasped loosely as he studied my face. His attitude was one of waiting. For comprehension?

I licked my dry lips. "I saw the wall. Not bad, eh?"

Relief relaxed his features slightly. "Here, have another."

"Zhoumnyar?" My voice was hoarse, but otherwise sounded okay.

"Yes. Fire grade." He smiled.

I tried to nod, and wriggled as a stray lock of my hair pulled under my elbow. I grimaced, but once again after swallowing more of the liquor some of the sickening coldness receded.

"Better?"

"So to speak. I have to be dreaming. I mean, vampires? Ruli had *Buffy* up there—oh, I get it, you're scamming me. Right. Got it."

"No. They're real enough." Tony brushed an errant lock of hair off my clammy brow. "Ruli likes *Buffy* because it's funny. And the vampires are so easy to kill. Quite cheering."

"So tell me about your vampires. Are they sexy?"

Tony gave me a look of disgust. "Some say my tastes are too undiscriminating, but I stop at carrion-reeking, fungus-cold walking corpses."

I began to laugh but it hurt too much. "They really stink?" I whispered.

"Yes. Unless you permit them to glamour you into liking the reek of old blood. We've a tenuous truce at the moment, the vampires and my folk, but no one sane seeks them out. They scare the shit out of me, if you want the truth. I bound up your shoulder as best I could. It should hold until we can get someone up here to tend it."

"Okay," I said, and shifted again, trying to find a comfortable position. But there was no comfortable position. "Why the ropes? I've never been into bondage, and I don't think I'm up to climbing walls."

Before Tony could answer, that raspy voice interrupted from somewhere behind me, with a flat American accent, "It's on my orders. Because if we have any more trouble with you I'm going to blow your head off."

Tony glanced up; from the direction of his reflective gaze I could tell that Reithermann was standing some ten or fifteen feet beyond where I lay. I also saw (for the briefest of instants but it was definitely there) that Tony was angry.

Clarity was slow in coming, but it was coming. "Something happened," I said.

Tony set the cup somewhere beyond my shoulder. "Alec seems to have objected to Maman's attempt to alter the disposition of affairs." He twiddled his fingers. "He and his brass-buttoned yobs stormed the gate at the same time you were making your tour of the family home."

"Alec? Here?" I repeated.

"Well, not here. But outside, somewhere. A classic stalemate. They hold the grounds and the sky suite, and we this part of the house. Middle level's no-man's-land. Alec seems to dislike the idea of a fight to the death deciding the contest, so we've sent someone to confer. Comfortable? Can I get you anything?"

"I'm cold." I went back to his earlier statement. *"Alec seems to have objected to my mother's attempt to alter the disposition of affairs."* What did he mean by that? I winced as my temples pounded. "So I'm part of the terms, is that it? Like, let you guys go or else?"

"That's it," Tony agreed.

Bertie Wooster whispered, *Neck-deep in the mulligatawny, and the flames are crackling around the pot.*

My voice was hoarse, but I successfully kept it indifferent. "Well then, how about another toast to my good luck?"

Tony smiled with instant appreciation. "More *zhoumnyar*?"

"You bet."

But this time I felt less of the restorative warmth, and my stomach protested faintly. I leaned my head back and shut my eyes, concentrating on breathing slowly and deeply. I noticed a trace of cigarette-stink in the air, and I remembered the cigarette hanging from Reithermann's mouth when he had watched me at Anna's wedding. I suspected if I said anything, he'd come over and blow it in my face.

Sounds were abnormally sharp; the shift of Tony's clothing as he got up from the piano stool and strolled away. His footsteps were quiet, measured; then there was the impatient scraping and rap of heavy boot heels as Reithermann did something. They exchanged a few low-voiced remarks. Tony's voice was mellow, humorous, the other's hard and tight and angry.

Tony said something about Niklos being slow but trustworthy, then

Reithermann uttered a lot of nastiness about Alec, then Tony said, "He'll listen."

Reithermann's language was peppered every two or three words with the usual X-rated cursing. If I cut the worst of it out, he more or less snapped, "You'd better be right, but I don't believe for a minute he's pissant enough to give a shit about this half-breed American bitch, unless we can swap her for your sister. Dammit! He's got to be up to something. I wish cell phones worked in this hellhole."

Tony sighed, walked back in my direction, and a pleasant weight settled gently over my limbs. I opened my eyes. An embroidered and fringed cloth covered me. Golden threads glinted and shimmered. Tony said apologetically, "It's the piano cover, but it should suffice."

"Thanks," I said, surprised it took such an effort to speak.

A cool lassitude was stealing over me; except for the increasing throb in my left shoulder, I felt as if I were floating in a swimming pool. My eyes closed again. There was silence for a while (or maybe only for a few seconds; my sense of time during this episode was completely distorted) and my thoughts went to Alec. Was he out there, or was that a lie?

I remembered Alec walking through the milling, talking, glittering crowd of dancers in the ballroom. I remembered promising to dance at midnight—

I remembered promising not to leave the city.

I opened my eyes. "You can't do that," I said.

Tony's back was to me; he was standing near a window, but he turned quickly.

I said as firmly as I could, "I won't be a party to it, making him choose between me and your sister."

"But it's out of your hands, cousin." Tony's smile was warm and kind, with emphasis on the word *cousin*. "You're here. And as you put it so aptly a moment ago, you're not going to be vaulting any walls—"

"I won't be a part of it," I said desperately, trying to sit up. A nasty feeling congealed in my guts. I couldn't fight it back. "I won't, I can't put him in that position."

"You should have thought of that when you crossed the border," he replied gently.

Not *when you tried to escape,* or even *when you left the city to come up here with my mother.*

The disorienting sensation that two conversations were bound up in the same words silenced me. I squeezed my eyes shut, trying to keep track of one of them, but what I saw was myself and Alec standing in my room, and Alec putting the necklace on me: the wordless offer again.

I said fiercely, "I hope he turns you down."

Tony had dropped back on the piano stool, and sat with his hands propped loosely on his knees. A boot scraped on wood behind me. Tony's fingers gripped his knees, then relaxed, and he murmured, "So do I."

Then he ran his fingertips across my forehead in a light caress.

Reithermann made a noise of disgust.

It bothered me I could not see that creep. It was like knowing a hungry carnivore is prowling and drooling behind you, but I ached too much to try turning my head to keep an eye on him. What could I do anyway? I'd tried my escape and lost, and that was while armed, without a bullet in my shoulder.

But I was not going to give up.

I closed my eyes again. The pounding in my head had steadied to a constant ache, and nausea flickered through me at my slightest move, which made me disinclined even to open my eyes again.

Sudden noise. Thuds, voices talking. I tried to gather energy to look, listen . . .

Reithermann's voice stabbed the air: "Anton."

Tony got up. Walked to the door. The voices melded. I was too tired to concentrate—

I must have fallen asleep, because I woke when a sharp pain under my chin pricked into my foggy mind, like lightning in a midnight thunderstorm.

My eyes flew open to see from the unwelcome perspective of pointee the steel tip of a hunting knife lifting my chin. Beyond that were the nastiest, coldest, angriest pair of eyes I've ever seen in any human being. Reithermann's thin lips creased into an anticipatory and utterly humorless smile.

In my head, Bertie said sadly, *And now the mulligatawny comes to a boil.*

THIRTY-SIX

THE KNIFE SLOWLY slid from under my chin.

Reithermann flicked it away, then casually tested its blade with one leather-gloved finger. He did this right at the level of my eyes, about two feet from me. He was sitting on Tony's piano stool, his khaki tunic rumpled and half-unbuttoned. A day's growth of beard did nothing for his hard-lined face. A cigarette hung from the corner of his tobacco-stained lips; I looked away, trying to suppress a shudder of revulsion.

His travesty of a smile widened. "So you've appeared to put in a claim for the family treasure." He then added gloatingly, "And you staked it in Alexander Ysvorod's bed. I find that resourceful. Enough to grant you a small share, should we decide to let you live—"

From behind came the scrape of a shoe and a word bitten off. I made a huge effort and turned my head. Three unfamiliar men stood on the other side of the room.

The guy in the center stood stiffly, his hands straight at his sides. He wore a Vigilzhi tunic, and his face was pale and set. Then I saw the heavy-gauge pistol pressed into his side by one of the other men. The third man flanked the Vigilzhi on the other side. A rifle dangled with seeming negligence from his fingers, the butt tucked under his armpit. Both the outside men wore the same khaki that Reithermann sported—khaki that could have done with an emergency appointment at the nearest laundry—and the rifle-clown grinned with enjoyment.

I looked back at Reithermann. So they were forcing one of Alec's Vigilzhi to witness the poor, weak female being questioned, eh?

Rage zinged through me. Glorious rage, with more firepower than the most supercharged *zhoumnyar* could provide.

Reithermann gave me that grin, like he was waiting for an answer. Fine. I'd answer. But one thing about sickos, my dad had said once: they love being called sickos, especially if you sound scared. So I said with puppy-dog sadness, "You are one sorry sad sack."

Reithermann's smile vanished. He transferred his knife to his other hand with a gesture so slow it was almost a caress. He lifted his right hand, held it posed as he flexed it once, then, *crack!* Hit me across the face.

Stars exploded. My head rang like the roar from fifty warring dragons.

"Now it is time to tell us where it is," he finished instructively, expelling a big stinking cloud of cigarette smoke right in my face.

"I don't know where it is," I replied, my voice sounding thick. My head reverberated like a gong. "And, what's more, I don't want to know where it is."

"That's what Anton said," Reithermann commented with such fake disappointment it was obvious he was putting on a show. "He insisted he knows how to get intel from smart-ass girls. I don't think so. I think it'll be much faster my way." He flicked another look at the audience, then raised the knife and grinned at me. "As well as fun."

It's a show, it's a show, I thought. *He wants me scared and broken. Because . . .*

"A Freudian would have a field day with you." I tried for bravado, though my voice shook.

He backhanded me harder, then closed his fingers into my hair and yanked so hard my eyes teared. As he jerked my head back and pressed the knife against my neck, he sent another assessing look at the three men.

He wants me broken to force Alec to surrender.

He began describing in a low, venomous voice the things he enjoyed doing to people, to "smart-ass girls." My head hurt too much to comprehend every word—not that I wanted to. I was creeped out enough by the gratification in his voice.

I had to send a message to Alec—if I didn't surrender, then he shouldn't, either. The only way I could see to do it was to make the audience laugh.

When Reithermann paused expectantly, I said, "Let's play horse. I'll be the front end and you be yourself."

There was a snort from the bully with the pistol. Reithermann raised a fist—then Tony spoke from somewhere behind, in a voice of lazy indifference. "I'm sure the fellow has gotten the idea by now, don't you think? At any rate Alec will, and we'll lose the cover of darkness in less than an hour."

Reithermann tweaked my earlobe painfully. "You and I will have plenty of time together soon." Another tweak. "You'll enjoy that, won't you?"

"Like a tax audit," I snapped hoarsely.

Reithermann got up, making a short gesture with his knife. His minions jerked their Vigilzhi out of the room.

As their footsteps clattered away I leaned my aching head back on my pillow, and took refuge in memory. . . sitting on the balcony of Ysvorod House after the concert in the cathedral, with distant music playing on the soft summer air. Alec and I in sitting the library, firelight illuminating his face as we talked. Alec and I standing side-by-side looking out over the city of Riev, as the children practiced in the—

"Kids?" he'd asked. When we were inside, he hadn't reacted to the sound. Nor had I noticed his lack of reaction. I'd been too distracted by everything he was telling me.

The flute music on the mountainside, leading me to the sign posts. Vrajhus, Miriam had said.

After what I'd seen this interminable night, it seemed more unbelievable to blame hallucination, or somebody tricked out in costume, or any other mundane excuse our brain produces in order to put a safe box around the inexplicable in order to control it. Tame it. Make it safely ordinary.

Those children were ghosts. They had to be telling me something—and Alec couldn't see or hear them, because he was so intent on . . .

He had been telling me something. Yes, the story about the festival, about the figures in the church. Something above that story, or below it, or behind it—something important, I had sensed, when I saw his expression as he gazed on those peeling plaster figures. The ghost girl gazing on them as well.

Telling me—

He'd been showing me the heart of his country. If the people were the hands and eyes, the economy the spine, this festival was the heart . . . and the heart sheltered—

Mary's face.

"I will, soon," he'd promised. *The statues, he would change the statues . . .*

He was showing me the *treasure.*

That's it, I knew it. It had to be. The symbolism was so right. And if so, what an irony! I tried not to smile as I thought: I know after all, Captain Sicko Reithermann, I'd stake my life on it—

And I'm probably going to have to.

I sighed. If only I wasn't so tired, didn't ache so much—

Voices. Indistinguishable.

"Time to go, love," Tony spoke softly, from close by. And then, even more softly, his breath warm on my ear, "Keep your head close to me. Whatever happens."

I watched with rather detached interest as he picked up the edges of the piano cover, its fringes dancing in the lamplight, and wrapped them securely about me. Then he slid an arm beneath my back, and the other beneath my legs, and lifted me up.

I couldn't keep back a hiss as a fresh battery of protests were registered by my whole left side. My hands dangled loosely in the warm cover, and I realized how insecurely they were tied. If I could move my left hand, I could probably slip the knots.

Sure. If I could even lift my left hand—

A cold pressure at my temple startled me. I saw from the worst possible angle (again from the position of pointee) that Reithermann was holding a heavy-caliber handgun to my head.

I felt like saying to Tony, "What do you expect me to do?" but his attention was not on me. He started walking, Reithermann close by with the pistol pressed hard against my skull, my loose hair swinging against Tony's side. They progressed slowly from the room, my head pinned between Tony's shoulder and the pistol so I could only see out of my left eye. Time measured out in the steady *lump-lump* of Tony's heart as we passed down an opulent hall, then through a heavy stone archway, and down a low-ceilinged hall with a cross-draft of stone-damp air. I caught a glimpse of silent faces in a doorway, men's faces, and once I heard the sound of a woman speaking in a low, angry voice.

More stairs, then a heavy door creaked open. Cold outside air fingered my hot face, fresh and pure and sweet.

I breathed deeply. Heard feet crunching on gravel and a distant twitter of morning birds; overhead the stars were shining through the hazy wisps of clouds. Tony's and Reithermann's steps were distinct as they progressed across a wide yard.

Then they slowed. Rolling my left eye as far as I could, I recognized the front of a jeep.

Reithermann stopped, hesitated, said shortly to Tony, "Get in." He backed away slowly, keeping the gun trained on me: I gazed straight up the barrel.

I closed my eyes—and two things happened.

A meaty thud close to my ear—Tony jerked. *"Govno,"* Tony grunted, and dropped me. That is, almost dropped me; his left arm slackened but he sank down to his knees, which broke my fall to the ground. My face hit the gravel as pistol shots fired from a distance, and then close by.

Tony's breathing was harsh. Ignoring the crawling sensation between my shoulder blades, I lifted my head. Reithermann knelt at the other end of the jeep, aiming his weapon over the hood back in the direction we had just come. As I watched he fired once, twice.

Tony grunted in pain, his breath hissing in. I wrenched my head round. Tony's right hand hefted a thin-bladed stiletto, smeared with black; his shoulder was oozing blood.

"Tony?" I whispered.

His body blocked me from seeing anything to the other side. His hand dropped down, holding the knife, and he brushed his knuckles against my cheek, his pirate ruffles whispering over my hot forehead. "Retreat but not a rout," he whispered, then he shifted his weight and raised his voice slightly. "Dieter? Over there."

A crunch of gravel indicating movement. Tony's good arm flashed up, wrist snapping. The knife spun away, then Tony dropped on top of me. My face ground against the gravel and the air squashed out of my lungs.

Reithermann yelled in inarticulate fury, and his gun went off twice, the last shot whining horribly near. The smell singed my nostrils and made me sneeze into Tony's arm, which was curved around my head.

Tony lifted himself slowly and breathed a laugh.

"What—?" I coughed.

A weak bluish light from the east highlighted lines of pain lengthening his face under the tousled hair, and glinted with red-gold highlights in the bristles on his unshaven chin. His right hand clutched at his left arm, which he held stiffly to his side. Darkness seeped between his fingers.

"What happened, what's happening?" I whispered, urgency fighting the instinct to hope.

"I wish I'd had you up here all these weeks." Tony smiled down at me. "The whole damn fiasco would have afforded us some fun, at least." He threw his head back then, and said in a sharp, clear voice, "Niklos! Back off."

"It's over?" Relief made my voice high, but I did not care.

He gave me a nod, his profile illuminated, brief and pale, as he squinted off over his shoulder.

I sighed deeply, several emotions struggling for supremacy. Annoyance, always so steadying, won. "Fun! If you mean what I think, we would have fought like dog and cat the whole time."

His laugh was breathless. "Maybe." He shifted his weight, took a fast scan, then bent over me. "You're safe from Dieter, love. The forces of righteousness are figuring it out and should be arriving shortly in full and holy wrath. I cannot see myself enacting the role of penitent—"

Shouts in the distance were followed by a couple of shots in rapid succession.

Tony got to his knee, and began, "I wish I could take you with me—"

I could not let him get away with the last word. "I know where the treasure is, and I won't tell you." I sounded like a sulking six-year-old.

The weak morning sun lit half his face, glowed lightly on the characteristically charming smile. I gazed back, keeping my own face stony.

"Au revoir." He got up, smiling down at me. "That's a promise."

I heard his footsteps crunch away, then pause. There was a clash of light metal. Keys! Then his footsteps dwindled rapidly, followed by another set of footsteps arriving from a different direction.

I lay there, wrapped like a giant worm in the embroidered and fringed cover, and passively listened to distant birds scolding from high atop the sky-brushing firs, and to the pinging of the cooling jeep engine near my head. The footsteps crunched and clunked around me like a herd of wildebeest.

A man said in Dobreni, "Reithermann's dead." And another, "Holy Mother of God! A knife through his throat—"

Fingers touched my cheek and Alec said sharply, "Kim?"

"Tony did that. I think," I croaked. "So he's handy with a knife, eh? I'm glad I didn't know that earlier."

Alec knelt down beside me. I couldn't see him but I could hear his breathing, hard and fast. "Here, can you sit up?"

"Nope," I said, as his fingers ran lightly along the sides of my exotic wrap and encountered the lumps my hands and wrists made.

"What's this?" he demanded, and then the scrupulous and gentlemanly Alec snapped out such a breathtakingly foul curse against Reithermann that I began to laugh helplessly. He stopped cursing and tried to check out my wound, but yanked his hand back when I let out a groan.

"Kilber!" Alec rapped out. "A knife—now."

Someone said, "Is the Lady Aurelia hurt?"

"There's a bullet hole in her shoulder," Alec snapped. "We'd better get her off this damned mountain fast. Kim, how long ago did this happen?"

"Seems a couple of years." I sighed. "Oh no," I added as my hands were suddenly free, and Alec started to lift me. "I would rather not move for a minute. I feel much better if I lie still—"

Alec cursed again, under his breath.

"Russian." I tried to grin. "Tony cusses in Russian, too. Do they have better cusswords?"

He gave me a brief smile in answer, but continued, slowly and tenderly, to lift me up.

I wished at this point I could have gracefully slid out of action: I couldn't help grunting "Ow, ow, ow, ugh, argh, ow!" as I was shifted about, and wincing when Alec issued orders in the sharp voice that made my headache twinge in protest.

He spoke in Dobreni, and the crashing in my skull sundered the connections between those words and their English or French equivalents. Running feet, answering shouts, several racing engines indicated a burst of activity, as I was sinking into irreversible passivity.

When I opened my eyes again, the pearl colored morning light glared. I squinted against it into Alec's face. We were in the back of a jeep, with me lying propped against him, my left shoulder free.

Alec's face was tired but alert; he too had the speckled shadow of a day's growth of beard, but on him the sight was disarmingly dear. I smiled.

He smiled back. "You need a shave," I said.

"Judging from the amount of mold you are wearing, you need a wash," he replied, then ducked his head down. And for the first time he brushed his lips against mine in the lightest of kisses.

Every nerve in my body flared diamond bright. I roused myself enough to say helpfully, "Tony ran that way." I rolled my eyes in the direction he'd taken.

"We saw him. Save your strength."

The jeep fired up, the engine so loud I grimaced and clenched my teeth. Once the driver peeled out of the castle courtyard and onto the pothole-dotted Dobreni mountain road I knew I was in for a rough ride.

Cold morning air tore over us, the roaring engine at first drowning all sound. The bright sun shafted between the shadows of ancient trees and speared my eyes. Alec held me against him, trying to absorb the shocks with his own body. I began to shiver, longing for oblivion until I became aware of a voice penetrating the increasing haze over my mind.

Alec bent over me, the wind whipping his fine dark hair into his eyes as he quoted poetry by the yard—Donne, Klopstock, Milton, in an effort to keep me awake.

I listened closely, but the sense of the words began to fade. Alec wanted me to listen, to stay awake, and I wanted to, but I could not remember what the poem was about . . . it was his voice that I liked listening to . . . it stitched together the cascade of images, from bright golden hair hanging in curls on a robe a l'Anglaise to the sad-eyed ghost drifting out of the dueling weapons room below the sky suite at the Eyrie. Meaning—I sensed meaning beyond my reach, but if I could only—

The jeep lurched, and I jerked awake.

"I got it," I said, struggling to sit up, to make him understand. "I didn't tell them. The treasure. You showed me—didn't you?" I peered up but I could not find his face in the fast-gathering darkness . . . wasn't it dawn? "I'm not bonkers. . . You showed me the treasure. . . Didn't you?"

"I did." I heard that before the darkness settled over me like a blanket.

THIRTY-SEVEN

ALEC'S VOICE. Urgent. ". . . fever."

A woman replied, in good old, peanut-butter plain Americanese, "Fever's to be expected. What worries me more is how much blood she's lost and if any bones were hit."

"Noooo." I gazed blearily at a vaguely familiar, cream-colored ceiling. It swam nastily, so I shut my eyes again.

Alec's voice again. "Shall I assist?"

The woman replied, "It'll go faster with some help—if you can do exactly as you're told. No fainting."

"I've had enough experience with field triage," Alex said, with a hint of a laugh. "Patching one another up when I ran with Tony's mates on the mountain, back in the bad old days."

"Then scrub. Fingernails, too. Get that gory shirt off first, and when you're ready there's an apron in that drawer."

"Oh, no," I groaned, chicken at the last.

The female voice was now beside my head, warm and humorous and tender. "Hey. You relax and mellow out. Before we lay a finger on you I'm going to knock you on your can with my handy hypo. You wouldn't feel a tackle from the entire Green Bay Packers."

And she was right.

From time to time someone woke me and coaxed me to drink something, after which I slid gratefully into dreamland again. I slept and slept, and finally woke feeling less like cashing in my chips and more like figuring out where I was.

And I needed to tell Alec something. That thought had persisted, with greater or lesser urgency, through the semi-waking and through my jumbled dreams.

When I woke for real, I recognized the small, crowded apartment belonging to Alec's M.D. friend Natalie. I was lying in her bed, my left arm straight at my side. My shoulder had quieted to a dull ache—though when I tried an experimental movement it twinged sharply.

"Ow," I said.

I heard a deep breath. I turned my head. What I had thought was a quilt plumped over a chair was a person, curled up, asleep.

"Good morning, Sunshine," a sleep-husky voice said in that familiar American accent.

"Nat?"

"Yo." She stood up, stretched, then yanked aside the curtain, letting morning light stream in. She was wearing sweats and a flannel pajama top. Her curly brown hair framed her face in a flyaway cap.

She flung off the pajama top and pulled on a ski sweater. She was short, and though in anorexia-land she would be considered chubby she had a magnificent figure. A round face, generous mouth, brown eyes darker than my own; I took her to be my age but later, when I saw her closer, I noticed the laugh lines, cheekbones, and blurred chin of a woman in her mid to late thirties.

"Almost seven," she went on. "Are you always such an early bird?"

"Nuh-uh." I hesitated, then said tentatively, "Alec was here. Wasn't he?"

She was folding up her quilt, and paused to shoot me a wry smile. "He was here. Last night, yesterday, and the night before. I kicked him out at midnight last night. I hope he's asleep now, but I suspect he's probably over at the palace playing Stadthalter. You've created quite a stir, dude."

I eased over onto my right side and started to push myself up. "I've got to know what's happened—"

"Where d'you think you're going?" She laughed, a rusty, pleasant sound. "Lie down. How 'bout breakfast in bed?"

"I'm not hungry, thanks. But I have to know what's—"

"I've got all the facts." She shook her head, grinning. "In some ways more than anyone. If you ever want the real dish, you get to know the local midwives, and I've got that wired. Tell you what. You lie down and let me play doctor, and I'll answer all your questions. And if anything stumps me, I'll send a messenger. How's that?"

"Okay," I said, trying to sound obedient and polite.

She stepped close, touched fingertips to my cheek, neck, forehead, then she slid a pillow behind me so I was sitting up comfortably. "Fever's gone," she said. "How's the shoulder?"

"Okay. Well, it hurts, but not nearly like it did. Thanks for fixing me up."

"You were damn lucky." Her mouth was wry, but the expression around her eyes was warm and kind. "Close range like that, anything larger than that pocket popgun could've taken your arm off. Or you could've had a bone shatter. But I can see my exciting medical news isn't what you want to hear. Hang on a sec."

She went to the window, peeked out, grinned, then she strode out of the apartment. Expert Dobreni echoed down the hall, followed by quick steps in the other direction. A minute later she was back. "Breakfast is ordered, and I'm fixing some of my Bunsen burner tea. With milk." She sat on a stool and slapped her hands on her thighs. "What do you want to know first?"

"Did they get Tony?"

"Nope. Alec didn't expect to, not after a couple of Tony's guys covered his exit from the castle courtyard. Alec says Tony's as at home in the mountains as he is in his castle and he was pretty much lost for good after that first chaotic ten minutes. But Alec's letting a few of the Vigilzhi content themselves with a search."

"What happened there, at the end? One minute we were walking out, and that creep Reithermann was pressing a gun right here." I touched my temple. "Then Tony dropped me and had a knife." I winced, remembering. "I think it was in his shoulder. He was bleeding."

"Brrr." She shivered. "That must've been a hell of a night, eh? Well, this is what Alec told me. Reithermann was going to off you unless he and Tony and you, as hostage, were allowed to leave the grounds in that jeep. At that point Alec's men had used the keys they took off the duchess and had gone up some hellhole secret passage that Ruli pointed out, to a secure part of the house. Everything wrapped up, more or less, but the two head snakes and you. The two wanted to bug out while it was dark, and Alec knew once they got half a mile down the road they could dump the jeep, melt into the forest, and be gone for good. So they had a single chance. Reithermann had you covered with the gun, but he had to get into the jeep and so did Tony. At the moment they split, Alec's lieutenant, this beefy old geezer—"

"Kilber."

She grinned. "So that's Kilber! I've heard about him. Been around here once or twice, last couple days. Anyway, he pulled off a piece of Bruce Lee knife-tossing, nailing Tony in the arm. Then Tony did a Bruce Willis by pulling the blade out and using it to nail Reithermann."

"I am so glad I did not see any of that."

"They gambled on Reithermann's sense of self-preservation being stronger than his urge to shoot you if they got Tony down. And they were right. Too bad Reithermann was too stupid to figure out that Tony was more dangerous than any of them." She chuckled. "Speaking of whom. They were counting on Tony not harming you, though Alec himself had a gun trained on him the whole time."

"What about my cousin and aunt? Aunt Sisi went to get help, is that what happened?" I sighed. "I couldn't figure it out."

She went to the door. "Hang on. My water must be boiling. I just got back from England. How's Fortnum & Mason crown blend sound? It's the breakfast tea for the servants over at your Aunt Sisi's, I found out last night. You'll naturally be horrified, I realize—"

"Oh, well, I'm totally used to first class all the way."

She laughed. "Back in a flash."

Back in a flash. It jolted me to hear home slang. *As if I'm being pulled away.*

There was no time to examine this idea further; she was back, carrying a heavy ceramic teapot, the milk, and the honey in unmatching containers. "You'll notice the Miller tea service. Eclectic. I call it neo-retro-fusion." She kept up a running stream of jokes as she fixed us each a cup, then sat back and held hers in both hands, her eyes half-shut as she sipped. She had avoided my gaze during all this.

Finally I said, "We left off at Aunt Sisi."

Nat made a face. "I was hoping you'd figured that out."

"Maybe I could if my brain hadn't shifted into neutral. Tell me."

"Here it comes, then. She set you up, Kim. That's the biggest pisser of all. I hate to be the one to slip you the good news."

"Set me up? You mean she shut me in the passage on purpose?"

"More'n that. She set you up from the beginning—I mean, soon's she laid eyes on you. Not only you but her daughter as well, but it was only you she deliberately put into danger. Maybe it's best you didn't figure out the scam the other night." Nat shook her head, then sipped again. "If you hadn't driven off with her she was going to have her butler tie you up so she could dump you on Reithermann's doorstep in trade for Ruli. Since Tony'd lost control of the castle—and the situation."

My insides cramped. "She said she had no one else to drive her."

"I take it you didn't find out that Danilov guy races the Le Mans in France every year, and one of those von Mecklundburg women has a Maserati."

"I don't know anything about any of them." I'd assumed they were all worthless because I didn't like them. Heat worked its way up into my face.

"Well, your Aunt Sisi didn't want you to. I'm told she worked hard to make sure none of you got to know the others. Anyway Alec said he'd been suspicious all along that she knew where Ruli was, but there wasn't any proof that would let him investigate. You can imagine the political hassles if he was wrong."

"Oh yeah."

"His suspicions spiked when you showed up at her royal dump with your big news a week or so back. He said that was a real close call. He also said that her first thought was not of rushing up to get her daughter, it was of cooperation."

"Yes—I noticed that, too—but I thought it was her superpowered polite training. That and her willingness to cooperate to get Ruli back faster. Yuck."

"That's mighty restrained of you." Nat wiggled her brows. "I'da been ready to snatch her bald. But since he couldn't prove it, Alec couldn't tell you."

"He did drop hints . . . I think I see it now. He played social games with her. He also made sure I never went anywhere with her alone. Was she in league with Tony?"

"Yeah, but Alec thinks she was running her own plot as well. She sneaked Tony into the ball, you know."

"He didn't steal Percy's costume?"

"Those von M poops are all pretty tightlipped about it, but Alec says they were all in on it that night, which is why, though he had Sisi's house watched, they smuggled Tony past. He was in the house during that dinner, wearing his own pirate suit. As soon as you were gone he got into the limo with them, in Percy's place."

"So that's why they wouldn't take us. And I thought it was a snobbish objection to me sitting with the chauffeur, since my skirts were too wide for me to fit in with them in back."

"The duchess pulled a snow job on everybody. When the Vigilzhi ordered to keep an eye on them followed the limo to the palace, Percy walked over, mixing in with a bunch of party guests also walking, and came in the back way through the kitchens. The servants were too busy to pay any attention to a wandering party guest, except to shoo him in the right direction."

"So what was Tony doing?"

"He hid out somewhere in the palace while Percy danced with you, so everyone could see him at it. And when Tony's guys were in place, they did the switcheroo. Percy confessed last night—he'd hated the plan from the get-go, and he was upset about you getting shot."

"So that's why he got so drunk at the dinner. Nerving himself up. I don't think cloak-and-dagger stuff is Percy's style."

"Nope. Empress Sisi strong-armed him into it. Him and the rest—her brother-in-law Robert hates her as much as she hates him, I'm told, but she roped him in by promising he could have the dukedom if she won. He's been encouraging Tony in his wilder exploits for years," Nat added, giving me a wry salute with her tea mug.

"Hoping he'd break his neck?"

"Or that he'd walk into someone's weapons fire," she said. "Anyway, the plan was, while Alec and all the government biggies were prancing around in one room with their masks and ruffs, Tony's gang would move in and pinch the lot of 'em. But none of 'em knew Alec had nosed it out and was ready. So all through the city that night, and in certain key points here and there, as Tony's boys drifted in they walked into the Vigilzhi's waiting arms."

I remembered those groups of men Alec waved to when driving me around—that had been a covert tour of inspection to make sure everyone was in place. But to anyone else, he was tooling about with his betrothed, showing her the sights.

"Waiting arms indeed," I said, appreciating how deftly Alec had played his double game.

No, triple. For he had showed me—not Ruli, but *me*—the treasure.

"Best thing was, they were so surprised there was no bloodshed. Not until the end. Thing is, Alec didn't know where Tony himself was—assumed he'd be out leading one of the assault units."

"Not Tony."

Nat laughed. "I told Alec he should've known Tony'd have to be in the main action, and as for everyone knowing him, what more obvious than a disguise? Anyway, while the empress deflected Alec and tried to round up the council for Tony's guys to grab, the other von M's kept everyone else away from you so Tony could waltz you right off the dance floor and into his tentacles."

I choked on a laugh.

"That was the only part of the plan that worked. By the time Alec was done with rounding up Tony's would-be council-nappers, you'd disappeared. The party was called off, people had to be escorted home, and so on. Tony must have told his mother where he'd stashed your corpse when he realized he'd been foiled by Alec, and she took it from there." Nat nodded soberly. "I hate to have to tell someone a blood relative is a skunk. She apparently had a mega-grudge against you."

I sighed. "To tell the truth, I never liked her, though I did try. But what about Ruli? Why'd Aunt Sisi let Tony keep Ruli prisoner?"

"Well, the plan with Ruli, to put it simplest, was to keep Alec out of the country searching for her until they could pull a coup. But when they heard that Alec had found Ruli and was partying with her—you—up and down the Dalmatian coast, the empress pushed Tony to run his coup early."

"Alec was on his cell phone constantly while we were faking the happy couple." *And I'd totally misconstrued the reasons for his tension.* But I was not ready to talk about that.

"Some family retainer who hated this Reithermann and his scumbags told someone who told someone else about Tony's posse gathering suspiciously, so from Split or wherever it was, Alec ordered the Vigilzhi out on maneuvers all over the main roads until he could arrive home. This was a few days before you turned up here and threw everyone into a tizzy. The von M gang was already antsy. Some of Duchess Sisi's European pals swore they'd spoken with Ruli, and of course she couldn't say no that's not possible."

"So that first day, when I walked around Riev, I was being watched? It sure felt like it."

"Both sides. But mostly they were watching each other, while Alec drove hell for leather to get back here under the radar, in case someone was lying in wait for him at the airstrip. Which is down in the valley. He'd maxed out the Vigilzhi watching the roads and guarding the city."

"So not all the von Mecklundburgs knew about Ruli being a prisoner?"

"Nope. That was Tony and Auntie's little secret until you showed up. By the time she had that party, where it woulda been clear in ten seconds you weren't Ruli, she'd had to do a lot of fast talking to get them on board."

"So Tony was running under his mom's command? This wasn't his idea?"

"That's what Alec can't figure out. He thinks Tony was getting her support for his own coup, but she was setting Tony up if he didn't win, so she could turn him over and be the good guy."

"Wow, that sucks."

"Last resort was letting Ruli marry Alec long enough to get her pretty paws on that treasure, so she could depose the both of them." Nat sipped tea, then put it down. "This stuff is good! I'll have to lay in a case or two before Alec closes us in."

I gasped. "So you believe in the Blessing?"

She grinned. "Sure." And shrugged. "When I first came up here I had the universe figured out. By the time I'd been here a year, I knew I don't know anything."

"What do you mean?"

She rolled her head back and forth, cracking her neck. "Need a better pillow! Hey, I've seen some seriously weird shit. Like those old Salfmatta ladies praying a spurting wound closed. People living long lives—cancer pretty much unheard of. Stuff you can't explain away, no matter how hard you try."

"I saw ghosts in the Eyrie, and Tony says he knows vampires. I don't think he was kidding. Or lying. But I guess one never knows."

"No, but there are people who insist the Devil's Mountain dukes have some kind of truce going with 'em."

"Truce?" A chill zapped through me.

"The midwives all insist that the magic those old folks work with their prayers and roses is warding vampires. And when someone dies, they make damn sure they're either buried and held down under a mighty monument, or else burned and urned."

"That's another thing I don't get. I thought mixing magic and the church was like the fast track to being burned at the stake. In the old days, I mean."

"It did happen, but a lot of that was political, and it didn't happen here. This is what I understand about magic. They use the forms of prayers to manipulate whatever powers there are—and we're getting into strange territory here—but by using prayers, they know they're not doing evil. As for the magic, there's *something* going on."

"That's what Alec said. But I'm here to say guns do work."

"But they don't always, especially in the back mountains, higher up even than the Eyrie. Which is why up in those border cliffs and caves Tony's gang fought the Germans and then the Russians sometimes with rifles, and sometimes with swords and bows. Those who do believe in magic say that this country is one of those places on earth where it's pooled a whole lot stronger. Because we're on some kind of liminal border."

"Liminal. That's the word Alec used."

"Yeah, well, I guess that's the latest term they're trying to fit over some stuff we don't have the vocabulary for."

I sat up, wincing at the tweaks and twinges in my arm. "What I don't get is why Aunt Sisi would want to rule. Alec told me that when she was a teen, Aunt Sisi came here and was met by cheering crowds. I thought that meant she was, you know, dedicated and loyal and all that. She has to see that Alec is not exactly the Dark Lord of Doom here. The people seem to like him, and he sure works hard."

"Try power crazy." Nat leaned forward and tapped her tea mug on the table. "Alec doesn't gossip about his royal pop, so I bet you don't know that from the time she was about sixteen, Empress Sisi was after old Milo, did you? She wanted him to marry her. He wouldn't. So she's been sighting her guns on his ass ever since."

"All Alec told me was that she married a guy in the other branch of the family. Kept the title and all that."

Nat snorted. "Her second cousin, who the title went to when her dad and uncle died. If you ask me, I think she would have married her own brother, if she'd had one, in order to be duchess. Anyway, the duke's a depressive sort, hiding on his estate somewhere in England. Raising race horses. Hadn't a chance against Duchess Sisi and her total domination drive."

"Midwives told you that?"

"Nope. I have other sources—in this case another one of Alec's sweeties, one in High Places." She wiggled her brows.

"I met none of Alec's high rank friends at those parties. It was always the relatives, or their friends."

"That's because Sisi did the invites. Beka is granddaughter of the baron, Shimon Ridotski, the number two man in the country. Hobby is orchids—"

"The orchid Napoleon? I danced with him! Talked about orchids a lot."

"That's because you were polite to him," Nat said with a grin. "His family cuts him off without compunction. Anyway, he's too important for Sisi to mess with, so he ignored her attempt to isolate you at the ball. And Sisi can't push Beka around like she can her own toadies, so she didn't invite her—or anyone else Alec likes or trusts. She didn't want you winning any sympathy. The council pretty much had to be on the guest list, but she turned that to her advantage by spending the whole night keeping those old geezers corralled so that Tony's gang could grab them."

"Tell me more about Beka."

"Sure. She teaches history at the temple school, and is on the university committee with me. We usually go out for coffee after hashing out some more ideas on how to build a school of higher education, and she catches me up on the skinny about the nosebleed league."

I grinned, then said, "So . . . tell me this. Tony told me once that he thought Alec pokey in his policies, like old Milo. But Alec told me he made mistakes—he tried to pull a Joseph II—and had to back off. He said Tony wasn't there to see it, but he was surprised Tony hadn't heard about it."

"That's an easy one." Nat finished her tea with a sigh. "Beka says when they were all kids, Aunt Sisi did her best to keep Tony and Ruli from teaming up with Alec, even when she had Alec over a lot. She was always running them down to one another—in the nicest way possible. She'd tell Alec how she wished her kids would be as studious and dedicated as he was. Tony, she encouraged to run around chasing Russians in the hills, or else to play around in Europe, and leave the boring old politics to her."

"Whoa. That explains a lot."

"Beka says the proof is that Tony and Alec got along pretty well when they were on their own, away from the family wolves. They used to harass the Russians together, when they were teens smuggled here for the occasional holiday, and the Russians were helping themselves to the mines. The empress did not like that—as soon as Alec became Stadthalter, she started ragging on Alec behind his back for being as big a stuffed shirt as dear old dad. And that Stadthalter—being king—was Tony's birthright."

I whistled. "So, what now? What's Alec going to do with her? Exile? He wouldn't put her in jail."

"No, because that'd mean a trial, and that's the worst thing for the country. But from now on she won't be able to scratch her ass without someone sending a memo. She knows it, too. Yesterday, in the smoothest and quietest way, he dismissed half her staff and had the French ones put on a train out of the country with cozy hints from the friendly Kilber about what might happen if he saw any of 'em again. So Princess Prissy-Sisi is going to stay right here until Alec decides what to do about her, and she'll hate every second of it."

"Serves her right." I saluted with my tea mug. "Where's Ruli?"

"Oh, she's at Alec's place. Everyone in the city knows she's there and you're here."

"That's . . . that's weird. Who spilled the beans the other night?"

"Ruli did. Alec was over at Vigilzhi HQ setting it all up when your chaperone called him after you and the empress took off. Alec was furious—"

"Oh, not with Madam Aradyinov!"

"No, no, he knew Duchess Sisi had done the Royal Decree number on her and the housekeeper, too, who I guess tried to talk Sisi down, to be told to can it and get back in her 'propah place.'"

"God, I wish I'd known that."

"She's smooth, that old battle-ax. I'm sure she was on the watch to make sure you didn't hear any of it. Anyway, when Alec and his go-for-blood gang of Vigilzhi met Sisi and Ruli on their way down the mountain, apparently there was *quite* a scene. I guess Sisi had been coaching Ruli, who was half in shock, in what to say and do when they got to town, but when Ruli saw the Vigilzhi and the guns and Alec, she started screaming about you being locked by her mother in a horrible secret passage with spiders."

I couldn't help it, I laughed. Though it hurt.

Nat grinned. "Sisi was shattered. Alec had a couple guys 'escort' her home, under guard, and someone else take Ruli to his place. Once they got into the sky suite there were enough of Tony's rats ready to jump the sinking ship—particularly when it looked like Reithermann was going to come out on top—they all helped him to take the castle. That's when the Vigilzhi got a load of your exploits with the sword. Guess you did a Cyrano de Bergerac on some of Reithermann's sleazes."

"Yeah, but they were all unarmed. Except one. Two," I amended, remembering the creep with the poker. And the fact that I'd been shot.

Nat smiled. "You're a hero. Get used to it. Look, we've been talking a long time, and you need to rest, if they don't get here with your breakfast. But I have one question, I've been burning to ask. Did you actually tell Reithermann he was a horse's ass?"

"Yep." My teeth ached at the memory.

"Did you have any idea what kind of guy he was?"

"Yeah, I saw it, all right, a psychopath. But I thought I should get a message to Alec, not to give in. Make the Vigilzhi guy laugh. Uh, it made sense at the time, but when I think back, I want to cluck and scratch for seeds."

She snickered.

"What makes someone turn out like that guy, anyway? Child abuse in early life?"

Nat jabbed her forefinger in my direction. "Mighta had the nicest parents ever, but some weird gene popped out of some maniac ancestor. We've all got 'em."

"He was too angry for nice parents, unless he was born angry. I wonder if they will grieve when they find out he is dead?"

"Dunno. Don't care." She shook her head. "About him, I mean. Yeah, that's mega-depressing, the idea that nobody would give a rat's ass if a person died. Anyway, the point is, you've got guts, and the city of Riev is yours. You could walk into any house or any store, take what you want, and they'd brag about it for years. A hero—except to the von M clan. They and their peeps got a bee in their pants about you, starting with your having made fools of them at that shindig at Sisi's."

"I wish I hadn't done that. But they were so . . ." I sighed.

"Before you got there your aunt made you out to be a hustler, showing up to cash in."

"I should have thought of that."

"Well, you didn't know what was going on. Ah." She got up, and swept up the empty tea things. "Here comes Alec's minion with your breakfast. He told me about your minions. I love that word. Minion! Can I be a minion?" She laughed again as she trod down the hall to the front door. She came back with a tray of fresh, buttered croissants, sliced peaches, a fluffy omelet with spring onions and two cheeses, and two kinds of pastry.

"Share?" I admired the abundance. "Looks too good to waste, and there's enough here for three."

"I'll get a plate. I never have tasted the famous Pedro's offerings."

"Pedro? Did Alec take him away?"

Nat helped herself to half the food. "Nope, but Pedro offered to cooperate on his own. It must piss Sisi off, but Alec wants to foster the happy family routine. His Vigilzhi were encouraged not to speak of Sisi's little oopsie. I hope they have." She picked up a croissant. "More tea? You need liquids. How about water?"

"Okay."

"Good. Eat up, then you're getting a bath. I'm afraid if I don't get those spider eggs out of your scalp they might hatch."

An hour later I was lying on the bed in Nat's fuzzy bathrobe, feeling human again. She had dealt with me with gentle hands, yet I got the feeling her mind was on something—or that she was about to say something.

I stretched, careful not to jar my arm. "I'm not taking you away from your practice, am I?"

"Nope. This is generally the time of year when they start 'em." She chuckled. "A couple local colleagues are standing in for a day or so. No one will bother us unless it's an emergency."

"The place is being guarded?"

"Nah. Watched, yes. If you want company, stick your nose out the door." She saluted me with a fresh mug of tea. "It'll do wonders for my business." Then she set the mug down. "I've known Alec for ten years, but he never talks about his own affairs. If I want to know what's going on behind the scenes at the palace, so to speak, I have to find out from Beka, or others."

I nodded slowly. She did have something on her mind.

"He listens to me rattle on about all the details of my practice. Nothing ever too inconsequential or too dull. Perceptive as hell—but his own emotions? For all you'd know he hasn't any. Or rather, they're hidden behind that polite wall."

"It's true," I said. "Talks about everything. Except himself."

She laughed again, mirthlessly this time. "You're like him, I can see it already. Pleasant, funny even, until something personal comes up and then up goes the wall. Look, Kim, I'm forcing the wall because you've got some heavy-duty decisions ahead of you, and you're going to need some straight facts, or at least some perspective."

"Decisions," I repeated.

She got up and stared out at the street, as she rubbed her fingers along the dusty windowsill. "I hate entanglements. Saw too much drama on the commune where I was born, and the result is, I have nooooo interest in even living with anyone. So I was good for Alec, for a while. No drama, no expectations."

She turned away from the window and studied me. "You okay with this conversation?"

"Sure," I said, though it did unsettle me. But I had to take responsibility for my own . . . what? There wasn't a relationship, not in the way anyone defined that. I said firmly, "Alec's personal life is none of my business. It's true I like him, and I know he likes me, but there's this Ruli mess, and things have gone so fast."

"It's going to get even messier. Faster. Anyway, that was his pattern until you came along. Didn't talk. But from the first night when I called from London to arrange for tickets back, the day you went missing up on the mountain, he's been talking about you. Never his feelings. He hasn't changed that much. What you did, said, your likes and dislikes, your parents, even." She tapped a fingernail on the table. "I know more about your mom and her cakes than I know about his mother—who he never met. But still."

"So," I said slowly, "you're telling me what?"

"I'm telling you what I told you. One more thing, and I didn't hear this from him." She was back at the window, looking out. "Jeez. I don't know if this is giving you the inside scoop or TMI. But you know he grew up knowing what he was going to be. One thing. Zip."

I remembered that conversation about vocation and avocation, and said, "He's mentioned that. He seems to love his work."

"True." Her eyes narrowed. "Okay, one more item. What's the only thing in that library of his that looks like he's actually been there? Not the CDs, a thing."

I thought rapidly, first of that gaudy platinum lighter, but no, that was the wrong track. "All I can remember is a book, with a bookmark. On the reading table. Milton's poetry?"

She brought her chin down. "And which poem?"

"'Lycidas.' I wondered if that was his or Milo's."

"What's that poem about?"

"It's a pastoral. Elegy. Super dense. About . . . somebody died, right? Elegies are always about death."

"On the surface, because that poem packs in a lot of stuff, Milton wrote it after a Cambridge schoolmate was drowned. Okay, I'm done."

"What?" I protested. "Nat, that is not even remotely too much information."

She looked out the window. "Sometimes TMI is betrayal of confidence, right? I told you, I don't do drama. So forget I even said anything."

Leaving me more confused than I'd been when I woke, only now it was about Alec and me, not about Dobrenica's politics. "At least tell me what is it you want me to do?"

She gave an exasperated laugh. "Do what you want. What you have to. I never give advice in heart matters. Hell's bells! Come to me with cramps, warts, a runny nose and I've got a chance of being right half the time. In the tangled world of emotions, nothing's the same, or right, ever."

Fighting a cold, sick sensation, I tried to sift out the warning I sensed in her words.

She sighed sharply. "In my mind, this was going to be easy. Like saying to a woman: you're pregnant. Here's a list of foods to avoid, and to eat, and things to watch out for. I should have known! I'll add one more thing, then butt out. At age nine or ten we cease to believe we are the center of the universe, but it takes another ten or twenty years to stop acting that way." Her voice changed. "Course, some of us never grow up. Take me. I'm the loving kind, but not the marrying kind. When I think about the satisfaction of pulling off a difficult birth, or getting a woman safely through a tricky pregnancy—lean your head back, I'm going to comb out that hair. Can you imagine, even in the twenty-first century, some of those mountain women were putting knives under their pillows to cut labor pains?"

"So superstition is foolish, but you tell me magic works?"

She threw her arms wide. "We're humans! How about the high-tech honeys at home who still check their horoscope? Won't go on a plane Friday the thirteenth? The women here ask for a novena and put a knife under their bed, because in their minds, both work."

She talked on about tradition, magic, and superstition as the rhythmic tug at my scalp soothed me.

First things first. Finish up the last of the marriage business. Gran's legal marriage, which makes everything work out perfectly.

Right.

First to Mt. Corbesc. Time enough for planning after that. I fell asleep, and when I woke, Alec was there.

THIRTY-EIGHT

WE STUDIED ONE another. I saw tenderness and exhaustion in his face. Then he lifted his hand and lightly touched my cheek and jaw.

How strange to be so attuned to someone. I felt the anger kindling inside him, and I said, "It's okay. I was so out of it I hardly noticed a few extra bruises, and it was worth it to make that slime-crawler mad. I'll admit I wasn't looking forward to round two."

"Tony sat and watched?" he asked, with a shade of grimness.

"Yes. But it made him angry. And he was the one who stopped it."

"Was he expecting you?"

"You mean, when Aunt Sisi locked me in the stairwell? No, he most definitely was surprised. Has he turned up?"

"No. But eventually I will catch up with him." He said it in his usual light tone, but I felt the undertone of promise.

I said, "Then, to be fair, another thing in his defense, though personally, if you find him and lock him up I'd rather help throw away the key. I think he could've disappeared at the end, there, when I got shot. But for whatever reason, he put himself back under Reithermann's gun, and for no more reason than I could see except to protect me from his so-called ally."

"All right. Thank you."

Au revoir. . . That's a promise. I wanted to get off the subject of Tony. "So how's everything else?"

"Busy. I can't stay long." He glanced at his watch. "Three meetings, one I should be at now. But Nat has forbidden late-night visits."

"Right on," Nat said in the background, and Alec gave her a quick, rather preoccupied smile.

"—so I stopped to see how you're feeling, and to ask you if you'd like to go somewhere for lunch tomorrow."

"Fine," I said awkwardly, wishing he would hold me again.

He left shortly after, and I resolved to make things easier for him by taking care of the last of my business before we met again.

I napped some more, then Natalie and I had dinner together. A Pedro-cooked meal of salmon poached in wine with baby potatoes and herb-sauced vegetables was brought to the apartment—the ultimate in food-to-go. Along with my suitcase that Tony's people had taken from the inn a couple centuries ago.

Nat played music, mostly old rock, right up to Jackson Browne's "Fountain of Sorrows" while we talked about home. Easy stuff, nothing personal relating to the here-and-now. She was funny about her days raised by hippies on a commune, and how aghast they were when she threw away her organic, non-gendered overalls, cut off her hippie hair, and went off to med school.

She described her friends and their exploits, and I told her about the infamous party at Aunt Sisi's. Nat laughed in gusts, and then listened with avid curiosity to my story of meeting Tony.

"I have to admit," she said when I'd finished, "I've always wanted to meet the guy, if only to see if he's half as hot as everyone says—and if it'd work on me."

"He's hot. But you can't trust him. I would be as happy if I never see him again." Even as I said the words, I knew they were not true, and I shifted impatiently, trying to will them to be true. I did not want the complication of Tony in an already overly complicated life.

"Little ambivalence there?" Nat wiggled her brows.

"Yes. But I also kept noticing how much he was like me physically, which makes everything confusing. I mean, is that incest, or narcissism, or what?"

"You're cousins at two removes, not brother and sister. Does it feel like incest?"

"No."

"He's got a rep for heavy-duty charm. Not anything he turns on or off at will, which I think would make him disgusting. The thing is, you've got it, too. And though you look so much like Ruli everyone says you two could be twins, she doesn't have it. Maybe that charm is in your genes . . . and when you and Tony are around each other, your radar jumps to high."

"Maybe. When he left, he said *'au revoir, and that's a promise.'* "

She gave a long, low whistle. "Sounds like the wicked count was definitely charmed with Kim. Okay, don't hurl—it's time for you to catch some Zs. I don't want you relapsing. Bad for *my* rep."

I agreed readily enough, for my shoulder was aching by then. But as I settled down on the bed and she curled up in her chair, a pile of professional magazines bought in England beside her, I said cautiously, "How long do I have to be invalid?"

"You're strong and healthy, and if you manage to stay out of action for a while you'll heal fast. So you can do pretty much what you want, outside of drunken binges or horseback-riding. You did lose some blood. Take it easy, and when you feel the urge to lie down, do it. I'll fix you a sling. Gravity is going to give you the most trouble now."

"So I can take a walk?"

"Take two!" She threw up her hands. "I'd wait until morning. It's raining outside right now."

I fell asleep concocting plausible excuses; I kept telling myself it hardly mattered anymore, but I still did not want anyone knowing where I was going. My instinct was strong and insistent—this last quest I had to make alone.

As it turned out, I did not need to give her any excuses. Someone rang her bell at about four AM and she slipped out quietly, garbed in her midwife clothes and carrying her bag. At seven I got up and dressed somewhat clumsily with my right hand. It was odd to see those clothes again, the ones I'd bought during my Ruli masquerade. Looking at them stirred memories and emotions.

I slammed the mental trunk hard, and turned to tackle my hair. Since I could not braid or put it up one-handed I brushed it the best I could and left it hanging. Then I found a paper and scrawled sloppily, "Be back at noon—Kim," slipped on the sling Nat had fashioned for me the night before, and went out.

The sky was streaked with clouds. The streets gleamed fresh-washed, puddles reflecting the sky, flowers glistening. The city was busy as usual; by seven the business day was already under way.

I thought Nat had exaggerated, but as I progressed down the street a flurry of attention seemed to move before me, like a scurrying wind. People smiled. Some even bowed. I was beginning to feel like I was outlined in neon.

The walk to the Waleskas' inn did not take long.

As soon as I got inside Anna came forward with a cry of welcome. I had planned to ask for my money and for a recommendation of someone to hire to take me up to the mountain, but Anna displayed her mother's energy. As soon as she understood what I wanted she yanked Josip from the back, snatched away his apron, and the two of us were bundled into an ancient Volkswagen—a vehicle that appeared to be shared by everyone on the street. The neighbors turned out as soon as they heard the engine start up and cheered us off.

Shy Josip crouched over the wheel, holding it tightly as we bounced and shuddered our way up into the hills. My shoulder hurt after a mile or so, and poor Josip sent so many anxious glances at me after each pothole I was afraid he'd go off the road.

He slowed to second gear, which sounded in that rusty metal shell like the engine of a 747 flying into a headwind, so I shut my eyes, held my shoulder with my good hand, and set myself to endure. At least the mystery would soon be solved.

A couple thousand years later Josip pulled the sputtering car before the gate of the high-walled monastery, parked, and assured me he would happily wait for me if I did not want his escort.

I thanked him and climbed out wearily. The last part of my quest was nearly done. It felt really, really weird.

The mellow dull gold limestone walls were smooth and well kept, and the massive wooden gate was as featureless as the walls. I found a bell pull and gave it a couple of hefty tugs. Half a minute later a small, narrow door set into one of the larger gate doors opened, and out came a young man wearing a cassock made of natural wool. He blinked enquiringly at me from behind wire-rimmed glasses.

I said in Dobreni, "Is Father Teodras in to a visitor? It's important," I added.

His brow furrowed. "I know no Father Teodras."

"He hasn't died?" Shock surged up in me, followed by the corrosive burn of self-mockery. I never thought he'd be dead. But what else, after more than half a century?

"I don't remember a Father Teodras ever being here," was his mild reply.

"Please, can you ask someone?" I put my hand out to stop him, though as yet he had made no move to shut the door. "Father Teodras. The Cistercian monastery on Mt. Corbesc. I know I've got the right place. He was here. This was . . . around 1940, or right before. He—performed a marriage. I need to talk to him about that. If he's alive," I added in desperation, and did not realize until I had ended that I had switched to German. "And if he isn't, I need to see the marriage records."

The monk studied my face. His eyes were black and slanted, their expression mildly curious. So different from Tony's. "This is not our day for visitors. May I ask you to wait a moment?"

"Yes, thank you!" I added fervently, and as the door closed I tried to still my breathing. My arm hurt, and my emotions were stirring up with a violence that surprised me. I rubbed my arm above my elbow.

No ghosts now, no mysterious faces. Only the breeze rustling my skirt, causing the clouds to play hide-and-seek with the sun overhead as the tall fir trees soughed and sighed.

I'd barely made these observations before the door opened again. This time it was a different man, a much older one, whose white cassock was belted by a black cord. He wore a crucifix on a long gold chain, and his hands were posed together in the same way depicted by monks in tapestries a thousand years old. He met my eyes directly; his were hazel, sunken with age, but they held that same expression as the other man's. Mild, only slightly interrogative. Mostly steady and—secretive? No, that was not it. "Please, come within. I apologize for Brother Marcus leaving you waiting outside," he said in accented German, his voice deep. "We are not accustomed to many visitors. You seek someone called Father Teodras?"

"Yes. I—" I swallowed. "I need to talk to him. He performed a marriage, of my grandmother. This was right before the Second World War. It was in secret. He was young, then. If he's still alive, please, may I speak to him?"

A smile narrowed the monk's eyes. "Secret marriages have been forbidden for many years, child." His smile faded; something of my stunned and sick reaction must have shown in my face as I followed him into a white-plastered hallway that gave onto a well-ordered garden.

A sun-touched white marble statue of the Virgin Mary stood gracefully above a bed of late lilies, her tranquil face bringing to mind the Mary of the treasure in the Roman church. Beyond this garden lay a plain building. Beyond that a back gate and a kitchen garden. Here and there white-robed figures moved about their business, some talking quietly, some solitary. The ambience was orderly, peaceful, and not particularly otherworldly.

The elderly monk trod with measured pace around the garden to the building. There we came to an archway. He gestured for me to look through as he said, "We do not permit the world beyond this point. But here you can see Brother Ildephonsas at work."

I glanced across an inner courtyard. Chickens cackled and pecked and wandered about the hard-packed ground. In between them sparrows hopped and darted. On a side of the yard was an open shed, in which a thin old monk stood on one side of a table with a still sheep laid on it. This monk held the sheep's head between his hands as a white-haired monk quickly stitched up the animal's side.

"A boar got in among the flock last night." The monk spoke at my shoulder. "Brother Ildephonsas has a talent with beasts."

Two long-haired dogs with thin, pointy muzzles galloped into the yard, plumed tails flying and tongues flapping pinkly.

One gave an excited yap and thrust his nose into the sinewy hand held down to him for a second. Brother Ildephonsas' long, homely face creased into a big smile, then he straightened up. When the sheep twitched and shuddered, he folded his hands around its head, and it relaxed. Totally absorbed, he never noticed us.

Remembering what I'd learned from Nat, I asked, "Is he a Salfpatra?"

"Yes."

"But it's Father Teodras I'm looking for. Does this man know him, is that it? May I talk to him?"

"Brother Ildephonsas cannot speak to you because he made a vow of silence many years ago, when he joined the order," the monk said gently, and he turned to go back.

I moved with him, but my steps were slow. "I don't get it. What does he have to do with—oh, no." Realization finally hit me, with awful finality.

The monk said softly, "There was once a young actor named Teodras Vinescos. He traveled in Romania and neighboring countries, and he was a friend to many young noblemen. But that man, that life, was left behind him more than half a century ago."

"So the marriage was a fake. That's what you were trying to tell me?" I said in a hard voice. "Took a while to sink in, but lately I haven't exactly been quick on the uptake . . ." Tears burned my eyelids, blurring the garden path before my feet. Furious with myself, embarrassed at the thought of climbing into Josip's car while blubbering, I fought them down.

My toe bumped a low step. I didn't remember a step on the way in. I'd been brought to a small room with the cream-colored walls so common in this part of the world. It was lit by windows high on a wall, furnished with long wooden benches. The only ornament was a simple wooden carved crucifix, mounted between the windows.

I rubbed my eyes fiercely as I plumped down onto a bench. The old monk sat next to me, his hands folded.

"I've got the story now. I'm sorry to have disturbed you," I said tightly.

"Your disappointment is understandable," was the even reply. "Your grandmother yet lives?"

"Yes." I took a deep breath, then expelled it. "At least, I hope so. She too has gone silent. We don't know why." I gulped in another breath. This time my voice shook less. "Did he—take that vow because of what he did to Gran? The false marriage, I mean?"

"That lies between Brother Ildephonsas and God," he said. There was no reproach at all in voice or face. He and the other guy looked like people who had found the answers. Or at least, for whom the questions no longer mattered in the face of what they had found.

"I see," I said, standing up. "Well, thank you for the truth."

The monk also stood up, gesturing toward the bench. "You are welcome to remain here for a time, if you wish. Brother Marcus will show you to the gate when you are ready to go."

"Sure. Thanks," I said again.

"Go in peace." He sketched the sign of the cross between us, then went out.

My legs sagged under me. I sat in the quiet room, listening to my own breathing. Still ragged. Poor Gran, I thought. Wearing that ring all her life—and it didn't mean anything.

I leaned my head back and breathed deeply, wondering what to say when I got home. If she would hear me. It was too easy to picture her being shocked beyond recovery, but then I thought, don't borrow trouble for Gran. Deal with your own issues.

What issues? I was exactly the same person I'd been before Josip drove me up. I was the same person as I'd been at birth. Everyone was the same. Ruli and Tony and Aunt Sisi—the situation was exactly as it had always been. So, outside of my mother's legitimacy, which she had never questioned (and my mother wasn't going to care about it when she did find out), nothing had changed.

I remembered Josip patiently waiting, and rose to leave.

Up the hallway a door opened and the first monk emerged. He gave me a placid nod and led me to the door in the big gate. With a courteous word of farewell he let me out.

Instead of the rust-black VW bug, Alec's red Fiat gleamed in the weak sunlight.

He leaned against the car door, contemplating the distant mountains, Riev Dhiavilyi—Devil's Mountain—crowned by the Eyrie silhouetted in the drifting haze.

Alec had not yet seen me. His sleeves were rolled to his elbows and the brisk wind ruffled through his hair and over the shirt but he seemed unaware of the cold.

As the door shut behind me with a quiet but solid thud he squinted against the sun's glare, then took a couple of swift strides to meet me. He studied my face, then said, "I'm sorry I did not tell you before. I'd planned to today. Both of us were going to."

"Both?"

"No one as yet knows that my father is here. He wants to meet you. Asked me yesterday to bring you up to have lunch with him. Are you up to it, do you think?"

I had difficulty making the transition, and said blankly, "Shouldn't I be dressed up?"

"Your appearance is fine. Are you too tired?"

"You knew all the time?"

"Your mother was born in Vienna, but she wasn't baptized until your grandmother reached Paris. Apparently Armandros always had some excuse, until right before they parted."

"And?" I asked, but I knew what was coming.

Alec said gently, "And she was baptized Maria Sofia Dsaret."

Up above, an eagle rode on a current of air, head twitching back and forth. The rising wind rustled through the trees.

"She knew," I said. "She knew."

"Armandros confessed the false marriage to her before he went back to fight against the Russians."

"So *that's* why they broke up?"

"The initial break was on ideological grounds, as I told you before. This is what I couldn't find a way to tell you: when he would not give up his plan to fly against Russia she begged him as a last act to go to church with her so their daughter could be baptized. Though he wasn't religious he apparently balked at lying to the priests about the baptismal certificate, which in those days was often the only form of ID a baby had. So he told her the truth. He hadn't know if she was serious or not about that 'last act,' but after that confession, well, it was the last time they saw one another."

"So she knew. I just don't get it. She's the most honest and straitlaced person I've ever known, but she wears a ring to this day!"

"On which hand?"

"On the left, of course."

He gave his head a shake. "In this part of the world we wear wedding bands on the right hand."

I tried to deal—but my brain had frozen.

"In those days, to be a single mother was serious business," he said. "The ring as well as the false name would be a bit of social protection during stressful times—for your mother as well as for your grandmother. After all, she'd thought she was married when she left home and when her baby was born. Kim, I'm sorry I didn't tell you. I should have—I meant to—but I didn't quite know how."

I sank into the car seat, and wound my hair slowly around my right fist so it wouldn't blow in the wind, as I thought wonderingly, *Everything has changed. No. Nothing has changed, except I know the truth that everyone else knew.*

He started the car and started down the long road. I said bitterly, "You would've told me in Dubrovnik if I hadn't reacted like General Gudarian leading the troops every time you opened your mouth. And I probably wouldn't have believed you anyway." Depression curled like cold fog at the edges of my thoughts.

"I should have done better at broaching the subject," he said. "I thought I was avoiding the accusatory, but I wasn't, or you wouldn't have been so angry with me. Rightly so. I grew up angry at your grandmother for what I regarded as a selfish act. Easy to condemn, isn't it, when one doesn't understand all the facts?"

"Totally." I let out my breath, and the last of my anger with it. "Totally."

Alec flashed a quick smile at me, but his eyes were preoccupied. "How'd you track the story down? Old palace servants?"

"At first. They told me about Salfmatta Mina—"

"Oh, the old governess." He nodded. "Everyone whispered about her for years, but she steadfastly maintained she knew nothing."

"She told me the whole story. That's who I was with, when I escaped from Tony that time. She was a witness at the wedding, or what she thought was a wedding. I'm glad she doesn't know it was fake." I grimaced, shaking my head hard.

He nosed the car down the driveway to the Assumption church, the one with the mosaic ledge at which the festival begins. The one with the treasure.

He parked and helped me out. Silently I followed him around to the nave. As we entered, an old woman stepped from a pew, knelt and crossed herself, and walked away.

Alec and I were now alone.

We walked up the center aisle. The statues were there, the arresting beauty unchanged. Eternal rapture on Mary's face.

"Wait." I held up a hand, and looked around. "No children—no ghosts." I sighed. "I not only saw ghost kids here last time, I heard them singing. But you say no one in the Dsaret family saw them?"

Alec said, "You do have two parents."

I drew in a breath sharply. "The Murrays? Why didn't I think of that? Maybe because everything here has been so much about Mom's side of the family tree."

"What do you know about your father's people?"

"Nothing, really. His folks were old when they moved to California, and there weren't any other relatives." I pointed up at the cracked plaster figures with the peeling paint. "I didn't dream *that,* did I?"

Alec murmured, "The statues underneath the plaster are solid gold." He smiled at my dropped jaw. "One of the few pleasant stories about the prewar years, and Milo couldn't write it down. If he's up to it, I'll ask him to give you the details, if you like, but the gist of it is, they took advantage of an already established process."

"You mean, replacing the statues?" I whispered.

"That had been under discussion for close to twenty years. When the king and the then-bishop took a hand, things did speed up. Did you notice the statue of Mary in the garden up there on Mt. Corbesc?"

"It's beautiful."

"That artist, a man named Janacek, was well known here. He was a Riev carpenter. In his free time he made religious art. The king began the conspiracy with Janacek, who was connected to the rabbi at that time through his wife. He was already involved in disguising the temple against possible invasion—everyone had heard what was happening to Jews in Germany."

"Is the Blessing behind how the religions get along? Because that sure doesn't match the rest of history."

He said, "Pretty much, yes. Anyway, his wife and daughter obtained work as laundry women at the palace, and among the baskets of linens she took away to wash at the close of the day were quantities of gold."

"So she sneaked it all out of the palace?"

"A lot of it. Milo and his cousin Grigorian helped, in countless wheelbarrows of sewage rolled right through the city. This was before the pipes were put in. Milo was supposedly overseeing the project, which was to be finished in time for the festival. Janacek had had the reputation for keeping his art to himself in his basement until he was ready to show it, or this never would have worked. Milo said that the night the statues were finished and they went down to see them, all gleaming golden in lamplight, is something he will never forget. This was early in August."

"And the plaster?"

Alec's smile deepened. "That was the fun part. They had to act fast, as the procession and installation were planned for the thirteenth. He and Grigorian and some artist friends—the sister of one of them is Emilio's wife, who was in on it as well—all sat up at night, drinking wine and plastering. Poor Janacek could not bear to watch. A couple days later they painted the figures, this time under Janacek's direction. On the thirteenth, the figures were unveiled, and the townspeople were astonished to find the great work done in plaster! But Janacek explained that the figures were solid oak underneath, built to last. The plaster was to further protect the wood, and could be changed every few years. The unlucky blokes chosen as bearers sweated the figures up the stairs and out into the streets on their way to the mountain."

"I bet they weigh a ton."

"That was the bad moment, Milo said. Wondering if someone would question their weight. But no one did. Oak is heavy, after all."

"And so they've been here all along, despite the Germans, and the Soviets, and Tony. That's great!" I laughed. "Are they all gold?"

"No, five have been converted. Milo found an artist who has been replacing the figures on Janacek's model, working from photographs. I've been overseeing the exchange, one at a time. She thinks the aging process on the plaster is to keep visual continuity. Hers are wood underneath. She doesn't know about the gold."

Aware of tiredness pulling at my muscles, my shoulder, I sank onto a pew and stared silently up.

I enjoyed the story, until the thought popped into my head that if Gran had not married Armandros she too probably would have been part of the conspiracy.

"Married" Armandros? *Oh, Gran.*

"Something wrong?"

He must have felt my change in mood; I bounced up again from the wooden pew and burst out, "I guess I can see Gran giving Armandros a fake name when she emigrated to the States, but what I can't get past is her wearing that ring her whole life. It's like she was living a lie."

"Do you think she was lying?" His gaze was steady. "How many people do you know whose marriages are absolutely legal and for whom the whole process means nothing? From everything you've told me about her, my guess would be that the ring was a symbol of her good faith, even if the priest blessing it was false."

I thought of people I knew who out of ignorance, or boredom, or greed, or transient lust, get married and then divorced and then married again a year later. I thought of Gran, who had not been able to make a meaningless marriage with Alec's father.

I thought of Alec, who was expected to make one with Ruli von Mecklundburg.

"Shall we go?" Alec suggested.

THIRTY-NINE

KING MILO WAS FRAIL, but he sat straight in his chair, and he looked kingly. There was nothing faltering in the deep-set gray-blue eyes or in the slow, precise French.

He was staying in an old stone-walled house down in the valley behind Our Lady of the Assumption. It was a quiet house, shaded by old oaks and perched on the bank above a deep-running river. I expect it was a religious retreat; a black-robed Benedictine brother opened the door to us, and there were religious symbols on the walls of the simply furnished rooms.

Milo remained in his armchair before a roaring fire and apologized for not getting up. His face was long and lined and craggy; except for the eyes it was difficult to see much resemblance to Alec. He had the same steady, reflective gaze, which narrowed to express humor the same way his son's did.

I sat on the edge of the other big chair with my hands in my lap and my ankles crossed, like a schoolgirl at a formal tea, and let him lead the conversation. He offered refreshment once, and though I remembered Alec's having mentioned lunch I sensed that the plans had been changed. I said "No thanks," then met Alec's eyes as he stood behind his father's chair, and he lifted his chin slightly in agreement.

The conversation was short. Milo asked me what I thought of Dobrenica and after I told him some of my impressions, he went on to ask a number of questions about Gran, and about my mother, about music and books and art.

Alec remained in the background, listening. After half an hour or so, about the time I finished my impressions of Vienna, I detected a shade of hoarseness in Milo's voice. I glanced Alec's way for clues, and caught a flicker of his eyes toward the door.

I finished up quickly, "And I saw the London Ballet. That's when I met Alec. You know the rest."

I didn't know how much he knew, but I left it at that.

Alec said, "How's your shoulder? This has been a rather long first day."

"I'm tired," I said truthfully, starting to rise.

"I'll take you back to town."

"Thank you for visiting me, Aurelia Kim." Milo extended a hand and gripped mine with brief but firm warmth. "I trust you will visit again."

"I'd like that," I responded sincerely.

When we were outside, Alec said, "I'm sorry about the lunch. He must have taken a bad turn last night and a messenger, if one was sent, did not catch up with me."

"Oh, yes. The unreliable phones."

He spread his hands. "There are many who still condemn the hydro-electric dam as frivolous. How do you feel?"

"Like week-old kitty litter. I think it was poor Josip's well-sprung chariot that did me in. You sent him home, I take it."

"Yes, with thanks, since he would not take money. Who is he, one of the Waleskas?"

"Just married the oldest daughter." I wound my hair around my hand again, and as the car started to roll, I leaned back and shut my eyes.

"Shall we stop somewhere for a meal, or would you rather we post-pone until dinner? If I go straight back now, I might be able to shake free of business by seven."

I sighed. "Perfect."

The clouds were disappearing, leaving a warm afternoon. The city had never looked so lovely.

Nat's door was unlocked, but she was not there. I found a bowl of fruit and a piece of yellow cheese wrapped up in white paper on Nat's main table, where the usual clutter had been shoved aside. Propped against it was a note in a hasty scrawl, *It's twins—might need a C-sec—make yourself at home! N.*

I nibbled some cheese, ate a plum, washed it down with water, then curled up for a nap. It was 6:30 by the time I had dressed and brushed the snarls out of my hair. Alec arrived soon after. "Nat not here?" he asked as he stepped in.

"Nope," I said, feeling inexplicably nervous. As if he had grown, or the room had shrunk. I rummaged busily, found her note to show him, and retreated.

He glanced at it, then at me across the room fiddling with a lamp, and smiled. "Shall we go?"

"Sure."

I picked up a sweater. Alec followed without touching me, and we got into the car. The air was summery; I twisted up my hair again, and crumpled the sweater into a ball in my lap as the car loudly made the climb out of the city.

The drive was not long. Alec pulled off the road onto a narrow track that bumped along for a hundred feet or so then ended under a grove of oak. "Here we are."

"What's this?" I said, looking about me.

"I thought you might like a picnic. I know I'd welcome a few hours without interruption."

"A picnic? Sounds great. As long as Tony's not invited."

"Tony? So he took you on a picnic, did he?"

"At Sedania. It's so pretty up there. More than Aunt Sisi deserves," I added.

"My father gave it to her when she was married," Alec said with a wry smile as he tossed the keys on his hand. We were still sitting in the car. "At her request. More of a demand, I suspect. I know he always regretted it, even though he doesn't believe that the site is a portal to the Nasdrafus."

"He should take it back. What's supposed to be the portal, that weird old archway?"

"That's the tradition. Did you see things there?"

"Yes. For a moment. I still don't get it. Six senses? I still don't know how much of what I saw is real and what isn't."

"Maybe we need to relook at what defines 'real,'" he said. "One of my friends, Beka Ridotski, has a great-aunt who is a Salfmatta."

"Isn't Beka Jewish? How does she reconcile using the Catholic novena to do her magical stuff?"

"She doesn't. All the religious traditions have their own forms."

I hit the car door latch. "Are there any forms outside of religious tradition?"

Alec got out of the car, and sprung the lid to the trunk. "Maybe. I don't know—since I have no proof that magic exists, I haven't pursued the methods by which it is invoked."

"Okay. My brain is about to explode from the idea of redefining reality. So I'm going to pretend I didn't hear that, and let me say that I hope your dad takes Sedania back, because it's so beautiful, and Aunt Sisi doesn't deserve it. Can I carry something? One hand's better than none."

"Here. How about this rug?" Alec held out a quilt and I tucked it under my arm as he picked up a basket and another quilt. He slammed the car trunk down and tossed the keys on the seat. "This way. We should make the spot before the light disappears." He added, smiling, "You are not being abducted, by the way. The keys are there in the car, and you'll find a light in the bottom of the basket if you decide to leave."

"And strand you up here?" I laughed.

"I know where I am. I hiked all over these slopes when I was small."

I followed him down a short trail, and then I forgot everything as we emerged on a ledge beside a small waterfall plashing into a stream. Below us lay the city of Riev, which was beginning to glow golden with night lights. Above, the sky was purpling swiftly, punctuated by glimmering stars.

"Nights this clear and warm are rare here," he commented, setting his basket down and spreading out the quilt. "I thought it would be a shame not to take advantage of it. And best of all—" He gestured for me to sit down. "Reithermann's evil twin could show up, or Tony could gather the remains of his boys and swoop down on the city, or the council could challenge one another to duels, and none of 'em can find me. For tonight."

"You've been on the run even more than I have."

"I am always on the run. Part of the job. That's both the joy and the pain of it."

I remembered what he had said about vocation and avocation and knew he was not complaining, he was stating a fact. "What d'you have? A Pedro-picnic again?"

"No, this I sorted myself. Pedro was busy preparing a consolation banquet for your aunt, who had the brass to throw a formal party in honor of her daughter's return, tonight. She can vilify me as much as she likes but I will not be there to hear it. Kilber will." He smiled, knowing I'd share the joke.

And I laughed at the thought of Aunt Sisi having to deal with Kilber's grim countenance. Whether she and her guests ignored him or not, he'd be a nice, big, grizzly gray elephant in her refined drawing room.

"Basic fare, therefore," Alec said. "Fresh bread, some turkey slices from the homely Ysvorod kitchen, an aged cheddar, medium-sharp—oh. Plums. And—ah! Half a chocolate bar. Good chocolate. For drink we have the Benedictines' home-brewed dark ale, and afterward, vintage Adam's ale there in the stream." He opened and flourishingly displayed each item as he named it.

"Nice! Um hmmm," I nodded primly each time. My mood had changed. Whether he'd planned it intentionally or not, there was no vestige of *droit de seigneur* in the place he had picked, in his manner, or even in the food he had selected. He could so easily have taken me to the royal castle and whistled up an army of minions to wait on us while we sat at either end of a thirty foot long table loaded with gold plate. Or we could have gone to some exclusive place that only the rankers knew about, where the food and the talk was international and sophisticated—and political.

Wherever in civilization we would have gone, the crown prince and his lady friend would have been watched.

Here we were alone, two human beings. We ate in easy silence, passing the ale bottle back and forth. I savored the sounds of the falling water, rustling leaves, occasional birds and small creatures. The summer air was fresh with the smell of water, and the scents of greenery.

When we'd eaten the last of the plums, I sighed, and sank back on the quilt to gaze happily up at the stars.

"Shall I fetch the water?" he asked. "I'm more handy than you at present—"

"Argh!"

"—at risk of a scabrous pun," his voice floated behind as he walked over to the stream.

When he returned he asked idly, "Are you finding Nat a compatriot?"

"She's great. Though at first it seemed weird hearing 'right on' and 'mellow out' here."

"She told me that hearing you talk was as good as a fresh-baked New York bagel."

He smiled at the twinkling lights of the city. I sensed any more had to come from me, so I said, "She also gave me the background on the Tony-Aunt Sisi mess, as much as she knew. I got the feeling she knew little about the military aspect, and cared less."

"True. Did you enjoy the conversation with my father?"

"I did. We have absolutely nothing in common, but he made me feel as if I were interesting. As if he enjoyed the conversation."

"I'm sure he did enjoy it. As for interests in common, there is music." Alec idly ran a blade of grass through his fingers. "He has always said he is not musically inclined, but he likes to listen to classical. You saw his LP collection in the Ysvorod House library, didn't you?"

"Yes. But—" I protested, flashing back to Mina and her hearth. "Your father can't have been that unmusical. Mina told me he played duets with Gran when they were young, and she was so good she would hardly have played with a two-finger chopsticks plunker—" I stopped, realization finally hitting me.

Alec commented, "He's never played since."

"Mina said he loved Gran," I said tentatively. "But that's not all of it. Right? He was in love with her."

"He's never said anything. But I believe it's true," Alec replied. "That is part of why I grew up angry with her."

I thought about that, retracing all the threads through all the conversations I'd had about Milo and Gran, with Alec, Mina, Nat. Even Tony, muttering *Shades of our fathers.*

The starlight beyond the oak-leaf canopy was not bright enough to illuminate faces or features. I was wondering why it was that, despite having had great parents and a trauma-free childhood, I instinctively kept aloof from most men to the extent that I'd never had a real relationship—just recreational dating—when Alex said softly, "So you have ceased to distrust me?"

For a measureless space, I contemplated the myriad implications.

Then I said, "I trusted you from the beginning—though I didn't want to. It was so much easier not to trust."

He waited, but more than that I would not say. It didn't seem right, until I talked to my grandmother. If that was even possible.

Alec brushed an insect away. Aware of his proximity, I lifted my face to look into his. He did not move, or speak. I reached with my good hand and touched his face, his warm skin beginning to roughen over cheekbones and chin, his fine, soft hair. He sat motionless under my hands as I traced the faint lines in his forehead; slow and deliberate, my touch slowed to caresses, and I felt the fine skin under my fingers relax.

I could not see, but I could hear his changed breathing, and I could sense his waiting, until I ran my fingers through his hair and cupped the back of his head, bringing it insistently toward mine. The fire of expectation sang through my blood and bones as slowly he blocked out the stars and breeze and rushing stream, and our lips met in a deep and antiphonal kiss.

I woke before dawn.

For a long time I listened to the sound of the stream and to Alec's soft breathing. To the sound of his slow and steady heartbeat, as the light outlining his shoulder changed subtly from shadowy and cool to warm and then flesh-toned. I was lying on my right side under the second quilt, my left arm tucked under his, and my head on his chest; when morning had banished all the shadows I lifted my head to contemplate Alec's peaceful brow, the dark eyelashes on his fine-drawn cheeks, his mouth relaxed with the shadow of a smile at the corners.

Gran, did you feel such transcendent joy when you looked on Armandros' sleeping face? I think I understand a lot, now.

It was a crow that broke my silent vigil. Crashing through a near bush, it scolded some unseen creature noisily, then flapped up into the sky cawing in outrage.

Alec opened his eyes, lifted his hand to run his fingers down and down through my hair.

He kissed me. Rekindled desire metamorphosed through tenderness, warmth. Finally we got up and splashed about in the shocking cold stream, gasping and laughing, and pulled ourselves together again. He helped me resume my sling, and with the grace of Prince Charming he slid my sandals onto my feet while I perched primly on a rock. We talked about childhood as we packed all the things, and when we climbed into the car we were singing an old Beatles tune, in a reprise of our drunken performance at the Vienna train station.

When we began the hairpin turns, the wind cool and bracing on our faces and in our hair, he was laughing as he told me about his early morning ritual when he was fourteen, of listening to the entire *Revolver* album, a ritual that lasted through an entire school year.

I told him about my instant success at an arts summer camp run by new age sorts, when I was eleven, by getting together three other long-haired girls and singing parodies of Beatles' songs under the sobriquet Beatles Reunited.

I was just ninety-four
And shaped like a door—
And before too long I barfed over he-er . . .

He laughed aloud at that, and I wondered why Nat had told me he was so inaccessible, because here he was, obviously enjoying something as silly and unsophisticated as it was possible to get.

But we didn't get to Milton and his long-ago dead schoolmate. Our reminiscences halted when we reached the outskirts of the city. And that's when his mood changed, the smile vanishing behind the Mr. Darcy mask. It acted on the fire of my euphoria like cold water.

I tensed up, tried to relax, tensed again, and turned to his sober, closed profile. "I do love you. It took me a while to catch up," I said in a rush of words. "But—I feel like I always have, somehow. And always will." I laughed uncertainly, my emotions whooshing up and down and around like a roller coaster at warp speed. "Always. That is, as much as a finite person can see into the infinite."

We were already on Nat's street. As Alec stopped the car, he began in a low, quick voice, "I was never in my life more undone than when I returned home and found that damned necklace lying there, and you gone—"

"Yo, gang!" A voice interrupted from behind. Nat was up in her window, her eyes ringed with exhaustion, her smile twisted. "Kim, I've got a visitor for you. Coming up?"

"Sure, hang on a—"

Another voice interrupted then, from a house on the other side of the street. A reedy female voice cried in Dobreni: "God bless you Aurelia Dsaret!"

Our heads whipped around to the steep-roofed house across the street where, in an attic window, a wrinkled face peered out. Black widow's weeds covered old shoulders and a snowy kerchief framed gray hair. Gnarled hands jerked, and a pure white rose sailed down and thumped on the hood of the car.

I reached over the windshield to fetch it. As I smiled and nodded, tucking the rose behind my ear, the half-seen old woman cackled a delighted laugh and called, "On Festival Day will you march with the Innocents? I shall then come watch!"

A few passersby slowed, smiling. Above, an unseen woman scolded, half-laughing and half-scandalized, "Mama! You come inside . . . you shouldn't . . ." The rest was lost.

Alec's face was blank, the same drained-of-reaction lack of expression I had seen all those weeks ago when I stood over him with my hair on his lap, obviously not my cousin Ruli.

I said, reluctantly, "I'd better go in. Later?"

I climbed out, my sling banging my side, and he looked up. "I'll find you another place to stay," he began, but was interrupted as a passing man called, "Good day to you, Stadthalter!"

Alec turned to smile and wave. I could feel the effort that took, and my newfound joy was tempered by confusion.

"Alec?" I muttered, aware of the passersby, who had not moved on. Instead, they gathered in ones and twos, curious, smiling.

I tried to shut them out as I studied him to find the key to his thoughts.

"Tonight." He met my eyes only briefly; his were squinted against the strong morning sun directly behind me.

Conscious of the watching crowd I backed away. I tried to smile casually, flicking my fingers up in a careless wave, then I made myself walk to Nat's door.

The urge to stop and watch him until he was out of sight was so strong it was almost painful.

At least I'll see him later.

I walked into the apartment, and stumbled to a stop when I smelled cigarette smoke.

Nat stood in her cluttered living room, looking tense and rueful as she held out a tray with two of her mismatched teacups. I turned to the hastily reassembled couch-bed to find, sitting in an elegant peach silk blouse and slacks, Ruli von Mecklundburg.

FORTY

HER FACE WAS beautifully made up, her hair swept into an elegant chignon. A dainty gold watch gleamed on one thin wrist, and a bracelet of crystal charms on the other. She was as out of place in Nat's homely, cluttered apartment as a swan in a henhouse.

Her perfectly painted red mouth thinned in a polite smile. Her gaze was furtive, uncomfortable—shy.

"I came to see how you are." Her fingers nervously settled her cigarette in a cracked ceramic saucer offered to serve as an ashtray.

I walked the rest of the way in, feeling like Frankenstein's monster. "How nice of you," I managed. "How are you?"

On the other side of the room, her head hidden from Ruli's view by the big lamp, Nat rolled her eyes.

"Fine, thank you." Ruli rearranged her feet and added, "I wanted to thank you. For helping me the other night. And I hoped to talk to you."

The world had closed around me again, and it knocked my mind spinning. But I was—at last—learning to think on the run, and not only about myself. "Sure. Look," I tried to sound easy. "I've got to go get something, pay someone I owe—why don't you come with me? Nat? How was it?"

"Twin boys." Nat laughed, voice raspy. "She finally pushed 'em out at three this morning."

"Bet you could use a nap, then."

She saluted. "You got that right! For about a month."

Ruli rose. "I see. You are a nurse, is that it?" she asked in her beautifully trained English.

"Doctor, in reality. But in Dobrenica a midwife. A miraculously good one," Nat said, smiling.

"I see now why you are here, Cousin." Ruli's brow cleared. "Maman said—" She broke off, her eyes wild.

It didn't take magical powers to guess that whatever Sisi had said about Nat or me wasn't anything we'd want to hear, so I said quickly, "Ruli, let's talk while we walk."

Ruli thanked Nat for the tea she had not drunk, and we left. When we got outside I pushed my hair behind me, aware of it hanging like an uncombed horsetail down my back. Recalling someone's words *she never walks* I glanced down at the heeled sandals she was wearing and said apologetically—in French—"It's about a mile."

She responded with unexpected humor, "After being closed in that pile on the mountain for all those weeks, anything is a pleasure. And soon I will be forced to do the Innocents March, so I may as well get the practice. How—how is your arm?"

"Okay. Nat fixed me up. It'll heal up fine."

"Is it true Dieter shot you?" she asked curiously, then flushed. "Of course if you'd rather not—"

"Oh, it's okay. Nightmare's over. I don't know who shot me, but I don't think it was he. I'd have recognized his disgusting voice. And he carried a whole lot more firepower. And probably wouldn't have missed."

She sighed in disgust, her gaze on the cobbled road in front of her dainty shoes. She did not appear to notice the considerable attention we were garnering; I looked down as well, afraid to meet any eyes, to elicit any more "Aurelia Dsaret" comments. "A horrid, evil person."

"It was pretty bad up there, eh?"

Her nose twitched, as if she'd whiffed something stinky. "They were always talking about killing. Dieter would go on about how he'd kill the new president of the United States if someone offered him enough money. How he'd kill this or that person. How he'd torture Alec to discover the hiding place of the so-called Dsaret hoard and then kill him. What he was going to do to you. And then Tony told me he was going to kill Dieter. That's all I heard that last week, killing, killing."

I grimaced in sympathy.

"Are you really from the States?" she asked.

"Yes."

"Your French. It's good." I knew she meant it as a compliment, but her voice carried shades of her mother's gracious condescension.

"Thanks to my grandmother. As for the latest idiom, I picked up a little of it in Paris a few weeks ago."

Her eyelids lifted in pleasure. "You were in Paris? It seems a hundred years since I was home. How were—but then, you wouldn't know—" she began in disappointment.

"Not likely," I said ironically, and she flushed as if rebuked. I added hastily, "I don't know anyone there. Too bad, too! It's a wonderful city. I would have liked to spend more time there." Inside, I was thinking, *She called it home.*

She hunched her shoulders and cast a furtive look about the busy street, but I had a feeling she didn't see any of the shops or people. Her hand fumbled in the elegant handbag and she half pulled out a cigarette case, then dropped it back. She said in a low voice to the tops of her shoes, "I wondered if you'd like to go on—" and stopped.

"Pardon?" I prompted cautiously.

"Trade places," she said in a desperate whisper. "Marry Alec and stay here."

Her words hit me with such force I felt dizzy—but I didn't see ghosts or goblins or anything that would have been relatively simple to define, compared to the new mess facing me. Instead I saw Alec's sleeping face as dawn began to paint his silhouette with color, and how badly I wanted to waken every day to that.

I don't know how long we walked like this, side-by-side and in silence, before I got control. *It's not all about me. And she isn't swooping down to give me what I want because I deserve it. So what does she want?* "But what about the Blessing?"

"I don't know," she—well, she whined, twisting the rings round and round on her fingers.

"You don't believe it'll work?" I asked.

She gave me a slanted glance, through eyes that were unsettlingly like my own. "I'm afraid it will," she said in a low voice. "Don't you see? If it does not, as Maman insists, then a marriage would not matter. I could live in Paris—Dubrovnik—do what I want and never have to be here except on state occasions. But to be married and imprisoned in the Nasdrafus forever . . ."

"What's wrong with the Nasdrafus?"

She shrugged listlessly. "It's a nightmare, from everything they say. Ugly creatures from stories walk freely, and there are no machines. Paris wouldn't be the real Paris—it wouldn't have elevators, or cars, or electric lights. Beka told me once that the Salfmattas say it looks more like the Paris of two centuries ago." She shivered.

"Your family doesn't believe in it?"

Ruli gave me a brief smile. "Maman doesn't want it to work, unless she can guarantee she would have the influence she has now." She gave a very French shrug. "My brother talks to the undead, and some say he knows the wild folk. But he says to anyone who will listen that magic is gone. Yet even so, they are all here for the Festival."

We were at the inn. I was trying to think of three things at once and doing none of them well when we walked in. Forcing my attention front and center, I introduced Ruli, who barely responded to their gratified nods and bows.

As soon as I named her, they retreated behind polite deference, which seemed to make it easier for her; she obviously had no idea how to deal with people outside of her circle. I could see that the artifice of social privilege was a refuge for her—she knew what to say and what to do.

By the time we'd refused offers of refreshment from each member of the Waleska family, Anna had disappeared and reappeared again with a scrupulously sealed paper package; Tania's lens-crafting shop had to be nearby.

As I brought out my wallet, with its slim pack of euros that hadn't been touched since my arrival, Anna backed away, hands behind her. "No, no, we will not take money, Josip told you yesterday! You will come to us again, soon?"

Nods, smiles, repeated thanks—they begged me to visit again—Theresa's intense dark eyes and her proud smile—I found a moment to whisper, "Thanks again for the rescue. Tell Miriam!" and Madam's obvious pleasure at the stir our appearance was bound to make. She would have liked to have kept us in the restaurant, seated by a window. Whatever else was going on, we'd be great for business.

As we walked away into the street, Ruli said curiously, "Who are those people? How do you know them?"

"That's the inn I first stayed at when I came to Riev."

"So you came alone?" she went on, and at my nod, "I wish I had a quarter of your courage." Her wry tone ended on a laugh breathy with desperation.

"It's not courage." I grimaced, groping for the truth, though I felt more awkward by the second. "I'm stubborn, not to mention pigheaded, and I really, *really* hate people trying to order my life."

"I'd like. Once. Not to have my life ordered. I want to be left alone. With my friends. In Paris, where I love living . . ."

I squashed down the urge to say, *Don't we all want to be left alone to live our lives?* "Why don't you want to stay? Is it the country? Or the trouble? Or—or Alec?"

She shrugged sharply. "I don't know. Since I was small I've been hearing about the idea of marrying him. I was willing enough when I knew he wouldn't interfere with my life. My child would inherit, and I'd have plenty of my own money at last."

"The Innocents' March, is that the young girls who walk down from the Roman church with candles on the Day of Assumption?"

"Young girls and brides-to-be," she said listlessly. "Four o'clock in the morning, and everyone flings roses in your face. Then a hideous long Mass, or service at the temple for the Jewish girls, and inevitably it will rain. The old women say that if the angels walk out with us, we will be in the Nasdrafus world." She made a gesture of repudiation, the crystal bracelet on her wrist rattling. "I think they pretend to see ghosts—Anton always used to tease me about the Bloody Duke in the weapons room, so I wouldn't pass it by, when we were little. But I never saw him."

"I see," I said, resisting the urge to touch the flower in my ear. "Uh oh," I added under my breath.

"I cannot tell you how much I hate the Eyrie. And this country," she went on, fierce and low. "And now, with Anton's trouble, and Maman acting so horrid. To be closed here forever—" She shuddered.

I nerved myself to ask the question central to my own interest. "What do you feel about Alec?"

Again, a shrug. "I've always known him. I could sleep with him, he's not repulsive, but I can't get what Cerisette is on about. She and Phaedra. "

Annoyance flashed through me, but I let it pass out again. I'd asked her and she had a right to her opinion. Things would be easier if she was totally into him—yet I was relieved that she wasn't.

She went on, obviously unaware of my reaction. "Alec was a horrid boy, a tongue like cut glass, but that was because Maman set Anton to rag him. He was nice enough to me, nicer than Anton was, anyway, though he made it clear he thought me boring. Boring! *He* always had his nose in a book. When he wasn't fighting with my brother, or running off with him into the hills to blow up Russian mining gear, when Maman wasn't around."

"Look, Ruli," I said. "Ah. How about if we sit down?"

We had reached the flower park before the temple. Ducks quacked and splashed in a pond, and on the other side, near a border of violets, two young mothers sat gossiping quietly while four children ran around yelling in a circle, their feet twinkling in the deep green grass. Ruli followed me, her gaze on the ground.

We sat on a stone bench, and as she eagerly pulled out and lit a cigarette, I said, "So you don't want to stay here?"

"That's why I thought of trading places." She gave her bracelet a couple of yanks so the dangling stones twinkled. "If you wouldn't mind stupid things, like wearing these ugly crystals." Her gaze was now back on her shoes. "You are a descendant, same as I. Tony even said something about a legal marriage—"

"It wasn't," I said.

She shrugged, a sharp movement. "I can't believe it would matter."

"If miracle there is," I said slowly, "I can't believe one can fool it."

"I don't know what to believe. I want people to be civilized, and pleasant." Her voice softened to a quivering whisper, eyes despairing. "Decent. Is that too much to ask?"

She rattled the bracelet, the crystals catching light and throwing it about in frantic rainbow shards. I wondered if the crystals I saw everywhere were not only for decoration.

"Why do you wear the crystals?"

"Beka Ridotski gave it to me. It's supposed to be magical protection. She went to school with me. How could she believe in magic? They all pretend to be civilized, but they chant ancient spells. Or under cover of darkness they grab swords or guns and run off into the brush to shoot one another. Anton more than any of them! Sometimes, even Maman seems—" She shook her head, and lifted a hand as if to push something away.

"Violence, cruelty, and greed are everywhere," I said, feeling my way toward the truth, desperate because events were fast outrunning my brain, leaving me to wade through emotional fallout. "Up close with swords, or at an anonymous distance, duels by e-mail and lawyers." And when she didn't react, "Ruli, even if there wasn't any Blessing, we can't switch places. You'd never be happy in a tiny Los Angeles house, though I know my parents would welcome you. I'm not rich, cousin. And if the kingdom was closed off by magic, would you have enough to live the way you want, if you went to Paris, and all your family was gone?"

She threw away her cigarette and pressed her hand over her eyes.

The train of reasoning moved inexorably, and the scenery got more bleak. But I had to ride it out: I owed it to us both—to us all—to find the truth. "Whether or not the Blessing is real, the idea, the *ideal,* is to bring about peace. Right now, that includes healing the breach between you von Mecklundburgs and the rest of the country. And so I—"

I make things worse.

Nat's voice echoed in my head, *"You have some heavy-duty decisions to make—"*

Now I knew why Alec's mood had changed as we left the peace of the mountainside and drove back down into civilization. Into his responsibilities, which never end. As always, he was right ahead of me on that train of reason, because he could never truly relax—he always had to be thinking ahead. Not for himself, but for an entire country.

I'd come here and found two guys who'd thoroughly disrupted my life. I was attracted to both, but there was only one I'd choose to live with, to share my life with.

But the hard choice had never been mine.

What was it he said? *"Easy to condemn, isn't it, when one doesn't understand all the facts?"*

Ruli said, "What's wrong?"

"The clue bat's finally hit me. I'm not facing Gran's choice, I never was. It's Alec who is."

"I don't follow, I'm afraid."

I pressed my hands over my forehead, where a volcano was threatening eruption. "'You were gone, and the diamonds were there.' Oh, God," I said, a cold and terrible numbness closing on my neck, my skull. "I wonder exactly when it was he found himself where Gran was, all those years ago, having to choose between love and responsibility?"

Ruli shook her head as she lit another cigarette. "Alec would never run away."

"No. Which makes this choice even rougher."

And my sitting here, waiting for his decision, makes it that much more painful.

I looked at her. Alec and Tony had said she didn't have a sense of humor, but I'd seen evidence of it. No one could watch seven seasons of *Buffy* without knowing how to laugh, even if she had no one to share it with. Her own mother had seen her as a tool, not as a person.

Had no one ever seen her potential? Though tears blurred my eyes, I had to convince her of it now. I gripped her thin shoulder with my right hand. "Look," I said, finding her eyes and holding her light brown gaze so much like mine. "I can't be you, you can only be you. Only *you.*" My throat closed with grief, and I struggled for control. "Only you can run away and leave the country divided, and open to the growing troubles outside, or you can use your heart and your hands and work to bring light and grace into it—" I stopped, a sob constricting my chest.

"Me?" she said wildly, her cigarette dropping ash onto her silk as she stared back, eyes wide and shocked.

I fought for control and went on desperately, "—and every decision, every problem, every triumph, you are asked to be a part of! I'd help Nat learn how to get medical knowledge match with magic—if it exists—and redefined so the superstitious can understand it, if not. I'd go up to the border and talk to the half-Russian Devil's Mountain people to get them to put down the knives, and I'd dance . . ." I fought for control. "And dance . . . at the weddings of people like Miriam, and Theresa, and love them as they'd grow to love you." My voice cracked. Fighting for balance, for humor, I added, "I'd be too busy to be bored!"

Her brow furrowed. "So you don't want to stay, is that it?"

"God! Beyond life I'd like to stay, Ruli, but I *can't.* Don't you see? There can't be two of us here. Only part of me is Dsaret. The other half is Murray. Your relatives hate me, and yeah, I asked for it, except they hated me before I walked in that door that night. To them I'm nothing but trouble. Tony and Dieter, with their guns and their knives, proved that much. Oh God, emotions, the glass knives that shatter . . ."

I hiccoughed, and let go of her shoulder.

"I don't understand," she whispered.

Would she have understood if I'd said *It's a matter of honor?* But that sounded so pompous, so self-righteous to my ears. And so I gasped, as always trying for humor though there wasn't any, and felt like there would never be any ever again, "Sisterhood is beautiful, Ruli," as I stared down at the package in my lap. The jeans, the cotton top. My passport, wallet, the airline ticket for a departure from London—

September 4.

"D'you think you can get me to the border, Ruli? Now, fast, without anyone knowing? *Fast,* Ruli?"

Tony had taught her to drive.

She got Alec's Fiat, which had been left at Ysvorod House. There was little more of any purpose said between us; she was terrified driving on mountain roads, and I—well, forget it.

From the western border of Dobrenica I must have used one of every type of wheeled conveyance known to modern life, splurging at last on a commuter flight from Frankfurt to London.

In a restroom in Frankfurt I changed into my jeans and top, and after trying unsuccessfully to figure how to carry the grubby dress I left it in the stall. I tore up the letters I'd started so disinterestedly on the train to Vienna, and then, carrying only my wallet and passport, with a white rose and a slim green dictionary tucked into my sling, I got onto the commuter plane.

In London I picked up some cheapo duds in an Oxfam then holed up in a Chelsea bed-and-breakfast for a day or two, sleeping and trying not to think as the last days of August burned toward September.

Finally I couldn't bear the four walls and I took a train north and visited all the Murray sites. Abandoning my sling, I tramped Culloden and Flodden fields, feeling as dead inside as those long-ago Jacobites who'd longed for a return to a lost world that had changed forever. The day was dark, pressed in with fog; ghostly figures seemed to drift in the slow vapors, but I was too dispirited to care.

A day or so before my flight I returned to London and wandered the streets of London aimlessly, looking, thinking. Remembering.

Finding myself in Charing Cross I was soon at Foyles' Bookstore. There I went into action with feverish intensity, and spent almost everything I had left of my money on purchasing copies of Tolkien's *The Hobbit* and *The Lord of the Rings*, and Harry Potter, and a host of other favorites about magic, and had them boxed up by the store to be sent by the quickest available method to Theresa and Miriam via the inn. They gave me a card to fill out as an enclosure, and my first impulse was to write "Rudolf Rassendyll."

I laughed unsteadily, and said, "Just get it there before the first. Or it might travel around and around the mountains forever . . ." Laughter is so dangerous, so close to tears; I threw down the money and ran.

The second dawned, and passed, and I endured the hours sitting in the garden at Hampton Court.

I nerved myself to look at the news on the third—but of course there was nothing. There had never been anything about Dobrenica, so quiet and removed it may as well be Brigadoon.

On the fourth I left for Los Angeles.

There were two bad moments on the flight. After food was served I could not keep still so I wandered about the plane. Anguish seized my heart at the glitter of a blue stone in a square ring on a male hand holding up a French newspaper; the paper lowered, and an elderly Middle Eastern man calmly turned the page before raising the paper again.

The second time was when I saw my mother's face.

My parents were at LAX, having known my arrival time when I bought my ticket months ago. I was the first through customs because I had no baggage—I left the Oxfam stuff in the airport restroom.

Mom's face was round and smiling, her short hair frizzing like a cream-colored halo around her face, the rest of her comfortable in her favorite flowered kaftan and sandals. Next to her Dad shifted from foot to foot, tall and rangy, his beard more straggly than I'd remembered, his eyes crinkled with good humor. He clapped his hands around me in an enthusiastic hug, until I groaned and backed away, wincing and rubbing my left shoulder.

Mama said nothing, her smile wavering, and after looking at her Dad spoke. "Welcome home, Oh Footsore Traveler! Or arm-sore . . . what happened?"

I shrugged. "Little accident." My voice came out too flat. Mom's brow puckered with quick worry.

He tried again. "Well, Rapunzel, I suppose I should do the fatherly and claim your burdens?"

"Aren't any," I said, trying for offhand, for a smile, but not quite able to yet. I held out the carryall I'd purchased in Frankfurt. "This is it."

"What? The airline lost your—"

"I lost it, Dad. Let's go."

"Kimli." Mom's voice was soft and tentative. "You look bummed. What's wrong?"

That's when I forced myself to meet her eyes. Her brow was serene, as I remembered, but instead of being smooth I finally saw the lines. But different lines from Aunt Sisi's. Instead of well-bred tension these were laugh lines—and instead of the military precision of Aunt Sisi's plucked brows Mom's were arched as nature made them.

I turned away, my eyes burning with tears I refused to shed. Instead I stared through the shaded windows into the blaring sunlight beyond as we began to walk down the long corridors. "It's okay, Mom," I said, when I knew I had a grip. "I found your relatives. And . . . and I think they are safe." My chest heaved; I closed my eyes, held my breath. Got control. Forced my eyes open, and my voice to sound normal. "But first, how is Gran?"

"The same," Mom said, searching my face with an anxious gaze. "Why don't we wait until we're home?"

"Okay." I looked away, groped for an easy topic and managed a normal LA question, "How's the traffic?"

"The usual!" Dad said in an attempt at cheer. "Cell-phone gabblers to the right of us, tailgaters to the left of us, folly and blunder. Your mom was so sure you'd be suffering withdrawal symptoms by now, from not having had any Mexican food, she suggested we have tacos for dinner tonight."

The door slid open, and the heat enveloped me uncompromisingly. Dust, smog, hot dry air, so alien, propelled me back into the old life. *Home life? Not home. Not home.*

As we drove up Sepulveda, I turned my aching eyes to the hazy horizon. A plane had taken off, engines screaming as they lifted the silver-winged shape into the air. I watched it soar into the glittering brown smog-haze as the fierce sun glared off its wings, and heat waves hazed the underside. It headed out over the ocean, and then began its wide turn up in the sky, vanishing into the glare.

I thought of the two continents that lay between myself and my heart, and of the hours, days, years that stretched ahead of me into this merciless sunlight, then somehow we were home, and getting out of the car, and there was my house, small and shabby and familiar yet strange. I knew I was seeing it through Alec's eyes.

There was our tiny kitchen, last painted before I was born. Mom thanked the neighbor who'd sat with Gran while they drove to the airport, and then we were alone.

Food had been half prepared, but Mom did not go to the stove to finish up the taco shells. Instead, she sat down at the table next to Dad, and touched an envelope lying next to one of Dad's clocks.

Mom said, "Kimli, maybe you've got a clue about what's happening here."

"Surprise came—express delivery for your grandmother, right before we left for the airport." Dad grinned, scratching his beard again, which bristled out, more demented than Rasputin's. "Go ahead. Take a gander."

I pulled the heavy paper from the envelope. My burning eyes took in the discreet letterhead naming some British law firm. The legalese prose below it was couched in finest British-reserve, making a jumble of the names . . . *Mr. Lavzhenko Emilio, agent for . . . Ysvorod . . . Maria Sofia Dsaret.*

Emilio's first loyalty was to Milo, who had loved Gran, who had been given charge of Gran's and her daughter's welfare. Milo had kept that charge faithfully for over half a century.

My mother said as she raised a hand to shade her eyes from the sun, "We took it for a Nigerian scam, or someone was seriously tripping. Those long foreign-sounding names, the mention of a big inheritance. But there's a heavy duty vibe in this paper with its engraved heading, and the overseas express delivery. You know what this is about?"

I stared at the paper in my hand.

There was Gran's name next to Mom's—both names, their fake ones and the real ones. Underneath was a copy of Mom's baptismal paper. *It's Mom's story, too.* My eyes ranged from the paper to the envelope, as if I could reclaim connection to the sender at the other end.

The world stilled, and only my heart beat, for the first time with hope.

Over the stamp lay a Dobreni cancellation mark, clear and sharp. The date: September 3.

They're still there. My emotions swooped between joy and anguish. *They're still there.*

"Is this stuff real?" Mom asked.

"Oh yes," I breathed. "Although I no longer quite know what 'real' is."

"Far out. Let's go to Gran's room, and you can tell us all. Dinner can wait," Mom suggested.

I held the letter as we went into Gran's room, where she lay in bed, for she had become too weak to rise.

I sat in her rocker next to the bed, talking in my old-fashioned but "pure" Parisian French as I told them everything, from the day I gave up on my search in Paris and took the train for Vienna to the day I sat in the temple square with Ruli. Sometimes my dad would stir, and Mom would shake her head, but they never interrupted.

Gran lay unmoving.

I finished up, "So, Granmère, it sounds like we'll have enough money to get whatever medical aid you need. So you're not to worry about that. Or anything else."

If she heard a word, there was no sign.

Dad said, "Maybe I should have told you this years ago, but it's only a single memory from when I was a kid. I still don't know what my dad meant. He was a tough old bird, I told you. Didn't like questions. But one night, real late, when I was considering a run to Canada to avoid the draft. I was eighteen, and this was right before the lottery, during the Vietnam War. I knew he'd be mad because he was pretty conservative, but I felt like I had to tell him what I was planning. He told me he was a runaway. Not to avoid war. He'd served in the navy during World War II. He'd crossed the entire continent to get away from his family's ghosts."

"Whoa," I breathed.

Dad felt in his pockets and pulled out a clock tool, which he turned over and over in his fingers, as he nodded toward the still figure on the bed. "Your grandmother was pretty definite about the subject of ghosts, so I kept that to myself."

"Was that ghost reference metaphorical?"

"If my dad ever recognized, or made, a metaphor, I'll eat that clock."

"So what you're telling me is that you think there might be a such thing as second sight, and that I might have inherited it."

Dad scratched his chin through his beard with the clock tool. "Stranger things have happened."

"Yeah. Well."

Mom had been silent, turning from us to Gran and back again.

"Kimli," she murmured.

Dad and I looked up.

"Will you speak a little of that language? I want to hear what it sounds like."

So I said in Dobreni, "They still talk about Princess Lily in Dobrenica. Salfmatta Mina said she wants to see her once, before she dies."

Gran's eyelids fluttered. She whispered in the same language, "Then we must go back."